An Hour Too Soon?

An Hour Too Soon?

CHRISTOPHER SANTOS

Copyright © 2010 Christopher Santos

The moral right of the author has been asserted.

Apart from any fair dealing for the purposes of research or private study, or criticism or review, as permitted under the Copyright, Designs and Patents Act 1988, this publication may only be reproduced, stored or transmitted, in any form or by any means, with the prior permission in writing of the publishers, or in the case of reprographic reproduction in accordance with the terms of licences issued by the Copyright Licensing Agency. Enquiries concerning reproduction outside those terms should be sent to the publishers.

Matador
5 Weir Road
Kibworth Beauchamp
Leicester LE8 0LQ, UK
Tel: (+44) 116 279 2299
Fax: (+44) 116 279 2277
Email: books@troubador.co.uk
Web: www.troubador.co.uk/matador

ISBN 978 1848763 883

British Library Cataloguing in Publication Data.
A catalogue record for this book is available from the British Library.

Typeset in 11pt Palatino by Troubador Publishing Ltd, Leicester, UK

Matador is an imprint of Troubador Publishing Ltd

For more information regarding the author visit
www.christophersantos.net

Printed in Great Britain by the MPG Books Group, Bodmin and King's Lynn

For the real Cindy

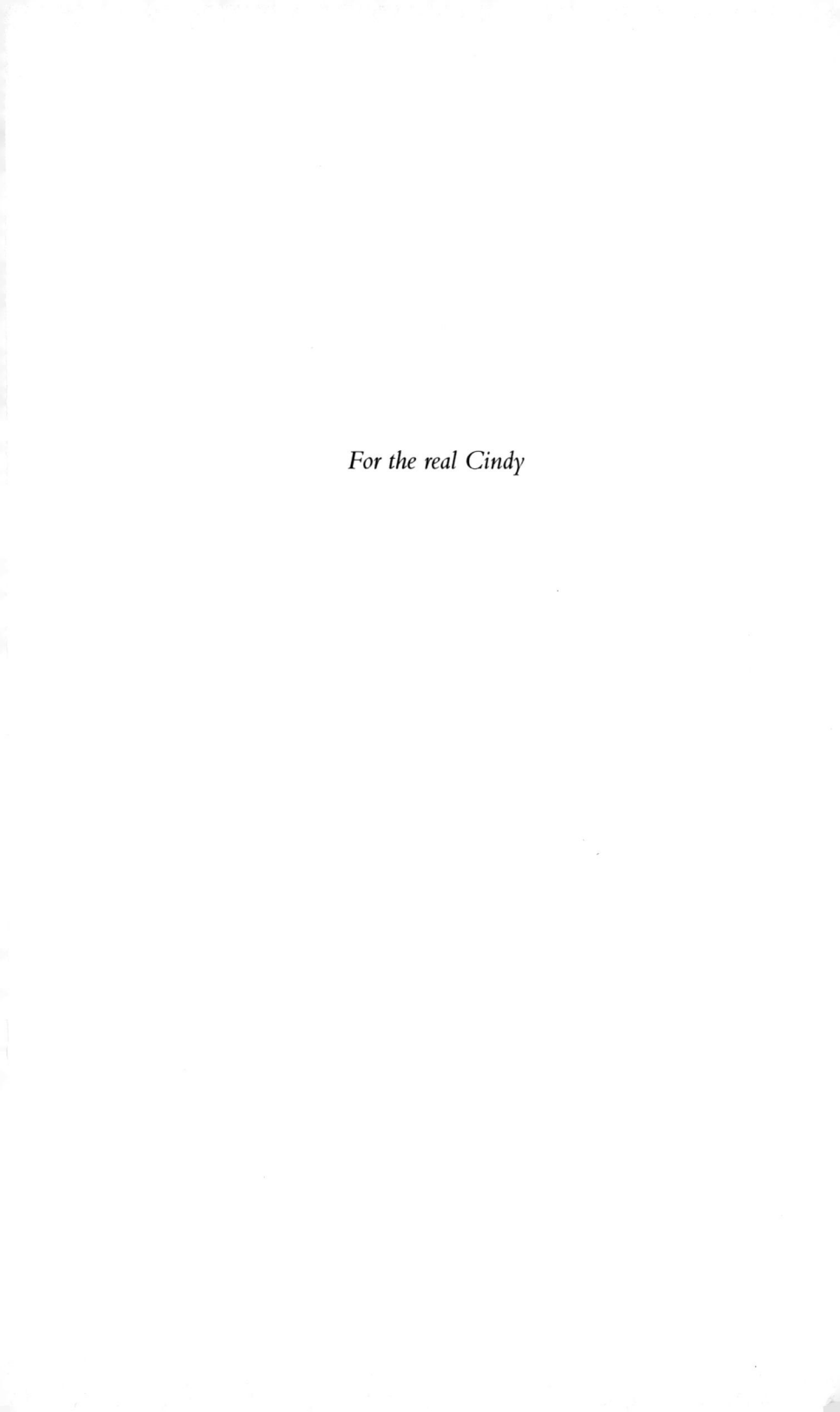

CHAPTER ONE

Sunday, 13th March 1994

*T*he high-pitched shrill reverberated around the stillness of the bedroom. Seventeen-year-old Cindy Howard wakened abruptly, grasping onto consciousness before reaching across to her bedside table to deaden the clock alarm. She lay back and contemplated her day ahead whilst listening to the gentle snoring emanating from the cat that slept contentedly on the bedroom chair. Smothering a long yawn with her thin right hand, Cindy pushed back the sheets and got out of her double bed. She briefly touched the small silver crucifix on the wall before drawing the curtains open and padding in bare feet to her en-suite bathroom.

Finally, dressed and with hair dryer in hand she sat on the side of her bed in front of the full length wall mirror gently brushing and methodically drying her long, fair hair.

Satisfied with her appearance she whispered goodbye to the cat and quietly let herself out onto the shadowy landing. She paused momentarily outside her parents' bedroom door. It was 7a.m. and all was quiet. Downstairs in the kitchen Cindy made herself her usual breakfast of fresh orange juice and dry brown toast.

Dressed in clean denim jeans tucked into equally clean green Wellington boots, a thick tartan shirt, which she had purloined from her father's wardrobe, and a large, sloppy woollen sweater her grandma had knitted for her, Cindy prepared to leave the house. Glancing at her watch she picked up her duffel bag and crept silently from the hall, making sure not to waken her parents as she gently shut the front door behind her.

With decisive movements she walked down the driveway, opened the black wrought iron gates with their gold painted spikes and stepped out onto the pavement, remembering her father's continuous reminders to close the gate behind her. She turned and her eyes lingered on the closed curtains of her parents' bedroom window. Her face suddenly became expressionless and momentarily it lost its youthful beauty.

Turning, she saw the old Land Rover waiting for her at the end of the cul-de-sac. She smiled, walked briskly towards it and opened the passenger door.

"Morning!" Cindy said joyfully to the elderly driver as she swiftly climbed in. Their journey involved little conversation, for Cindy, or Cinders as her father affectionately called her, was happy to sit back and visualise her day. As the Land Rover trundled along the deserted streets Cindy glanced into the passenger door mirror and peered at her reflection. She saw her face staring back at her and gave a self-conscious smile before turning to look out of the windscreen. Ever since she was a young girl, Cindy had frequently been told that she was beautiful and had often been compared to the fair haired, blue eyed *Sindy* doll that she had been named after.

It had been one Saturday afternoon when Cindy had seen the advert in the local free weekend newspaper. *Volunteers Needed To Help Out At Cat Sanctuary.* She had phoned immediately and offered her services for she had always admired cats and their philosophy towards life. The decision to work at the sanctuary had a double implication, for Cindy wanted to turn her talent for art into a skill for drawing and painting animals. The work would be rewarding and would allow her to get out of the house on a Sunday. There had been a slight disagreement with her parents when she had suggested Sunday work. Her mother, a church-going Catholic, had only agreed on extraction of a promise that she would continue to attend Mass at least once a month. Her father, a non-Catholic, had said yes without making any fuss. "But do you think you will fit in?" Pamela, the grey haired, middle-aged supervisor of the cat sanctuary, had asked the hauntingly attractive girl with the nervous smile and impractically long fingernails. Pamela had immediately recognised the dark maroon blazer, maroon kilt and cream coloured shirt as belonging to Saint Margaret's, the prestigious local independent girls' school. Cindy in turn had seen the scepticism in Pamela's eyes and gave an open smile that made her blue-green eyes sparkle.

"I'll tie my hair back and wear jeans and boots," Cindy had offered in a quiet well-modulated tone.

"And what about those long nails?" Pamela had asked.

It was a vanity that Cindy knew she would find hard to get rid of. Her hands were thin and artistic and she was very proud of her well-manicured nails. "I'll compromise," she had said reluctantly. Initially she had cut her nails down to an acceptable length but now they were as long as ever.

Pamela had agreed a month's trial period, but it was evident to her from the first weekend that Cindy and the cats were compatible.

One wet Sunday morning, Cindy had opened the cardboard flaps of a box that had been placed anonymously on the office doorstep. Peering in she saw an emaciated kitten whose unblinking eyes stared up at her. It gave a plaintive meow and without hesitation Cindy reached into the box, scooped the kitten up and hugged it. She felt its sadness as the small pink mouth opened to give out another heart-rending meow. Although the kitten was blind it was the first cat Cindy had immediately felt an affinity with. She took the kitten home and called her Pandora.

Cindy's parents had been concerned about the arrival of a kitten into their neat and orderly house. Pandora's disability had caused Cindy's mother, Susan, concern but it was her father, Grant, who had pacified her into accepting it. Cindy had reassured them that the kitten was her responsibility, so Pandora in her sightless world had moved in.

Cindy's weekend work at the sanctuary had become a regular part of her life. Here she found a much needed peace within herself. Her tenacity to stick at the job had surprised her parents, but not Pamela.

The Land Rover turned down the pot-holed lane. Cindy got out and pushed open the old rusty gate, allowing the Land Rover to move forward. She followed on foot to the small red brick building that housed the office, store, small veterinary surgery, reception and viewing area. The cats were all housed in kennels to the rear of the building. It was a charitable institution and depended heavily on donations and legacies.

Cindy's day had been tiring but rewarding. It was now 4.30 p.m. and she made her way to the small cramped staff room to collect her coat and duffel bag. As she pushed open the door she heard raucous laughter and hesitated before entering, knowing that the conversation would be sexually based.

Barbara and Gail, both in their early twenties and well entrenched with boyfriends, seemed to Cindy to be always discussing their sexual experiences. On numerous occasions Cindy had seen Gail being picked up after work by her boyfriend. Gail seemed quite content to don a helmet and sit behind him astride his old motorbike.

"Not for me!" Barbara had said to her with a disdainful sniff. "I like mine to have cars, preferably with a large comfortable back seat." And she had winked knowingly at Cindy.

Under the pretext of gathering her things together Cindy could not help but overhear that Gail had been seeing an older man whilst still living with her boyfriend.

"Playing away, eh?" Barbara said with a laugh. Knowing Cindy was listening she turned to her and asked if she had a boyfriend yet.

Cindy merely smiled, not wishing to be drawn on the subject, but Gail continued, "I wouldn't mind getting a grip of the guy who picks you up after work!" The joke, if you could call it that, was in poor taste as they were referring to Cindy's father.

Cindy wanted to remain aloof from the conversation as she placed her portable CD Player into her bag. It wasn't that Cindy disliked Barbara and Gail, for they were both good with the animals, it was just that they were not people with whom she had anything in common. She couldn't understand their sense of humour nor their constant wish to talk about sex. What irritated Cindy more was the knowledge that they thought she took herself far too seriously and, like now, often liked to tease her with crude innuendo.

Back in the main office Barbara and Gail said their goodbyes to Pamela and made their way to the door. At that moment a tall, sun tanned man entered the office and they gave self-conscious giggles as they walked past him.

The man closed the door after them, giving a broad smile, showing perfect white teeth beneath a dark moustache.

Pamela looked up. "Hello Mr Howard." She immediately recognised Cindy's father and felt his attire of colourful shirt, denim jeans and tan shoes more in keeping with a Spanish beach than her small office on a damp Sunday afternoon. "Cindy will be with you in a minute," Pamela said as he glanced at his gold watch.

Grant ran a hand through his dark hair in a self-conscious gesture. He usually collected Cindy on a Sunday and he rarely let her down, although he would have much preferred to be at home watching the football on television. Grant allowed his eyes to scan over the various charity posters in the office and then put his hand in his trouser pocket and extracted a five-pound note. He walked over to the desk where Pamela was working and tapped the note into the donation can. Pamela looked up giving him an appreciative smile.

Cindy entered the office with her duffel bag slung over her shoulder and Pamela saw her eyes meet those of her father. She felt rather than saw an imperceptible communication between them.

"Thought you were never coming, Cinders!" Grant said in an over-jovial manner.

"We've been very busy!" Cindy replied with a warm smile directed at Pamela.

"I'll see you next week." Pamela watched Grant place a fatherly arm round Cindy's shoulders and guide her from the office.

Slowly Cindy walked across the dimly lit car park to the waiting Mercedes, seeing the outline of her father's face etched against the gloom of night. He turned and she saw his eyes watching her from behind the gold-rimmed spectacles. Everyone had told her that he was a classically good-looking man. He was also popular with all her friends for his easy, casual manner and they envied her for having such a trendy Dad.

Grant smiled as he opened the passenger door for Cindy and watched her get into the car. It never failed to amaze him that he and Susan had produced such a beautiful daughter. He could still remember the pride he had felt when they'd told him he was the father of a girl. She was his and he would protect, love, advise and occasionally spoil her.

They had been very close when Cindy had been younger. He felt she needed his fatherly protection and had enjoyed taking her out every Sunday morning round the park; it had been his special time with her. Later, as she'd started to grow up, he'd wanted to recapture their times together and had taken photographs and colour slides depicting Cindy changing from a child into a beautiful young woman. Grant sometimes found it difficult to accept that Cindy had grown up but he still enjoyed her company.

He asked how her day had been and Cindy knew he would be in a talkative mood for the journey home. Her father had a laid-back attitude that she felt was sometimes a charade. Contrary to what people thought, he *was* concerned about peoples' opinions, and could get annoyed if mocked – it all seemed at odds with his strong name. Recently she had been secretly embarrassed by his need to be popular and wished he would dress in a more conventional manner for a man in his late forties, like the fathers of her school friends. Ironically they wished they could substitute their fathers for him.

"You look tired," Grant went on and as he drove along the pot-holed lane. He bent down and extracted an item from his car door pocket. "For you!" he said.

Cindy fought a smile for it was her one indulgence – *Toblerone* chocolate. Grant had handed her a small triangular bar and Cindy, unable to resist the temptation, opened the box, broke off a triangular piece of chocolate and placed it in her mouth. She savoured the taste before breaking a second piece off, leaning across, and placing it carefully in to her father's mouth.

CHAPTER TWO

Monday, 14th March

Susan Howard felt a glow of contentment. If the kitchen was the heart of the home then good food had to be the lifeblood. Hers was a pleasant and spacious kitchen in a well-proportioned house, which stood at the end of the cul-de-sac along with five other houses of individual design. The house, *Henderland*, lay back from the road behind black wrought iron gates and a neat wall. A mock stone well provided a focal point on the long stretch of perfectly manicured front lawn. The part-time gardener they employed had cultivated a wide border of colourful shrubs and the pebbled driveway led to a double garage. A white ornamental wheelbarrow, spilling yet more colourful spring flowers, offset the white, pillared porch and impressive front door.

Susan had planned every aspect of the house and had overseen all the major alterations. It was almost 15 years, she realised with surprise, since they had moved to the outskirts of this village. With that move Susan had achieved one of her aims in life. It had been part of her childhood dream to have a steady marriage and to move up in the world from the inconspicuous semi she had lived in with her parents.

Susan poured the sauce over the vegetables and chicken,

placed the dish in the oven and meticulously set the timer.

She smiled in a self-satisfied manner, remembering how she had decided to marry Grant only days after they had been introduced at a friend's wedding. Her decision had caused parental pressure on both sides of the family, but her parents had been mollified by Grant's reassurance that any children would be brought up as Catholics. Grant's mother had not been so accommodating.

When she had met Grant, Susan had already been going out with a boy named Jack. He was a hard-working boy but destined to be an artisan worker all his life. They had never been lovers but there had been hot, searing nights when she had wanted him. But Grant had prospects. He was good-looking, well dressed, had a car and money in his pocket. He had matched her dreams. His rather light-hearted manner, as she later discovered, hid an inner diffidence. His conversation and interests had been limited but were always interjected with humour. From the moment they met Susan had known he wanted her. She loved him, was proud of him and always enjoyed sex with him. It was so easy for him to *arouse* her. She had never been promiscuous but had found that with Grant she could be overtly sexual. Going on the pill had been a trauma, but he had coaxed and cajoled until, in the end, she had had to put her faith on hold.

Susan had been ambitious for them both. With her help Grant had learned conversational skills, public speaking, and of course social graces. Now he was the sole owner of a company that supplied intruder alarms and CCTV systems for commercial buildings. It was a small operation with a part-time secretary and a dozen servicing vans, but it was surprisingly profitable and over the last year Grant had won four lucrative new contracts. Susan, who had always wanted to be her own person, had successfully carved a niche for herself in the field of voluntary work and speech therapy. It was an extension to her main pastime as actor, producer and sometimes prompter with the local amateur dramatic group. There was no part Susan did not feel capable of tackling. The last production had been, *Three Sisters* by Anton Chekhov. She had been cast as Natasha and it had been the crowning glory of her acting career to date. Unfortunately the reviews in the local paper had been unnecessarily dismissive, implying they had played to a near empty house and the production had been too ambitious for a small local group.

Grant had no acting ambitions or abilities, but he would often come down and help out with set building and on occasion stand as Front of House Manager. He was very popular with the younger members of the cast. Cindy had shown no interest in acting but would always come and watch Susan on stage although she would not replicate Grant's over effusiveness when applauding.

Susan finished clearing the cooking utensils away and glanced round, admiring her kitchen.

The icing on Susan's cake had come two years ago with Grant's appointment as a Magistrate. She couldn't resist the glow whenever she had occasion to casually drop his position into conversation, or whenever she saw letters addressed to Mr Grant Howard, JP.

Of course, from every silver lining ... Susan's cloud had been none other than Grant's mother, Olive. She was a cranky, devious, possessive woman who had clung to Grant in a pathetic attempt to stop him marrying. Yes, Susan still thought of her mother-in-law as a venomous old witch. Looking back she realised that Grant must have felt like a pendulum swinging between two women who were both frightened of losing him. Their engagement period had been an ordeal.

First, there had been the letters, demanding attention, vicious in their attacks on Susan. They were followed by a string of midnight phone calls, all demanding Grant's help to deal with imaginary problems. Then Susan had suffered an early miscarriage, with Olive almost gloating at her failure. Susan had tried hard. No one could accuse her of not extending the hand of friendship, but the gesture was neither appreciated nor reciprocated and in the end Susan had given up. The birth of Cindy had done nothing to alleviate Olive's possessive jealousy; in fact it enhanced it. The baby's baptism into the Catholic church had engendered spiteful and vitriolic comments. Well, her mother-in-law was now well away, in a home, so she could no longer deliver her accusations. Only Grant visited her. Susan didn't wish to know about such visits and never enquired. It had been a battle and she had won.

She shuddered as she walked across to the sink, turned on the tap and watched as the cold water gushed into the kettle. She made instant coffee thinking about her own upbringing. It had been very different. Her parents, Emma and Clive, were ordinary people who had faced hardship, redundancy and poverty. Their belief in God held them together through the bad times. Their relationship had been so close that Susan had often felt the outsider. When her father died, Emma had been rudderless but Susan had been adamant that she could not live with them. It had been Grant who had found Emma a small terraced house in the village.

Life was indeed good. There was no doubting that Cindy had grown into a very beautiful young woman. She had gone through a disruptive period and could still be difficult, but what teenage girl wasn't? There had been worrying incidents when she wouldn't eat properly, but she had grown out of that and Susan was very proud of her daughter. "The sort of daughter every mother wishes for," a friend had once said. Subconsciously Susan found herself humming the song that Cindy always played when she was in her bedroom. Snatches of the words came into her mind. It was a fast, catchy tune but Susan could never understand why Cindy played it over and over again. On occasions Susan wished she and Cindy had a closer relationship and envied Grant's easy rapport with her. Perhaps it was her own fault. She had been brought up to encourage independence and did not indulge in the cloying, pseudo sentiment some mothers and daughters shared. Playing at being sisters with her daughter was not for her. No, she had always treated Cindy as a person who was entitled to her own thoughts and privacy. She was not overly inquisitive about boyfriends or what Cindy did. If Cindy needed to tell her she would do so, and as her mother she would listen. Susan assumed it was a relationship that suited both of them. Grant, well, Susan smiled, he was an old softie where Cindy was concerned. Some mothers Susan knew would be jealous of the attention he lavished on her. At times Susan got annoyed at Cindy's occasional lack of appreciation. But Grant was an affectionate man and he would often put his arms round both their shoulders and say, 'How are my beautiful girls today?'

She didn't like to think about the few hiccups that had disturbed her marriage. Susan had discovered early that Grant had a roving eye. After Cindy's birth she had been tired and inattentive to him. All her time and energy had been spent on her daughter. "I needed someone to make me feel wanted," he had said when she had accused him of infidelity. They had weathered it all and now, after the stormy years, had come the tranquillity and the rewards.

She finished the coffee and placed the mug in the dishwasher. There was, of course, a part of her dream that had not yet been fulfilled: her daughter's marriage. But more than that, Susan wanted to be a young grandmother.

Cindy disliked travelling home from school by bus and had recently started to drop heavy hints about having her own car, for she desperately wanted to be the first in her form to have one. However, to date it had all been to no avail.

Today it was raining. She was late and anticipated the journey home would be more unpleasant than usual. She loathed public transport, resenting the invasion of her personal space and had refused to get on the first bus that had offered standing room only and steamed up windows. Feeling slightly irritated she waited patiently for another and now, standing alone at the windy bus stop, she noticed three youths from the local comprehensive school walking on her side of the pavement. Instinctively, she pulled the hood of her school regulation duffel coat over her head, wishing to remain inconspicuous. But it was not to be. Cindy had to endure a series of wolf-whistles and salacious comments as they passed her.

Finally, a second bus trundled into view and choosing to avoid the chattering crowd of shoppers on the lower deck she clambered up the stairs. There was just one double seat left and Cindy quickly slid in next to the window. She pushed her duffel coat hood off her head, allowing the cascading tresses of fair hair to form round her face. She swished it back impatiently, conscious of the admiring glances from the other passengers. Now she dug into her blazer pocket and produced a white paper tissue with which she carefully wiped the condensation off the window to make a small peephole in the glass. She meticulously folded the paper tissue into a small square before placing it back in her blazer pocket, flicked an imaginary speck of dust off her kilt with her thin hand, then straightened the maroon tie with its gold shield, a sign, along with the gold braid on her maroon blazer, that she was a school prefect. She gave a quiet yawn, putting her hand across her mouth before turning to gaze out of the window, idly clicking her long fingernails back and forth.

The bus continued its uncomfortable journey, stopping and starting every few minutes.

"Hi!" a voice said and Cindy felt the thump of a body sit

down next to her. She glanced up seeing David Carter, a nineteen-year-old neighbour who lived with his parents and younger brother. Cindy considered him relatively good looking but found his manner a little forward. He had asked her out on numerous occasions but she had always politely declined.

Today David had been caught in the rain; his mid-brown hair was plastered against his head. He explained that his car was in the garage for repair. They were soon chatting easily together and she was glad of his companionship to pass the tedious journey home. Their conversation was interrupted as a woman carrying a young child and two large shopping bags struggled to sit down across the aisle from David.

"Sorry, love," the woman apologised as she caught his shoulders whilst trying to push the bags beneath the seat and balance the child on her knee.

David helped stow her parcels in a safe place but the bus lurched again so the child fell heavily against him and jogged Cindy.

"Hard work carrying bags and a baby." The woman gave a weary smile.

Cindy glanced across at the child who had started to whimper, seeing the cheap clothes, the flushed face, the wet mouth and the tear-filled eyes.

"He's not well," the woman whispered to David. "Got to have an operation, poor mite. He's been in and out of hospital." She leaned forward and hugged the child to her. She sniffed and dug into a plastic bag, finally retrieving a paper tissue that she used to wipe the child's running nose and eyes. But the child started crying in earnest.

Cindy turned her face towards the window, ignoring the sympathetic comments from David and the cries from the child. Quite suddenly she felt nausea rising in her stomach.

"You okay?" David asked as he peered at Cindy, noting her strained expression and sudden quietness.

"Just a headache," she mumbled not turning to meet his eyes. The child's cries grew more plaintive and even louder. Cindy could hear his raspy breath and whimpers of distress but still refused to look at him.

"Sorry about the noise," the woman muttered, cradling the child close to her. David acknowledged the apology but Cindy continued to stare out of the window, praying that the woman and her crying child would get up and move. In the end she could stand it no longer, so, two stops away from her destination, Cindy suddenly made to get up.

"I've got to get off, my head is splitting," she muttered to David who had no option but to get up and help her off the bus.

Cindy felt the rain baptise her face as she stood on the pavement. David, slightly perplexed by her actions, walked with her along the puddle-strewn pathway. Cindy was now chatting in a gregarious manner, as if the incident on the bus had never happened.

CHAPTER THREE

Susan was dressed in what she termed her practical outfit of jeans and a loose shirt. With an apron protecting her clothes, she stood in the kitchen putting the finishing touches to the evening meal, an open cookery book in front of her. She did not hear the front door open, or see Cindy standing quietly in the hall, a contemplative expression on her face.

"Hello Mum," she called.

Susan turned round with a smile. "Hello, darling. You look wet. Put the coat in the utility room."

Cindy kissed her mother on the cheek.

"I hope the rain eases off. Your father gets his new car today. He'll be disappointed if it is wet."

"With Dad's luck it will clear up," Cindy replied as she walked into the utility room. The new car had been the focal point of all conversation for the past two weeks. "Smells nice," she said returning to the kitchen and giving an appreciate sniff of the aroma. "I'm just going to change."

When Cindy was out of the house she always left her bedroom door slightly ajar, angled just wide enough to allow Pandora to come and go. Despite Pandora's blindness, the cat coped well and now, fed with good food, beautifully groomed and contented, it would be hard to notice her disability.

Cindy's glance went immediately to the bed where Pandora

was stretching luxuriously at the sound of her entering. The room had been decorated to Cindy's requirements, with a long desk space beneath the window. On it was an easel, an assortment of paints and papers, and charcoal and pencils neatly stacked into jars. The bookshelves were well organised and comprised of titles like: *Myths to Live by*, *Alice in Wonderland* and *The Mists of Avalon*. Posters and leaflets for animal rights were stuck on the wall with blu-tac as Susan prohibited the use of drawing pins.

Cindy's was a well-used room, although there was nothing messy about it. Her clothes were always put neatly into the wardrobe next to the en-suite bathroom, and the room kept tidy, although Susan at times felt it was a little too tidy. The double bed, with its ornate curtain-matching cover, dominated the centre of the room and a lace-curtained window overlooked the front garden.

Instinctively Cindy walked across to her impressive hi-fi system and activated the CD Player. She selected track number six from Supertramp's *Breakfast in America* and sang along to the words. The song, *Take The Long Way Home,* evoked memories of a time she had wanted to forget but Cindy felt it was part of her penance to remember and pay tribute to what should have been.

"Oh Pandora!" Cindy now bent to stroke the cat as it lay curled up on her bed. It purred at her touch, its large eyes staring blankly at her. She picked Pandora up, hugged her before whispering into her ear, "How was your day?" She placed the cat down gently on the floor whilst she sat on the edge of the bed and kicked her school shoes off and removed her school uniform. Standing now in front of the full-length wardrobe mirror she looked at her slim figure, clad only in her white silk underwear. She liked to wear expensive lingerie for in doing so felt she was putting a high value on her body. A frown creased her brow as she gazed into her own eyes.

Some days she asked herself if she really wished to be this beautiful. She was after all her parents' little angel – this person who attracted lots and lots of attention, the wolf-whistling men, and envious back-stabbing women. Or did she really have a secret wish to be plain, so no one would notice her slinking into anonymity? It was a dichotomy.

Once she had taken the kitchen scissors and stood with a bunch of long golden hair in her hands ready to cut it off. But the other Cindy said you have a right to look like this. So, she had reasoned it was not she who should change and continued to reassure herself that she neither flaunted her beauty nor hid it. But she still felt a terrible unease within herself and often hated her reflection.

Now she gave a faint smile. Perhaps that was why she liked cats; they just didn't care what you looked like, although she reluctantly acknowledged men and cats had one thing in common – they both got their own way through flattery. Slowly she reached down to pick up Pandora and in doing so caught a fingernail in the bed sheet. She quickly inspected the nail to see if it was damaged, recalling her father's words, "File them down, they are like claws."

Now she went into her en-suite bathroom to fully undress and have her usual afternoon shower. The warm water was soothing as it cascaded over her. She poured the soap-gel into her hands and gently massaged her body, feeling her breasts and then down to the pubic hairs, washing, soaping and massaging. She showered twice a day with ritualistic precision. "Talk about cleanliness being next to Godliness!" Susan had exclaimed one evening.

Cindy stood in her bedroom hugging the towel round her damp body, gently rubbing herself dry. She shuddered as she stood in front of her full-length mirror and slowly let the towel drop onto the floor. She looked at her body, seeing the youthfulness of the breasts, the firmness of her hips and flat stomach and suddenly her whole frame started to shake. The sight of her naked form instigated a mild panic attack. It swept over her like a vicious wave, pulling her down so she could barely breathe. The room felt like it was spinning as she staggered to the bed and lay down. She stared at the ceiling. How many times had she lain thus, frightened and alone? Her head ached and she hugged Pandora for reassurance.

A few minutes later she opened her eyes. The room was quiescent and her heart had stopped pounding. Was there a word for menacing nightmares that invaded your mind during the day?

Now, staggering from the bed she walked across to the wardrobe, grabbing a pair of black jeans from their hanger and a black T-shirt from the drawer. She often wore black; it was a non-colour and she felt it suited her moods.

The noise of car tyres on gravel drew her to the window from where she could see the gleaming white Jaguar convertible with the black canvas roof. Her mother had run out, discarding her apron and disregarding the thin drizzle of light rain. Cindy stood by her bedroom window watching her father laughing as he put his arm round Susan's shoulder and hugged her. Grant got into the car and activated the horn. Cindy knew he did it to attract the neighbours' attention.

The other week she had watched a television programme on psychology. At first it had been a little boring but then it had caught her attention and she had found herself starting to analyse her actions, her parents and their relationship as a family. She had gone to the library and looked at books on the subject, but they had started to disturb her and the more she read the more confused she had become. But she had recognised her father's need to create that careful image of the man he felt every woman wanted. It was probably all to do with his bleak childhood and his mother's possessiveness. Now Cindy stood by the window she tried to feel an understanding for their ostentation and pity for their need to let people know they had, as Susan would say, *finally arrived*. They all played their make-believe roles of pseudo-respectability, hiding their origins and their secrets.

Cindy sighed, and recalled a poem by A.E. Houseman:

Oh how am I to face the odds,
Of man's bedevilment, and God's?
I, a stranger and afraid,
In a world I never made.

"You are such a sceptic," a teacher had once told her. Well, perhaps she was. But respectability was a word that belied so many actions. Sometimes she felt sorry for Susan who tried so hard to play out to perfection her role of the ultimate wife and mother. Perhaps there was no role to learn! Her mother was a good actor, Cindy admitted, but she held the opinion that all actors were subconsciously unfulfilled. Why on earth would you want to pretend you were somebody else unless you disliked being yourself in the first place? Perhaps I should become an actor, Cindy thought.

Her friends' parents varied from those who quarrelled loudly in front of anyone, to those who seemed to be overly concerned about each other with nauseating overtones. Then there were the friends that Grant invited to his parties; empty-headed people who came to be entertained in their candle-lit conservatory after consuming drinks in the bar that Grant had built in the dining room. The evenings always ended up with communal singing in the lounge. Singing was a feature of all their parties. "I can't understand it," Cindy would often say to her grandmother Emma. "It is so juvenile and embarrassing."

Emma would nod in agreement and murmur, "Well, they are not doing anyone any harm." But secretly Emma too found Grant's style of entertaining a little hard to understand.

Cindy had also recently taken to reading books on human behaviour patterns, and Britain's unfair justice system but none of them had answered her many questions. She was currently reading *Dad, Help Me Please*. It was the story of Derek Bentley but the title could so easily have been used for her own autobiography.

Did children love their parents and vice versa, or did they just co-exist through necessity or habit? You didn't have to love your parents. It was not a requirement of childhood. Parents were an automatic package, demanding your attention, your love. Love was another strange word that evoked so many images. Did a soldier really love his country sufficiently to give his life for it? Did squalling babies love you? Love wasn't sex; love was without demands. She loved Pandora. Her father was always saying he loved her, giving her hugs and kisses, demonstrating his words with an outward show of affection. But he could also withhold love. No, it was a word and an emotion that she did not understand. She looked down, watching Susan fuss around the car. Her mother, this person who seemed only to conjure up emotion when there was an audience present. That sounded cruel, but she felt there was little warmth between them, no real empathy, they were just named mother and daughter. Did they really like each other? Susan, unlike Grant, was not a person who engendered intimate conversations. Cindy frowned as her parents bestowed adulation and words of praise on the car.

She moved away from the window. This was a moment to be recorded. There was time before her mother called her down for dinner. She bent down and searched beneath the mattress of her bed for the sketchpad. Pandora gave a small meow of irritation at being disturbed. Cindy placed the pad meticulously in the centre of her desk and then sat down, flipping over the pages, one after another; sketches of her family and how *she* saw them. She stopped for a moment and looked down at the lined face, the elderly eyes now devoid of any expression, blank pools of unknown depth, the lips grim, so like him, and yet so strange and so frightening. Grant's mother, Olive. She could still remember that terrible visit. It had been cold and clinical; the old woman's eyes watchful and knowing and the hands busy. She flicked the page over and the same face, but with the mouth smiling, looked back at her. They were all Cindy's family – paper people drawn by a master hand.

She retrieved her gold *Cartier* pencil from the inside pocket of her school blazer, holding it for a moment between her fingers. She preferred to sketch with this pencil for the smoothness of its case was mystical to her touch. It had been given to her by a wizard who made things disappear and she used it now to create the pictures that videoed through her mind; memories to be expiated onto the virginal paper. Slowly she turned the bezel to obtain the right amount of lead. The white purity of the new page was before her and she guided the pencil to make the first strokes.

Susan had called Cindy for dinner and they were sitting round the kitchen table discussing the virtues of the new car. Cindy gave Grant a rear window sticker promoting the Cat Sanctuary. Grant offered to collect Cindy from school one afternoon and was rewarded with what he considered was a large appreciative smile.

"Well!" Grant sat back a few minutes later and beamed round the table as he finished drinking his mug of coffee. "Here sits one happy man. You've seen the car, now I'm going to take your mother for a spin."

Cindy stood in the kitchen doorway as Grant lowered the convertible's roof and reversed the Jaguar out of the drive. She could not contain a smile as, despite it being the middle of March, they headed off, hood down, hair blowing in the wind, towards the dizzy heights of the village centre.

Quickly and efficiently Cindy finished clearing the kitchen and, satisfied all was tidy, went upstairs. She walked purposefully into her bedroom and switched on her hi-fi. She knew every word of *Take The Long Way Home* but like an addict she had to have her daily fix. She set the volume to high and the CD Player to repeat track six.

"Is there nothing else you can play?" her mother would say but there was nothing else she wished to listen to. Every time she played the tune the words took on a different meaning and she felt she was living the song. Perhaps one day she would not need this mantra. The words reverberated round the house as she went into her parents' bedroom. It was, by her standards, untidy. She strolled across to Susan's dressing table and fiddled with the jars and beauty aids. Then, on an impulse she could not understand, she opened the louvered doors of the wardrobe to stand and gaze at Grant's brightly coloured clothes before fingering his expensive blue double-breasted blazer.

Cindy felt her heart start to thump as she slipped it off its hanger and slowly inserted her arms into the sleeves that dangled below her wrists. She hugged it close to her body, the aroma of her father's after-shave filled her nostrils and she closed her eyes as a kaleidoscope of images came and went. The song was infiltrating her thoughts. Suddenly she was crying. She paused in front of Susan's dressing table mirror and her tear-filled eyes narrowed, for the reflection in the mirror was not of her, but that of her father.

Slowly she removed the jacket and, pushing a lock of hair from her eyes, she gave it a cursory brush with her hand before returning it carefully to its hanger in the wardrobe.

The song now restarted.

She went to her bedroom and felt herself start to shiver as she sat on the bed staring at the bedroom door. It creaked and she gave a startled jump, but it was only Pandora nudging her way back into the bedroom.

She lifted the cat up and buried her face into the warm fur. Then as Pandora settled herself down on the bed Cindy lifted the corner of the mattress to retrieve her sketchbook.

She sat down at her desk and again placed the book precisely in the middle of the work surface. A deep thoughtful frown formed on her face. Slowly she flipped over the pages until she found herself staring at a head and shoulder sketch of Grant with Susan. The more she stared at it the more she became convinced it wasn't quite right. With a robotic movement she picked up the gold pencil and twiddled it round in her fingers before starting to make slight changes to the sketch. Her head started to ache as she returned the sketchpad back under the mattress before lying down beside Pandora to close her eyes and listen to the words of the song.

Susan and Grant's excursion in the new car was interrupted by a faint drizzle of rain that necessitated Grant having to stop and raise the roof. Now, Susan was sitting back with a contented expression on her face, commenting on the expensive smell of new leather. Grant agreed that the car was everything he had hoped it would be and gave her a smile. "I should have suggested dinner, sorry!" he commented as he turned the car into the car park of The Langden Chase Hotel.

He stopped the car to allow Susan to get out at the main entrance whilst he went on to park. Before he got out he sat running his hands over the wood and leather trimmed steering wheel that he had paid extra for. It felt good to his touch, almost sensuous. After taking a small pocket comb from his breast pocket he gave a cursory glance in the vanity mirror, pleased with what he saw. He dreaded old age, losing his looks and his ability. Golf, well that helped to keep him fit and the twice weekly visits to the health club prevented him from getting a potbelly. Some of his friends were huge and his main motivation was to avoid becoming like them. Out of the corner of his eye he noticed two females getting out of a Rover. They were smartly dressed in sharp suits, faces well made up, briefcases in hand. He watched as they approached, allowing his eyes to roam over their figures, not disguising his appreciation. One gave a reciprocal smile; the other ignored him. He often thought monogamy was so restrictive; one woman for life, no real excitement once the honeymoon period was over. He liked to think of himself as someone who had many chances and sometimes he had even been tempted. But he knew there was too much to lose. He thought about Cindy and the joy she had brought to their marriage. He had always wanted another child but Susan had not been keen.

Cindy had been, no, he corrected himself, *was*, very spoilt, inclined to want her own way far too much. Mercurial, but then that was the price of having a teenager. He made no pretence that he worried about her, and knew the dangers of young girls getting mixed up with drugs, drink and sex. Perhaps he was too easy with her, maybe he should have been stricter, but it was too late now to play the heavy father role. He preferred to be her friend. It was true that he and Cindy had gone through a rough patch but that was all behind them. "She is exerting herself, finding her own boundaries," a friend had said.

He got out of the car, activated the alarm and allowed himself a small smile of satisfaction as he gave the car a surreptitious pat on the bonnet before walking to the hotel entrance.

They sat in the comfortable lounge in deep, chintz covered chairs as a waiter sidled round dispensing drinks. They ordered coffee and Susan had a brandy. They talked in a contented manner with Grant cracking the odd humorous remark. Once the talk had focused on Cindy, school reports, friends and outings. Saturdays in town, buying clothes for Cindy, parents' nights and school concerts. But their lines of communication had changed as their parenting roles altered.

Entertaining, parties and a more active social life had replaced the parenthood role and this was due mainly to Grant's large disposable income. He seldom talked about his work but religiously wrote down all his experiences in his journals.

Susan had never been what she termed domesticated. The household chores had been a necessity. Unlike her mother, Emma, who considered dusting, washing, and ironing to be an essential part of a woman's life.

Grant took a sip of coffee and listened as Susan talked incessantly about amateur theatre.

CHAPTER FOUR

Thursday, 17th March

Cindy liked to think she had the mental ability never to become bored. In Cindy's opinion to be bored meant you didn't have a good self-image. Her self-image was, she knew, fragile to say the least, but she was intelligent enough to be able to fill an empty space with constructive work. She would not admit that this was just a way of blotting out unwanted thoughts. Contemplation, that was how she liked to describe the time she spent on her own, and this was not due to boredom but more to an inner need. She required the silence and space in order to file and compartmentalise her thoughts. Sometimes they overpowered her and she was glad when the parish priest, bound by the confessional, listened to her faltering words before eventually absolving her of guilt. But she knew the ultimate sin was not hers. Father Patrick, a sympathetic elderly man, had talked to her about many of her worries and that had gone some way towards relieving the tension she often felt within herself.

This particular afternoon she had some free study time and she had decided to spend it in the town library. Dressed in her school uniform, she walked down the High Street towards the undercover shopping area. As she entered she noticed a young woman with a child in a scruffy pushchair. The girl seemed no older than twenty and was poorly dressed in a grubby denim jacket and long black skirt over dirty white training shoes. Cindy saw her approach two smartly dressed elderly ladies, who refused to listen and side-stepped their way round her. Now as Cindy tried to sidle past the pale faced, poorly dressed child she saw that it was clutching a half empty bottle of what looked like orange juice. It stared up at Cindy, who quickly averted her eyes. But suddenly she felt a hand on her blazer. Turning she met the pale blue eyes of the young woman who stared at her in desperation and muttered, "Please, could you help me?"

Cindy had no option but to stop.

"I've lost my purse," the woman continued and tears welled down the thin white cheeks.

"I'm sorry," Cindy replied and made an attempt to continue on her way.

"Oh, please," the woman begged. "I've got to get the bus to the hospital. My mother, she's ill." Watery eyes met Cindy's. "I know it sounds…" The woman gave a loud sniff. "I can't ask the men. They think… well, you look nice. I thought you could help."

Cindy sighed. Her father had often said that she must never give money to people. What's more, Cindy felt this woman was attempting to con her and wasn't at all convinced by her mumbled story.

But the woman saw Cindy hesitate and continued, "I'll pay you back, I promise. Please."

Cindy knew she wouldn't really miss ten pounds and as she steeled herself to look down at the child she felt an overwhelming urge to help this stranger. "Oh here!" She dug into her inside pocket of her blazer, extracted a ten-pound note and thrust it into the grimy hand.

"What's your name, luv?" The woman grasped the note gratefully.

"Cindy."

"That's really nice. God bless you." Cindy watched as the woman turned and pushed the squeaking pushchair away to mingle with the crowd of shoppers, knowing full well that the bus stop for the hospital was in the opposite direction and that was the last she would see of her ten pound note.

Forgetting her intention to study at the library, Cindy continued to window shop and stopped after a while at a small café for refreshments. Opening the door, she glanced round. The place was almost full and she paused to read the large menu displayed on the wall, before choosing a corner table.

"Yes?" the waitress, asked, pad in hand, "What can I get you?"

Cindy glanced up and smiled as she ordered and paid for a coffee and a sandwich.

When the sandwich arrived Cindy cut it into neat little triangles and then gazed down at her coffee, slowly stirring the liquid round and round. It brought back a sudden memory. "You'll melt the spoon!" Cindy could still hear his voice. In this very café she had looked into his eyes and smiled. It was as if he was still with her, sitting across the table and giving her that very special smile that told her that she, Cindy Howard, was his girl. But the smile did not remain on her lips, for he'd betrayed her. Like everything else in life, it had been so good in the beginning. He had been very knowledgeable. She remembered his kisses, his experience, and his hands on her body. It had been her secret time. Susan had been too busy with voluntary work to notice any of the changes in her.

"You watch the boys," Grant had warned her from an early age. "With your looks they'll be queuing up at the door," he had joked, but there was always the undercurrent of concern.

So no one had really known about the boyfriend who had come into her life and gone out of it as quickly. She had been too young and very inexperienced. Her life was full of secrets and lies. Lies. She picked up her coffee cup and took a sip of the liquid. Well, they were not really lies but untruths, to protect those she loved. But who did she love? She had replaced those secret moments with more mundane thoughts. There had been no one else, well, not really.

Cindy put the cup back on the saucer and dug into her bag to extract a new *Toblerone*. She tried to remember the faces but they seemed to melt away from her, blending into one laughing, smiling face. It could almost have been his face, but somehow not quite. Then her face, those blank eyes, staring out from the emptiness within. She shuddered involuntarily and placed a piece of chocolate in her mouth. Her life seemed so confusing and she tried to get a semblance of order into her thoughts. They were blurred visions of long ago; too long, but not long enough. Cindy couldn't concentrate. She tried hard to remember what had happened. He would meet her after school; they would walk through the park. They would stop in a country lane. He would kiss her. She frowned. The scenes in her head were suddenly a mishmash of faces, hands and words. It was him. Of course it was.

The gentle hum of conversation in the café was suddenly interrupted by a wolf-like howl that made her jump.

"It's that poor dog," the waitress announced to everyone. "He's been tied up outside and has got himself into a tangled mess."

Curiously Cindy stood up and peered out of the window just as the dog's owner returned and untied him.

"So what are you up to?" A soft, well-spoken voice broke through Cindy's thoughts and she found her school friend, Elizabeth Morgan, standing by the table.

"Just looking at that man with his dog," Cindy said with a startled smile.

"What is it with you and animals?" Elizabeth laughed as she dumped her belongings on the chair opposite before sitting down next to Cindy. Elizabeth was a tall, slightly angular girl; with mid brown hair, freckles and warm brown eyes. Her personality matched her looks. "Want some company?"

Cindy nodded.

"How's dishy Dave?" Elizabeth asked, giving Cindy a knowing look before helping herself to a quarter of Cindy's untouched sandwich.

Cindy frowned, momentarily regretting the frequent remarks she had made about David Carter's constant attempts to persuade her out on a date. She could see that Elizabeth was unsure whether to believe her. But it wasn't a lie. David had asked her out many times, and she had just said no.

When Cindy had finished her coffee, she and Elizabeth made their way down the long corridor to the ladies.

They giggled as Elizabeth rummaged through her bag and brought out a small make-up case. Standing in front of the mirror they carefully applied eye shadow and mascara and Cindy saw her face transformed from a schoolgirl's to that of a woman. Finally, Cindy flipped the clasp from her hair so it flowed round her face.

They walked out of the ladies' room. Cindy had her eyes downcast so she was not conscious of the admiring glances from the group of male students at one of the tables.

They strolled nonchalantly down the High Street, chatting animatedly until a middle-aged man in an obvious hurry, bumped straight into Cindy, causing her to drop her bag.

"Sorry!" they chimed in unison and she thanked him as he bent down and picked up her bag.

"The pleasure is all mine," he said gallantly.

Cindy felt herself start to blush as she saw his eyes glance appreciatively over her face and figure.

"I know where we will go," Cindy said suddenly as they approached the formidable building of the town's Magistrates Court. "I think Dad's on duty. Let's go in and have a look round."

They were met at the entrance by two security guards and their bags were searched. Then the doors opened and they were admitted into a large cathedral-like concourse. They saw the people waiting, sad faces, grim faces and youths with a studied air of boredom.

"Can I help, Miss?" A gowned usher with a sheaf of papers in hand swept towards her.

"We are on an educational visit," Cindy said confidently. "Is Mr Howard in court today?" As Elizabeth hovered in the background the clerk referred to his papers. Shrugging his shoulders, he suggested they look into Court Four.

Another gowned usher opened the door for them, Grant was just entering the court and there was a noise as people got to their feet.

"Good afternoon." Grant gave a nod to the waiting clerks and solicitors. Then gesturing for them to be seated, he and his two fellow-magistrates sat down. Cindy allowed the usher to direct them to the rear of the court where they joined four other people.

"Gosh your Dad's so sexy," Elizabeth laughed as she sat down noisily. Grant shuffled through papers and then leaned over the bench to speak to the clerk. Cindy froze in embarrassment as the usher shot a cold stare in their direction.

"Is Vincent Walter here?" the clerk asked the usher who consulted a piece of paper and then with a nod disappeared out of the court. They watched as Grant turned to whisper to the attractive woman Magistrate on his left. Cindy saw him flick an imaginary speck of dust from his impeccable, pin-striped suit, saw the flash of gold from his watch and wedding ring as he straightened his old school tie against the white shirt she had seen Susan iron so carefully the night before.

At that point Grant, as if suddenly conscious of their scrutiny, glanced down into the well of the court. He stared at Cindy in surprise and then Cindy saw his eyes move slowly from her face to Elizabeth's and he smiled, that warm embracing smile, and Cindy knew Elizabeth would be reciprocating. Grant turned and his eyes met hers and she lowered her gaze for she knew instinctively that her presence had surprised him.

Grant looked down at his list of appearances, tapping his gold pen impatiently. Why on earth had Cindy come? He had always emphasised that his court work was a civic duty, not a family event. Susan had visited to the court once. "Just so I know what I am talking about," she had said. But Cindy had shown no interest until now. Her watchful gaze disconcerted him and he felt his hand go subconsciously to the knot of his tie and then to his moustache. Then he realised that she would recognise the nervous gesture, so he stopped.

He found it difficult to concentrate for her appearance had taken him by surprise. She looked grown up, almost a woman. He removed his spectacles and blinked before retrieving a white handkerchief from his breast pocket and polishing the lenses. Grant was aware that the usher kept glancing not only at Cindy but also at the four youths that occupied the seats behind her and who were quite obviously competing for the girls' attention. Their presence was somehow disrupting his court.

Grant slammed his hand down, berating the whispering boys in his most authoritative voice. "Quiet, otherwise I will have you removed from my court."

"I like a man of authority," Elizabeth giggled behind her hand and Cindy now wished she had not suggested they come to the Courts. Elizabeth had spoiled her afternoon; she had wanted time on her own and should have said a firm no when asked if she wanted company. Cindy knew she allowed herself to be persuaded and cajoled far too much. But she did not like disputes or arguments; they upset her. A long time ago she had realised it was easier, well perhaps not easier, but less complicated to say *yes* rather than provoke displeasure.

As thoughts cascaded through her mind her left hand instinctively went to the inside pocket of her school blazer to extract her gold pencil. She held it in her hand, running her fingers over the initials of the inscription. The familiar words from her song crept into her mind. She had no wish to remember how she had acquired the pencil and slowly she started turning it between her fingers. Her eyes never left her father's face.

Grant addressed the man who stood waiting for the pronouncement, but his eyes darted continuously from the accused to Cindy.

"You habitually shop-lift and appear to have no remorse for your actions." His voice was stern and he paused for effect. Cindy realised he was enjoying his moment of power over the man. "We have therefore decided to ask for reports. You must now comply with the Social Workers' request and you will return to this court for sentencing at a later date."

"There are no further cases to call, your Worships," the clerk announced.

"We will retire." Grant stood up and the court rose with him.

"That's it, Miss," the usher said.

"Is that all they do?" Elizabeth asked in a loud voice. "Not worth the fuss!"

The usher smiled in silent acknowledgement and returned to his own small desk at the side of the court.

The youths started sniggering and Elizabeth giggled at their winks and innuendoes.

"Come on Elizabeth," Cindy urged, wanting to leave the court before her father.

"Perhaps your Dad will give us a lift home," Elizabeth said.

"His car only has two seats," Cindy replied but Elizabeth was not to be discouraged and followed the usher's directions round to the back of the building. Cindy found herself following until she located Grant's Jaguar. Elizabeth put her bag down beside the car and leaned against the passenger door. They heard Grant's voice and laughter as he approached, briefcase in hand, with the attractive female Magistrate who'd served alongside him.

Cindy knew he had been about to invite her for a drink, until he saw them watching him.

"Hello girls!" He smiled and Cindy sensed he was surprised they had waited for him. "My daughter, Cindy and her friend, Elizabeth," Grant introduced them.

"Hello," Cindy said in a friendly tone and watched as the woman walked towards her car.

"You looked great in court, Mr Howard," Elizabeth babbled. "So stern and judge-like."

"And so authoritative," Cindy added and saw her father preen himself at the compliment. There was a pause and his eyes darted from Elizabeth to Cindy.

"You both look very nice." Grant smiled, giving them an appreciative look. There was an awkward pause.

"Look, it's Elizabeth's birthday next week," Cindy hastily said the first thing that came into her mind. "I've got to let her choose something, so we'll be off." She gave Elizabeth a meaningful glance, but Elizabeth chose to ignore it and continued to chatter to Grant.

"Would you like to join us, Mr Howard?" Elizabeth asked with a provocative arch of her eyebrows.

Cindy was a little taken aback at Elizabeth's invitation but placed her arm in her father's and said, "Come on, Dad. You can treat us to a cream tea." She winked at Elizabeth.

"Why not? I have a free afternoon." Grant opened the car boot and threw his briefcase and Cindy's bag in. "Come on then." He walked in the middle of them and, placing an arm round each of their shoulders, guided them to the precinct.

CHAPTER FIVE

"Why are we going in here?" Cindy glanced round in embarrassment as Elizabeth guided them through the shopping arcade to the cheap and gaudy lingerie shop. Grant watched Cindy's discomfort with a sudden surge of amusement.

"Oh, just look at this!" Elizabeth laughed as she pointed to a black nightdress. "Cinders would look great in that."

"Elizabeth!" Cindy gasped but Elizabeth was now fingering another nightdress and Cindy picked up a sexy scarlet slip. For a moment Grant stared at her, their eyes meeting. But neither was able to read the other's thoughts.

"Oh, buy this for her, Mr Howard," Elizabeth teased as she held up a black lace nightdress. Cindy gave her father an appealing smile, suddenly noticing the two assistants glancing at each other.

Grant winked at the assistants before retrieving his wallet and producing his gold credit card. He placed the nightdress on the counter and defused the awkward situation by saying, "Daughters!"

"God, your Dad's great!" Elizabeth whispered in Cindy's ear.

"Time we went," Grant announced as he handed Cindy the package.

"Thank you!" Cindy said obsequiously before reaching up to kiss him on the cheek.

"Let's have that cream tea!" Elizabeth urged as they walked towards the *Olde Tea Shoppe* with its mock Tudor beams, rickety tables, floral tablecloths and laden cake-stands. Grant glanced round, smiling at the groups of chattering blue-rinsed females. Their aimless talk stopped for a moment as his head hit a beam with a thud.

"Oh, poor you!" Elizabeth said, her voice full of sympathy as Grant rubbed his head self-consciously.

"Come on. Find a table," he muttered brusquely and Cindy knew he was embarrassed.

"Over here, sir." The voice belonged to a matronly woman who guided them smilingly to a small table beside a window. "I'm afraid tall gentlemen do tend to knock their heads on the beams."

Cindy and Elizabeth sat themselves down; Cindy straightened her kilt and swished her hair back from her eyes.

"He'll have to minimise his attraction!" Elizabeth said laughing. There was a note in her voice that made the woman raise her eyebrows.

"My daughter and her friend," Grant said as he saw the querying expression on the woman's face and the under-the-lid glance from Cindy. He ordered hurriedly.

"She thinks we're his bits on the side!" Elizabeth whispered behind her hand and they both giggled.

"Girls!" Grant said jokingly.

"Sorry, we were just having a laugh," Cindy said softly, momentarily putting her hand over his.

The waitress returned carrying a tray. "You'll pour, dear?" The remark was directed at Cindy. The woman placed the teapot and hot water jug down in front of her and then busily arranged the china teacups. "Enjoy your tea."

Cindy watched Grant from beneath lowered eyelids as he carefully spread the butter, then the jam and finally layered it all with cream. She observed him with amusement as he bit into the scone, leaving a frosting of cream on his moustache. Without thought – or was it to prove something to Elizabeth, she did not know – Cindy reached over and ran the forefinger of her right hand across his moustache, gathering up the cream. Then, slowly, she brought her finger to her lips and licked the cream off. She stopped, seeing the startled expression on Elizabeth's face.

"Thank you, Cindy," Grant winked across at Elizabeth and wiped his moustache with the napkin.

"Cindy tells me you've promised to teach her to drive?" Elizabeth said.

Grant nodded. "Yes, but school work first."

"Did you like your time at school Mr Howard?" Elizabeth leaned forward her face showing interest.

Cindy saw the hand holding the scone freeze in mid-air as Grant raised his eyebrows at the question. "Well, I wasn't as clever as you two, that's for sure!"

"Tell us," Elizabeth urged.

"I was more interested in getting into trouble than studying," he looked directly into Elizabeth's eyes. "And as the only son of a widow..." There was a touch of bitterness in his voice as he remembered the hardship of trying to please a possessive, jealous, unpredictable mother, who could praise and punish within seconds. He had been smothered and subsequently been a bit of a bully at school. He could still hear the cruel taunts that he and his friends made to a fellow pupil, Craig Cooper. Whatever time Craig left school his mother would be at the gate, waiting. Grant recognised the irony for Craig's mother was just as possessive as his. Looking back Grant had felt the burden of responsibility of trying to please Olive and figured he bullied Craig in an attempt to forge his own identity and relieve himself of the tension he received at home. There were so many incidents involving Craig, but one immediately sprang to mind. A group of Grant's friends had got Craig drunk, pouring liquor down his throat, opening his shirt and soaking his body in cheap red wine. Then the girls who'd always flocked around Grant wrenched Craig's trousers off and threw them away. They had shouted cruel taunts at Craig before his mother had intervened. "Mammy, here's your little lad," Grant had shouted and remembered Craig's mother's expression of total disgust as she looked down at Craig's wine soaked body.

"Get up, get up!" she shouted and Craig had followed behind her like some mangy lap dog.

Years later Grant had met Craig accidentally when on a business trip to London. They had gone for a drink together and discussed their school days. Craig didn't bear a grudge and Grant had found him to be good company. In the end he had invited him and his wife to dinner one summer evening. Now they exchanged Christmas cards.

Grant blinked as Cindy snapped her fingers in front of his face.

"Sorry!" He smiled and watched as she refilled their cups then gave a quick glance at his watch. "Look, girls I must be going soon." He turned to Cindy. "Are you all right for cash?"

She nodded unconvincingly.

He gave her a faint exasperated sigh then dug into the inner pocket of his jacket and produced his wallet from which he extracted two ten pound notes. "You are a very expensive young lady," he murmured.

As he passed the notes across he momentarily saw the raised eyebrows and the sardonic expression on the faces of the two women at the next table. He raised his eyebrows and smiled across at them.

"Thank you," Cindy whispered.

Grant finished his tea and glanced at his watch. "See you back home," he stood up and gently ruffled Elizabeth's hair and then bent down and kissed Cindy on the cheek. They watched him leave.

"Gosh you are so lucky! He's the sort of father you dream of having," Elizabeth said and asked Cindy if she would like to come back to her house for dinner. Cindy agreed for she always enjoyed going home with Elizabeth. Theirs was an old house covered in Virginia creepers and set well back from the road in a dishevelled garden. The house always seemed to be full of people coming and going and nobody minded that it was untidy and yes, often undusted. Two golden retrievers welcomed Cindy by licking her hands with their sloppy tongues.

Elizabeth's mother, Elspeth Morgan, greeted her from the ramshackle family kitchen with its *Aga* range. Elizabeth's two younger brothers and elder sister would not be far away. Their father, Alex Morgan, a tall, rough looking man, badly dressed, with callused hands, and a ruddy complexion from continually working outdoors, watched it all with a relaxed air. Precisely what he did had never been mentioned, but he never seemed short of money. The whole atmosphere in the house was one of a close and loving family.

"Sit down, Cindy," Elspeth Morgan said as she saw her hovering in the doorway. Elspeth was a plump and yet surprisingly attractive woman with an easy smile, who never seemed to get hassled when extra people appeared at mealtimes.

They all sat round the large scrubbed wooden kitchen table, which Alex had apparently made himself. Everyone talked at once, but Elspeth had time to listen and offer friendly advice as they related their day. To Cindy it was reminiscent of the television series *The Waltons*.

"How's the cat sanctuary?" Alex asked and Cindy blushed, knowing all eyes were upon her.

After supper everyone helped clear up. There was no dishwasher just a rota for helping in the kitchen. Cindy was given a tea towel and told to dry the dishes. "Earn your supper, girl!" Alex joked.

Elizabeth shared her bedroom with her elder sister. It was a large, messy room with clothes and magazines, compact discs and books scattered round. But nobody seemed to worry.

In the bedroom, they sat talking and listening to music, and Cindy relaxed and wished her home was less formal and more friendly. She reached down and idly picked up one of the many magazines scattered on the floor. It was an ironic choice for she had read this particular issue many times before and she surreptitiously leafed through to page 12 seeking the article *Daddy's Girl* by Shona Widdry. The words jumped out from the pages, it was so real she could almost feel the writer's anguish.

"Take it if you want," Elizabeth said casually.

"Thanks," Cindy murmured as she folded the magazine and placed it in her inside blazer pocket. Then she glanced at her watch and stood up. It was ten o' clock. "I'd better go."

"Suppose so," Elizabeth laughed in exasperation.

"What I need is my own car," Cindy said as she gathered her things together, "then no one would have to worry about me."

"Can't see you getting that."

Cindy frowned. "Why not?" she challenged.

"Well, " Elizabeth prevaricated. "I just don't think your Dad would get you a car!"

"Oh yes he would. I just have to say, Dad I want a car!" Cindy raised her eyebrows confidently.

"Okay, prove it!" Elizabeth challenged.

Cindy stared at her, wishing for a moment that she had never made the rash statement. Then she smiled. "Okay, I will."

Elizabeth's father had offered her a lift, but she welcomed the fifteen minute walk back to her house because it gave her time to think.

The evening was cold with the stars shining brightly from a

clear sky and a thin haze round the moon. Cindy had intended phoning from Elizabeth's to say she was on her way home, but after Elizabeth's challenge about the car it seemed a good opportunity to let her parents worry about her being out, making them realise that a car was more a necessity to her than a luxury. She mulled it over in her mind until she felt confident that she could persuade Grant to buy her one.

Grant arrived home after his night at the health club at ten minutes to ten and found Susan, her face flushed with irritation as she paced up and down the lounge, a glass of red wine in her hand.

"Why is she so late? She telephoned from Elizabeth's to say she was having a meal there, but why so late?" Susan asked without preamble.

Grant sighed as he placed his sports holdall and Cindy's school bag on a chair and slipped out of his jacket. "It's only ten o' clock. You know what girls are like." He was dismissive and just wanted to relax with a small Scotch and tell Susan about his day in court and the party he had arranged for the weekend, but he could see she was in no mood to listen to the menu he had planned during the journey home.

"I'm going to phone Elizabeth's parents." Susan glared at him. "If you're not concerned, I am."

"Oh, I'd leave it a few minutes." Grant tried to placate her, but knew it was useless; she had worked herself up into a state. He offered to telephone the Morgans.

As if on cue they heard the key in the front door lock and before Cindy could walk into the sitting room Susan had marched into the hall and snapped, "Just where do you think you've been my girl?" Her face was flushed with anger and her eyes were hard and unyielding as they bore into Cindy's.

Momentarily Cindy contrasted this with the easy reception she had received in Elizabeth's house and felt a swift rush of resentment. But not wishing to become involved in a family dispute she shrugged her shoulders and said, "Sorry, but I did tell you where I was." She looked at Grant who gave her a conspiratorial wink. "Sorry Dad, but after we left you this afternoon I went to Elizabeth's. I did tell Mum."

Grant was nodding slightly as he ran a finger over his moustache. "Well, as long as my girl is all right." He walked forward and put his arm round her shoulders and she allowed him to hug her briefly before pulling away.

"Sorry I worried you." She yawned. "It would be so much easier if I had my own car," she murmured.

"We'll have to see about that," Grant replied as he walked back into the lounge. "Now, can we discuss the party at the weekend?"

"Not another party?" Cindy asked, envisaging the house once more full of people. Grant had not heard the remark and Cindy picked up her school bag and the carrier bag from the lingerie shop and walked upstairs. Well, she had asked for the car and although her father hadn't said yes, he had not said no either.

Back in her bedroom she prepared to undress but her hands instinctively went to her blazer pocket and retrieved the magazine Elizabeth had given her. She leafed through the pages until she found the article *Daddy's Girl* by Shona Widdry. Then she switched on her hi-fi and carefully read every word as the song infiltrated her thoughts.

CHAPTER SIX

Friday, 25th March

Cindy could not remember how her parents had become involved in what they termed the *party scene*. It had started with a quite ordinary end of production party that Susan had thrown for her theatre group. Then it had been nothing more than drinks and nibbles, but it had escalated.

Grant had found he enjoyed being the host and had built up a reputation amongst Susan's friends, the golf club, and indeed all he came into contact with, as a party animal. It was as if, Cindy thought, he metamorphosed and cast off his inhibitions to become the person he wished people to assume he was. Initially Susan had found it difficult to adapt to the parties and the change that came over her husband's personality on these occasions, and had talked it over with her mother, Emma.

"I think it is to do with his deprived childhood," Emma reasoned. "The remnants of teenage rebellion and the fear of growing old. At least he is not straying."

Susan had accepted that perhaps it was easier to party and observe Grant rather than disapprove and drive him away. If he wanted to recapture the part of his youth his mother, Olive, had deprived him of, then it seemed harmless enough.

Cindy had come to dislike the parties. She felt a deep embarrassment in her father's perpetual wish to dress up in garish clothes. He had allowed his hair to grow a little longer and suddenly the grey round his temple had turned jet black.

"Oh, he enjoys himself." Susan had dismissed Cindy's protests. "He works hard and this is a form of relaxing. He is doing no harm."

Cindy distanced herself further as the party format went from the original drinks and nibbles to what Grant termed *theme nights*. As the year went on the summer barbecues with the colourful garden lights and the occasional fireworks were replaced by candlelight suppers in the conservatory.

Grant had also taken to cooking. *Coq-au-Vin* he found was the easiest and most rewarding dish to prepare. His starters were always well thought out and Cindy could not deny the trouble he went to.

When she arrived home from school on Friday afternoon, preparations were well in hand and Grant had already taken up his position in the kitchen to prepare the chicken.

The dining room and bar were festooned with balloons and stocked in readiness with the usual cask of beer. Large jugs stood in readiness for the Sangria, which Grant prided himself on making, flanked by drip mats and glasses, all awaiting their guests. Without even glancing at the corner Cindy knew the hi-fi would be ready with Grant's favourite seventies music. The idea of singing had come to him after a holiday on the Costa del Sol when they had sat in an English Bar one evening and listened to Karaoke. Cindy could still see Grant, his face tanned, his orange silk shirt open to the waist to show the display of Spanish gold chains round his neck, stride forward to grasp the microphone. He had grinned down at the audience and sung the Rod Stewart song, *Do you think I'm sexy?* She had felt herself blush as the crowd clapped in time to his singing. Susan, whose inhibitions had been pushed aside by her last glass of Spanish brandy, had followed him with her rendering of *Paper Roses*. Grant had returned home and bought a guitar. He soon found he had neither the time nor ability to learn and so he had invested in his own karaoke equipment with a microphone and suitable lighting.

Whether the guests enjoyed making what Cindy termed *complete prats of themselves* was debatable. Some, she noted, never returned, so there was always a stream of new so-called friends passing through the house.

Grant's repertoire had grown with the years and now included, *Jail House Rock* and *Pinball Wizard*. His guests gathered round the bar until the early hours of the morning, singing. The flashing lights, the car horns and the loud goodbyes had brought mild comments and some complaints from the neighbours.

But Cindy had also seen her father put his arms round the females, kiss them and then dance, holding them too close. And her mother seemed to enjoy flirting with the men, and broke into ridiculously girlish giggles whenever a compliment came her way.

Candles were their latest innovation.

"Cuts down on the face wrinkles," Susan said jokingly.

The conservatory was waiting in readiness; candles in ornate holders had been strategically placed on the window ledge and on small tables round the room. The centrepiece on the coffee table was a large glass bowl of coloured water on which ten small candles floated, waiting to be lit.

Cindy found it hard to understand her parents' need to entertain the lightweight people they did. She had listened to the trivial conversation, heard the back-stabbing comments, the flirting and innuendoes. It was, she felt, so out of character with the other image they wished to portray.

Saturday, 26th March

When Cindy opened her eyes she could see the sun shining from behind her bedroom curtains. She did not want to get out of bed, preferring just to curl into a ball and cut herself off from the world, but she had promised Susan that she would go to eight o'clock Mass at Saint Andrews before starting work at the newsagent. She felt a wave of fatigue sweep over her as she thought of the day ahead. The last of the party hangers on had remained until half past two in the morning and she had not been able to get to sleep until dawn.

It always surprised her that even after a hectic night's entertaining both Susan and Grant got up bright and early, and cleared the house up. Her father, she realised, almost had a fetish for tidiness. She felt it was an unusual trait in a man but then so was an exuberance for cooking. Whilst Grant never prepared the evening meals he always helped with the dinner when Emma came round and Christmas was his speciality. In the summer, he loved nothing more than barbecuing. This was a new innovation and Cindy had felt embarrassed the first time he had stood, chef's hat on his head, stripped blue and white apron round his waist, turning sausages and bacon with panache.

Cindy entered the kitchen that was already precision tidy, muttered a brief, "Morning," and pulled up a chair.

Susan smiled across at her from the stove where the usual Saturday morning fry-up was sizzling.

"I don't know how you can eat that after last night," Cindy

said, looking with distaste at the eggs, bacon and fried bread. *The gut-buster* as Grant complacently called it.

"Toast?" Susan placed the rack in front of Cindy's plate. She then stood behind Cindy's chair and gently ran her hands over her long locks.

"Please Mum!" Cindy said pulling her head away.

"Don't you think your hair is a little long to be worn loose?"

"No!" Cindy jerked her head away and a strand of hair fell across her forehead.

"I like it," Grant murmured as he put The *Daily Telegraph* down and smiled across at Cindy. "She is my beautiful angel with the long fair hair."

"Yes, Dad." There was a tetchy note in Cindy's voice and, Grant, noting Cindy's mood, returned his attention to the paper.

This was the only time Susan served food that she did not really consider to be healthy for her family. She liked to quote her mother's, "It puts a lining on your stomach." Emma still subscribed to the notion that a healthy portion of fat and grease were essential to your diet.

"Cindy, do you want an egg?" Susan asked.

Cindy wrinkled up her nose. "No, thank you."

"You don't know what you're missing," Grant said, digging a piece of fried bread into the yolk. Cindy winced at the thought of eating all that fatty food. She ate her toast in silence, listening to their rehashing of last night's party.

Saturday was Susan's morning for a round of golf while Grant took a trip to the cricket club for his mid-morning drink. Her own morning would be spent working in the local newsagent, listening to the girls' giggling as they chatted up the local lads. In the afternoon she'd visit Emma, who lived in a few miles away. Cindy enjoyed the visits that Grant mockingly referred to as *duty calls*. Emma was lonely, Cindy sensed that, yet she had never interfered in their lives and only came to their house when asked.

Cindy tried to visit Emma each Saturday. As they talked,

Emma would stagger up and place the white lace tablecloth over the extended gate-leg table. Then in would come the tray, carrying cups, saucers and spoons. The table had to be properly laid before Emma would bring in small sandwiches and cakes. Emma was a perfectionist and Cindy always appreciated the trouble she took to prepare and serve tea. "I believe in keeping up standards," Emma would say. "Just because you live alone doesn't mean you have to become sloppy."

"You've not opened your letter. This came for you." Grant interrupted Cindy's thoughts, reaching across to the dresser and fumbling amongst the morning's mail. He pushed a large pink envelope across the table.

Cindy stared at the outrageously coloured envelope in surprise, then gave a slight shrug as she picked it up and examined it. Her thoughts went immediately to David who lived two doors away.

"Very nice, looks like an invitation," Grant commented with a grin. He did not continue eating his toast, but sat watching and waiting whilst Cindy picked up her unused side-knife and gently slit the envelope open. She could feel their curiosity as she extracted the card. It was large and expensive. Cindy stared at it, catching her lower lip between her teeth as she read the card's hand written message.

CINDY: YOU'RE GORGEOUS.

She stared at it for a moment before throwing her head back and laughing.

"What is it?" Grant said, curiosity apparent in his voice as he leaned forward and took the card from Cindy's hand.

"So, who thinks you're gorgeous apart from me?" he asked after studying the card.

"I don't know," she replied. "Perhaps it is David, it's the sort of thing he'd do." She took the card from Grant's hand and replaced it in the envelope, studying the postmark and handwriting.

"Mmm," Grant frowned and glanced across at Susan. "Our daughter has an anonymous admirer it would seem." He paused and tried to make his voice sound light. "You're not seeing him are you, Cindy?"

Cindy stared at him, surprised at the question, and then shook her head. "David! No, of course I'm not seeing him, we're just friends!" She could tell from her father's expression that he was not convinced. "Anyhow, I don't know whether he sent it or not, do I?"

She saw the consternation in his eyes and touched his arm reassuringly. "You're still the only man in my life, Dad."

Saint Andrews was a short walk away and its congregation was local and friendly. Saturday morning Mass was always well attended with a good mixture of parents, children and the elderly. Confession followed but Cindy would not take part today for she felt she had confessed her soul dry and no absolution would absolve her from the guilt she continually felt.

She nodded to a few of the parishioners as she entered the church and took her usual pew, five rows away from the communal rail. The Mass commenced and to Cindy's surprise and disappointment, Father Patrick, the elderly priest she liked and considered her friend, was not taking the service.

The celebrant priest welcomed them and Cindy joined in the first hymn, glad it was one she knew. She enjoyed Saturday morning Mass, it was peaceful and she found the prayers and readings oddly comforting. Now, as she stood before the priest and heard the familiar words, *The Body of Christ*, and felt the wafer placed on her hand she whispered *Amen* out loud and *forgive me* in her mind. Walking back to the pew she knelt until the final hymn and genuflected to the altar as she left. As she made her way out of the church she was stopped by a hand on her arm.

She turned and smiled at Andrea, a parishioner she had met during a ten-week course called *A Journey in Faith*. It had been a small class that had congregated in the church hall on Monday evenings, where groups of people had discussed their faith and how it had helped them over the years. Andrea was a nurse who had been divorced and was now married to a bank clerk she had met the previous summer. According to Andrea, Father Patrick had listened to her predicament and, being the considerate person Cindy knew he was, had agreed to bless Andrea's marriage on its first anniversary.

"Haven't seen you for sometime," Andrea said.

"No, school work and all that," Cindy replied softly as they stood outside the narthex. "I was sorry Father Patrick wasn't the celebrant this morning."

"Oh, he's not with the us any more," Andrea said with a shake of her head. "It's shame because he never got to bless our marriage. He's on a sabbatical, or so they say!"

"Oh! But I never said goodbye to him!" Cindy frowned and there was disappointment in her voice. "I would have thought there would have been a farewell party; he's been in the parish for years."

"No party; no goodbye. It's almost as though he never existed." Andrea paused. "You know what surprised me?"

"What?" Cindy asked.

"There have been no prayers for him either."

Andrea left to make her own way home and Cindy walked thoughtfully down the avenue of trees remembering Father Patrick and the series of confessions she had made to him. Andrea's remarks had worried her. It was out of character for the caring priest to have left without saying goodbye. But then she found herself at the newsagents and it was time to face the day ahead.

CHAPTER SEVEN

Susan stood in her bedroom, admiring herself in the mirror. She was still an attractive woman and her trim figure was being shown to advantage in her new checked golfing trousers, a burgundy shirt with the club emblem embroidered on the pocket and this season's *Burberry* golfing jacket. As vice-captain it was right and proper that she dressed the part, she thought, stepping closer to the mirror for a final check on her make-up. She had learned the art through years of practice with stage-make-up and knew how to apply the right amount of eye shadow to enhance the blue of her eyes, how to pencil her eyebrows in a perfect arch and how to paint her mouth the ideal shade of red, dark enough to enhance its allure as it curved into a smile. Her dark hair was expensively cut and styled.

She picked up her *Rolex* watch, an extravagant present from Grant. They lived to the limit of their income, and that worried her, but if she queried what they spent he would sulk and say, "No pockets in a shroud!" Susan wandered across to the window and stood looking out at the back lawn. The gardener was becoming costly but the result was definitely worthwhile. The conservatory had been a good idea too, not least because her house had been the first in the cul-de-sac to have one. The cane furniture with the chintz cushions added that touch of class. Yes, *Henderland* was a tasteful house. She was always on the lookout for new ideas. "You copy everyone!" Cindy had remarked when the new television in its wooden case with the two opening doors had arrived. "I don't!" she had snapped in annoyance at the truth of the statement. The water-colours at least had been her own idea. Costly, yes, but you didn't get quality for a song.

Now they needed a garden lounger, one with a canopy. Susan could imagine herself sitting there in the summer, gently rocking back and forth. But that was on hold for the moment. Susan had a list of planned acquisitions and was slowly ticking them off one by one. The trouble was that as soon as she purchased one item of furniture or clothing she discovered a desperate need for something else. The list never seemed to reduce in length.

Susan was often beset with worry as to what, precisely, to purchase. Her car had caused her great consternation and she had finally settled for an Audi Coupe that been an ex-demonstrator, choosing it for its style and potential to cause envy among her friends, rather than its practicality and huge saving.

She picked up her jacket and prepared to leave the house.

Monday, 28th March

Cindy saw the large, pale pink box lying on the front door mat as she came downstairs that morning. Instinctively she knew it would be addressed to her and frowned as she saw it was unstamped, meaning it must have been hand delivered.

"You're late, Cindy!" Susan snapped as she came into the kitchen.

Cindy knew her mother was tired after a night with the committee at the theatre. "Didn't it go too well last night?" she asked sympathetically.

Susan sighed and managed a bleak smile. "No, it did not. An evening spent in disagreement. What's that?" she pointed to the box in Cindy's hand.

"Something for me!" Cindy murmured quietly.

Grant adjusted his spectacles, lowered his paper and stared across the table at Cindy. Susan gave him a surreptitious glance as they watched Cindy pick up her side knife and slowly and methodically insert it into the sticky tape that held the top of the box in place.

She heard her father give an impatient sigh and said, "Patience father, all will be revealed in good time."

"Come on!" Grant said with a smile, knowing she was deliberately choosing to make them wait.

Susan and Grant watched as Cindy slowly extracted a

white party cracker from the box and then retrieved the small message card.

"Well, does it say who has sent it?" Grant could not refrain from asking.

"All it says is CINDY: YOU'RE A CRACKER!"

"Well someone has good taste," Grant winked at Susan. "You must know who's sent it?"

Cindy shook her head and then said casually, "I think it has to be from David."

"David, eh?" Grant raised his eyebrows. "He seems a nice enough lad to me." He buttered another slice of toast. "From a respectable family as well."

"Oh Dad! There's more to it than coming from a respectable family."

"Cindy's right," Susan said with a sniff. "You either like people or you don't, and Cindy has more important things to worry about than boys who can't even sign their name on a card."

Saint Margaret's School building had once been a convent, and for the last forty years it had played an integral part in the life of the small town. Over the years the school had grown and developed to become a modern learning centre for girls with a strong academic bias. The school boasted that it was always listed in or near the top twenty of the most productive schools in England and the high term fees meant the number of pupils remained at a manageable level. It was also a strict establishment with even the senior girls having to wear full uniform. Susan had always wanted to educate Cindy at Saint Margaret's and it hadn't taken much persuasion on her part to convince Grant that as Cindy was their only child it would be in their best interests to give her a good start in life. And Cindy had certainly made best use out of the opportunity. While she was not quite top of her form, she was near it. She was also popular enough to have been elected a prefect though, unfortunately, she had missed out on being head or deputy head girl.

The cards had been on Cindy's mind all day and she had even taken them to school to show Elizabeth during their lunch in the school's old-fashioned refectory. The two of them had giggled as they discussed David and other boys they knew. When Elizabeth asked if Cindy would go out with David, she had prevaricated.

David was in his second year as an apprentice car mechanic and had always had his eye on Cindy. Living next door, David would often see her walking along the pavement en-route to the bus stop. Although he had ample opportunity to talk to her, Cindy never made it easy for him and he felt that talking to her was like trying to get blood out of a stone. But today would be different. After saving long and hard he had just taken delivery of his second-hand Mazda MX5 sports car. He was now parked outside Saint Margaret's School, irritated that a thin drizzle of rain had prevented him from lowering the convertible roof. Knowing Cindy always took the bus home he waited impatiently for her to emerge, looking forward to offering her a lift.

He heard the school bell ring at 3:45 and it wasn't long before a sea of girls, all dressed in maroon, walked past his car. Then he saw her, she was one of the few girls holding an umbrella above her head. Her long fair hair was tied back into a ponytail and he was surprised she was on her own.

She walked past his car not noticing him.

"Cindy!" he called. She stopped, lowered her umbrella and turned round.

"Fancy a lift?" he asked in a friendly tone and Cindy felt her face blush, knowing all eyes were on her. "Come on," David cajoled.

It didn't take long for Cindy to give in to David's

persuasion and she got in carefully, straightened her uniform and put on her seat belt. "Is this yours?" she asked.

David nodded proudly before saying. "Did you like the cards?"

They laughed in unison.

David drove home slowly, wishing to make the journey last. When they arrived at the cul-de-sac he asked her out on the Friday, but Cindy shook her head saying that her father wanted her to study for the forthcoming exams. But she nodded when David suggested a rain check and with a warm smile got out of the car.

Thursday, 7th April

The wedding invitation was on the snug mantelpiece alongside more mundane invitations to the Magistrates' annual dinner dance and tickets to the local amateur production of *Hamlet*. It was for the marriage of the son of an old school friend of Susan's and would be a smart affair. With only sixteen days to go Susan was becoming very concerned about what she was going to wear.

"I'll take you both to London," Grant had suggested, knowing that a day out would appeal to Susan.

Cindy had not wanted to go. She had more than enough clothes in her already extensive wardrobe and knew a day shopping with her parents would be an exhausting waste of time. But her excuses had been pushed aside.

She had been having sleepless nights recently. In the dark she could see a face and yet it was not a face. She could feel the hands on her body but there were no hands there. For some reason Olive's face would come floating ghostlike before her eyes. To escape these unsettling visions, Cindy often got up in the night, listening to the silence of the house then creeping slowly downstairs, avoiding the known creaks and going into the kitchen to stand barefoot on the floor tiles, feeling their coldness seep through her body. She'd make herself a hot drink, anything to take her mind off the disturbing thoughts pounding through her head. She felt a prisoner in her body, like being in a room with a locked door, wanting to find the key to get out, but never succeeding.

"You look tired," Susan commented.

"Just exams," Cindy replied, relieved yet irritated to see her facile explanation so easily accepted.

Susan had decided they would go to London by train and had driven them to the local station in her car. They were now sitting opposite each other in the first class carriage. Susan, happy and relaxed, was starting to go through her various shopping lists. Cindy saw Grant wink conspiratorially at her and managed to reciprocate with a small smile.

"We'll start at Knightsbridge," Susan announced, "Harrods. I always like to shop at Harrods for a special occasion."

Cindy turned to look out of the window. She began to click her nails together and stared out as the countryside sped past. She felt the familiar wave of travel sickness and cursed herself for forgetting to bring her tablets. She closed her eyes, but the prospect of rest was abruptly shattered by a sudden noise. She desperately tried to block it out. But it seemed to get even louder. From the second-class carriage the cries of a young child, plaintive and wailing, obliterated all other sounds.

"Are you all right, dear?" There was real concern in Susan's voice as she leaned forward and peered at her daughter's pale face. "You've gone quite white!"

The underground service to Knightsbridge was uncomfortable. Cindy hated standing, hanging onto the overhead strap so that the men could sit leering at her. Grant seemed to be enjoying it. He was smiling and joking with Susan. When he winked this time, Cindy turned away.

Harrods was its usual chaotic self, but choosing an outfit for Susan was easier than Cindy had anticipated. "I think she's bought it more for the label than for the style," Grant said, nudging Cindy as Susan disappeared once more into the changing rooms. The assistant packed the garment into a large, clearly marked, *Harrods* bag.

Choosing for Cindy was more fraught for she resisted trying on anything that Grant suggested. She found herself irritated at his interference and by the way he smiled at the assistants and kept on saying. "I think this will look good on you."

"They are too young for me, Dad," Cindy protested as Grant lifted outfit after outfit from the racks. In the end it had been Susan who, seeing Grant's growing irritation as Cindy continued to reject his choices, finally pointed out something that seemed suitable.

Cindy stood in the dressing room and stared at her reflection.

"I'm sorry Mum, this is just not me," she said and Susan had to agree. The dress looked terrible.

It was then that Cindy went across to Grant, who was now sitting down, exhausted by the whole affair. "I'd rather use something from my existing wardrobe," she said.

Grant shrugged. "If you want." It was Grant who then persuaded Susan to let Cindy have her own way. When, after much deliberation, Susan finally agreed, Grant winked again at Cindy.

After that Cindy asked to go off round the store on her own and they agreed to meet at far end of the food hall in 45 minutes.

Cindy was not keen on Harrods. She felt it sold everything under the sun at ridiculously inflated prices, and as she pushed her way through the throngs of people her opinion did not alter. But she was enjoying the break away from her parents.

They met up in the food hall as arranged and lunched in the store. Cindy would have preferred somewhere quieter, but Susan was glancing round, chatting to Grant and basking in the euphoria of being in Harrods.

"I was thinking." Cindy smiled, "Poor Dad! We should buy you something."

"Oh, that's a lovely idea," Susan nodded.

Cindy ignored Susan's obsequious tone. "A silk tie ... that's what you need for the wedding. It'll be our present."

Cindy and Susan left Grant wandering round the electrical department as they made their way to the men's department.

Cindy picked out one of the most expensive ties and handed it to Susan. "This will go with his dark suit."

Susan raised her eyebrows as she examined the orange motif. "It's pricey," she muttered.

"Surely he's worth it?" Cindy goaded her mother.

It was impossible for Susan not to meet the challenge. She signalled resignedly to the waiting salesman, handing over the tie and her credit card.

They finally left Harrods in the early afternoon, deciding to walk across Hyde Park in the spring sunshine to Oxford Street. By the time they took a taxi to a crowded Euston Station they were all exhausted. The journey home was tiring, tedious and terrible.

CHAPTER EIGHT

Though she was exhausted after the day trailing round the shops in London, Cindy couldn't sleep. Pandora was snoring, a gentle comforting sound at the foot of her bed. Cindy got up, walked to the window and pulled the curtains back. Her room was bathed in moonlight. Swiftly she walked to her hi-fi and turned the volume to low. She listened to her song, but she could not relax. It was one-thirty and all was still. The light from the full moon illuminated the garden, outlining the trees, which in turn cast finger shadows over the lawn. She looked up at the moon, which seemed to be watching her like an all-seeing, all knowing Goddess.

She shivered, but it was not with the chill of the night. The words of the song ran through her mind but it was her thoughts she could not control. Her heart had started to race and the pain was back in her stomach. The moonlight seemed to dance around the room with its single, glowing beam. She thought of the horrible dresses she had tried on and was glad her parents had eventually agreed not to buy any of them. It had seemed a wasted day. Suddenly she remembered a long forgotten incident of a pink party frock with white petticoat frills that Emma had so painstakingly made for her, along with a beautiful blue velvet cape with lining to match the dress. It had been her seventh birthday present.

Then her father had said, "You're beautiful, the prettiest girl in the world." He had held her high against his chest with her long hair flowing over his face as Susan clapped her hands with Emma looking on with pride.

But even then she had been afraid. She had hated hearing stories of wicked fairies, giants and two headed monsters. Susan had taken her numerous children's picture books and pasted over the nasty pictures with blank paper but there had been other horrors that couldn't be eradicated as easily. She remembered an incident at junior school when she had seen a drawing of King James the First of England who seemed to have big round eyes and an overly long tongue. The teacher had put an illustration on the blackboard and gone to great lengths to describe these peculiarities. It had made her feel sick and she had fainted in the classroom, much to the amusement of her classmates. Another time she had been at Elizabeth's when the family were watching a horror video. The faces and monsters had interwoven with her own demons and she had made an excuse to leave. She could still not look at horror films, and wondered why people felt the need to frighten themselves when life was really frightening enough already.

Tuesday, 19th April

Susan had planned a small family dinner party to celebrate Cindy's first day of work experience at the local commercial radio station. In their final year, pupils from Saint Margaret's were allowed out into local businesses. The radio station had selected Cindy and Janet Hughes, another girl in her class, to experience a week in the life of a business serving the local community.

"They must think a lot of you," Grant had said, pride in his voice as Cindy had told them what would be involved.

Susan had asked her mother to join them for dinner, knowing how lonely she was since Clive had died. As they had been a devoted couple Emma had forged no interests or links outside the home. Susan had tried to encourage her to join the local Catholic Women's League, but Emma had declined, saying she preferred to sit at home with her knitting and reading Agatha Christie novels. She was quite opinionated and would support her arguments with quotations from *Readers' Digest* (at times, Grant would regret having paid the yearly subscription). Emma was seventy-two; a small, thin figure with motley brown hair which had never, to her great disappointment, turned the silver she longed for. Her face had remained youthful and she would remind anyone who cared to listen that this was down to the fact that she seldom drank and had never smoked. She dressed in a conventional manner, skirt, blouse and cardigan with the inevitable string of pearls and the cord from which her spectacles hung round her neck.

They were all having a pre-dinner drink when Cindy came home. "What's this, a party?" she asked, looking from one to the other, her face animated before walking across to kiss Emma on the cheek.

"It's a little dinner party for you," Emma replied, smiling up at Cindy. "We thought it would be nice to let you know how proud we are of you for doing so well at school."

"You look pleased with yourself," Grant said as he came into the conservatory carrying a small silver tray with two glasses of sherry and a gin and tonic carefully balanced on it.

"I got a lift home from David. His car is fantastic," Cindy beamed.

Grant raised his eyebrows and handed a small glass to Emma and then one to Susan. "Someone has their eye on my Cinders!" he said in a humorous tone. "This young lad has even sent her anonymous cards," he explained as he sat down and took the first sip of his drink.

"Cards?" Emma murmured.

"Oh, just silly boy to girl cards, nothing nasty," Grant added.

Cindy made her excuses and went upstairs to change, knowing her grandmother would milk the topic as much as she could.

In her bedroom she slowly stripped off her school uniform, shaking the creases out of her kilt before placing it on a hanger. She folded the tie and sweater before putting the shirt into the linen basket. Then she showered, feeling the water cascade over her body. It had been a good day and she felt light-hearted and happy. She now dressed in her familiar black jeans and T-shirt.

As Cindy walked into the dining room Grant was opening

a bottle of *Lambrusco* wine. "Here we are, Cindy," he smiled at her, "you can have the first glass."

Emma, the *matriarch*, sat at the head of the table and Cindy gave an inward smile as she wondered what topic would be chosen for them to discuss. She knew all about inter-relationships and what was expected from each member of a family; the pecking order, and where you stood. She realised you never really knew anyone, not even yourself. Here we all are, she thought, sitting round the table, my family. She stretched her face into a smile and her grandmother responded. Now they see me smile, she thought, my nice open smile, my eyes bright, intelligent and innocent. Her outward shell, the body, the name, but who exactly was Cindy? Where was she? What did anyone know about her and those black velvet thoughts that sifted through her mind?

"Here's to a happy family!" Susan raised her glass to her.

"Yes, you have a lot to be thankful for," Emma said.

Her mother had obviously gone to a great deal of trouble. The table was beautifully set, with candles flickering. The lamb was cooked with rosemary, and the vegetables were Cindy's favourites. Grant smiled as he looked round them before standing up to carve the leg of lamb whilst Susan served the vegetables. Emma was asking Cindy about her day and Cindy, her face flushed with enthusiasm, was sitting back smiling.

"Janet, came with me." She explained the selection procedure and elaborated on the morning, remembering how nervous she had felt as she and Janet had entered the radio station's reception lounge. They had sat on the settee drinking coffee from plastic cups. Cindy had been surprised that Janet, a pleasant but plump girl, with pale blue eyes, a round face and lanky fair hair, had been chosen for the assignment. Her size made her the butt of many classroom jokes, but Janet took it all with good humour and survived with a tenacity that Cindy admired. She secretly wished she possessed the same quality to laugh off personal remarks rather than take them to heart and dwell on them.

"Janet?" Susan was now saying, "Isn't she that rather plain girl?"

"She has a hard time with all the comments at school, it's not easy for her," Cindy said defensively. "Her father has been made redundant; they've got money problems. She eats stupidly and she bites her nails. I advised her to get a Saturday job and I even offered to put in a word for her at the sanctuary."

"That's really nice of you," Emma cut in.

"Did you see any DJ's?" Grant asked.

Cindy nodded. "Oh yes, I saw and spoke with Bill Smith. He offered me a photograph."

Susan's eyes lit up with interest; she often listened to his afternoon programme.

Cindy got up and went into the hall and came back with a smile on her face. "Here you are, Mum, I know you like him."

Susan took the coloured photograph and noticed the dedication was to Susan.

Reading her mother's thoughts Cindy added, "I asked him to sign one for you."

Susan placed the photograph down on the table and Emma leaned over and said, "My, he's good looking."

Cindy raised her eyebrows as she sat down. It was a lie. Bill Smith's photograph showed him looking quite sensational, young and good-looking, but the reality was that he was old, with dyed hair and a potbelly. "It's just a con-trick," she said quietly. "Nothing is as it seems; it's all make-believe. They're just actors on a set, a figment of their own imaginations."

"Oh darling," Emma shook her head glancing across at Susan, who shrugged her shoulders, "You sound so cynical for one so young."

"Well, you have to have illusions to be disillusioned," Cindy replied, her face now still. Only her eyes moved slowly round the watching faces.

Emma frowned; it seemed an odd remark to make.

"Don't you sometimes think that we are all just showing people what we want them to see?" Cindy continued. "I mean – you don't know me and of course I don't know you. We're all icebergs, with that secret part of us hidden from sight!"

"It's all too deep for me," Grant said with a yawn and then laughed. Cindy too forced herself to laugh in a light-hearted manner.

Only Emma seemed disturbed and Susan saw her finger the pearls round her neck, knowing from the gesture that Cindy's comments had made her uneasy.

"Are you saying that nobody knows you?" Emma asked and Cindy glanced up as if surprised at the question.

"I suppose I am. You see what you want to, but in here," she tapped her head, "is the real me." She shrugged. "I could be a druggie, a prostitute or even a mass-murderer, and you wouldn't know."

"Oh darling!" Susan exclaimed in horror.

"Mum, I didn't mean it literally," Cindy gave a disarming smile.

Emma saw the blush sweep over Susan's face and was suddenly reminded of her husband, Clive, and the friction that had existed between him and Susan. He had never been able to accept that women had opinions of their own. It had been hard for Susan; she knew that, although she had never taken Susan's side against Clive. She remembered the time when Susan – she had been what, sixteen? Emma couldn't quite remember – had come in and stuck a membership card under her father's nose.

"What is this?" he had said coldly.

"I've joined the Conservative Party."

She could still see the anger on Clive's face. Clive was a

Labour man born and bred. It had never been the same after that; the political point scoring escalated and the atmosphere in the house was somehow soured for good. She sometimes thought that it was as well he had died when he did. Susan's lifestyle now stood for all he had loathed and for her to have married a non-Catholic would have been the final disintegration of their relationship.

Emma now glanced across the table and saw the contemplative expression on Cindy's face and wondered just what was going through her mind.

CHAPTER NINE

Saturday, 23rd April

Susan woke early. It was *Saint George's Day* and it looked as though the weather was going to be beautiful for the wedding. She felt a tingle of anticipation at the prospect of showing off her brand new, and expensive, outfit in the company of her handsome husband and her beautiful daughter. She could already imagine the admiring glances that would come her way.

She turned on her back and gazed at the ceiling, and sighed contentedly while Grant gently snored beside her. She gave a sideways glance at his sleeping figure. I love him, she thought, wondering where the years had gone. She wished the family atmosphere could last forever but soon Cindy would be going to university and the family bonds would start to loosen. All the more reason to make today a day to remember.

Glancing at the bedside clock, Susan knew she didn't have to rush.

"You always arrive hours before any event," Grant had joked, adding in mock exasperation, "You're the only person I know who does routine reconnaissance."

"I believe in being on time," she had retorted. Today would be no exception. Although she would not admit it to Grant, she had been to the church and had timed the journey. She had even picked out the pew. The whole object was to find the best vantage point from which to see the guests and the bride and groom. The hotel had also come under Susan's scrutiny. It was not quite the place she would have chosen, and was a little vulgar, she thought. The furnishings were, well, just that little bit too worn and the ladies room, her most trusted gauge of a place, was only surface clean.

An hour later, Susan was smiling with contentment as they sat round the kitchen table in their dressing gowns.

"I don't suppose you have any idea how long it will take to get to the church?" Grant said to Susan, winking across at Cindy.

"Traffic permitting, exactly twenty-three minutes," Susan replied with a smug expression.

"And the ladies toilet?" Grant continued. "Did that pass your test?"

Cindy opened the wardrobe and took out her favourite skirt. It was well fitting and fell below the knee, with a slit at the back. She wore it with a yellow silk shirt and a man's brightly patterned silk waistcoat. The family hadn't seen the waistcoat; she had bought it in town one Saturday afternoon after visiting Emma.

Cindy checked her appearance in the mirror, content with what she saw. Giving her hair a pat she remembered the final touch to her image and retrieved the sun-glasses case from her bottom drawer.

She leaned down and kissed the top of Pandora's head and stroked her fur, hearing her purr in contentment, and then went downstairs.

"You look very nice," Grant clapped his hands with approval as he came into the hall from the kitchen.

"Oh does she indeed?" Susan snapped. "And what about me?"

Grant smiled, "Both my girls look very nice." And he placed an arm round their shoulders and guided them out of the house.

Once outside Susan put her arm through Grant's as he walked her to the car, but he accidentally caught his trouser leg on the car's bumper. "Grant!" she said in exasperation and bent down to brush the mark off with her hand.

The church, *Saint Francis of Assisi*, had once been part of a monastic order and did not possess any external architectural beauty. The once expansive grounds where Franciscan monks had walked in contemplation had now been absorbed into a large car park, with only the occasional bush, tree and statue left as a reminder of its past glory. From the car park was a well-trodden pathway flanked by mossy headstones with indecipherable inscriptions.

Susan smiled graciously as she led her family up the three steps into the narthex. She dutifully dipped her fingers in the holy water before being shown to their pew by the usher. Cindy genuflected; Grant just sat down. It was not the position Susan had wished for, but it did offer her a reasonably favourable view.

After kneeling to say her usual prayer, Cindy straightened her skirt and fiddled with the gold chain round her neck. Gazing round she admired the intricacy of the stained glass windows, and the vivid colours. She also noticed a few young men glancing in her direction.

If the exterior of the church was bleak it was well compensated for by the internal beauty of the stone pillars, side chapels and altars. She sat back and closed her eyes and through habit began to click her fingernails back and forth. Suddenly she heard the dismal wail of a baby crying behind her. It stopped as quickly as it had started and without any reason her thoughts went back to the previous Friday afternoon.

"Miss Brown wishes to see you," she had been told by the Head Girl, on entering the prefects' room. Immediately the air was filled with the teasing jibes of the other girls, suggesting that she was in trouble. Cindy had gone immediately to the headmistress's study where she had waited in the secretary's office before being allowed into what the girls called the inner chamber.

Miss Brown had been the head teacher of Saint Margaret's for twelve years and was a plump, middle-aged woman who spoke in a clear, clipped northern tone. She peered over the top of her half moon spectacles as Cindy came quietly into the room. "An envelope came to the school addressed merely to Cindy. As you are the only pupil we have of that name I am assuming it is for you and I have to ask you to open it in my presence." Miss Brown reluctantly handed the brown manila envelope across the desk. Cindy took the small envelope, secretly praying that this was not one of David's jokes, but try as she might she didn't recognise the writing.

"I do not approve of personal mail coming to the school," Miss Brown warned her.

Without answering Cindy ripped the envelope open and took out two five-pound notes. There was also a leaf of paper that had been torn out of a cheap notebook with a message saying, *Thanks for the loan of the ten pounds*. She stared at the money in amazement; she had long ago forgotten the incident with the girl in the precinct.

She related the incident to the astonished headmistress and added, "She really did keep her promise."

Now, waiting for the wedding ceremony to get under way, Cindy felt a stab of remorse and silently reprimanded herself for doubting the girl's character. She was deep in thought and continued to click her long nails together. She was abruptly interrupted by Susan's hand on her arm.

"Stop that," Susan hissed.

The ceremony began and the congregation rose. As Cindy listened to the priest and then whispered the responses she had given so many times on so many occasions, Cindy felt her hands begin to shake. *Would God forgive her?* She gave a faint shudder and felt rather than saw Susan's eyes on her. Cindy's head ached and the readings washed over her. Suddenly she thought of Olive. There would be no Requiem Mass for her, just a cold burial. Why think of her grandmother now? What was really so wrong with Olive? She knew too much, that was it. Those hands with the grotesque nails and the rings that jangled; the saliva on the lips. But the face in Cindy's mind was becoming blurred and it was no longer Olive's.

She felt Susan's hand cover hers and saw that Susan had also taken Grant's hand, binding them together as a united family.

Grant too was thinking about his mother, that covetous old woman who had so nearly managed to pull him back into her possessive orbit. She had been old to have a child; an only child and a son at that. Why had his father left? Allegedly he had died of cancer but there was no grave to visit, only a single picture of a man she said was his father. There was no proof she had actually been married. She called herself Mrs and wore a wedding ring, but she had no photographs, no friends or family to confirm her story. Grant had thought of applying for a copy of their marriage certificate – but did he really want to know? No! He had his own family now.

Grant remembered how he and his mother had lived, or existed, in the small terraced house in a grim northern town. He had tried to love her, to please her, to understand her anguish and her poverty of mind and spirit and purse. She had rejected him, yet possessed him. He would never understand the complexities of that relationship.

Grant could still see his mother's cheeks, deeply furrowed

with bitter lines, her mouth grim and unsmiling. He remembered her hair, streaky grey and invariably pinned at the nape of her neck. And how could he ever forget the disturbing, and disturbed, eyes with their discomfiting stare. Grant stroked Susan's hand in his as he thought of his mother's long bony fingers and her habit of perpetually dry washing her hands, like Cindy's irritating habit of clicking her long nails.

Grant had often wondered who had loved his mother enough to want her sexually; or whether he had been the result of one sordid encounter. Had she been unwilling? Had he been born out of hatred not love?

Susan had not been his first woman. She liked to think she was, but he had looked for the warmth his mother could not give him long before Susan came on the scene. Susan had been different; she was a girl a man wanted to marry. He remembered that Sunday morning when he had told his mother he was getting engaged. He had survived the nightmarish difficulties of growing up, going to college, trying to leave home, but had always been drawn back in. Susan had offered him a way out and he had welcomed it and her strength. But he had not been prepared for his mother's vindictiveness or his own feelings of guilt. Olive had wanted to control their every move. He had not been able to cope, not with two women pulling him in different directions. One had had to be sacrificed. In the end it had been his mother. And now her face and the hatred that had distorted it as a result of his rejection haunted him. Months after he and Susan had married, Olive had turned up at the door of their flat, pleading with him to leave Susan. Grant had slammed the door in her face. He had contacted her again when Susan was pregnant, hoping the news would bring peace between them. It had been a false hope. Olive sent a note to Susan, saying that she hoped the baby would be born dead; that it was better if women had no children to hurt and harm them. He had jotted his thoughts for this period in his journals.

Grant gazed down at the hymnbook clutched in his hands, trying to concentrate, but Olive's face was there, staring back at him. He felt the sting of guilt and bit his lip. He had had his own mother committed. It had been very quick. A couple of conversations, a couple of forms to fill in, the police, the doctor and that had been it. He would not speak of it, but he had made himself visit Olive, a parody of the dutiful son. The thought of that sterile room with the chairs circled round made him shiver. He had tried to introduce Cindy to her *other* grandmother. Poor Cindy had been terrified. There had been weeks of nightmares, when she imagined all sorts of horrors. The stir of movement around him finally brought Grant back to the present.

Cindy followed Susan from the pew to join the queues waiting to take communion. Then it was her turn and she watched the priest raise the host and murmur the comforting words. The wafer was placed in the palm of her hand. "Amen," she whispered and put the wafer in her mouth before returning to her place. The aisle was crowded but all she could see was Grant's eyes fixed on her. She returned to their pew where she knelt, her mind a turmoil of thoughts as faces blended into one another. In the distance she heard the choir singing. The bride and groom were kissing. There were tears in Susan's eyes. Finally they moved slowly along the aisle and out of the church.

"I'm hungry," Grant said as they walked back to the car. "That's the problem with these late weddings, they do nothing for your appetite."

The reception was tedious. Cindy had been placed at a separate table from her parents and next to another fair-haired teenage girl called Jessica. They did not speak initially but exchanged meaningful glances as they listened to the interminable speeches. Finally, the formalities drew to a close and everyone was ushered into the lounge for a break before the dancing commenced.

"They should have had Robbie, my boyfriend, as the photographer," Jessica muttered in an attempt to break the ice as she and Cindy sat down on a settee. "He's just sitting at home doing nothing."

"Phone him," Cindy said as she started to yawn. "No one will notice an extra guest."

Jessica stared at her and then shook her head. "I couldn't. Suppose someone found out?"

"Who's going to bother? Anyhow I'll back you up." Cindy gave Jessica a small push. "He's probably sitting at home hoping you'll call."

"Do you think so?" Jessica said, already getting up.

Cindy watched Jessica walk out into the lobby, before turning to smile at the old lady who had sat down beside her.

"Hot, isn't it?" The old lady puffed as she started to fan herself with a hand, beads of perspiration on her forehead and lip.

"Would you like a drink of iced-water?" asked Cindy.

"Would it help?" The tired eyes met Cindy's.

"I think so. We can put a cube of ice on your forehead." Cindy stood up and went to the bar, returning a few minutes later.

Cindy held the glass out, "Put it to your forehead. It will cool you down. My grandma always says it helps." She opened her bag and took out a small spray of refreshing mist that she sprayed onto a tissue and dabbed at the old lady's neck.

"Are you all right, Mum?" The bright voice belonged to a reedy, middle-aged woman.

"This young lady has looked after me." The old lady gave Cindy a grateful smile.

Cindy watched the two of them go off arm in arm, the old lady still hugging the glass of iced water that was now dribbling on the carpet.

"He's out." Jessica's voice was distraught as she flopped down beside Cindy. "I phoned his flat and then his Mum. She said he'd left early. Gone to London!" She gave a faint sniff. "He didn't say anything to me. Told me he'd be in all day."

"That's men for you!" Cindy said in a sceptical tone.

The dancing was the usual wedding mixture of old and new, with the bride and groom taking the floor for the traditional first dance. Susan sighed with disdain, as she watched the men quickly divest themselves of their jackets, to show off their braces, belts and beer bellies. Some even rolled up their shirtsleeves and took off their ties. The ladies, in their too tight skirts and cleavage-spilling dresses, seemed to expand as seams were stretched to the limit.

Jessica had been talking incessantly to Cindy about her job as a hairdresser. Cindy nodded at the appropriate times until a jacketless, tieless, paunchy man shambled across the dance floor, his eyes on Jessica. He eyed her up and down before saying. "How about a dance?" He held out a podgy hand and Cindy heard Jessica sigh as she shook her head.

"Enjoy yourself!" Cindy laughed.

The man asked again and finally Jessica reluctantly got to her feet.

"Well," Grant said with forced jollity. "I think we'll dance." He held his hands out to Susan. She laughed and placed an arm round his waist as they moved to the dance floor.

Cindy watched Grant pull Susan closer for the slow, smoochy waltz. Her mother's hand was entwined in Grant's hair. He was whispering in Susan's ear and she was laughing. Then as Grant spun Susan round he looked up and his eyes met Cindy's. He smiled, that special smile to her. Without fully knowing why she pushed her way onto the dance floor and tapped Grant on the shoulder. He turned and the smile returned as he and Susan drew apart.

"Cindy!" his voice was soft as silk. The music was loud and she felt strangely like an observer to the scene she was creating. "My," he said with a mocking smile into Cindy's eyes. "I am in demand from my women tonight."

Susan, whose feet were aching, was glad of the interruption and missed the veiled confusion in her daughter's eyes as Cindy moved into Grant's arms.

"You've a handsome husband, dear. Who's the pretty girl he's dancing with?" an obese lady asked as Susan returned to the table.

"Cindy, our daughter," Susan replied with pride in her voice as she watched Grant and Cindy slowly circle the floor.

"She's a real beauty, easily outdoing the bride!" the lady continued.

With the dance over Grant and Cindy returned arm in arm to the table, where he released Cindy's arm and went to kiss his wife on the forehead. Cindy moved past them to stand outside the circle, watching. Most of the guests had had too much to drink and she thought how stupid they all looked. Jessica was still in the tight embrace of her partner. Cindy could see her obvious discomfort and gave a faint giggle as they drew alongside. Then the dance ended and Jessica appeared to go off to the ladies' room.

Across the room Cindy saw a group of youths standing, pint glasses in their hands, laughing and sniggering as they looked across at her. She knew what they were thinking and turned away, hoping they wouldn't pursue her. It was then she wished she had brought David with her.

"Dance?" a voice asked. She turned to see the acne-pitted face of a youth hovering beside her. His expression was a livid red, his hair dark with sweat, his eyes beseeching her to say *yes* as they constantly darted across to his waiting peer group who were watching the scene avidly.

"No thank you," she murmured, ignoring the hurt in his eyes and seeing, with relief, that Jessica was returning.

But to her horror, Jessica said, "Go along, Cindy. Dance with him. It's what people do at weddings."

Cindy felt the thumping of her heart, as she looked at the waiting boy. She didn't wish to be the centre of attention. She just wanted to say no and walk away. But suddenly his hand was on hers and he was pulling her onto the heaving dance floor. She saw him raise his thumb at his gawping friends. Cindy felt his arms encircle her, pulling her far closer than she liked, and placed her own hands stiffly on his back. Without further encouragement he gyrated against her, his lower body rubbing against her groin.

"I'm Scott!" he said.

"Just cool it," she murmured, trying to appear calm and in control of the situation. But she could feel a hot hand on her breast. Quickly she guided it back to her shoulder. But he persisted in pressing closer. His other hand was making a surreptitious attempt to open the buttons of her shirt and he was again pushing his hand against her breast.

She pulled herself away from him.

"Who you with?" he whispered in a hoarse voice.

She did not reply but glanced in Grant's direction. She managed to catch his eye and saw the flash of surprise that crossed his face. Swiftly she sent out a signal of distress but he had already turned away and was speaking to Susan. Then other dancers impaired her line of vision. Scott was panting, his face sweaty, his lust-glazed eyes gazing down at her. She could feel his penis through his trousers as he pressed against her. Furiously she extricated herself from his embrace. "Leave me alone! If you don't I'll get my Dad on you."

Scott laughed into her face, "Get your Dad then," he

mocked but she was already walking away.

Feeling agitated and embarrassed Cindy made a hasty retreat to the ladies' room. She was splashing cold water on her face when Susan entered.

"I saw you with that obnoxious young man. Good job you pushed him away." She stared at her daughter thoughtfully before saying, "Make your face up, and don't mention it to your father."

Cindy watched as Susan went into a cubicle and then turned to stare at her reflection. She felt tarnished, knowing she had allowed Scott to invade her privacy and felt a wave of nausea engulf her as she dabbed the cold water on her face. She stared at herself then took her hair and pulled it back off her face. If it were cut off perhaps she would be more ordinary. Ordinary, so men would not regard her as merely sexual.

The youths were still there when she returned to her table, leering across the dance floor at her. Ignoring them, Cindy sipped her soft drink. In the corner she saw the youths giggling as Scott approached them, carrying a tray. She knew they would be talking about her.

"Are you all right?" Jessica asked, "I saw that guy coming on a bit heavy with you!"

Cindy shrugged. "I took care of it."

The music started once more and not to be deterred Scott again approached the table. "Got you a drink," he said, handing Cindy a glass of white wine.

"She doesn't want it," Jessica said.

Scott gulped his beer down and wiped his hand down the seat of his trousers. "What's yer phone number?" he slurred.

"Why?" Jessica replied for her.

"Can't she speak for herself?" He pointed to Cindy.

"Try asking her properly," Jessica suggested.

"Gimme yer phone number." He fumbled in his rear

trouser pocket and produced a tatty piece of paper and the stub of a pencil. He handed it across the table to Cindy, but it was Jessica who took it. Scott grinned back at her, his confidence restored.

Jessica wrote on the paper and smothered a smile as she handed it back to him. The confident grin vanished as he looked down at the paper, replaced by a startled expression. Defeated he walked away, but not before he muttered, "Bitch."

"What did you write?" Cindy asked.

"Fuck off!" Jessica said and they both laughed.

CHAPTER TEN

Wednesday afternoon, 27th April

Cindy had the day off to prepare for her forthcoming exams. She had eaten an early breakfast and told Susan she was going to the library in town.

She had lain awake all night, wavering between decisions. Perhaps it had been more than coincidence that she had met Jessica at the wedding, for her mind was now firmly made up. She left the house casually dressed in ankle boots, jeans and a denim jacket. Her hair was aggressively pulled back. As she walked down the cul-de-sac she saw David's car reversing out of his driveway.

"Want a lift?" he shouted to her.

She hesitated and then accepted. He gave her a frowning glance as she got into the car, wondering why she was wearing such a grim expression. They chatted inconsequentially as he weaved the car skilfully through the early morning traffic. She told him of her plans to get a car that summer so she would be independent.

"If you want any help with driving lessons, let me know," he offered with a broad smile. "Fathers teaching daughters to drive isn't always a good idea." He went on with an amusing story and Cindy relaxed.

"Okay, you can teach me," she murmured with a faint smile as she visualised Elizabeth's face when she told her.

He grinned. "So, where are you off to then?"

"Hairdressers," she told him. "I'm having it all cut off. It's more bother than it's worth."

"No! Don't do that," David cried in astonishment but Cindy chose to ignore him.

When he pulled up outside the shopping area he was still frowning. "I don't like women with short hair!" he told her as she got out and thanked him for the lift. She simply shrugged and watched as David turned his car to rejoin the traffic. Then she walked purposefully towards the salon.

Jessica greeted Cindy and said she would have a ten-minute wait. Cindy sat in the small reception area idly glancing through the out-dated women's magazines. Women posing, women smiling. Women! Women! Women! Unconsciously her hand went to the restricting hair band at the nape of her neck, she pulled it and in doing so felt the familiar hair tentacles falling round her face.

"Cindy, we're ready for you," Jessica announced as she held out the dark brown nylon cover.

Cindy stood up and allowed Jessica to take her coat. Covered in an overall and towel she moved towards the washbasins. She stared at her reflection in one of the wall mirrors as Jessica drew up her working trolley and took out a small brush.

"Cindy, you have great hair!" Jessica said as she started to brush it. "How much do you want off?"

There was a long pause as Cindy looked at her reflection in the mirror. "Just a wash," she eventually said, realising that at this stage in her life getting rid of her long hair would be like cutting off her right arm. She could not live without either.

Cindy returned home mid-morning. As Susan had two pupils coming round that afternoon for elocution lessons, she would spend her afternoon in her room revising.

At precisely two o'clock the front doorbell rang and Susan

answered it. It was the first of her pupils, smiling sheepishly on the doorstep, and behind him Susan saw the figure of Elizabeth standing in the porch, her long straggly hair falling over her face, her bright red lips giving a smile.

"Cindy in?" She had a voice that Susan had always felt would benefit from her skills.

Cindy had not anticipated Elizabeth's visit and was sitting on her bed with Pandora going through a pile of letters and slowly devouring a *Toblerone*.

"Hi!" Elizabeth didn't pause to knock before pushing open the bedroom door.

"Liz!" Cindy said, trying to sound friendly, but Elizabeth was too busy struggling out of her coat to see the irritation in Cindy's eyes. She had hoped for a peaceful afternoon.

"What secrets are you hiding?" Elizabeth peered forward as Cindy tried to gather the letters together, scooping them back into their large brown envelope. Elizabeth frowned at the telephone directory open on the bed and at Cindy's frantic efforts to push the letters out of sight.

"So, what are you doing?"

"Nothing much," Cindy replied, making no effort to disguise her irritation. "I am writing for some summer work."

"Summer work?" Elizabeth queried. "But it's only April."

"Got to be first in the queue," Cindy temporised and helped herself to a chunk of chocolate.

The next half-hour was taken up chatting and giggling at Cindy's experience at the wedding.

"He couldn't have been that awful, " Elizabeth said.

"He was, believe me!" and they both collapsed on the bed laughing. Elizabeth stretched out and Pandora meowed in protest.

"Move cat!" Elizabeth gave a flick of her hand and Pandora jumped off the bed, her back arched in anger.

"Leave her alone," Cindy said abruptly.

"Oh, leave her alone!" Elizabeth mocked.

Cindy got up, walked across to Pandora and scooped her up. "It always irritates me when people are cruel to cats." She paused before adding, "You know a dog is a dog, a bird is a bird, but a cat is a person!" Cindy kissed Pandora on her face.

Elizabeth raised her eyebrows and said, "You own a dog, you only feed a cat!"

"Touché!" Cindy smiled and replaced Pandora on the bed, just as Elizabeth was taking out what looked like a newspaper advert from her jacket pocket. "What's that?" she asked curiously.

"Cast your eyes over this, " Elizabeth said smugly, giving a self-satisfied sniff. She watched as Cindy peered at the cutting of a newspaper advert showing a special edition Ford Fiesta from a local Ford dealership.

"So?" Cindy said with a shrug of her shoulders.

"Well with you saying you'd ask your Dad for a car, I thought I'd ask mine for one and guess what?" Elizabeth remarked with as much self-modesty as she could muster.

Cindy shrugged.

"My Dad's buying me a brand new car!" Elizabeth could not contain the excitement from her voice. "I beat you to it!" she added in an attempt to rub more salt into Cindy's wounds.

Cindy tried to mask the envy she felt flooding through her. But Elizabeth was preening herself and announced, "I take my driving test on Tuesday and I get it next Wednesday."

Cindy now screwed her nose up. "You might fail your test," she paused for effect before adding, "I don't like Fiestas. I want a Golf GTI."

"But all you have, my dear Cindy, is the bus!"

There was a knock on the door and Elizabeth's attention was diverted so she did not see the look of indignation on Cindy's face as she got up and opened the bedroom door.

Susan swept in. "Tea for my girls? We're having a break

downstairs," she said beaming at Elizabeth and Cindy, who smiled in appreciation of her mother's gesture.

Susan put the tray down on Cindy's desk, seeing as she did so the disgruntled expression on her daughter's face.

"I was just telling Cindy that I was getting my first car," Elizabeth beamed across at Susan. "Dad's ordered it specially for me." She pushed the newspaper cutting into Susan's hand.

"Oh very nice indeed," Susan said with a smile, realising why her daughter seemed so out of sorts.

Cindy pushed a lock of hair from her face and picked up a mug of tea and handed it to Elizabeth, saying, "I wish Dad would buy me a car."

Susan could not resist giving a faint laugh. "I don't think that will be on his agenda, but he might buy you a bicycle!" she turned to Elizabeth and laughed as she left the bedroom. She did not see the flush on Cindy's cheeks or the humiliated expression in her eyes.

They had drunk their tea and nibbled at the biscuits and Cindy was surreptitiously glancing at the bedside clock wishing Elizabeth would leave. She wanted to sit down and plan the approach she would make to her father that evening. Suddenly a car was all-important, but perhaps not an expensive Golf GTI. In reality anything on par with Elizabeth's Fiesta would do.

"Whatever happened to that – what's his name – James? He went up north, didn't he?" Elizabeth asked as she helped herself to the last biscuit.

"I don't hear from him often now," Cindy replied abruptly. "We talk on the phone sometimes, that's all."

Elizabeth glanced up sharply but she couldn't read the expression on Cindy's face and decided to leave.

Saturday, 30th April

Cindy arrived at the newsagent early. In the back office she enjoyed a quick coffee whilst chatting with the paperboys. Then on the instructions of the Manageress, Sarah, she went into the main shop to sort out the magazines.

"It's like a public library," Sarah complained. "Everyone comes in, reads the magazines and no one buys them!"

Cindy smiled at the middle-aged woman who seemed to be engrossed in a magazine article. The few remaining copies of the local newspaper had become trapped behind one of the racks and Cindy struggled to dislodge them, knowing her mother would be expecting her to bring a copy home.

"Just a lot of unnecessary gossip and loads of estate agent adverts," Grant complained, and had even attached a sign to the gatepost saying he wished for no free newspapers to be delivered. But when Cindy brought the paper home, he read it nevertheless.

Cindy arranged the newspapers into a neat pile and suddenly the headlines jumped at her from the page.

Local priest in child sex allegations.

With a deep frown Cindy scanned the article with growing horror and a feeling of utter disbelief. Father Patrick, her priest, the man she had confided so much in, a man of God, had apparently abused young boys years ago in another parish. She felt nausea rising in her stomach.

The middle-aged woman, having finished reading, glanced over Cindy's shoulder and muttered, "These priests, they make me sick."

Cindy wasted no time in agreeing and admitted it was an appalling story; one that made her feel very bitter and betrayed.

Cindy did not enjoy her morning at the newsagent. The story regarding Father Patrick had upset her and hearing peoples' comments about the alleged incidents did not make her feel any better. She decided to walk home as it was a sunny day and was glad she was wearing comfortable trainers and jeans. There seemed little point in queuing for the bus only to be squashed by Saturday crowds, half of them football fans going out of their way to annoy her. It was a good thirty-minute walk and it gave her time to think. She took a route that ran alongside the cricket club. It was a nice tree-lined avenue and she enjoyed walking there, seeing the patterns of sunlight coming through the trees. It made her feel quite spiritual.

In the distance Cindy saw the somewhat incongruous bunting and felt, not for the first time, that a garage in such a peaceful area was out of place. As she approached the building slowly took form and on the forecourt was a selection of second-hand vehicles, one being a Ford Escort in dazzling red paint, with a sunroof and sports wheels. Curiosity got the better of her and as she approached the forecourt she stepped over the small wall to peer more closely at the car. She was still irritated at Elizabeth's constant asking when she was getting a car. She had broached the subject with her father again but he had merely said, "We'll see!" But now, looking at this eye-catching vehicle, she knew this was the car for her. She glanced up at the price ticket on the window.

A young, smartly dressed man with slicked back hair, stay-pressed trousers, a blue blazer and an abundance of after-shave approached her. "Good afternoon, Madam!" he said in an unctuous tone.

Unsure as to how to conduct herself, Cindy said she was merely looking at the car.

"A beautiful car for a beautiful lady!" The salesman knew from the expression of irritation on her face that Cindy did not care for his patronising remark. He went on quickly to outline the virtues of the car, even saying interest free credit was available over twelve months. He then produced a set of keys from his pocket and inserted them into the driver's door lock, the door clicked open and he invited Cindy to sit in and familiarise herself with the interior. Elegantly, Cindy slid behind the steering wheel and the salesman took no time in adjusting her seat to ensure she was more comfortable. Cindy felt he was just a little too close as she gripped the steering wheel and pretended to select the gears whilst the salesman stepped back and shut the door, allowing her time to admire herself. She glanced round the cockpit and saw the dials, radio cassette and the brightly coloured upholstery – yes she liked it. She opened the driver's door and stepped back onto the forecourt.

"It suits you," the salesman remarked and this time he was rewarded by a smile.

Cindy laughed. "Well I do like it!" she said.

"You may like it, but can you afford it?" the salesman replied.

"My father can." And with another smile Cindy left.

Thoughts of Father Patrick swirled around in Cindy's mind as she walked the remainder of the way home. A mish mash of scenes all unrelated to one another flashed before her eyes as she tried to analyse the accusations made against him. Father Patrick did not seem like an abuser, but Cindy accepted that you could not pick out rapists or paedophiles; they didn't walk round with horns on their heads. Perhaps they should.

Her thoughts went back to the Ford Escort she had seen. There was no doubt in her mind that her father would buy it for her.

Arriving at her house she made her way to the back door.

"Hello, Mum," she smiled at Susan who was sitting at the kitchen table reading a newspaper. There was a deep frown on her face as she looked up at Cindy. Cindy could see that her mother had already read the article in the local paper. "I brought it home for you to read," she said as she placed her copy down on one of the work surfaces.

"Your father got the paper at the petrol station." Susan shook her head. "I am devastated. Father Patrick! I mean, he is such a nice man. Someone with a vindictive mind is out to smear his name."

Cindy did not offer any comments but filled a glass with cold water and took a long drink.

"He is a good parish priest," Susan continued and as she met Cindy's eyes, she shrugged saying, "Mum will be so upset."

Cindy sat down at the kitchen table with Susan. "And what happens if the allegations are true?" she asked quietly. "Perhaps we should think about his victims."

Susan dismissed Cindy's remark and as she got up from the table she muttered, "Allegations like this can ruin a man's life."

She did not see the thoughtful expression that appeared in Cindy's eyes.

CHAPTER ELEVEN

Bank Holiday Monday, 2nd May

Cindy had dropped numerous hints about *her* Ford Escort, even leaving the sales leaflet on the kitchen table. But Grant's attention was fully occupied by newspaper reports on the previous day's fatal accident of racing driver, Ayrton Senna. Susan was also preoccupied by the allegations regarding Father Patrick. But eventually the leaflet had disappeared from the kitchen table and Cindy felt confident that the car would be hers. She even bought a set of L-plates and left them in a prominent position on the hall table.

Grant had surprised her.

"I've got a present for my girl," he said after dinner. His voice was warm and Cindy felt that special glow that always came when he called her his own. Her heart beat fast with anticipation as she waited for him to slide a set of car keys across the table. Instead he got up and walked into the hall returning with a large, square box.

Cindy frowned.

"What is it?" Susan asked curiously.

Cindy took no time in peeling back the extravagant gift-wrapping. This was no set of car keys, she realised with a sinking heart.

Susan gasped when Cindy finally revealed a small remote control colour television with built in video recorder.

"So what about a kiss for your father, eh?" Grant asked.

Dutifully Cindy got up and put her arms round his neck. "Thank you," she murmured, feeling his warm breath on her face as she nuzzled into him.

"You deserve it!" Grant replied; his face now slightly flushed.

As much as she wanted to, Cindy could not bring up the subject of the car – it would seem too ungrateful.

After dinner she retreated upstairs and was now safely enclosed in the uterus of her room. Her thoughts were not on the television but the car. She knew that if Grant didn't buy it for her she would lose face in front of her school friends, especially Elizabeth.

Sitting on the edge of her bed, Cindy's attention went to the teenage girls' magazine Elizabeth had given her. Casually she sauntered across to her bedside table, opened the drawer and retrieved an identical magazine she had bought for herself earlier in the month. Sitting back on the bed, she glanced through the pages before subconsciously going to the article called *Daddy's Girl*. She lay back on her bed with her head resting on the pillow. It was sometimes difficult to remember; at others it was so very easy. She rocked her head back and forth, starting to hum *Take The Long Way Home* in her mind. She had heard the tune that fateful morning; it had been emanating from the radio. The song was now a reassurance to help her through the bad times. But small incidents still made her remember, and as she lay still and quiet she turned her head towards the door of her bedroom and her eyes remained fixed on the handle.

Her demons often came at night. She couldn't exorcise them, except through her drawings. People were stupid, stupid, stupid, fools.

How old had she been – eight – nine – ten? What did it matter? She could hardly breathe; she was suffocating now. Her breath gulped down her throat, her teeth ran over her dry lips. She clasped her hands over her breasts. She always needed protection. She moved them down to cover that secret part, the tunnel of exploration. He was coming nearer and nearer, she could see his naked outline, standing shadowy and menacing, watching her. She could hear his breathing and feel his breath against her face. She could feel the hands as they pulled back the bedclothes and hear his swift intake of breath as he murmured, "Oh, you are so lovely." Then he was kneeling down beside her bed. She felt his hands hard on her shoulders and she could feel his hot breath on the nape of her neck.

His hands moved down her shoulders, to caress her, before moving down, down, touching and feeling over her flat belly. He was faintly muttering obscenities mingled with endearments. His hands were between her legs, gently pulling them apart. He moaned and shuddered as he moved his face down, down to that private part. She could see the back of his head and the gleam of his naked white shoulders. His wet tongue was caressing her, searching, probing. His hands gripped her thighs, hurtful and hard and his tongue no longer gentle, his lips no longer caressing as he moaned.

Slowly his head lifted and he stared down at her. She could not see his face, not now; only his voice lay filed in her memory. It was harsh and raspy, like no voice she had heard before. He spun her round so she was sitting on the edge of the bed but now she had shut her eyes – tight.

"No ... no!" Her lips were dry, her voice hoarse. "Don't hurt me, don't hurt me!"

"Kiss me. Kiss me!" She could feel and smell and taste him pushing against her lips.

He held her on the bed, hard and demanding. His face flushed as he lay against her. He stroked her hair. Then they were struggling on the bed. It was creaking. They moved up and down, down and up and that thing was between her legs.

His teeth bit into her neck as he forced himself on her. His tongue had pushed into her mouth. He had invaded her, intruding into her body. She didn't resist any more; she lay limp, his puppet. Her thoughts were sinful, the guilt over powering.

Then she'd been alone, hurting and bleeding. Cindy remembered showering and noticing the bruise on her neck. And she hurt. She had ached and her head felt as if it had been split open by an axe. Was this what it was all about? Was this sex? Those things he had done to her were horrible. But then he'd wanted her – hadn't he? Who had wanted her? She couldn't remember the face.

Then he was gone; she was left, bruised and alone. The thoughts in her head clicked on and on and on and on and on. Then the thoughts became a voice – a quiet voice that had come to her before. It comforted her when she was alone, telling her that everything would be all right. But now she felt the sweat break out on her body and her heart suddenly started to pound madly. Pandora was here so it was today and not yesterday. But where had yesterday gone? She could not remember. It was all out of focus and she felt the tears coursing down her cheeks. Tears for what she had lost.

She walked into the bathroom to rinse her face with cold water, and then looked at herself in the mirror. Her eyes were veiled, hostile, dark and deep, her face still. She stood transfixed by her reflection. It seemed to her that the inner voice was growing stronger, warning her that she would never be free unless she came to terms with her horrendous past. Should she tell them or should she just kill herself? Everything was so confusing. Only God knew the truth and only Cindy knew how much she needed help.

Saturday, 21st May

After work on Saturday, Cindy decided not to make her regular visit to Emma. She wanted to go into town instead and asked Elizabeth if she would meet her at the newsagent. Much to Cindy's disappointment, Elizabeth had made other plans but promised to meet up with later her in a café in town.

Saturday in town was hell with throngs of people, crying kids and disgruntled parents. Cindy saw her reflection in one of the shop windows, seeing that her tight jeans, short denim jacket and high-heeled shoes all accentuated her slimness. She stopped under the pretext of looking at the window display but she was really studying her own reflection. This was her image and she saw her own attraction as if she was looking at a stranger for the first time. Gone was the gawky schoolgirl of last year. This was the beginning of womanhood. Was this narcissism? Perhaps it was. She would look it up in her psychology book. Was it possible to be two personalities? She liked to be beautiful but did not always like the attention it brought. Sometimes she felt she was on a perpetual seesaw. When she was up she felt at peace, but when the seesaw was down, the world was bleak and invaded by gloomy shadows, and she despised herself. Did other people have such dark thoughts, such extremes of emotion? Elizabeth seemed so boringly contented. Suddenly she was conscious of the time she had spent staring at the window and she moved away. She browsed around several more shops before losing interest and heading towards the park.

She noticed an elderly woman sitting on a bench. She reminded Cindy of her grandma. Not Olive, but Emma, a homely old woman who looked like a grandma should. The old woman was feeding the pigeons from a bag of crusts.

"Look at the mess!" The man's voice was loud. "If the police won't move her on, I will."

Cindy felt explosive anger course through her as this pompous twit approached the old lady. She could not hear what he said to her but all the pleasure and contentment left the wrinkled face. The old lady gathered her bags together with shaking hands, then, with the man standing like a sentinel of righteousness, she shuffled slowly away through the carpet of birds, her eyes downcast. As she passed, Cindy saw tears running down her cheeks and on impulse put her hand out.

"Don't go!" she cried. Then, seeing the startled expression on the old woman's face, said gently, "He's not the police. He's no right to move you on. Come with me." Gently she turned the old woman round and, holding onto her arm, guided her back to the bench.

The man stood there glowering at her. "Right," he snapped. "I'll report you."

"You do that," Cindy said, throwing him a disarming smile as she reached across and opened one of the bags of stale bread that the old woman had left on the bench. She crumbled the bread in her hand and threw it down for the greedy birds.

The old lady watched and then, regaining her confidence, she too resumed feeding the birds. They did not speak, but there was empathy between then. Finally as they threw the last crumbs down, Cindy stood up and opened her carrier bag and took out one of the boxes of plain chocolates she had bought for her grandmother. "Give yourself a treat!" She saw the puzzlement in the faded eyes as the hand reached out and added. "Don't let people bully you. It's your park as much as theirs."

A few minutes later Cindy entered the café where she had arranged to meet Elizabeth. It was crowded and she walked straight across to the ladies' room.

She washed her hands then reapplied lipstick to her mouth and adjusted her hair. Back in the café she found a vacant table and was immediately distracted by the four youths at the next table who were eyeing her and making innuendoes. One of them got up, shambled across and sat down opposite her.

"Hi!" He was good looking with an appealing smile.

She pretended to glance at her watch, trying to think of some way of discouraging him without making a scene, but thankfully Elizabeth chose that moment to arrive. The youth, seeing the disinterest in Cindy's eyes, returned to his laughing friends. Elizabeth sat down at the table and in an over-elaborate and theatrical gesture threw her car keys down so that they skated across the table. The action irritated Cindy. Ever since Elizabeth had got her car she had been rubbing her nose in the fact that she had yet to be given one. Added to that, a scrawny little girl in her form called Mary, who was quiet and unassuming, had also turned up at school in a new Mini. Cindy was consumed with irritation because she had not been the first person in her year to get a car, nor even the second! Despite her frequent hints, Grant had merely shrugged and said he would continue to *think about it*. On one occasion when he had driven her past the garage she had pointed out the car to him. Although he had slowed down to give it quick look he had not offered to stop and get out. Instead he had asked, "Who is going to pay the insurance, petrol and running costs? You haven't even passed your driving test!"

Cindy had rashly announced that she would give up her job at the cat sanctuary and obtain a full time weekend position. And in the summer, she promised, she would get a proper job. But to Grant's obvious amusement, she had immediately changed her mind, knowing full well that she couldn't give up her Sundays with the cats.

"I'll certainly get a summer job," she had said.

"And when the summer is over," Grant challenged, "and you go to university, how will you manage then?"

As usual he had tied her up in knots and her observation that her friends' parents seemed to cope, did not alter his opinion. "I will think about it," was his only reply. That irritated Cindy so much that she now declined to bring the car into conversation.

"You're dreaming," Elizabeth said, snapping her fingers in front of Cindy's eyes.

Elizabeth took a sip of her orange drink. "I've just bought myself a nice air freshener for my car," she said, not noticing the flash of irritation on Cindy's face. "Drove past the garage this morning; your Escort is still there!"

Cindy wanted to snap back but wouldn't give Elizabeth the satisfaction of doing so. "I know," she murmured.

"How's the bus?" Elizabeth went on and Cindy's patience was finally exhausted.

"Will you shut up about your bloody car," she hissed.

"Oh sorry," Elizabeth remarked in a high-pitched tone. "We are touchy!"

Cindy lowered her eyes and took a sip of her drink.

"It's not my fault your Dad won't buy you a car," Elizabeth purred.

"I'll get a car, just you wait and see."

But Elizabeth was not convinced and merely shrugged her shoulders.

They spent the afternoon in town but suddenly there was an edge to their friendship. Gone was the giggly, school-girlish rapport. Elizabeth now appeared more mature. She was independent, had her own transport and the more Cindy thought about it the more the resentment festered inside her.

It wasn't even as if Elizabeth was a competent driver. She crashed through the gears, rode the clutch and had narrowly missed two pedestrians in the short distance between town and Cindy's house. On a slight incline at a set of traffic lights, Elizabeth had stalled the car, not once but three times. That incident was overshadowed minutes later when Elizabeth, who was busy staring at a grubby white Transit van that had, *I wish my wife was this dirty* written on its back doors, almost drove into it. She stamped her foot on the brake at the very last second, bringing the Fiesta to a screeching halt in a fog of burning rubber. By the time they trundled into the cul-de-sac Elizabeth's *joy de vivre* at having a car was somewhat tarnished, because she knew Cindy had witnessed all her driving mistakes.

Cindy couldn't resist saying, "Thanks for the lift. I think you need a little more practice!" She got out, smiling sweetly as she waved goodbye.

CHAPTER TWELVE

Cindy watched Elizabeth chug out of the cul-de-sac before walking swiftly up the gravel driveway. Her temper was simmering dangerously and she was thankful her parents were out. She stood in the hall for a moment, trying to calm her thoughts. Such heated feelings were alien to her because she had trained herself to always remain in control, to restrain her temper. To her mind it was a wasted emotion. But now it bubbled up within her.

It was her father's fault. He had broken his promise to her, and made her look stupid. Not just to Elizabeth but to everyone in her form. Certain that she would get her own way, Cindy had confidently told everyone that she was getting a car. It was bad enough that two other girls had beaten her to it but everyone was really laughing now that her much boasted car had still failed to materialise. She walked into the kitchen and automatically set about making herself some coffee as Elizabeth's gloating face flashed before her eyes.

Her request had been modest, she thought. And she did not think she was acting in a spoilt way – quite the opposite. After all, she had not asked for a new car. Her father had lots of money, Cindy was sure of that, so he could obviously afford to buy her a car, if he wanted to.

Coffee mug in hand Cindy stood in the centre of the kitchen listening to the house. It was very quiet and she walked slowly into the dining room, absorbing the atmosphere. Slowly her anger subsided and gave way to resentment as she entered the lounge. She went across to Grant's expensive *Bang & Olufsen* hi-fi system then she ran her hands over the back of the leather three-piece suite before going into the conservatory to look at the comfortable cane furniture.

Her car was all-important, consuming her thoughts to an extent she would not have believed possible. "I have to persuade him," she thought, almost desperately.

The sound of Grant's car on the gravel outside brought her mind back to the present and she made her way to the lounge window from where she watched her father as he sat back in the driving seat waiting for the convertible roof to close. Unusually for a Saturday he had been working at the office. He was dressed casually in jeans, blue blazer and an open neck shirt and Cindy was captivated by his physical appearance. Her mind flashed back over a series of memories of the happy times they had spent together. But now he had abandoned her to ridicule. She did not want an argument, confrontation always upset her, and yet she knew the subject had to be approached again.

She opened the front door and greeted him warmly. She took his briefcase from his hand and placed it on the hall chair. "Would you like a cup of coffee?"

"No thanks," he said, "I've some paper work to look at."

"Dad," she linked her arm with his, glancing up appealingly into his eyes as she guided him into the kitchen.

He stared down into her face. "Oh Cinders," he sighed. "Please, not the car again." She couldn't miss the exasperation in his tone.

"Oh Dad," she heard her own pleading voice. "I had to suffer Elizabeth's bad driving to get home from town today. Everyone at school with parents like you has a car. That Escort is still for sale. It's made for me."

Grant closed his eyes and shook his head. He was tempted to give in, to say, "Yes, my darling, I'll buy it for you." But this time he was determined that Cindy would wait. Of course he would buy her a car, but he didn't want it to come too easily for her. Whatever she had wanted in the past he had bought for her. But Cindy wasn't a child any more and it was time for her to learn the art of patience. Yes, he told himself, he was doing his duty as a good father. He would have to put up with her sulks, but in the end, he would have retained control over her. He had a sudden, uncomfortable memory of his mother. She had always pulled the strings to make him dance to her tune. But he was not doing that to Cindy. He was simply teaching her a necessary lesson.

"Dad, please?" There was a brief moment when Cindy thought she had won and she waited in anticipation for him to turn round and say, "It's yours." He had done it many times before so why not now? But as he turned and she met his eyes she knew that the answer was still no.

"No, Cindy, you can't have everything you want just when you want it. Now stop pestering me, I've work to do."

Cindy was taken aback at his tone for he was rarely so abrupt with her. Her expression changed. The affectionate pleading look in her eyes was replaced by a hard, unyielding stare and Grant was reminded of his mother when she didn't get her own way.

"But Elizabeth..," she started to say.

"I don't want to hear about Elizabeth."

"You promised."

"Leave it!" Grant said, turning on his heels, picking up his briefcase from the hall chair and retreating to his study.

Tuesday, 24th May

Cindy had woken up feeling off-colour. She brought her knees up to her chin and knew without even looking at her diary it was that time of the month. Her periods often came without any warning and were always irregular and painful. It was a time she hated; the pain, mood swings and a feeling of guilt often engulfed her. No matter how hard she tried the first two days left her tired, exhausted and feeling disgruntled.

"It's normal," Susan had sympathised. "You'll get used to it!"

"Perhaps," she had replied, adding, "I don't know why God made women suffer."

Susan always listened to her daughter when she needed to talk and Cindy was glad of a confidant. But her mother didn't know it all. That first horror of blood on the bed sheet … the face, the voices and the tears, so many tears that would stay with her forever. Slowly she got out of bed, patted Pandora and walked into her en-suite bathroom.

She ran the tap and filled a glass with cold water and then, reaching into the bathroom cabinet she took out a bottle of pain killers. Glancing into the mirror she noticed deep smudges beneath her eyes as she gulped down the pills. The shower was warm and helped the pain but it was not a good start to her day.

Dressed in her school uniform, Cindy said her good mornings as she entered the kitchen and heard Susan's friendly greeting. But she had no wish to talk, wanting only to go back to bed, curl up, pull the bed clothes over her head and forget. Forget about the pain and the day ahead.

Over breakfast Grant had teased her and she fought back a smile when he gave her a half promise that he would meet her after school.

Cindy's day dragged on and it was not enjoyable. Elizabeth constantly chattered on about her car whilst Cindy struggled against a rising feeling of nausea. I just want to go home and have a bath, she thought as she made yet another surreptitious glance at her watch.

"Sorry I can't give you a lift," Elizabeth said breezily as they walked together across the quadrant after the final bell.

"It's okay, Dad's meeting me," Cindy replied and watched Elizabeth join Mary as they walked across to the small area that was now designated as a pupil car park. She saw their cars and heard the laughter and then the starting of engines as they tried to outshine each other. Cindy felt the now familiar swell of resentment as she made her way out of the school gates and looked round for her father's Jaguar. He hadn't come; hadn't kept his promise and she had no option but to trudge to the bus stop with the wind teasing at her kilt and blowing strands of hair across her face. Suddenly there was the sound of a car horn. She turned half expecting to see her father arriving late but it was Elizabeth waving to her as she drove past.

Wearily Cindy arrived at the cul-de-sac. She wanted only to undress and soak in the warm bath she had been thinking about all day. As she neared the house a frown appeared on her forehead for in the drive was her father's car.

Pushing the front door open she called out, "I'm home." Dumping her bag on the hall chair she heard Susan call, "Hello." She found her mother standing in the middle of the conservatory with a golf club in her hand and a golf ball in front of her on the carpet. She was practising her putting shot.

"Where's Dad?" Cindy asked.

Looking up Susan frowned at the interruption. "He's gone in a taxi to town." She was dismissive, her mind absorbed on the golf club.

Cindy felt a wave of disappointment. "He promised to meet me from school!"

Susan continued practising her shot. "I'm sure he didn't forget on purpose."

Cindy shrugged her shoulders then noticed the array of new golf clubs stacked against one of the cane chairs. Propped up next to them was a new red and white leather golf bag. "Very nice, whose are they?"

Susan hesitated for a moment and then with a wide smile she beamed, "Mine!"

"I thought you already had a set?"

"I have, but well …" She shrugged. Seeing the flicker of a frown appear on Cindy's forehead as she stood staring at the clubs, Susan realised that Cindy was mentally adding up their cost, no doubt comparing them to the price of that car she was constantly nagging for. Guilt trapped her into saying that she would be selling her old clubs and, attempting to further pacify Cindy, she added, "I am sure you will get the car … eventually."

"Perhaps!" Cindy whispered as she turned away, unable to conceal the irritation she felt. She was conscious of a surge of jealousy against her mother as Susan started proudly placing the clubs one by one back into the golf bag.

"We can't always get what we want when we want it," Susan went on. When she saw the sulky expression in Cindy's eyes she wished she had not uttered the words, but felt obliged to continue. "Try not to let disappointment cloud the day."

"It's all right for you," Cindy's voice was uncharacteristically harsh as she pointed to the clubs. "You always get what you want."

"Well, Cindy, I am his wife." There was a gentle note of reproach in Susan's tone.

Cindy felt the impulse to go across to Susan and put her arms round her shoulders and murmur how nice the clubs were, but she stubbornly rejected it. "I am sorry if I sound ungrateful, but I am the laughing stock of the sixth form at the moment."

Susan heard the small catch in her daughter's voice and suddenly realised that Cindy was vulnerable, and understood how deep was her disappointment over the car. She gave an inward smile, knowing that Grant would not let her down. "Oh, come on." She placed her arm round Cindy's shoulder. "You know you always get what you want from your father, just be patient."

"Do I indeed?" Cindy muttered and pulled away from Susan's embrace. She removed the clasp from her hair and allowed it to flow reassuringly round her face. Agitatedly she ran her fingers through the long locks. "So I have to be patient?" There was an edge to her voice that made Susan stare at her, for it was seldom that Cindy answered back in such a way.

"There's no need to be rude," Susan chided.

"I'm not being rude," Cindy replied tartly without meeting Susan's eyes. The build up of disappointment regarding the car now mingled with what she thought was her mother's lack of understanding and complacency got the better of her. "I'm going to my room. I'll leave you with your new clubs."

Susan chose not to answer. But Cindy could not resist adding, "You have no idea how upset I am with Dad."

"I am sure you are," Susan said, "And he doesn't deserve

that from you." Then, wishing to close the subject she said. "If you've nothing better to do then go and set the table for dinner. It's your father's favourite – grilled sirloin steak."

The remark infuriated Cindy. "Of course, his repayment!" She took off her school blazer, slung it over her shoulder and made to leave the conservatory.

"And what exactly is that remark supposed to mean?" Susan's patience snapped.

"Well, Dad never does things for nothing does he mother?" Cindy's voice was not more than a whisper. "A favourite dinner for new golf clubs, not a bad return. I wonder what my payment for a car would have to be?" Cindy stopped herself going further but the unexpected edge in her tone made Susan look up.

"Well it's time you understood, young lady, that you've got to earn things in this life!"

"Don't patronise me mother." Cindy was allowing her temper to win, she had almost lost control for the first time in her life. "I have more than paid for everything I've got."

Susan stared at her, shocked by the change in her daughter. "Anyone would think you were badly done to. But you have everything you could want. Much more than most girls of your age. Don't be so ungrateful."

Cindy saw the anger in her mother's eyes and shook her head furiously. "Mother, give it a rest. I've paid for it all." Then Cindy closed her eyes and bit her lip, annoyed with herself for allowing the situation to get out of control.

Susan watched her daughter closely. There was something very odd about how Cindy was acting. "What do you mean by that?" she demanded.

In the silence that followed, Cindy balanced her scales of justice. She had often wondered if there would be a right time to take the key and open her forbidden box of memories, thus allowing her dark hidden secrets to be exposed to the light. She had always sworn that she would never utter those experiences out loud, only Father Patrick and Pandora knew exactly what had happened, but Father Patrick had recently proved that he was not the right receptacle for her confidences and she had a deep need to share them with someone else.

Perhaps the horrors of the past should be re-awakened. The memory that lurked in the shadows of her consciousness had to be addressed, brought out, otherwise she would slowly go mad. Mad like Olive. As she obviously wasn't going to get the car, what had she got to lose? Only her peace of mind.

Cindy gave a small choked sob, and slowly raised her tear-stained face. "I am so sorry but I …" she gulped for air and was obviously distressed as she brought her hands up to cover her face. Cindy now found herself at the bridge she promised herself she would cross when the time came. But how much traffic could this particular bridge carry?

"What on earth is the matter, Cindy?" Susan asked, placing a comforting arm round her daughter's shaking shoulders as a sense of foreboding enveloped her.

"There is never going to be a right time to say this." Cindy felt the sweat on her hands and the power of emotion surging. Slowly she inserted the key into her box of memories, the rusty-hinged lid creaked open and she knew there was no going back.

Cindy moved away from Susan's embrace and sank into one of the cane chairs. Her body language was that of defeat. She looked as if she had fought a world war single handed – and lost. There was an unreadable expression in her eyes and she paused as her mind visualised the word she was going to use. It was a horrible word but yet so descriptive.

"I have been raped." How casual it sounded as it dropped from her lips. She heard the sudden intake of breath and noticed the naked fear on her mother's face as she sat down on the small settee.

"What do you mean you have been raped?" Susan stuttered. Then, in a monotone voice, Cindy started talking to her mother, speaking as though she was a child again. Her head was lowered so a curtain of hair shielded her face and her body was shaking with gut wrenching sobs. "I have been raped, over and over again." She gave a small choked cry, and slowly raised her tear-stained face. "Mum, help me ..."

But Susan sat like stone and could only repeat in a faint voice, "Raped?"

"It's a horrible word. I hate it." Cindy shook her head. "But what else can you call it, violation, intrusion, penetration?"

"Don't! Please." Susan stared at her as she desperately tried to muster some control. At last she managed to get herself out of the chair and then knelt by Cindy's side. "Tell me everything." She whispered, trying to remain as calm as she could, hearing the emotion in her own voice. Cindy continued to cry, a low, sobbing, disconcerting noise. Her eyes were closed, her face tight.

"Was it rape?" Susan prompted her. "I mean ...?"

Cindy interrupted. "What is rape?"

"Well..." Susan floundered. She could feel the sweat on her hands and suddenly her heart seemed to be pumping faster than ever. She didn't like this conversation.

"I'll tell you," Cindy said. "It's someone nice; someone you trust and love creeping up on you. You feel dirty and used. Every time I see my body I remember and I will never trust men ever again. You never stop hating. Just hate and more hate. It haunts you all the time. That's what I'm talking about. That's rape!"

"My God!" Susan let her head fall into her hands. She felt the sweat breaking out over her body, the tears in her eyes. "I would have known," she muttered. "I would have known. This man, this fiend – did you know him?"

"He said it would do no good to tell anyone – he made me

swear not to. He said I would be taken away, put in a home. No one would believe me!"

Susan raised her head, her eyes filled with bewilderment and unshed tears. "Taken away? Who said that? Why didn't you tell us? Your father would have sorted it all out." Her voice was filled with disbelief.

There was a silence, then Cindy started to cry again. Susan watched in horror as her daughter seemed to crumple before her eyes and fresh tears poured down her cheeks.

"Who said they'd lock you away?" Susan asked as calmly as she could.

"Daddy." The word fell slowly from Cindy's lips as she saw Susan's face drain of colour. "He said I'd be put away like Grandma, in some home, if I told anyone about what happened." Cindy started shaking. Her teeth were chattering and her face was white and drawn.

"You're saying it was Grant? Your father? He said you'd be locked away?" Susan asked faintly.

"My father raped me." Cindy had stopped shaking. She now sat quite still, staring at her mother with a blank expression in her eyes. There was silence.

Susan felt Cindy's words hang over her like a cloud. As if in slow motion she felt her mouth move. "Where ... where was I when this happened?"

"Being busy!" Cindy's reply bit through the red hot mist between them.

It was a lie, a damned, horrible lie, Susan thought as she got to her feet. "You little liar! How dare you! All this because you don't get a car when you want it!" Susan stopped, seeing her daughter's river of tears, but felt an urge to continue. "You spoiled little bitch."

"It's nothing to do with the car," Cindy spat back. "I'm his little angel – but not in the way you think." She cringed at the remark.

Unable to control her anger Susan lashed her hand across Cindy's face. The smack was loud, leaving a red mark on her daughter's cheek.

Sobbing from the impact, Cindy ran upstairs.

In the conservatory, Susan stood up gulping heavy, gasping breaths. She felt like she was drowning, submerged in a bottomless well. Her head span as the implications of her daughter's words slowly seeped into her mind. The absolute horror of the allegation filled her with disgust. She felt nausea rising and dashed to the downstairs cloakroom, lifted the toilet lid and vomited into the pan.

CHAPTER THIRTEEN

With tears streaming down her face and her heart thumping in her chest, Cindy stumbled across the landing into her bedroom and threw herself on the bed next to a disturbed Pandora.

The stricken expression on Susan's face would, Cindy knew, be imprinted on her memory forever. She started to shiver uncontrollably and felt Pandora's warm body press into hers, as though the cat understood her distress. She put her hand across her face feeling where Susan had slapped it.

Words, so many words that could not be retracted. Horrible words for horrible deeds. Her father. What on earth had she done to him? What had she said, and why? Her mind resembled a jigsaw with only half the pieces present – but where they really missing or had she just ignored them? Until they all fitted together and made some cohesive picture she would never be a complete person. She needed help. So many of her thoughts had been kept hidden that sometimes it was difficult to know the real from the fantasy.

Her allegation had been received like a French kiss at a family reunion. But how had she expected her mother to react? Would there have ever been a right time to tell her? Yet why shatter their comfortable life? Why ruin her mother's life? Questions, questions, questions.

"My darling angel," his loving words haunted her. She

remembered his kisses but they were never those of a father. But then how did fathers kiss their daughters?

Incest. She felt sick at the sound of the word and even more nauseous at the thought that she had been a victim of it. Yes, of course it was real. It had happened. Her bedroom door had frequently creaked open and it had been him standing there. Her father. He loved her, he had told her that often. But rape? If he loved her why did he have to rape her? Tears made her vision blurred. Her mind no longer seemed capable of focusing. He had betrayed her or had she betrayed him? She had not meant to hurt Susan; to shatter her dreams. She loved her. She even loved her father – but not in that way. She felt the pain in her stomach, always the same pain. As she slowly got up from the bed, images flashed before her eyes. She screwed her eyes tight shut, trying to block them out, but he was there laughing at her. Who was it? She staggered to the mirror. Her face was red and blotchy, her eyes puffy through crying. Oh, she had cried before, rivers of tears for the dead, but this time they were for the living. She walked to the desk and picked up the thin gold pencil and brought it to her lips. It was as smooth as silk just like his voice and his gentle hands on her body. But there was always blood. And a concerned voice warning her, "Cindy, this is our secret."

She threw the pencil down on the desk and covered her ears with her hands in an attempt to stop the voices from within. He should have protected her from these thoughts. He should have made sure that she could never reveal what had happened. The car. That bloody car had been their downfall. If only he had bought it for her. So, was she doing this merely for revenge? Revenge for what? For not buying her the car, or for something else?

Dimly she heard the sound of car tyres on gravel, like waves on the seashore. But it wasn't the seashore, it was their driveway at home. Cindy peered through the lace curtains and stared down as her father got out of the car. A red car! Her car! She shook her head, feeling the living nightmare close around her. He was staring up at her bedroom window smiling that wide, all-loving smile. He waved and pointed to the car.

She was frozen. She ran her tongue over dry lips. Please God, can I take it back, move time, go back an hour?

She heard Susan's voice come from the front door. Suddenly his face changed, the smile was replaced with concern as his eyes moved from her bedroom window to Susan.

Cindy lay back on the bed. Had she made her accusation an hour too soon? Instinctively she got up and went across to her hi-fi. There was only one song she wished to listen to.

Grant stood, white-faced and taut. A small tic pulsed at the corner of his eye. He was staring at the intricate pattern on the lounge carpet and momentarily found himself wondering what had possessed them to buy it.

"For God's sake say something!" Susan demanded, her eyes glazed from crying, her voice harsh with despair.

Grant shook his head in sheer bewilderment. What on earth had possessed Cindy to make such a vile accusation? Suddenly he saw visions of men who had stood before him in court. Dirty, perverted, sick men who had sexually attacked children. Was this how Cindy saw him? There was little he could say; he was overwhelmed by the accusation. He sucked at his dry lips and rasped, "Susan, it's...it's too disgusting even to contemplate." He stuttered over the words as Susan stared at him but there was a look of scepticism in her eyes that sent a bolt of cold fear through him. "You surely don't believe her? I mean, what sort of man do you think you married?"

"Oh Grant." She moved closer to him, her arms reaching out to embrace him, comforting and believing.

The only explanation Grant could offer was the non-appearance of the car that Cindy so desperately wanted. Had they raised her to be so shallow, so selfish that when denied something she wanted she would react with such dreadful venom? They continued to sit, locked in silence, their minds frozen, neither able to comprehend what had possessed Cindy to say such a thing.

It was there though, that small niggle in the back of Susan's mind. Could he, she wondered, could this man with whom she shared her bed and her body, have interfered with their daughter? Suddenly Susan felt entirely alone. "Did you do anything to her? I have to ask, I must know," she whispered.

The pain was visible in his eyes. "I'm your husband and her father, not some bloody monster. What do want me to do? Swear on your Bible?" He stopped, knowing that losing his temper would solve nothing. Suddenly his whole frame seemed to sag, like a puppet whose strings have been cut. "I don't understand it," he finally managed to say.

"But she seemed so positive," Susan replied without thinking.

"Well she would be! She's obviously worked out a story. Doesn't it seem odd that this has come just when Father Patrick has been accused of child abuse; it's almost too coincidental." It was clear that Grant was now on the defensive.

"She meant it; I am sure of that." Susan dabbed her eyes with her sodden tissue.

"And you believed her?" He started to pace up and down the lounge.

"No, of course not, but ..."

"Ah yes, a but ..." Grant looked at her angrily. "Susan, there should be no 'but'. How could you think ...?"

Susan did not reply. She sat as if rooted to the spot, part of her wanting to take him in her arms, hug him close and reassure him. But that small niggle made her say, "Why has she made such a dreadful accusation?"

"I'll tell you why. Because she is a spoilt little madam who always wants her own way." There was anger in his voice and he spat the harsh words out. "It's because of the bloody car, that's why."

Susan wanted to believe him, and yet, what sort of a girl could make up such a horrible story? Maybe Grant was right. The car had seemed to be a focal point in Cindy's accusation. Was it some sort of weird test? Buy it and I don't tell; don't buy it and I will tell. And now the car had been bought. What did it all mean?

"Get her down here," Grant's voice was rough as he stood at the bay window of the lounge.

Cindy was still in her bedroom staring in horror at her reflection in the mirror, listening as the song's words seeped into her mind. She knew her parents were arguing about her. The impact of her accusation was slowly sinking in. The gold pencil lay sensuously between her fingers and through the distance she could hear his voice and soothing words. Her mind was terribly confused. It had happened hadn't it? She felt as if her head would explode; that her body would shatter into a thousand pieces. Then she heard her mother's voice. "Cindy, turn the music off and come downstairs. Now!"

She came quietly into the lounge.

"Right, my girl," Grant said as he met her eyes. "This has gone as far as it's going. Here." He dug into the pocket of his jacket and dangled the set of car keys in front of her. "Your car. I kept my promise. Now, just tell your mother it is completely untrue. Tell her that I have never done anything to hurt you."

There was a long pause before Cindy whispered, "I'm sorry Dad."

"That's all right then. Apologise, take the car and we'll try and forget it. We'll put it down to overwork."

There was another long period of silence and then Grant said again, "Cindy, tell your mother it's lies." When she remained silent he took her arm and shook her. "This is not a game, Cindy! Tell your mother that your accusation is nothing more than the result of your overactive imagination." He seemed to realise that he was gripping her arm too hard and dropped it like it was contaminated.

Cindy saw the thin line of sweat on his forehead as he ran a hand over his eyes. She bit her lip. His voice came to her from a distance. He was her trendy, good-looking father, the envy of all her friends. How could she have said those things about him? But there had been so many deceptions. She heard Susan start to sob. It was too late; too late for any of them. Under it all she was aware of the steady ticking of the grandfather clock in the hall, a sound that was so much a part of her everyday life that she had ceased to notice it years ago. She wished it was possible to turn the minutes back, make it just as it was.

Their secret.

"For God's sake, Cindy, say something!" She heard her mother's voice and saw her as if through tunnel vision, so small, so insignificant. Had she been telling lies? Sooner or later she would have to lie. Well, not lie but perhaps tell half-truths. Why had she said it? Why had she allowed those secret velvet words to escape from her hidden well of misery?

She gulped as she felt her father's hand on her shoulder, his fingers digging into her flesh. Suddenly a collage of faces formed in front of her eyes, but whose was the face in the centre? She heard the scream come from her lips, a long wail of forgotten memories. Even as her mother rushed towards her, unnerved by the scream, Cindy heard her voice, a monotone now, as she whispered, "You came into my bedroom. I was eight years old." Cindy closed her eyes, trying to remember the painful details. "Oh Dad, just say you remember. I was standing in front of the mirror with no clothes on. You put your hands on me. You kissed my shoulders. You moved your hands, down ... down to ... to feel, to grope me, to touch me."

"Cindy!" Susan cried.

"No! I did no such thing!" Grant shouted, his face flushed. He replaced his spectacles and the light caught them, making his eyes appear as opaque as Pandora's. "You are lying Cindy and you know it." He stared across at Susan who was sitting listening, unable to believe what she was hearing. Where had she been? Surely she would have known? Grant creeping into Cindy's room, doing things to her, then returning to their double bed. It was horrible. Too horrible to contemplate and certainly unbelievable.

Cindy was looking at Susan for help as Grant asked, "Where was your mother?" He snapped the question at her.

She stared at him and ran her tongue over her lips. Her mother, where had she been when she had cried out? Mothers should know. But Susan hadn't known. "I can't remember ..."

"Of course you can't remember. Because it is all in your head!" Grant roared. "Now you just think about what you are accusing me of. You're lying. You know you are. Just tell us the truth, Cindy."

Cindy clenched her hands. It wasn't meant to be like this. She had blurted it all out without thinking. But now that it was out in the open, why wouldn't her father admit it? Why couldn't they sit down and talk it through, try and make sense of it? Then she could try and come to terms with her fears. Instinctively she got up and walked across to Susan in a plea for understanding. "Mum, please, I am not lying, I need to talk... I need to get you to understand... There is so much to tell."

Cindy waited for her mother to respond, saw the anguished look she threw at her husband but then, slowly, Susan placed an arm round her daughter's shoulders. "Cindy, please tell us it was all make-belief," she begged.

Cindy stepped away from her mother and shook her head. "It is all true and if Dad admits it then we can face it together." She took a deep breath and turned to face her father, meeting his eyes unflinchingly. "Dad!" There was a desperate note of appeal in her voice. "Please, tell Mum how it was. Help me, please?" She looked at Grant's face. His eyes met hers steadily, angrily, and his jaw was set in hard, unyielding lines. He said not a word. Looking back at her mother Cindy saw only confusion.

Cindy's head ached as though from a pounding with inner hammers, beating, beating and beating behind her eyes.

"You're lying!" Finally Grant spoke.

"But why would I lie?" She heard her own voice ask. "I don't want to hurt anyone. I'm the one who's been hurt. I wakened this morning and felt my body burning up. I felt the disgust of my periods and I can't stop remembering what you did to me."

Susan was unnerved by the reply. It seemed almost too clinical. Could Cindy really have made this accusation because she thought her father was not going to buy her the car she wanted? Or was it because her friend, Father Patrick, had been accused of a similar incident? No, she reasoned Cindy just wasn't that sort of girl.

"So, why now? Why, if I did such dreadful things years ago, why didn't you tell someone?" Grant was now the accuser.

"You said you'd lock me away; said no one would believe me. I'd be like your mother ... mad!" Cindy stood before them, a small, thin figure, her shoulders hunched, her face white and her hands twining round and round each other.

"Jesus! I've never heard such bloody rubbish!" Grant snapped. "You need help! You need to see someone!"

"Yes, I do need help," Cindy whispered. The room gently start to spin, round and round. Voices came and went. Her father's face grew into that of a monster with large eyes while her mother began to shrink into the floor. Suddenly everything was black. She did not feel the impact as she hit the floor.

Her bedroom was dark and still. Someone had laid her gently between the sheets, stroked her forehead and whispered words to cast away her fear. No, it was not then, it was now. She heard the gentle snoring from Pandora and knew this was reality. In the distance, as if from another lifetime, she heard the murmur of voices and knew her parents were talking. What had she expected from them? Had she thought that her mother would automatically take her side, all women together? Their belief in her, that was all she wanted; just someone to believe her. It had gone too far; there was no turning back, and like an avalanche it would gather momentum, destroying them all.

Grant felt there was nothing more to be said. He wanted space and needed to get away from his women, for they possessed and manipulated him. Memories of his childhood penetrated his thoughts as he walked to the front door. "Going out," he called. No one answered and he let the door slam behind him as he strode down the driveway past the now infamous red Ford Escort. At the gate he turned to look up at Cindy's bedroom window. What was she doing? More importantly, what was she thinking? She had seen the car. Did she know he had kept faith with her? Why had she accused him of such a horrible deed? He pushed the gate open and saw his neighbour, Andrew Manson, cutting the hedge.

"Hello Grant, don't often see you walking!" Andrew's voice was friendly and he obviously wanted to talk.

Grant pulled his face back into a smile. "Got a headache. Thought a breath of fresh air would clear it," Grant said bleakly as he edged away, not wishing to get involved in trivial conversation. He wanted to appear normal. But how could you appear normal when your beloved daughter had accused you of being some perverted sex beast? He found his pace increasing with his pent up anger and a thin line of sweat formed on his brow. He remembered his mother and her taunts, her continual condemnation and ridicule, never praise for achievement. He had been determined to praise and love his daughter, to be a friend as well as her father. And this was his repayment. He turned swiftly into the local pub, not one of his usual drinking holes, a place where he was unknown. He ordered a double whisky and a pint of beer. What had his Scottish friend called this combination? A *Boiler Maker*, that was it. Well, it added to the furnace of his hurt. He sat down at a corner table, his eyes downcast. In the back of his mind he knew what was required to resolve the situation. He had to talk to Cindy, get her to withdraw her accusation. And then he would ask her to apologise.

Susan heard Grant leave and slipped into the lounge to pick up the telephone handset. "Oh Mum," she whispered, "the most dreadful thing has happened."

CHAPTER FOURTEEN

Emma replaced the receiver with a shaking hand. She shuddered, then slowly moved to slump into the armchair. Did Susan doubt Grant? Surely not. But the alternative, to believe that her beautiful granddaughter was capable of making such a filthy accusation against her own father, was unthinkable. Who was lying and who was telling the truth?

"It's appalling, but perhaps Cindy's desperate for your attention. You know how much pressure she's been under at school. And that business of her wanting the car." Emma had tried hard to be helpful.

"So she accuses her father of incest? That's what we're talking about, mother. I feel as though the whole episode is a hideous nightmare, not happening to me at all." Susan's voice had risen alarmingly and after listening to Emma's practical suggestion, agreed to call Cindy's bluff and take her to a private hospital for an examination. Discretion was of the utmost importance to Susan.

After reassuring her daughter, Emma felt a surge of panic as she remembered similar stories she had read in the Sunday papers. This just didn't happen to middle class families, or did it? She closed her eyes, concentrating on Cindy. The Cindy she knew was always so loving and attentive. She was kind, polite and considerate and seemed to be coping well with the pressures of growing up. So she wanted a car. Well, young people wanted a lot these days and her friends did have one. Then she remembered the strange remark that Cindy had made over dinner a few weeks ago. "Don't you sometimes think that we are all just showing people what we want them to see?" Now those words seemed loaded with meaning.

I'm too old to be involved in all this, Emma sighed to herself. I don't understand how any father could do such a thing. Emma could not bring herself to even think of Grant in those terms. She and Susan had never discussed the sexual side of their marriage, but they seemed a happy, loving couple. Emma had always thought of Grant as an ideal son-in-law. He was a strong husband for Susan and a caring, generous father. Maybe she didn't always agree with Grant's over-the-top parties and his attitude to important things could sometimes be superficial, but he had been nothing but generous to her. Yes, she liked him.

Emma frowned as she looked back over the past. Even with the benefit of hindsight there was nothing she could recall that had seemed even remotely remiss in his relationship with Cindy. He was immensely proud of her, that much was obvious to anyone. But how would anyone know if a father were abusing his daughter? She tried to imagine what Clive, her husband, would have said. He was so sensible, his judgements well considered. She would think it through; try to be detached, to help them cope.

Thursday, 26th May

With some reluctance, and with Grant's knowledge, Susan approached Cindy about a medical examination. She had hoped that Cindy would decline, break down and retract her accusation, but to her surprise and consternation, Cindy had, after a thoughtful pause, agreed.

So an appointment had been made at a private clinic in the next town and Susan was now sitting in the waiting room, idly flicking through out of date magazines. No matter what happens, Susan thought, my life will never be the same again. Their lives were already in suspense. She had cancelled her elocution pupil for the afternoon, unable to bear the thought of strangers in the house. She had also called Saint Margaret's, saying that Cindy was unwell. Unwell! What an understatement! They had to face the real possibility that Cindy could be mentally disturbed. Susan closed her eyes, letting her mind course over the recent events. The car – that dreaded Ford Escort – had been placed in the garage, out of sight and out of mind.

Is my beautiful daughter ill? Susan thought, remembering with a shudder, Grant's mother that sick, possessive old woman. There had been a time, when she was very young, when Cindy had been almost obsessively possessive over Grant. "I am Daddy's little angel," she would say and climb onto his knee. But didn't all young girls do that? Grant's mother and her insistent, vicious campaign of hatred, her attempts to break up their relationship and then the family had been very stressful. Her letters had been full of reproaches, pleas, and muddled emotions, veering from fact to fantasy with no indication that she was capable of separating one from the other. Then there had been long periods of silence when Grant's guilt would lie unspoken between them until the arrival of more cards and letters set the whole sorry sequence in motion again. "Have you forgotten you have a mother?" her mother-in-law would write. "You and that bitch of a wife?" Susan intercepted as many of these as she could, putting them in an envelope marked *Return to Sender*. Susan remembered how upset Cindy had been after visiting Olive in the residential home. For months afterwards she had had a terrified obsession with her grandmother's wrinkled and curled hands and there had been frequent nightmares. Susan couldn't remember ever having taken them very seriously. I should have listened, paid more attention, she thought.

"Mrs Howard!" The nurse's voice broke through her thoughts. "The doctor would like to see you."

Susan felt fear chill her body as she got to her feet. Visibly shaking, she entered the consulting room. The middle-aged, female doctor motioned to Susan to sit next to Cindy.

"Well, Mrs Howard, I have examined Cindy," the doctor said as she rifled through some notes.

Susan glanced across at Cindy; her daughter's face was impassive as she sat listening and clicking her fingernails.

Later that afternoon Cindy stood gazing out of the small bedroom window, watching her mother and grandmother at the garden gate. All she wished for now was to go to university and start her art career. The gold pencil was in her hand and unconsciously she ran her fingers over its smoothness. She'd been ordered out of the family home and sent to Emma's. Her mother had kissed her, promising that it would be for the best if they all had space to think. Poor Pandora! Cindy turned to look at the cat dozing away in the cage. She wouldn't like it here on a strange bed; it would take her time to get used to her new surroundings.

Cindy opened her small suitcase, throwing the few clothes she had packed onto the chair. Perhaps it was better, after all, to be here, away from her parents. Lying back on the bed she gazed at the ceiling. I am being punished, she thought, then started to sob quietly.

Gently the door opened.

"Cindy, I've brought you a mug of tea." Emma gently slipped into the room. She stood beside the bed looking down at her tearful granddaughter, meeting the pale face and the beautiful eyes that looked up at her. "Your mother is very upset," she commented, placing the mug down on the bedside table.

"I'm sorry, Gran. I didn't plan for this to happen, but I need someone to help me through this, to believe what I say." There was a pause as Cindy looked at the floor. "I have been over this in my mind hundreds of times. I knew what would happen."

"Cindy, this isn't revenge because your father wouldn't buy the car when you asked him to, is it?"

"No." It was all Cindy offered.

Emma tried to perch on the bed, putting a hand out to Cindy, but uncharacteristically Cindy turned away.

Taking off her jacket, tossing it carelessly over the banister, Susan wandered into the kitchen to open the fridge and help herself to a glass of carrot juice. The kitchen was precision tidy. Almost subconsciously she crossed the hallway, mounted the stairs and went into Cindy's bedroom.

Standing at the window looking out across the cul-de-sac, Susan slowly and painfully started to go over that morning's trip to the doctor. Cindy was no virgin, that much had been confirmed. Susan had phoned Grant and told him the result and he seemed equally dumbstruck.

Susan's shoulders began to shake and she started to sob uncontrollably. The noise of car tyres on gravel informed her that Grant was home but her mind was full of Cindy. Was she on the pill? Susan was floundering in a sea of despair. She rubbed her hands together nervously, aware of the awful atmosphere that was building up in the house. Theories for Cindy's accusation were pounding through her head. All afternoon, since the doctor's clinical voice had shattered her last hope, she had tried to make sense of it. In desperation, she had suggested that Cindy leave the house and stay with Emma while they all gave themselves space to think.

Grant stood silently in Cindy's bedroom doorway. "This is tearing me apart." His eyes were on Susan's face. "We are a family, we need each other."

Susan looked at him. He looks just the same, she thought. Nothing has changed. But what had she expected? Surely she would have picked up some signs of child abuse? But what would the signs have been? She confessed she didn't know. She hadn't even been looking. Did any mother deliberately look? Now Grant stood in front her, dressed as immaculately as ever, almost as if those dreadful words had never been uttered. "Oh, Grant!" Susan said. "We'll come through this, won't we?" She knew she did not sound convincing. "You do understand why Cindy had to leave the house for a little while? We cannot all live together at the moment, you do understand that, don't you?" Susan's voice was quiet as she walked across and placed her arm round his waist.

"I don't." he replied. "It is as if you don't trust me."

"Or perhaps I don't trust Cindy," she murmured. "I feel torn in two, Grant. Someone is going to be hurt, so terribly hurt."

"And you'd rather it was me?"

She looked away from him. "I'm going for a shower, I feel …" Susan shrugged and left the room.

Now Grant was alone in Cindy's bedroom. He stood by the window and looked down at the garden. He remembered the family summers they had enjoyed together, the barbecues and the laughter, how proud he had always been of his angel. "Oh Cinders," he whispered, "why have you said these things?" Out of the corner of his eye he saw a stupid teenage magazine lying discarded on her dressing table. What made him pick it up, he didn't know but pick it up he did and sat on the bed as he flicked through the pages. Nothing interested him and he was about to throw it into the waste paper basket when he noticed an article entitled *Daddy's Girl* written by Shona Widdry. He read it with growing disbelief. It was almost word for word. Often he had thought Cindy lived in her own world … but this? He stood up, anger welling inside him as, magazine in hand, he walked out of Cindy's room and pounded into his own bedroom where Susan was preparing for her shower.

"What do you make of this then?" He flung the magazine down on their double bed in front of Susan, who picked it up.

"Page 12," he said.

Susan glanced at the article.

"Well, now we know, don't we?" There was a note of triumph in his voice.

It had seemed a logical decision when Susan had made it but now, sleeping alone in the spare room, it seemed as if she was accusing Grant. She could not sleep; the events were spinning around her head. It seemed inconceivable that Cindy would one morning wake up and decide to say that Grant had abused her. The more Susan thought about this situation the more convinced she was that the article Cindy had read in the magazine had been a trigger point. But had it been a trigger point for the truth or fantasy? In horror Susan had read and re-read the article *Daddy's Girl*. She had felt repulsed by the story but had to reluctantly acknowledge that the writing bore a resemblance to the phraseology Cindy had used to describe what she claimed had happened to her.

There were so many questions going through her head and the answers could only come from Cindy.

It was morning and Grant had left for work. Susan sat in the hall staring at the telephone. Calling her mother's number she spoke to Cindy and asked to meet somewhere neutral.

Finally, after much deliberation, Cindy agreed and Susan chose a quiet pub in their village, arranging to meet at 8 o' clock that evening.

Susan arrived at the Durham Ox at ten minutes to eight and ordered herself a glass of white wine and an orange juice for Cindy. The minutes ticked by and at eight-twenty Susan was wondering if Cindy would come. Ten minutes later she had come to the conclusion that Cindy had decided not to come and she stood up, ready to leave. That was when she saw Cindy standing in the doorway observing her.

"I've missed you," Cindy said as she sat down, though she did not meet her mother's eyes.

They sat polarised at either end of the small table. The talk was desultory, until Susan said firmly, "Why say it now?"

There was a pause; Cindy's eyes were downcast as she murmured, "Don't you understand? I had to." Her voice was rough with suppressed emotion. "I couldn't go on with this hanging over me. What he did was so wrong. It seemed as good a time as any."

Susan frowned and gently shook her head. "But you seemed so close to your father. I always envied the easy friendship you had with him." The remark caused Cindy to think about her answer.

"I loved him," she replied eventually. "He would have been a fantastic father had it not been for his perversion."

Again there was that strange choice of words, words that Susan had read in the magazine story. "But it still doesn't explain why you were so friendly with him. If he really did these things to you, why did you put up with it?"

"Because, like you, I love being part of the family. Where else could I go? The family was important to me."

They ordered their meals and ate in silence. Susan picked at her food. All trace of appetite had vanished under the weight of Cindy's accusations. She was surprised to see that events had not caused Cindy a similar problem. She waited patiently for Cindy to finish then asked, "I need to understand. When this happened, what did he do?"

Cindy ran a hand through her hair and with a weary expression on her face said, "I told you. He raped me."

"When was the first time it happened?" Susan persisted.

"I was in the bath. Looking back it seemed quite innocuous. He sponged me down and dried me with the towel. I just thought his hands happened to touch me by accident."

Susan frowned. "I thought you said you were standing in your bedroom?" She stopped, seeing the look of irritation on her daughter's face.

Cindy shrugged and without making eye contact said, "I can't remember the exact details."

The answer didn't satisfy Susan. "How old were you?" she fired the question at Cindy.

"Eight."

"And what happened after that?"

"Initially he wanted me to undress in front of him when he put me to bed. He would kiss me on the mouth, slap my bottom. It progressed from there. I had to kiss him. He would put my hand on, well you know." There was a break in her voice.

Susan closed her eyes. It sounded absolutely disgusting and yet so clinically told. But she knew it was imperative that she did not break down, that she allowed the whole sordid story to come out. This meeting was so important and she had to maintain Cindy's confidence. I can't believe it, she thought. It just doesn't sound like Grant. And yet she saw the obvious distress Cindy was feeling. Subconsciously she rubbed her wedding ring.

"When you went to evening classes on a Thursday afternoon, Dad always met me from school and brought me, but not always directly, home. Sometimes we'd have a cream tea and sometimes we'd just go down a country lane." Cindy still did not meet her mother's eyes but her innuendo was not lost.

Susan rubbed her aching head, wondering how much worse this could get. Could Grant or any man commit incest with his daughter in a public place? The risk seemed horrendous. Cindy in her school uniform and Grant taking her down some lane, either to have sex or commit a sexual act with her. The whole thing seemed totally out of character for Grant who, when they were courting, had been reluctant to kiss her in public.

As if reading Susan's thoughts Cindy went on, "The risk seemed to excite him."

There was a long pause as each contemplated what had been said. It was Susan who broke the silence by showing Cindy the magazine article.

If Susan expected Cindy to go on the defensive she was disappointed. In a soft voice Cindy replied. "I can't tell you how much I admire Shona for writing that article. If more people were like her and had the guts to come out and tell the world about their experiences then people like Dad would find it hard to practice their sexual games."

As much as Susan desperately wanted to disbelieve Cindy and find inaccuracies in her story she could not. But still there remained a niggle of doubt.

Monday afternoon, 6th June

There were no words left. A gulf had come between them; a gulf so wide that neither seemed capable of building a bridge across it. There was no anger, only many unanswered, unresolved questions. They got up, made breakfast and lived as best they could.

Susan found comfort in Cindy's bedroom, where she sometimes sat on the bed for more than an hour. She hoped that by trying to absorb the atmosphere in the room some message would come to her. But there was nothing except confusion. The past week had been a nightmare of uncertainty. They did not live now as husband and wife, merely existed in the same space. The accusation and the doctor's confirmation had scorched their minds. Every minute of the day, Susan tried to reconstruct an incident from the past in the hope of finding an explanation.

That afternoon, with Cindy back at school, Susan had gone to visit Emma, taking with her the family photograph albums. They sat at Emma's dining room table, sifting through memories.

"Oh, she was so pretty!" Emma sighed as her old hands ran over photographs of Cindy. "Her lovely long hair in that red ribbon. You dressed her so beautifully. It was just …" Emma stopped and they both stared down at the picture of Cindy sitting on Grant's knee. "Well, Cindy wanted so much attention. You must remember how demanding she was. If Grant gave you a kiss then she had to have one too. It was amusing, but ..."

"But?"

"Oh nothing. She could be a jealous mite sometimes."

"Of me?"

"Mothers can get jealous of daughters and daughters of their mothers."

Susan continued to peer at the photograph as Emma got up to make a pot of tea. Whilst she was out of sight Susan slipped across to the small bookcase and took out a magnifying glass, which Emma used for reading small print. Now Susan peered closely at the photograph of Cindy and Grant. His hands, where were his hands? Peering closely she saw they were merely holding Cindy's in a fatherly way. This was so morbid, but nevertheless she continued. There were many holiday snaps showing Cindy in her bathing suit and Grant in his shorts. They were laughing together, hugging and kissing, but there was never anything untoward. They were normal family photographs, with nothing at all suspicious in them. In another album she found a school photograph of Cindy aged eight and then a later picture of her at twelve. A four-year gap. What had happened in those years? She peered from one to the other but they told her nothing. Should I have known? It was a question that haunted her.

Susan asked Emma, who shook her head, reassuring her that there had been nothing for her to know. But Susan couldn't get it out of her mind. "I have failed somehow," she said. "Perhaps by not finding out why Cindy was having nightmares, why she wasn't eating properly. But I told myself it didn't matter."

"You haven't failed," Emma soothed as they sat drinking tea. "You've been ... you are," Emma corrected, "a wonderful mother and wife. You really couldn't have done more." She paused as she picked up a photograph showing a young Cindy in the bath. "You can drive yourself mad, imagining all sorts of things if you've a mind to." She handed the photograph to Susan.

Susan looked at it, remembering how Grant had enjoyed bathing Cindy.

"They are just family snapshots," Emma reminded her briskly. "Nothing more and certainly nothing sinister."

"I know, Mum. I can't help myself."

"But what do you hope to find?" Emma asked.

"I don't know. Nothing! I want to find nothing." Susan pushed a hand through her hair. It needed cutting but she had not been to the hairdresser. She couldn't face the inane questions.

"You've always expected life to be perfect. Well, it isn't and it can never be. You've been lucky up to now, in having no serious problems," Emma's voice was low. "Life isn't perfect. You can't make it so. You simply have to accept that, believe in the strength of your marriage and deal with whatever comes up."

"What about Cindy? What can I think of her?"

"That she may well be a very disturbed young woman."

"She is no virgin, mother. We can't ignore that."

"Susan, girls today are often promiscuous."

Susan shook her head. "Cindy is not like that."

CHAPTER FIFTEEN

*I*t was sobering for Susan to realise that they had no close friends to turn to. Not that she would in any case have wanted to talk about her predicament. It was difficult to face the ladies at the golf club. What if Cindy pressed charges? The thought of that was too frightening to contemplate.

The atmosphere in the house remained tense. Susan and Grant continued to look at each other furtively. They had tried to talk, but it was no use. She believed him. Of course she did, but the niggle was there now, gradually eroding her resolve to be strong. Grant seemed to age suddenly, his eyes sunk in their sockets through lack of sleep. He felt incredibly weary. He cancelled his magisterial duties, saying he couldn't face making judgements. Their social life was non-existent.

Susan was standing again at Cindy's bedroom window. Her hand slammed down on the ledge in anger as tears started to make their familiar journey down her face. She turned and kicked the bed hard, ramming the mattress to one side. Mad with frustration, she started to rip the sheets off her daughter's bed and in a rage threw the pillows across the room. One pillow smashed into a pot plant, which in turn fell to the floor. The pot broke, sending soil all over the carpet.

Susan paused, gasping for breath. Losing control solved nothing and getting angry solved even less. She had to be rational or at least try to look as if she was on top of the situation. She knelt down beside the bed and slowly collapsed in anguish on the floor. The bedclothes were strewn around her.

She thought about Grant and his withdrawal from the family. He had tried to talk to Cindy, tried to get the family to act as a unit but Cindy would not communicate with him and they had become more and more withdrawn. Life was no easier with Cindy staying at her mother's. How long could she remain away from the family home? Susan convinced herself that it was a postponement, a waiting period for confirmation. Confirmation that Cindy was lying?

It was an impossible situation and Susan had been tempted to seek help, but who could help her? Twice she had picked up the telephone and dialled a counselling service. But she couldn't talk; there was nothing she could say. It was a private, family affair.

Susan brushed the back of her hand across her eyes. Blinking, she tried to focus and was about to get up when she saw the corner of what looked like a book protruding from under the mattress.

Without much interest she pulled it out, seeing at once that it was not a book but one of Cindy's sketching pads. Curiously she started to flick through the pages. Then, as she gazed down at the sketches, Susan felt numbness chill through her body. Turning the pages rapidly, she saw the pencil sketches, the familiar faces, one after another.

"In the name of God," Susan whispered through dry lips as she crouched, half sitting, half kneeling by the bed, gazing at the perfectly executed pencil sketch. It was one of many, drawn meticulously, showing the face in a range of different expressions. The eyes, so gentle and tender, the mouth so sensitive. The drawings clearly conveyed to Susan her daughter's love for the face she had captured so naturally. It was Grant.

Emma watched as the Audi drew up outside her house. She stood at the window as Susan got out, slammed the door and activated the alarm. She realised for the first time that her daughter was middle-aged. Well, she herself was old, far too old for these problems. She watched Susan approach dressed in her navy blue blazer, jeans and white loafer shoes, with a large manila envelope under her arm, purposefully making her way down the small path.

Emma moved away from the window. She walked into the hall and opened the door before Susan had time to ring the bell.

"Where's Cindy?" Susan asked without any preamble.

"She's upstairs asleep. Go into the sitting room, dear."

For all her show of being in control, Emma could see that Susan was suffering. Worry lines were etched round her eyes and her make-up was not as meticulously applied as it usually was. Susan sat wearily down, clutching the envelope, her fingers continuously tapping it in an annoying rat-tat-tat.

"Would you like a cup of tea?"

Susan shook her head. "No. I've come to see Cindy. I wanted to find some evidence. Well I have, and now I'm sorry." Susan's hands shook slightly as she opened the envelope. Taking out the sketchpad, she handed it to Emma.

Sitting down Emma flicked through the pad. The appalling brilliance of the sketches made her wince.

"I don't understand."

"Just turn to the last sketch."

Emma adjusted her glasses and flicked to the last page. She gasped at the perfectly life-like sketch of the man. "But ... it's Grant." Her brows furrowed. "I don't understand. Cindy's drawn him as if ..."

"Yes," Susan cut in, her voice rising, "Like her lover!"

She got up and paced the room, her hands pushed into the pockets of her jeans.

Emma gazed once more at the sketch and then turned over the pages of the pad. Images of Susan and Grant met her eyes.

"I want to see Cindy. Find out what it all means."

Susan's eyes were angry. Emma got up out of the chair. She put an arm round her daughter to comfort her.

At that moment, both women looked up to see Cindy enter. Her eyes looked sad and lifeless.

"How are you feeling?" Susan asked, her mind on the sketches.

Cindy stared at her mother for a moment before pulling her mouth back in a grim smile. "I'm all right."

"I think it was wise for you to return to school. It'll take your mind off things," Susan said bluntly.

As Cindy looked at Susan, a surge of pity overtook her. Susan's perfect family was shattered. But it had had to be said, she had to grasp on to that simple thought.

"Cindy," Susan tried to keep her voice on a level tone as she walked across the room, picking up the pad that Emma had placed on the coffee table. "I have to ask you about this." Susan leafed through the pad and held up the last sketch of Grant.

"You've been into my room!" Cindy frowned and snatched the pad from her mother's hand. "This is my business! You've no right going through my things."

Susan was taken aback at Cindy's reaction.

"I was changing your bed. I was not prying," she said coldly. "But I want to know what all this means."

Cindy looked from her mother's face to her grandmother's. They looked back at her like accusers. Cindy clutched her pad to her chest. They had no right; it was like taking the lid off her head. Finding her thoughts, sifting and filtering them, keeping only what they wanted and discarding the rest.

"I'm waiting." Susan was impatient.

Cindy stared from her mother to her grandmother, her eyes suddenly full of tears.

Emma put her arm round Cindy and guided her to a seat, in a sobbing voice Cindy said, "I am not stupid. You all seem to think that I have no idea what will happen. I haven't lied. I tried to forget it all. It happened. Mum used to go out of the house for evenings, learning bridge ... "

Emma glanced across at Susan who slowly nodded her head.

"That's when it started. I was his little angel," Cindy shuddered. "He said angels are heaven sent, and I'd been sent for him." She closed her eyes tightly and shuddered again. "Mum, I know you think I said it because I thought I wasn't getting the car, but it wasn't that. I just need someone to believe me!" She tailed off, waiting and hoping for some gesture from her mother and grandmother. Instead Susan could only dwell on the drawings, saying again, "But these sketches, why did you do them?"

Cindy sighed as she stared down at the floor. I have to make them believe me, she thought. She had gone over and over in her mind what she would say at this crucial time, knowing she had to try and convince them she was telling the truth. She knew it would be hard to shatter her father's image, to bring out the monster that lurked beneath his genteel manner. Had she left it too late? Body language, Cindy knew how important that was. She must not appear too assertive, too competent. She must be fragile, cynical and sad. She must be the weak female, the daughter besmirched by her father's hand. "I was remembering," Cindy whispered. "I didn't want to remember, but I have to. I have to make you believe me. I am not lying. I've pushed everything into the back of my mind for so long. It was the only way I could live with myself. These people here," she tapped the sketchpad, "became my family. I wanted to love my father, I just wanted to love him as a father." Cindy handed the sketchpad to her grandmother. "See. See," she flicked to a new page, "what she looks like?" Cindy held up the pencilled sketch of an old woman, with gnarled, hook-like hands, a face vacant, but unmistakably like Grant's. "You didn't see this one, did you? I've drawn shackles on her hands and feet. A prisoner! That's what he made his mother, a prisoner."

Emma sat back. Her heart was beating fast. Dear God, I almost believe her. She saw the stricken expression on Susan's face as Cindy made her impassioned plea for understanding. And yet why do I feel this is a masterly performance? Why am I so sceptical? She is seventeen, afraid, unsure, and she is accusing her father of a terrible crime. My heart should go out to her, yet I cannot help but feel I am being manipulated. The sketches, the story, why would she make it up? She wished she were not involved, she wished Susan would stop looking across at her, as if age had given her the wisdom to deal with such a situation.

"No, Grant could not do it. He is a kind, generous man, I couldn't have found a better husband." Susan's voice was rising, indignant. "His mother was impossible. But he hated putting her away, believe me."

Cindy stood up. "I've told you what happened. It's the truth. I'm tired, grandma, I'm going to lie down." She closed the sketchpad. "I know you want to brush it all under the carpet, but it happened. Be glad I left it so long before I did tell you."

"But why draw Grant looking so desirable?" Susan challenged. She was rewarded by a faint look of irritation in Cindy's eyes as her hands tightened imperceptibly round the sketchpad. There was the faintest of pauses before she said, "It meant nothing, Mum." And seeing the sceptical look on Emma's face she opened the door and left the sitting room.

Grant sat at his office desk, his mind a nothingness as he watched the unrelenting rain pouring down outside his office window. Concentrating on his work was hopeless. Grant wanted, no, needed physical contact; he had to prove something to himself. Susan had returned from the spare room and submitted to his lovemaking, his need to prove he was normal, a man who couldn't have done those dreadful things to his daughter, but he had the impression that her heart was not involved.

He had tried to convince Susan that his outward affection for Cindy – the hugs, kisses, generosity and love, always lots of love – had been distorted into something disgusting. Was every father who kissed and loved his daughter to be a suspect? Was there so much being made of incest that girls like Cindy could imagine it happened? He had read somewhere about false memory syndrome. Was that what was happening here?

He had treated Cindy fairly. Yes, he had bought the car but it was out of pride at her achievements at school and certainly not a bribe to keep her confidence. He wanted only the best, the very best for her. Was this how he was to be repaid? A daughter who was throwing his love back with horrendous accusations? He had tried to understand but he couldn't. So why? What reason was there for Cindy to accuse him? He closed his eyes. Surely she had known she would get the car? Why had she been so impatient? If he had bought her the car sooner, would Cindy still have made the allegations?

He had tried talking to Susan in an effort to reassure her, but how did you reassure a wife, or convince anyone for that matter, that you were not some degenerate pervert with a need to grope and abuse your own flesh and blood? How did you really make someone believe you were not guilty? Grant could not help but accept the irony of the situation. He thought of all the court cases, the accused pleading their innocence. Now here he was, pleading his own case.

As he drove home he felt utterly alone. There was so much help for women but where did men go for advice?

He turned his key in the front door lock and pushed the door open. The house was quiet and waiting for him. He threw his briefcase on the hall chair. Taking off his jacket, he loosened his tie as he made his way to the dining room, to stand behind his bar. He was drinking too much, he knew that, but it dulled any unpleasant thoughts. Grant poured a generous measure into the tumbler and took his first gulp of the evening. He breathed a grateful sigh as the whisky scorched his throat. Then, taking the bottle, he wandered into the kitchen.

He saw the brief note from Susan on the kitchen table, telling him she had left his dinner in the oven. But the thought of food made him feel nauseous. He refilled his glass and took it upstairs. Cindy's bedroom door was closed. Grant paused outside it as he had done so many times in the past. Listening, somehow expecting to hear her movements from within. Griping the door handle, Grant felt it silently turn beneath his touch. He sensed his heart start to thump as he swung open the door. He half expected to find her lying there, but the room was empty. He gave a faint shudder, remembering the many times he had been there with Cindy. Then she had been glad to have him with her. She had welcomed him then, he had been a loving father and she a carefree daughter. Grant bit his lip at the memory and closed his eyes, seeing her now, in his mind's eye, so beautiful, so pure. Her arms open to him, her eyes wide and wondrous. His little angel. How proud he had been of her! She had responded to him. He was her father and she was all that had mattered to him at one time. He had blown away her fear of the darkness, comforted her on those nights she had bad dreams and been her friend when needed. He walked to the window and looked outside.

He saw her face. It haunted him. His mother, malevolent, waiting, as she always had done, querying his every move. Grant could not admit, even now, that he hated her. Thoughts of her used to bombard him; he had had to prove he was free. He'd taken his daughter to see her, his mad old mother, sitting in her chair, watching and waiting, no longer able to possess him. Cindy had been badly frightened but he had reassured her that it was all right. Grandma Olive was locked away – forever.

Memories were disturbing him regularly now. Grant liked to take things at face value. Exploring the depths of the unconscious was for shrinks, not for him. He moved round Cindy's bedroom looking at the pictures. Opening the wardrobe, he touched her clothes. He sat at the dressing table; his fingers caressed the small objects that she had left, including a bottle of perfume. He placed his glass tumbler down and picked up the perfume bottle, sniffed at the contents, remembering the smell on Cindy. Pouring a little onto the palm of his hand, the aroma brought back a vivid memory.

He took another gulp of Whisky. Cindy's face became merged with that of his mother. Grant shook his head in confusion, conscious of the tears in his eyes, conscious of the pain in his heart.

Cindy had decided to have an early night. But she could not sleep. Shadows made strange configurations on the wall. This was not her bedroom and she didn't know whether the reflections were friends or enemies. They looked like long pointed fingers that could run over her skin and tear it open to reveal more blood.

She had seen it, crimson red on the sheet; her body torn to shreds so she had bled. It had scared her to see her own blood – a part of her seeping away, which she had no control over.

Then she'd showered again but still she'd bled. She wanted to tell her mother but she wasn't there. She gave a shudder as she remembered how it had been.

Every month after that she hated being a woman. The loss of blood made her feel dirty, unclean and she'd taken to showering sometimes three or four times a day. Scrubbing and scrubbing, trying to rid herself of that horrid memory. But each month it returned and haunted her. It was always there. Like a curse. Red on white – and always on her mind.

God would never let her forget what happened. It was a penance she had to pay for the rest of her life.

She sat up in bed and switched on the small bedside light. Its weak bulb gave off an orange glow. Pandora yawned and stretched herself out on the bed as Cindy got up and stood by the window. She had nothing now, except the few things she had brought with her.

She was irritated, no more than that. Why had her father denied the allegation? Why was he making her out to be the liar? Why had she come to her grandma's? It was as if she was the guilty one.

Grant heard the sound of car tyres crunch up the driveway. He got up from the bed quickly, straightening the covers before furtively peering out of the window and then at his watch. It was half past ten and Susan was back. Gulping down the remains of the whisky, Grant closed Cindy's bedroom door. He felt guilty and yet why should he? He had done nothing wrong. He started to make his way down the stairs. I don't want to see Susan, he thought suddenly, as he heard her insert the key into the lock.

Susan jumped in surprise as she saw him hovering on the stairs.

"What on earth have you been doing? You look a mess," Susan rasped, her eyes full of pent-up anger. "Have you been drinking? Here I am, worried sick, and you come back to indulge your self-pity. Sit down. Have you had anything to eat?"

He shook his head and followed her into the kitchen, watching as she opened the oven door and slammed the desiccated meal down before him. His stomach lurched as he picked at the food on the plate while Susan busied herself with the dishwasher. Grant pushed the remains of his dinner away. Sinking his head in his hands, he gave an involuntary moan. Susan felt her temper snap as she sat opposite him.

Susan leant across and opened a drawer. She pulled out a small plastic bag and pushed it across the table towards him. "Open it!" she instructed.

He stared dumbly at the bag. Peering in he asked, "So?"

"What do you mean, 'So?' Take it out! Look at it!"

He tipped the contents out on to the table and rummaging among the tissue sheets, he extracted the box.

"Open it," Susan commanded.

He did and stared down at the black lace nightdress.

"Whose is it?" he asked.

"I found the bag in Cindy's room with this in it."

She handed him the credit card slip with the name of the shop and his signature on it.

Grant stared at it as realisation suddenly dawned. He remembered the incident with Cindy and Elizabeth at the lingerie shop.

"Look," he started weakly, "It's quite innocent." And he went on to relate what had happened.

"You bought her this! A black lace nightdress! In the name of God, Grant."

He stared at her and shook his head. "It was a present. I swear to you, it was just a present."

"Don't you think it's rather an unusual present for a father to give a teenage daughter?" Susan's voice was acid.

No matter how Grant tried to explain how unimportant the gesture was, her scepticism was unshakeable. Slowly he was realising how innocent gestures in the past could now be brought back and misinterpreted and he felt an overwhelming fear.

CHAPTER SIXTEEN

Thursday, 9th June

*G*rant had not seen Cindy since she had made the accusation. He had expected to hear from her, but he hadn't. Susan had been adamant that he was to stay away from Emma's house and was not to try to contact Cindy. "It would be far too upsetting for mother," she said.

Grant couldn't let it rest. He had to speak to Cindy, which was why he was sitting at a table in the corner of the café that he knew Cindy and Elizabeth often used after school.

This was his third attempt and he was willing her to come today. Looking at his watch, he decided he could justify another five minutes; then he would leave and resume his vigil the next day. Downing his mug of coffee he was about to get up when the door jingled open and he heard her laugh.

Grant felt the sweat on his hands as he saw Cindy walk in. There was no sign of trauma, no hint of the nervous, pale young woman that Susan had talked about. Her hair was glossy, her face was animated as she laughed and chatted with Elizabeth. She looked, he thought, as though she didn't have a care in the world.

He got awkwardly to his feet. "Cindy can we talk?" Grant tried to sound light and friendly but as she turned towards him he saw a veil of hostility in her eyes and knew she was about to refuse. But Elizabeth and a third girl hovered and it was Elizabeth who unwittingly came to his aid.

"Hello Mr Howard," Elizabeth said with a wide smile. "We'll be over there, Cindy," she said tactfully and they moved off.

When Elizabeth was out of earshot, Cindy whispered, "I don't want to see you."

"Cindy," he cajoled, "we have to talk. We must sort this out. Please? Let me get you a coffee. And sit down; it makes things easier."

Reluctantly Cindy dragged back a chair and sat down, her face impassive as her father got up to get two mugs of coffee. "Would you like a scone?" he called. He noticed her hesitate before giving a disinterested nod.

Putting the tray on the table, Grant sat opposite her. Cindy looked at him from beneath lowered eyelids, and then she shrugged her shoulders and cut her scone up, hastily smearing on the jam and then the cream.

"You always did like a cream tea!"

Cindy fought a smile, remembering how greedy she had been, and for a brief moment there was empathy between them. Then the lights in Cindy's eyes went out, like shutters closing out the sun. Or so it seemed to Grant.

"Look, " his voice was low. "You and I, we had such a good relationship. We were always that little more than just father and daughter. We were real friends. Well, I liked to think we were. I know over the past couple of years you've been growing up and you've had new interests and new friends and that's how it should be." Grant knew he had Cindy's attention. "But you were always very special to me. You were my little angel!"

She wiped a smear of jam from her lips and muttered, "Dad, not here!"

He smiled. "Am I embarrassing you talking about love?"

"We're not talking about love," Cindy snapped. "We're talking about you and me and ... "

"You know it's a lie." He paused and sighed before adding. "The car. If that's what it's all been about, it's at home in the garage. It's yours. I'll even pay the running costs."

She met his eyes across the table. "A bribe?" Her voice was cynical.

"Cindy, this accusation, it's got out of hand!" His voice was almost a whisper. "I would never have harmed you. What you told your mother was not true." Grant leaned forward. "Cindy, you have to tell them I never hurt you."

Cindy's face was impassive. She could sense his nervousness and it gave her an advantage. She shook her head. "I don't want to talk about it."

"Why are you doing this?" He was conscious that he came over as wheedling and ineffective when he should be sounding strong. "Cindy, you're hurting all of us. This has gone on long enough." Grant tailed off lamely. But Cindy did not reply so he continued. "I can't work. I can't think. The family is disintegrating before my eyes. I have to keep us together, all of us!"

She glanced up, seeing the beads of sweat on his forehead. For the first time Cindy noticed a strand of grey in his hair.

He watched her repeatedly click one long fingernail across the other, a habit she knew irritated him.

Grant placed his hand over hers. "Stop that!" His eyes met hers as she separated her hands. "So where do we go from here then?" he asked in resignation. "You can't stay at your grandma's forever. You've got to come home at some stage. We need to be a family again." His voice was persuasive.

Shaking her head, Cindy replied, "You and I can't ever be in the same house again. Don't you realise that?" She looked pitifully at her father. "It's you that has to leave home. Surely you know that." Her eyes were merciless.

He stared at her, disbelief spreading across his face. Then his eyes became hard and his mouth drew back into a grim line. "Leave home! And go where? This sounds like revenge. Is that it? I'm to go because of your stupid accusation! Don't think I don't know the way you're manipulating the situation? Don't think I don't see through you."

She met his eyes, saying quietly, "I don't know what you mean."

"Oh yes you damn well do! That bloody nightdress you made me buy, an innocent gift ..."

They faced each other across the table for a second. A frown appeared on Cindy's forehead. "I don't know what you're talking about."

"Oh yes you damn well do! Your mother found it in your wardrobe."

"So?"

"Your mother thought it was a very odd gift." He tailed off.

Cindy shrugged. If they would go searching through her room it served them right if they didn't like what they found.

Grant sighed. "There's no point in talking." He reached down for his briefcase. Turning his face away, he stood up. He couldn't bear to look at his daughter for fear he would hit her. Smack her so hard that he would feel he was knocking some sense into her. His own daughter had become a malevolent stranger. "I'm leaving. I hope you'll think about what I've said." He did not look at her. Cindy watched him go before picking up her mug of coffee and walking across to join her friends.

Although Susan had wanted to throw the magazine containing the article *Daddy's Girl* in the bin, inexplicably she had put it in a drawer for future reference. Now she found herself turning again to page 12, but this time her interpretation of the article was different and she wondered if perhaps it brought back unpleasant memories for Cindy.

But was Susan merely grasping at straws? First she had thought all this had happened because Cindy didn't get her car, now she was wondering if it had anything to do with an article in a magazine. One thing was abundantly clear, it was too great an allegation for there to be an easy solution. And as Cindy's mother she had a duty to take it seriously.

The whole truth of the allegation seemed to hinge on one question. Who had taken Cindy's virginity?

Saturday, 11th June

After her morning at the newsagent Cindy returned home knowing the house would be empty. She walked upstairs to her room. They had violated it. She knew they had been here, hands opening drawers, peering and prying and looking for evidence. But only she had that.

Here in this room he had come in the night, pushing the door open and entering stealthily. Here on this bed, he had knelt beside her, his face ... his tears ... his pleas. In this room, on this bed it had happened. She felt sick; her head had started to ache as the tears pricked at the back of her eyes. The room blurred as she blinked; tears rolled down her cheeks as she slowly started to rock her head back and forth. The ceiling was a white cloud, there had been blood, pain and guilt, always guilt.

Cindy heard the hall clock in the distance chiming the hour. The moment of sadness passed. Dabbing her eyes with the back of her hand, she lay back on the bed, and dozed off. Twenty minutes later she staggered to her feet and stripped off her clothes as she walked into her bathroom. Emma's shower was a makeshift extension pipe from the bath taps that had to be encouraged to emit even a lukewarm trickle of water and Cindy longed to feel the invigorating force of her own powerful shower.

Ten minutes later she dressed in fresh jeans, underclothes

and a shirt. After drying her hair she walked to the bed, straightened the cover and reached under the mattress. But then she remembered that Susan had found it, her book about her family. Now it was in her grandmother's house. But there was something else she needed.

Cindy knew all her secrets had been hidden with care. Only Pandora sensed their location. Removing her shoes from the floor of her wardrobe, Cindy pulled back the carpet to reveal a loose floorboard that she prized up. Thrusting her arm into the dark space she dragged out a dusty bin liner. A small brown parcel lay within the liner, tied with string. She retrieved it and returned the bin liner to its hiding place in the wardrobe then meticulously replaced the floorboard, the carpet and her shoes.

Cindy placed the brown parcel on the bed before methodically removing the string and peeling open the wrapping. There it lay, neatly folded. She felt a moment's nausea when she saw it, recalling the pain and how she would lie awake until it died away, how she would feel with her hands where he'd been. In the morning she'd pretend it had never happened.

Cindy's thoughts were interrupted by the premature arrival of Susan's car. Quickly she wrapped the parcel and picked it up. She walked to the top of the landing and watched silently as Susan opened the front door and entered in her golfing gear. But there was none of the usual verve in Susan's actions as she took off her jacket and hung it on the stair post.

How old she looks, Cindy thought. So dull and middle-aged. A floorboard creaked under her foot and the noise made her mother jump.

"Who's there?" Susan looked up, her eyes fearful.

"It's me," Cindy came slowly down the stairs. She followed Susan into the kitchen and placed the parcel down on the table.

"Do you want a coffee?"

Cindy nodded at Susan, who busied herself with the kettle.

"So?" Susan attempted a smile. It didn't work; it looked more like a grimace. "How are you?"

Cindy sighed, not wishing to talk but knowing she had no choice. Briefly she told Susan about her meeting with Grant in the café. She hesitated before saying, "But that's not why I'm here. I came here today because I remembered, and I hate remembering. I can't seem to stop now. It just goes round and round in my mind." Susan made as if to speak then paused seeing the expression on Cindy's face.

Her mother seemed to have aged fifteen years over the past weeks. Her skin looked sallow and was creased by worry lines. To know that she had been the cause of this deterioration in her mother gave Cindy a moment's unease. Susan had done nothing wrong and it seemed unfair that she was being put through so much. "You don't believe me, do you?" Cindy said softly.

"I don't know what to think any more," Susan admitted with a sigh.

Cindy hesitated and then said quietly. "It was hard for me to do this, Mum. I'd pushed it away, but it wouldn't go for long." She tapped her forehead. "It comes and it goes, the memory of it. Sometimes it hurts. I wouldn't have mentioned it but the article made me want to be clean again. It's so hard to put into words, Mum. But I've something here. I need to show you." She looked embarrassed as she handed Susan the package. "Open it!"

Susan stared at the package suspiciously, wondering what fresh horror was about to be revealed. Slowly she untied the string and spilled the contents onto the table. Susan frowned as she saw what looked like a bed sheet. "In the name of God what is it?"

"Do you recognise it?" Cindy's voice was a whisper.

Susan glanced up at her daughter, seeing her taut white face. "It looks like that bed sheet that went missing. But that was years ago."

"I kept it. I had to." Cindy stood up, frantically clicking her nails.

"Stop that!" Susan commanded. "Stop it, it gets on my nerves."

Cindy glanced at her hands before grasping them together so the knuckles showed white.

"Why have you kept this dirty sheet?" Susan asked in bewilderment.

"Why do you think it went missing?"

Mother and daughter looked at each other across the table on which the sheet lay. Then Cindy leaned across and unfurled the sheet. A few brown stains, then a patch in the centre caught Susan's eye – muddy – as if coffee had spilt on it a long time ago.

"I don't understand, Cindy." Susan put a hand to her head and closed her eyes for a brief moment.

"Mum it's the bed sheet. The one that was on the bed when it happened. The first night! Those are bloodstains you're looking at. My blood!"

Susan wanted to dismiss it but couldn't. Cindy was shaking, her face white as she waited for Susan to react.

"You have to believe me, Mum. Someone has to believe me," Cindy was pleading.

Susan stood looking at the bed that she and Grant shared. She was thinking about the physical side of their marriage. She knew it had always meant a lot to Grant, but she had to admit that over the past few months she had been distant. She obliged him, gave him his rights, nothing more. God, what a terrible expression to use in this day and age.

God damn you Grant! Susan flung herself on the bed, pounding the quilt with her hands. What have you done to us?

As she lay there Grant's Jaguar came up the driveway. She got up quickly and ran a comb through her hair. God, I look a mess, she thought as she walked down the stairs.

Seeing his outline against the frosted glass in the front door, Susan watched as he inserted his key and slowly entered. He should look like a monster, she thought, should be different in some way. But he wasn't. Grant attempted a half smile. But Susan could not respond and could only watch him silently as he placed his briefcase down on the hall chair.

Then suddenly the strain of the day took its toll and she exploded in anger, "You miserable, self-satisfied bastard!" she screamed. She wanted to goad him into losing his temper, to make him say something. Anything! In the kitchen, she stood in front of him, her face pinched with accusation, her body shaking. Grant placed a hand on her shoulders but she shrugged him off.

"Don't touch me," she pulled away.

"Susan, what do I have to say? We've been married twenty years. Why can't you believe me when I say I have done nothing to Cindy?"

"I don't know what to believe any more." Picking up the parcel, Susan shook out the bed sheet.

Grant stared down, a small tic twitched in his left eye. "What is it this time?"

"This sheet was on Cindy's bed the night it happened. Look! " She pointed to the muddy stains. "Don't you remember these sheets? They were part of a set and then one mysteriously disappeared. Well, this is the one. Cindy dragged it off her bed the night you went in," she hesitated, pausing for breath.

"For God's sake, woman!" He could not keep the bewilderment from his voice as they stood confronting each other. "Are you telling me that you think this is proof that I ..." he balked.

"That is what Cindy has told me."

"And you obviously believe her!"

"I am trying to believe you," Susan was tired.

"But obviously finding it difficult in the face of one dirty sheet. God! What sort of a wife are you?" He slammed his fist into the wall in an act of desperation.

"I'm trying hard to be wife, mother and now counsellor. Cindy says this is her blood. She was young, a virgin. She would have bled if anyone had sex with her!"

Grant shook his head at Susan and then looked down at the sheet. "For all we know these could be coffee stains. She probably hid it because she knew you'd be cross. How do you know it's blood? In any case, don't young girls start periods at that age? Don't they bleed? I'm appalled you could even consider ..." He broke off. "I'm going to get a drink. Dear God, I need one!"

He stormed out of the kitchen across the hall and into the dining room.

Susan followed him. Her head ached as she felt the burden of depression smother her.

Grant stood with his back to her. "This has got ridiculous! God knows what Cindy will do or say or find next!" He turned to her, glass in hand. "You confront with me with this tatty bit of sheet as if I'm some bloody criminal! What sort of a man do you think I am?"

Susan did not want to think of the answer.

CHAPTER SEVENTEEN

Monday, 13th June

The previous night Emma had gone into Cindy's room, sat on the bed and tried to get her granddaughter to talk to her. Cindy had given nothing away. Her eyes were clear and wide and yet full of misery as they met her grandmother's. But she had opened her arms and snuggled into Emma murmuring, "Oh Gran, I am so sorry for what has happened."

"Why did you wait so long, Cindy, before telling anyone?" Emma asked the question that had been bothering her from the beginning.

There was a long silence and Emma felt Cindy's body stiffen and pull away. In the dim light, Emma saw the tear stains on Cindy's cheeks as she whispered, "Promise not to tell Mum, not yet."

Emma nodded. "I promise."

"I was afraid, you see." Cindy paused and bit her lip. "He'd started to come into my room again. I'd hear the stairs creak and see the door start to open. I put a chair under the handle. I was frightened."

"Are you saying that Grant...?" Emma balked at actually uttering the words.

"Yes, Gran. I came home late one night. The next day Mum left him to talk to me, and well ... " she paused, took a deep breath and said, "He got too close..." Cindy's face screwed up into a tight grimace and she turned away.

Emma listened quietly to this latest confession but despite Cindy's persuasive performance, there was something, just something about it that she found hard to believe.

Grant made the decision to move out of the house. The difficult part was breaking the news to Susan. But it was obvious that the situation between them had become intolerable. His family was broken and bruised by Cindy's devastating allegations and they seemed to have reached a stalemate. Something had to change so that they could have the chance to move forward, and that something had to be him.

He went back to the office and told his secretary that he would be away for the remainder of the afternoon.

The Green Park Hotel was a small, privately run establishment. It was tastefully decorated and offered comfortable accommodation with tea-making facilities, television and a small en-suite shower room. They offered breakfast but no evening meal. Grant made the necessary arrangements and went home to tell Susan he was moving out.

For a moment there was a stricken expression on her face but then she turned on him with an icy look and said, "That is almost an admission of guilt."

He lost his temper, brought his fist down on the table so hard that the plates rattled. "I can't stay here, don't you see that? You're watching every bloody move I make."

In the end Susan pleaded with him to stay but it was too late. He threw a few things into his overnight bag and left.

Now he sat in the solitude of the hotel room and for the first time since the accusation he felt a surge of peace. Perhaps now he would be able to think clearly, to make some plans for the future. He had a niggling temptation to pack it all in, to get away from these women who were dominating and ruining his life; to simply disappear, just like his father must have done all those years ago.

He took off his spectacles and rubbed his eyes. He wanted to let all the emotion flow away, but he couldn't. He knew that men don't cry.

Susan was right, he thought. Leaving would make him look guilty, especially after the latest twist in the allegation. There seemed to be no way out. If he went to the police he would be condemned before he even began. To do nothing meant Cindy could carry on, inflicting more and more hurt until eventually he lost everything. Grant put his head in his hands. Try as he might he was unable to find a satisfactory solution.

During the mid-morning free period, Elizabeth brought up the subject of the gold pencil, asking, not for the first time, where Cindy had got it.

"From a good-looking man," Cindy admitted and the words were out before she could stop herself. Seeing the flash of curiosity in Elizabeth's eyes, Cindy knew she had to go further.

Who had given her the gold pencil, Elizabeth wanted to know? Where had she got it? As if it mattered. Eventually Cindy heard herself saying that it belonged to a tall man with silver hair. A memory flickered before her eyes like a video and the song came into her head. But the pencil had been with her a long time. She had seen it on his desk, glistening in the sunlight. Then he had left her, and she had picked it up, feeling the smoothness against her fingers. She didn't remember putting it in her pocket, but she must have done, because she'd had it with her that night when she got home. Perhaps he'd given it to her. Cindy couldn't remember. Did doctors give patients their pencils?

Elizabeth was unable to get Cindy to reveal anything else. "I bet it is your father's."

But Cindy remained quiet and eventually Elizabeth gave up and changed the subject to how she wanted someone called Robert Fletcher to accompany her to the forthcoming school dance. "He's a hunk!" Elizabeth remarked.

Cindy shrugged casually. She wasn't interested in Elizabeth's romantic notions. This Robert would be like all other men, just after one thing. No, that was unfair. She shouldn't compartmentalise everyone like her father, but she had lived through too much to allow any sentiment regarding the male species to cloud her judgement. She knew only too well that men and her were a volatile combination.

"You didn't tell me you'd been out with him," Cindy commented as she replaced the pencil into the inside pocket of her blazer.

"Well I haven't actually been out with him," Elizabeth confessed. "It's just, well, you know when people want to ask you out. You get that feeling." Elizabeth was struggling a bit under Cindy's appraising eyes. "I met him at a party. We played a game and at the end, well, I knew what he was after."

Cindy wondered if Elizabeth was lying. Lying was easy. Making others believe you, that was the hard part.

"Didn't he telephone you afterwards?" Cindy asked curiously.

"Of course! He works in the chemist in town and asked me to call round to see him any time I was passing. He has his own flat." Cindy's obvious lack of interest only fuelled Elizabeth's lies. "I'll go over to the shop and see him today," she announced confidently.

At lunchtime they walked down to the shops. Elizabeth had brushed her hair and put on lipstick.

"He's in there!" Elizabeth confirmed as she surreptitiously glanced into the chemist's window. The shop doorbell rang loudly and heads turned as they entered. Cindy stood by the make-up counter, wondering why she had been coerced into becoming part of Elizabeth's childish antics.

Elizabeth walked over to the counter behind which a white-coated figure stood. "Hello, I'm Elizabeth," she said giving a coy smile. "Remember me?"

"Hello." The young man gave a grin before his eyes darted over to where Cindy was standing.

"You said to call in." Elizabeth saw a flash of appreciation in his eyes but much to her irritation they were focused on Cindy, who was nonchalantly inspecting the make-up products.

He raised an eyebrow and gave a knowing smile but his eyes were now assessing Cindy's figure. Even under the school blazer he could make out the shape of well-developed breasts. Her tie had been pulled down and the top button of her shirt was open. He looked at the face. Wow! She's beautiful, he thought.

To her intense humiliation, Elizabeth could see he was more interested in Cindy. Without saying another word she stormed out of the shop.

"What happened?" Cindy shouted after her as she tried to keep up with Elizabeth's fast pace.

"You know all too well," Elizabeth snarled as she strode purposefully back to the school.

Cindy was perplexed. She had no idea what Elizabeth was talking about.

"It's you!" Elizabeth finally admitted. "All the men see you, but they don't notice me."

Cindy stared at Elizabeth. Is that what they all thought? She remembered Janet had said something similar at the radio station. Not for the first time Cindy wished that people could see the person behind her attractive mask. She caught her reflection in one of the shop windows and momentarily hated the face that looked back at her. I am sick of being leered at as if I am just some sexual object, she thought sadly.

Susan walked into the tidy, empty house. It was almost unbearably quiet. She made herself a pot of coffee and took it into the snug. Feeling exhausted, she kicked her shoes off and rested her feet on the small footstool. Her lunch with Grant had confirmed that nothing had progressed. It was at a stalemate.

She closed her eyes and sadness welled up inside. Supposing they never managed to get back together as a family? So much water, dirty, murky water, had gone under the bridge. She wished she did not have to dwell on the practicalities, the house, and the mortgage. If Grant left, who would pay for it all?

"There's nothing to reproach yourself with," Emma had reassured her.

At the back of Susan's mind there was a warning light. She had thought about it the other night as she lay alone in the large double bed. On the edge of sleep she had put her hand out and cried to find Grant not there. It had revived a sudden memory of a time when, like now, he hadn't been there. That time it had been her fault. They had been out. It had been a successful evening and Susan was mellow with the inner warmth of wine. She been alcohol-flirtatious and Grant, never one to miss a moment had caught her, held her close and kissed her. He'd undressed her as she lay half asleep on the bed. His caresses had awakened her and her desire, which was usually so dormant, had come surging forth. She had wanted him so much, as passionately as when they had first been married. Her mouth had been on his and then her body had covered him as her desire exploded. "Come on, now!" Her voice had been urgent. Her hand had found his manhood, expecting it to be ready, pulsating, wanting, but it had been dead and cold. She hadn't understood.

"Come on, Grant, please."

She could remember the look on his face. "I can't," he'd muttered and turned away from her so she couldn't see his shame.

"What do you mean you can't?"

"I can't. Not now. I'm too tired."

Pushing him away savagely, Susan had sneered at his limp manhood.

"What's the matter with you?" she'd asked, her body burning. She had been too angry to care about the hurt in his eyes as he shuffled off to the bathroom.

He'd not returned and she'd slept alone that night. The next morning, she'd found him slumped on the settee downstairs.

It was a time of strain for both of them. Susan had started to feel that she was losing her sex appeal. Grant seemed to have lost interest altogether, for each time she turned to him in bed he rejected her. When she tried to arouse him he didn't respond. Night after night they had lain side by side, staring at the ceiling, each feeling a sense of terrible inadequacy.

They became embarrassed with each other, shying away from any physical contact. In front of their friends they pretended that everything was all right, putting up a show with meaningless glances, kisses and innuendoes that fooled everyone but themselves. And that was when Grant started throwing his parties. Eventually they had managed to get their relationship together and the sex had resumed. But it had never been quite the same; Susan could only just admit that to herself.

Friday evening, 17th June

"Where on earth are you going?" Emma noticed Cindy coming down the stairs in heavy make-up and a seductive, low-cut dress.

Cindy had hoped to slip out of the house without her grandmother seeing. "It's a party," she replied brightly. "I know! You're going to say I look a sight." She waited for the inevitable tirade and when it didn't come, challenged, "Well, don't I?" Still her grandmother kept her silence and Cindy felt obliged to continue. "Elizabeth and I are going to this disco, at the school. We have to dress up – overdo it – it's a joke!" She was fumbling for a good excuse but her grandmother looked sceptical. She changed tack, pleading, "I need to get out, to forget."

Emma hesitated.

"Look! You can ring Elizabeth if you don't believe me."

"Oh no, dear. I didn't mean to suggest that," Emma was flustered, torn between her promise to Susan to keep an eye on Cindy, and wanting to show some trust in the girl. Finally she admitted, "It's just, well, you do look a little tarty. I'm not sure whether your mother would approve of you going out like this."

"I'm meant to look tarty, Gran." There was a note of exasperation in Cindy's tone. "Look, do you want me to spend all my nights in?"

Emma shook her head. "No, of course not. But you seem to have been out an awful lot lately. And I don't really know where you're going. You must remember that I am responsible for you."

"Oh Gran! It's a dance for the sixth form at school. I'm going with Elizabeth. It's the end of my school days; it's a celebration," Cindy's tone was soft and reasonable and Emma felt she had no option but to agree.

It was well after eight in the evening when Grant stood on the doorstep, his finger depressing the doorbell. He had his house key in his pocket but somehow he didn't feel he could enter unannounced. He waited patiently as the door swung open and then stood paralysed by a sudden wave of embarrassment.

"You still have a key," Susan murmured as he reached forward and gave her a cursory kiss on her cheek. He shrugged his shoulders without replying as he followed her into the conservatory. They sat down and exchanged pleasantries with an air of constraint. Susan wanted to tell him that she felt as though she was living in hell and beg him to come home, but, like an interested stranger, she merely asked him how he was coping.

He gave another shrug, wanting to ask her how the bloody hell she thought he was coping without his family? Instead he said, "I saw Cindy."

Now he had Susan's attention and she glanced up, her eyes sharp and bright. "You saw Cindy? Where?"

He ran his fingers over his moustache. "I was waiting at a set of traffic lights and I looked across at the car alongside me. It was the noise that attracted me. You know – loud music? Anyway, Cindy was there in Elizabeth's car. She didn't notice me." He refrained from adding she looked very pleased with herself and quite untroubled by the events.

"Elizabeth was probably giving her a lift home from

school!" Susan temporised, seeing his hidden anger in the tautness of his body and the thin line of his lips.

"I hardly think so." Now the edge of sarcasm had crept in. "This was ten minutes ago."

Grant's tone was not lost on Susan. "They'd just be going to Elizabeth's house. Cindy's in no state to be out enjoying herself, Grant. She can barely face going to school."

"I wonder if she's saying one thing to you and Emma, and doing the complete opposite when she's out of your sight?" Grant paused before adding bitterly, "She looked as if she had not a care in the world." He stopped, suddenly sensing he was saying too much. But he knew his remarks had hit home. And it was true – Cindy was not acting like a girl who had problems – quite the opposite.

Emma could not sleep. She lay on the bed with the bedside light on, watching the minutes of the clock pass ever so slowly. Pandora had joined her and was lying across her feet, silently sharing her vigil. Emma had spent many sleepless nights recently and it wasn't until half past one that she heard a car draw up outside. Pandora, ever alert, was up and onto the window ledge.

By the time Emma had got out of bed and moved across to the window, the car was pulling away. Seeing Cindy standing on the pavement, she put on her dressing gown and went downstairs to open the front door.

"Cindy?" Then she stopped, seeing the dishevelled figure before her, the smeared lipstick, the bleary eyes and the messed up hair. "Get in!" she snapped, hoping the neighbours hadn't heard. Emma took Cindy by the shoulders. "Do you know what time it is?"

Cindy gave her a blank stare. It was then that Emma smelt the alcohol on her breath.

"You're drunk!"

Cindy giggled.

"Get into the kitchen. Get into the kitchen this minute!" Emma pushed Cindy again but the push sent her stumbling against the wall.

Cindy tried to retrieve some control and with as much dignity as she could manage she ran her fingers through her unruly hair. "We broke down," she slurred.

"We? Who was driving you? You told me you were going to the school with Elizabeth. I'm in charge of you when you're under my roof and just look at you! You never went to the school. Who did that car belong to?"

"Elizabeth!" Cindy was defiant. Her head was beginning to ache and her grandmother seemed to be swaying backwards and forwards in front of her. She blinked and her grandmother's face swam into focus for long enough for her to see that Emma's anger had been replaced by distaste. Cindy knew she must look a mess. She half-expected her grandmother's arms to go round her as they usually did, but Emma remained cold.

"We'll talk in the morning, Cindy. Now get to bed," she commanded, pushing Cindy in front of her. Emma watched as the girl staggered up the staircase to crash onto the bed fully clothed.

CHAPTER EIGHTEEN

Saturday, 18th June

*E*mma was woken abruptly the next morning by the sound of her bedroom door opening. She was startled and glanced at the clock. It was early. For a moment she couldn't get her mind adjusted and then she remembered the previous night.

"Gran, I've made you a cup of tea," she heard Cindy say.

Emma turned wearily towards her granddaughter. Cindy was fully dressed, standing beside the bed with the cup ready to put on the small bedside table.

"Look Gran," Cindy said quietly as she sat on the bed. "I'm so sorry about last night."

Her face was now scrubbed clean of make-up, her eyes were wide open and fresh looking, her hair was neatly tied back and there was no visible sign of the previous night's excess. Emma shook her head in disbelief and pulled herself into a sitting position.

"Gran," Cindy repeated and leaned forward. "Can you forgive me? Elizabeth's car did break down. Honestly – we had a flat tyre. We were stuck there. I had had a drink, and well," she laughed shyly, "Half a shandy would send me stupid. I'm not used to drinking and I think it must have gone to my head."

She glanced across at her grandmother, who was sipping her tea in silence.

"I knew you'd have been worrying and I just wanted to tell you I was all right. I'm sorry. I'm honestly sorry." There was no mistaking the contrition in Cindy's voice but Emma was not prepared to be so easily manipulated.

"Cindy, I don't believe you. I think you deliberately lied to me last night. I think you had made arrangements to meet some man who gave you a lift home."

"That is not fair! I am telling you the truth," Cindy protested vehemently as she met Emma's eyes full on. "Why would I lie? I don't have a boyfriend. I was with Elizabeth. You know she has her own car. It's unfair! Nobody ever believes me." She turned away and flounced out of the bedroom.

It was then Emma decided that it was time Cindy returned to her mother's care.

Later that afternoon Elizabeth made an unexpected visit to Emma's to see Cindy. Elizabeth had continually asked why Cindy was staying at her grandmother's house.

"We're having the house decorated." Cindy had said the first thing that came into her head.

Emma glanced out of her sitting room window and saw the Ford Fiesta draw up alongside the kerb. She watched and waited, fully anticipating a young man to emerge.

"Is that your car?" Emma asked Elizabeth as she greeted her on the doorstep.

"Yes! Dad bought it for me. It's brand new," Elizabeth boasted. The reply caused Emma to frown for she recognised the car as the one she had seen the night before. She had been wrong about Cindy. She hadn't lied; it was she who had jumped to conclusions.

Monday, 20th June

Grant reluctantly admitted that he, and his family, needed professional help. He did not know where to start but the *Yellow Pages* seemed as good a place as any. Initially he picked out four counselling agencies in out of town locations. He certainly didn't wish to be seen locally. On Wednesday lunchtime he drove out to survey the venues, noting that one of the agencies offered extended opening hours on a Thursday. He remained in his office late that day, sitting silently, head in hands, staring down at the number before picking up the phone and dialling.

"Is that The Family Counselling Service?"

He felt sweat on his hands as he gripped the receiver and stuttered his enquiry.

"We offer a personal and confidential family counselling service," an educated, well-modulated woman's voice told him.

"Are you trained psychiatrists?"

"No," her answer was emphatic. She explained to him that the organisation consisted of four trained counsellors with backgrounds in AIDS counselling, social work, trauma and behavioural and sexually related therapy. "I should add," she said, "that all our counsellors hold recognised diplomas and are very experienced in family matters. There is nothing that would shock us or that we won't have heard before."

"So how does it work?" Grant asked, feeling more confident. He nodded to himself as the woman outlined the service they provided. She assured him that they listened to all sides of a story, explaining that most people held the answer to their own problems and found that discussion brought those answers to light.

"We are not," she went on, and Grant could almost feel the professional smile in her voice, "an information service. Neither do we offer advice."

"So basically it is just talk?"

"With someone trained to move the talk in a positive and searching direction. Family problems often occur through lack of communication and those silences breed mistrust."

"Oh, I see." Grant now sounded unsure.

"I can understand your scepticism, but the service we offer has helped countless families, I can assure you." She went on to explain that the service was privately run and outlined the basic counselling charges. "Obviously, without knowing your needs, I cannot tell you how many sessions would be required. We usually consider an introductory session, a follow-up, a group family session and from there it would depend on the individual situation."

He muttered that the charges seemed acceptable. She was eager to emphasise that the service had no links with social services or any other statutory body and that what was discussed between client and counsellor was completely confidential.

"Are there any circumstances in which you would break confidentiality?" Grant cut in.

There was a pause. "Only if we think someone is in danger; in which case we would contact the appropriate authorities. No action would ever be taken without informing the client first."

There was a silence as Grant balanced his thoughts. It

seemed the only way forward was to talk. After a brief interval he heard the woman ask if he wished to make an appointment. "I have just had a cancellation for Thursday the twenty third, with a very experienced counsellor, Doctor Fiona Stevens."

"Doctor?"

"Fiona Stevens's doctorate is in chemistry. As I said, we're not medical doctors."

Grant concluded the conversation by making an appointment.

Doctor Fiona Stevens was an attractive forty-five year old who specialised in family problems. A divorcée with a teenage daughter to support, she had shoulder length blonde hair and sharp, intelligent blue eyes. She was also a health fanatic, working out regularly to keep her slim figure in shape.

The Counselling Centre was situated in a large Victorian house that had been subdivided to incorporate other agencies. Now she sat behind her desk in a small but comfortable interviewing room and smiled gently at Grant Howard. She could see his disquiet.

"It is difficult in the beginning," she nodded reassuringly. "But remember, I am trained to hear and evaluate; I am not here to judge or condemn. You said in your phone call that it was a family matter?"

Grant lowered his head and she saw from his body language his reluctance to reveal any confidences at this stage.

After Doctor Stevens had gone through the usual formalities, which she always found helped people to relax, she leaned back in her chair. "Tell me about your family," she asked gently. Fiona saw the hesitancy in Grant's manner and gave him an understanding smile. "Take your time. I know this is difficult."

He gave her a grateful nod and then slowly and with obvious diffidence, started to relate incidents leading up to

Cindy's accusation and the subsequent result of the medical examination. A flicker of a frown was drifting across Fiona Stevens's forehead. Although she was an experienced counsellor on issues of rape she had to admit this was the first time the father had presented himself to her as a victim. She asked in detail about his background and family and listened without interruption as he spoke lovingly of Susan and Cindy. Occasionally she jotted down notes on her pad. She prodded him gently as to how he saw his role as the father of a teenage girl. She commended him in her mind for his modern style of upbringing and saw the confusion in his eyes as he told her the exact accusation. She heard him sigh and then he paused and quickly lowered his head, but not before she had seen that his eyes were brimming with tears.

"Why do you think Cindy chose to make this accusation now?" Doctor Stevens asked.

Grant shook his head. "I don't know."

"If there is anything, however trivial, please tell me," she urged.

After a moment's pause, Grant continued. "Cindy is not a vindictive girl, you have to understand that." He ran his finger over his moustache and removed his spectacles, rubbing his hand over his eyes. "There appears to be a pecking order in her school. I suppose once it was about trivial issues but now it is the status symbol of girls having their own cars. She likes to be at the top."

Fiona nodded.

"Cindy's friend was given a car. I suppose my daughter felt I let her down in not buying her one immediately."

"You had promised her a car?"

"Yes, but then I just procrastinated. And then there was the business with Father Patrick. It all seemed to happen at the same time. It must have been very hard for Cindy." He reached into his inside pocket of his jacket and extracted an envelope, which he passed across to Fiona. "This explains it better than I can."

Fiona took the envelope and extracted the newspaper cutting. Grant waited as her eyes sped over the contents. She glanced up.

"It's her parish priest," Grant said in answer to the unasked question.

"You think this has some bearing on her accusation?" Fiona asked.

"Perhaps."

Fiona nodded her head. "Let's leave Father Patrick for the moment. Why would your daughter suddenly accuse you of rape? What would she have to gain?"

He paused and leaned forward and then related the gist of the magazine article he had found in Cindy's bedroom. "I know it all sounds coincidental, but Cindy has always fantasised a little, been over dramatic."

Fiona frowned, not fully understanding his reasoning. She saw again his diffidence and realised he felt he was betraying Cindy in an effort to clear his name.

He reached down to the floor and opened his briefcase. Fiona saw the nervous shake of his hands as he handed her the magazine. "I think you should read page 12," he said.

Fiona was surprised at the amount of evidence he had collated but nevertheless took the magazine and swiftly located page 12. Her eyes scanned the article. "Tell me, do Cindy's accusations mirror this article?"

"It's hard to say. She made the accusation before I'd seen the article. But yes, I suppose they do."

Fiona could see Grant struggling to remember and she had the impression he was answering too cautiously. She picked up her pencil and made a few more notes. She wanted to dismiss the article; it was too melodramatic. The words were overly dramatised and she briefly wondered if the article was factual or not. Father Patrick's allegation seemed more of a focal point. Although she wasn't a Catholic herself she could still understand the horror Cindy must have felt. The theory regarding the car did not sit well with her; it seemed too flimsy. Try as she might, Fiona could not get a picture of Cindy in her mind. On the face of it she sounded a disturbed, vindictive and spoilt girl. Yet, Grant spoke of her only with affection. She asked why Grant had eventually bought her the car.

"Because she deserved it, " Grant replied simply.

Fiona encouraged him to expand on his answer. "In what way?"

"She did well at school."

He paused when she asked him about his own childhood, and she immediately saw his discomfort. Finally, in clipped tones, he spoke of his mother's unbearable possessiveness.

"And now you have three women in your life. Are they all possessive?"

Grant shrugged his shoulders, shaking his head. Doctor Stevens could see he was still very tense. "No, Susan is very much her own woman. Cindy, well, you know I had never really thought about her possessiveness." He frowned, "But then, I always assumed daughters could get a bit possessive over their fathers."

Doctor Stevens raised her eyebrows. "May I ask how you arrived at that assumption?"

He drew his brows together. "I don't know. Perhaps because I thought girls looked up to their fathers. The first man in their life and all that." He gave an embarrassed laugh. "Maybe I am wrong!" There was a pause, and he started rubbing the forefinger of his right hand across his moustache again, eventually saying diffidently. "Cindy, she always wanted so much more when she was young, demanded a great deal of my attention, and," he shrugged his shoulders, "I tended to, well I still do, spoil her."

"This attention, was it reminiscent of your mother's demands?"

Grant stopped and stared at her. "I never thought about it like that."

"May I suggest you do think about it, seriously? I'll come back to possessiveness later. Tell me again about Cindy's request for a car."

"Like I said, it was to keep up with her school friends, a status symbol. Without a car Cindy felt disadvantaged. Elizabeth, her friend's parents are...." He coughed to cover his embarrassment. "Their circumstances are, in my daughter's eyes, lower than ours. She felt that I could easily afford to buy her a car. In fact she began to imagine it was her right to have one." He stopped, biting his lip. "It's very confusing!"

"Why is it confusing?" Doctor Stevens asked quietly.

"It turned out that I bought her the car an hour after she had made the allegation to Susan."

"So you really feel that if Cindy had had the car earlier her accusation would not have been made? You believe your daughter said this vindictively?"

Grant nodded.

"I understand Cindy attends a single sex school. This must mean there is some rivalry for boyfriends, some boasting about conquests." Fiona gave a gentle smile. "We do tend to forget our teenage years and the importance then of what, in later life, is trivia. Today the loss of virginity is a status symbol to boast about. As a father would you think Cindy could be promiscuous?"

"Good God no!"

Grant was plainly shocked by the suggestion. She placed her pencil down and leaned forward in a friendly reassuring manner. "I know this must be painful for you, but then so is the allegation." She paused before asking. "Your daughter is not a virgin?"

He lowered his eyes and muttered, "I believe that is what an examination proved."

There was a pause as Fiona sorted her thoughts. "The examination that Cindy had is not believed to be a hundred percent conclusive, the results can be open to misinterpretation."

Grant looked up but Fiona continued.

"But the thought of Cindy having sex is hard to come to terms with?"

He looked up. "Yes. I was shocked. Even more shocked because Cindy implies I am the cause." Suddenly Grant's face contorted in distaste.

"You've remembered something?"

Briefly he described Cindy's flirtatious friendship with David Carter, and the incident at the wedding reception.

"So now you are questioning this picture of innocence?" she said quietly.

Grant lowered his head. "I don't know."

Doctor Stevens made more notes before saying. "Let us go back to that incident at the wedding. You and your wife were dancing?"

Grant nodded, describing with amusement how Cindy had cut in on the dance.

"Susan didn't mind?"

"Oh, she was glad to get off the dance floor."

There was a pause before Doctor Stevens asked, "Why would Cindy make up such a serious allegation and risk breaking up what sounds like a very comfortable home life?" Doctor Stevens referred to her notes. The nucleus of an idea was nudging her thoughts and she had written one word on the pad under the heading *reasons*.

Grant's voice was desperate. "Look, Doctor Stevens, I need you to tell me why my daughter has lied. My life is in pieces. Cindy is just throwing accusations around." He told her of

Cindy's insistence that he had gone into her bedroom again recently.

Doctor Stevens leaned forward. Her voice was low as she reassured him. Grant began to calm down and felt a tremendous relief to know that she was not judging him. But would she actually be able to help him or was he putting himself through this agonising hell for nothing?

At the end of the hour Doctor Stevens glanced at the clock. "Just before we end this session, have you ever, in any small way, for whatever reason, touched your daughter in a manner she could have misinterpreted?"

"What is a manner she could have misinterpreted?" he asked. "I have kissed her, hugged her, loved her as any father would his daughter. What father could hurt his own child?" Grant broke off.

"Unfortunately far too many," Doctor Stevens replied quietly.

"But I'm not that sort of man," Grant insisted.

"What is that sort of man, Mr Howard?"

He stared at her. "I don't know!"

She gave a gentle smile. "That is it. Nobody can ever imagine or understand the type of parent who assaults their own child."

He stared at her, adding, "Or the type of daughter who accuses her father of such a crime, knowing he didn't do it?"

"You have a point, Mr Howard," and she opened her desk drawer. "I would suggest I pencil in a few sessions." She glanced up, "I'd like to see you on Monday to go over it again and then we will take it from there."

When Doctor Stevens returned to her desk after Grant had left she took out her notebook and continued making notes. His question, *Why would a daughter accuse an innocent father?* was important; indeed it could form the basis of a chapter in her forthcoming book.

CHAPTER NINETEEN

Monday, 27th June

Grant had expected to see Doctor Stevens in the same room, but this time he was shown into a small, comfortable lounge with easy chairs and a table on which sat a small pot of tea and two cups.

"Sit down," Doctor Stevens said after they had shaken hands. "I prefer the second meeting to be less formal. I would like to call you Grant; you may call me Fiona. Tea?"

She had studied the notes of the case over the weekend. Cindy intrigued her and she wanted Grant to talk about her.

"Mr Howard, I'm sorry, Grant." She gave him a friendly smile. "Child abuse is in the media nearly every day. It's at the forefront of public consciousness and people demand retributive justice. Your daughter has not made any charge against you to the police?"

He stared at her and rubbed his hands together, his eyes wide with horror. "Good God, no!"

"Why not?"

"It's obvious surely? Because her accusation is a lie."

"You do realise that if Cindy went to the police they would investigate further? Public sympathy would not be in your favour. You say the story is a lie but they would ask why your daughter would make up a story of such a damning nature.

The general feeling towards matters like this is there's no smoke without fire!"

"Don't you think I know that?"

"What do you think of Cindy now she has accused you?"

"I don't follow you."

"Do you think she could be ill, disturbed? What is your opinion of her state of mind?"

Grant paused before answering. "She has to be ill."

Fiona made notes. "Tell me a little about your wife and her relationship with Cindy."

After a pause he related a few of the incidents he could remember; times Susan and Cindy had spent together. Then, delving further back, he talked of how Cindy used to climb into their bed, so many years ago now, wanting to snuggle in between them.

"Wanting you to herself perhaps?"

"Well ..."

"It must have been a bit flattering; the only man in a household of women. How did Susan feel about your closeness to Cindy?"

"No, you're wrong. Susan has never been jealous of my attention to Cindy. She is a good, loving mother."

"And Cindy, is she jealous of Susan?"

"Good God no! Why would she be?" Grant leaned back in his chair and raised his hands in resignation. "I see what you mean." He recognised he was being disingenuous and could see Fiona's line of thought. It was a possibility. Almost as if thinking aloud, he began to tell her about small, insignificant incidents.

"And your wife. Tell me again about her reaction to the allegation?"

The hour passed quickly and Grant sat back exhausted. "I don't know where this is getting me or how I'm ever going to prove I'm innocent," he said.

"Patience, Grant!" Fiona said, glancing at her watch.

He got the message; their time was up. He reached into his wallet and waited while she wrote a receipt. "Friday?" he asked, bringing out his diary.

Fiona nodded and then dropped her bombshell. "I would like that to be a family session."

"I don't think Cindy will come," Grant said with a frown.

"I think you will find she will," Doctor Stevens replied with a gentle smile.

Fiona walked Grant to the reception and booked in a family session. Then she returned to her office. The case intrigued her. What father exposed the accusation and proclaimed his innocence when no formal allegations had been made? Unless there was no foundation for the accusation, it seemed an enormous gamble. Grant had come here of his own volition, answering all her questions in what seemed to her to be a logical and truthful manner, but something about the situation did not satisfy her.

She sat staring at the two pictures on her desk, her former husband, affable and wealthy, and her teenage daughter. Not for the first time, she wondered how she would have coped if she'd found that her husband had interfered with their daughter. She looked at the picture of Joely, a pretty fourteen year old, with all the potential of life ahead of her. It hadn't been easy, the divorce, the decision to place Joely in a boarding school during the week, but it had been necessary and it didn't seem to have harmed their relationship. Perhaps it was too early to tell. Relationships, she smiled sadly, were so difficult to sustain without compromise. They had always fascinated her, the politics and interaction in a family, how the members bounced off each other. Fiona frowned now. Grant Howard was an interesting man. But far more interesting was Cindy.

Fiona had started taping her interviews, changing the names and the extraneous circumstances to prepare case studies for the book. The material was growing steadily. She intended to devote a large section to the inherent complexities of the father and daughter relationship. Her talk with Grant had expanded her understanding of the relationship's perimeters and problems. Yes, Mr Howard would provide her with a very valuable insight. She could not afford to lose him.

Friday, 1st July

As Fiona Stevens had predicted, Grant had no difficulty in persuading Cindy and Susan to attend a counselling session.

"Anything!" Susan had confided to Emma. "Anything to get us out of this nightmare. If we have to talk, then that's what we'll all do. Doctor Stevens must be used to situations like this."

Cindy, much to Susan's surprise, had also expressed interest and had made no objections.

Now they all sat in the waiting room, each cocooned in their own thoughts, avoiding eye contact. Cindy, dressed casually in jeans, ankle boots, T-shirt and a jacket, sat staring blankly at the wall opposite. She was aware of her father's eyes darting repeatedly in her direction, as if willing her to look across the room at him. She had given him a surreptitious glance on entering the waiting room, conscious of the lines of worry on his face, but as soon as he looked at her she turned her gaze away. He was suffering, she could see that and felt a moment's sorrow for him.

"I hope she is on time." Susan glanced at her watch and then, for a brief second, Grant's eyes met Cindy's in a flicker of acknowledgement about Susan's punctuality fetish.

Susan saw the veiled amusement in their eyes. "And what do you find so funny?" she snapped at Cindy. "It's because of you we're here."

Cindy frowned and muttered, "No, it's ..." but she was stopped mid sentence as one of the doors opened, revealing Doctor Stevens.

Fiona immediately sensed the tension and animosity in the atmosphere as she allowed her eyes to speed from Susan, to Grant and finally Cindy. She smiled and invited them into the office. Once inside Grant introduced his family and they all sat on comfortable armchairs.

"I hope this will be useful." It was more a plea from Susan than a statement.

Cindy surprised Fiona. Here was an attractive, no, an exceptionally pretty young lady, who watched her with wide-eyed curiosity. She had an air of confidence and competence that Fiona had not anticipated.

"I am pleased you have all come as a family," Fiona said quietly, seeing a brief flash of scepticism on Cindy's face as she continued. "I have no magical powers; I cannot make a lie into the truth or vice-versa. I can't offer you miracles. I believe we all know what we are seeking. We know that there is a truth, and that someone is lying." She paused. "What I do believe is that by talking, listening and evaluating, we can discover a way to the truth. And perhaps also find a reason as to why it may have been distorted."

"What you are really saying is that you want to prove I'm lying," Cindy cut in.

"No..." Fiona started to say but Grant interrupted.

"You know bloody well you've lied!" he snapped. "What we need to know is why."

"I have not lied." Cindy's voice was gentle but emphatic.

"For God's sake," Susan said as she glared from one to the other. "It's no use bickering about what we are here for." She expected Fiona to interrupt, but she just sat back, watching the interplay, seeing a shadow form over Cindy's face, making the attractiveness give way to an inner darkness, giving her an almost mystical aura. Then, as if by an unseen hand, the darkness was wiped away and Cindy sat back in the chair, her face devoid of all expression. But Fiona was aware of an uneasy watchfulness in her eyes and knew she was on the defensive.

Susan was uncomfortably aware of being an observer under observation as Fiona noted the interplay between Cindy and Grant.

"Susan," Fiona said into the silence that had engulfed them, "You must have a question?"

"Only one." Her voice was bitter. "What would make a daughter accuse her father of such a terrible thing?"

"I haven't said anything that isn't the truth," Cindy reiterated in a quiet, almost broken voice. "I didn't want it to be like this."

Grant sighed and slumped forward in his chair, letting his hands drop forward between his knees. His whole attitude seemed to be one of weariness. "I don't know what to say or what to do any more," he said. "I have moved out of the house. Can you believe that? I am living in a small hotel. And why? Because my daughter, whom I love, has somehow decided I am a pervert. Me!" His voice rose. "A loving father, for that is what I have tried to be, suddenly accused of the most despicable actions towards his daughter."

"I didn't want it to be like this," Cindy repeated, lowering her eyes.

"How did you want it to be Cindy?" Fiona asked softly.

Cindy shrugged and then looked up, her eyes wide and trusting, meeting Fiona's. "I wanted a proper family, a father who just, well, was like other fathers. I didn't want ..." She sniffed turning her head away.

"But you have made a very serious accusation against him. Is it true?"

"Yes."

"He sexually abused you? Committed incest?"

Cindy's body language changed, a tautness came into her face. She closed her eyes, leaning forward and clasping her hands together so her knuckles were visible. "I thought, when I was younger, that this was how fathers loved their daughters. I didn't know. There was no one to ask. Secrets, you see, couldn't be broken."

Grant took a deep, gasping breath. "I loved you as a daughter! There was never anything sexual between us. Fathers do hold their daughters and kiss them and that is all I ever did. Not these filthy accusations."

"Cindy, tell me what happened," Fiona encouraged.

"Do we have to?" There was revulsion written all over Susan's face.

"Yes, we do have to," Fiona replied firmly.

Slowly Grant straightened up in the chair, his hands now resting on the arm. "What did I do to you Cindy? What harm have I ever done you?" There was an appeal in his voice but Cindy chose not to look in his direction.

Cindy bit her lips and flicked her hair from her eyes and then, as if preparing herself, she gave a sigh that seemed to reverberate round the room. "Shall I shock you, mother? Shall I tell it as crudely as it happened? Shall I describe to you how he committed virginal and anal rape?" She ignored the small gasp that escaped her mother, the groan that came from her father's direction. "Is that what you all want?"

"When you're ready, Cindy," Fiona interjected coolly.

There was silence. Grant brought out a handkerchief and ran it across his forehead and Susan felt the beating of her heart.

"It's difficult." Cindy bit her lip and paused, conscious of the tension in the room. She lowered her eyelids before saying. "Once I tried to phone *Child-Line*, but I couldn't speak. I couldn't say anything. I suppose I started to live in my own world. I made it a fortress surrounded by a large moat. I wanted it to be impregnable, safe from his constant intrusion. I learned to pull up the drawbridge on a regular basis." she stopped and they saw her tension and Susan suddenly wanted to get up and put her arms round her daughter's shoulders and whisper that it was all right. But was it all right? She didn't know. All she could do was listen to Cindy who was now talking in a low, monotone voice.

"I could never control those events that happened during the night. Even today they haunt me and I frequently ask myself could I have done anything to stop them?" Cindy glanced up and Fiona could see unshed tears in her eyes as she continued. "I can still see the dark shadow, the outline of a body and a face I never wanted to identify."

There was a gasp and Susan put her hand to her mouth to stifle a sob, as instinctively she turned her head towards Grant. His face had gone a greyish hue. Cindy's voice carried on in a quietly disturbing tone.

"I was seven and I woke up suddenly. My bedroom was dark but I knew there was someone in the room. I went to curl up in bed when a voice whispered, "Don't be afraid my angel." This dark shape was standing at the foot of my bed. It was my father. He started to tuck me in, and I put my arms round his neck. I was glad to see him. He stroked my hair. His hands slowly removed the duvet. I could feel his hot breath on the nape of my neck. I pushed him away but he didn't do anything, not then. He just kissed me over and over again."

"I thought you said it happened in the bathroom?" Susan shot the question at Cindy, who ignored it and carried on.

"I thought of telling Mum, but I settled for imagining it had been a dream. It didn't happen again for quite a while. It was about a year later when he started creeping into my bedroom again. I never knew why. Perhaps I had done something wrong." Cindy clenched her hands and her distress was obvious to the onlookers. "It always started with the bedroom door handle. I can see it now, slowly turning, followed by the door creaking open. He would come like a shadow. I couldn't see his face but I sensed he was smiling. "My little angel." His voice always sounded strange, as if he could barely speak. He would kneel at the bed and his hands would creep under the sheets to lift my nightdress." She gulped and waited for a few seconds before going on. "He then removed the duvet and allowed his hands to move slowly over my stomach. He would mumble all sorts of words. Nasty words. He wasn't my Dad then, just some horrible beast that wanted to hurt me. He would bite and nibble my neck, breasts, buttocks, genitals…"

Fiona noticed that Grant had put his hands over his ears and was shaking his head whilst there was a look of naked fear and revulsion on Susan's face.

Cindy continued, "He didn't care about me. At first he just wanted to enjoy the sensation as I lay there gasping for air. I would try and push him away, but he was far too strong. Then he wanted more, so much more. He would sometimes use a handkerchief to cover my eyes." Cindy paused and wiped a tear from her eye. "I could see his outline, naked against the moonlit wall. He would stand looking at me. I could hear his heavy breathing, and then suddenly he was either beside me in bed or on top of me. I wanted to scream, but he was my Dad and it seemed inappropriate. He told me that angels were heaven sent and I had been sent for him and this was what real Dads did if they loved their little girls! I didn't know any better. I mean, who could I ask? He would pull up my nightdress and then I could feel …" Cindy stopped for a moment. "I could feel his breath against my face. I could feel his hands on my legs as he pulled them apart and his fingers and then, I couldn't stop him …"

They sat like stone, Susan could think of nothing to say. Grant merely stared ahead blankly whilst Fiona made occasional notes.

"He told me little girls liked to please their fathers. He told me to relax as it was pleasure not hurt. But it was hurt. I was so frightened. He could be harsh and demanding. He expected me to do all sorts of things. He would tell me I was lovely but sometimes he was brutal, and said nasty things like I wasn't loving and liked to hurt him. He started wanting more things that were horrible. I had to lie on my stomach and he would try and penetrate my bottom. It hurt and when I screamed he put his hand over my mouth. He would use his tongue, in me, searching, probing. Then his tongue would be no longer gentle, his lips no longer soft as he moaned."

"I can't listen to any more!" Susan's voice was verging on the hysterical. She looked pale as she gasped, "Please, tell us this is fantasy, something from a book, something you've imagined." She turned with tears streaming down her cheeks to stare at Grant.

"I think we need to remain calm and let Cindy finish," Fiona gave them a reassuring nod. "Cindy …"

"It was like … as if he wanted to make me a sort of sex slave, to degrade me. He bought me so many presents, told me what clothes to wear. I got confused, it seemed I was doing it to get things. Then he wanted oral sex. It made me physically sick. He wanted me to feel his testicles. So many other things and when I said no he got cross. He would hold me on the bed and kiss my breasts. His mouth would suck at my skin as he forced himself into me. Then, when he was finished he would get up, kiss me on the forehead and whisper, "Sleep well my angel." The next morning when I saw him at breakfast I had to pretend nothing had happened. It was, as he said, our secret."

The silence that engulfed them was broken as Susan started to cry in long, body-racking sobs.

"Look what you've done to your mother! You should be utterly ashamed of yourself." Grant got up from his chair and walked across to place an arm round Susan's shaking shoulders. "Susan, it is all lies. How could I have done such wicked things to her and you not know?" He turned and looked across at Cindy who sat with her hands clasped together, her face shrouded by a curtain of hair.

Fiona allowed the scene to impinge on them all before asking, "Cindy," Fiona's voice was gentle, "did your father penetrate you?"

"Good God!" Grant spun round on his heels and stared at Fiona. "What sort of questions are these?"

"Necessary questions I'm afraid," she replied.

"Yes, many times," Cindy whispered and then tears ran down her face before she reached into her jacket pocket and retrieved a fresh paper tissue.

Fiona knew that tears were merely a guide to the emotional upheaval that Cindy was feeling. They were not an indication of the truthfulness of the statement. It would have been easier if Cindy hadn't broken down – but to Fiona's disappointment Cindy was sobbing.

It resembles a morbid game, Fiona wrote. Cindy is goading Grant so he will return the shot. Attention. She wants all of his attention. And he cannot keep his eyes off her. His body language implies he is waiting for her question. He feels threatened by her; she knows she is in control. Susan is passive, unaware of Cindy's masterly manipulation. Fiona scribbled her notes and Grant lowered his head, clasping his hands together in a gesture of defeat. But Cindy's account seemed so hauntingly vivid that Fiona hesitated for a moment, briefly unsure how to continue. Whilst she believed Grant there was a small niggle of doubt at the back of her mind. Could any girl have made that up about her father?

"Are you sorry you made the accusation?" Fiona asked, glancing at Cindy. Grant's head shot up as a look of confusion came over Cindy's face.

"I told you I didn't want to break the family up." Cindy gave a faint sniff.

Fiona frowned and asked gently, "Why don't you report him to the police?"

There was a pause and Cindy did not answer.

"Come on, Cindy. Why don't you report him to the police? If what you say is true, then surely you must have considered contacting the authorities?" Fiona saw the conflict on the girl's face. "Is it because you don't wish to get him into trouble?" There was still no response from Cindy so Fiona continued. "Why accuse him?"

Cindy sat, her eyes downcast as she clicked her nails. Eventually she said, "I couldn't stand up in a witness box, have people listen to me, having them know what happened. It is too horrible. making family business public."

"But you have come here. Do you regret that?"

Cindy shrugged and there was a long silence. Fiona allowed it to settle over them before she fired her final question.

"What did you think when you read the article?" Fiona asked, trying to throw Cindy, to change the repetitiveness of the conversation. She saw the glazed expression that came over Cindy's eyes.

"What article?"

"Oh don't be so stupid, Cindy." Grant's voice had risen again. "The article in your magazine."

"Oh that." Cindy shrugged. "I could have almost written it myself, it was so accurate."

Fiona realised that Cindy was adept at dealing with difficult questions. I want to ask her more, Fiona thought. The girl intrigued her. There is a far greater depth to Cindy and there must be a reason for what she's doing.

"Have we achieved anything?" Susan asked as Fiona brought the interview to a close.

"Just bared our souls," Cindy said quietly.

Fiona watched them leave, a confused and conflicted family. She returned to her office, sitting down to study the notes she had made and wondered briefly if she should contact Social Services.

It was a dilemma and past training had taught her to always inform the authorities if a child might be in danger. But Cindy was seventeen and had come willingly to see her. At this stage she did not know who was telling the truth. No, she decided, she would handle this case herself.

Under the headings of Susan and Grant there were lines and lines of written observations whilst under Cindy's name there were just three words: *above average intelligence*.

Turning to her typewriter, she started to type the outline of her initial assessment.

CHAPTER TWENTY

Tuesday, 5th July

Susan was unsure why Fiona had asked to come to the house to see her. What did she hope to find? At first she had been reluctant to agree and had talked it over with Grant.

"It'll give her an insight into our family life," he had reassured her. "We have nothing to hide, Susan. She can see we have a good standard of living, that Cindy wants for nothing."

So Susan had agreed.

Susan tidied the house, polishing all that could be polished, hoovering the carpets, inspecting the downstairs cloakroom, putting in clean hand towels, as well as replenishing the air freshener and soap. She was fussy, she knew, which was probably why she had never managed to keep a cleaning lady for longer than a month. She now felt it necessary to show Doctor Stevens that she was not slovenly.

Did it matter what this Fiona Stevens thought? Yes, Susan felt it did. Her home showed that she was a caring mother and a good wife. She had baked scones for their tea and laid out a tray with china and some small linen tea napkins that Emma had given her. The silver milk jug and sugar bowl gleamed after a thorough polish. The scones lay cooling on the rack as she prepared the cream and filled the small dish with strawberry jam.

Doctor Stevens would see she was used to entertaining and used to coping. No, she sighed. It wasn't done to impress; merely to fill in time. She wanted to get the interview over. She wanted to put her point of view forward, to show the house off; let her see Cindy's bedroom. Show her that it wasn't some dirty, tatty room full of posters, but a light, bright room, beautifully furnished and meticulously maintained.

Susan dressed, after much deliberation, in a summer skirt and matching top in mint green. Did it look too frivolous? She was about to change into something more sombre when the doorbell rang. It was three o'clock precisely.

"Doctor Stevens." She believed in formality, this was no social call.

"Mrs Howard," Fiona smiled and admired the garden and the house, whilst Susan noted her expensive outfit. She was glad that Fiona had also taken the trouble to dress for the interview, for that was what she considered this meeting to be. Susan explained that Cindy was still living at her mother's and seemed to be enjoying the break from the house but would be returning home shortly. "I'll show you round. We can talk as we go, then I can fill in whilst we have a cup of tea."

Fiona Stevens put her briefcase down in the hall. Then, having second thoughts, picked it up and followed Susan up the stairs, admiring the decor. They stopped on the spacious square landing and Fiona noted the closed bedroom doors.

"From habit I keep them shut to stop Pandora, Cindy's cat, wandering in. I don't like cats on the bed, although she does sleep on Cindy's." Susan opened one of the closed doors. "This is Cindy's room." The scene of the crime, she thought sardonically. The women stood together in the centre of the room and Susan knew it was not as Fiona had anticipated.

"A most attractive room and so tidy. Most teenagers' rooms have walls plastered with posters, clothes lying around and an overflowing desk," Fiona observed as she compared it with her own daughter's lair. She also noted Cindy's double sized bed.

"Not Cindy," Susan confirmed. "She is very particular, very tidy. Mind you, I'm a little like that myself."

Fiona nodded moving across to peer at the books neatly stacked on a shelf. "Does Cindy read a lot?" she murmured her eyes scanning the titles with surprise.

"Odd books!" Susan sniffed.

"The Occult, Astrology, Buddhism, quite a variety," Fiona commented. Then one title caught her eye. She frowned with a vague recollection, but was unsure. She took the book from the shelf and started to flick through the pages, finally turning to the preface. She was just about to start reading when Susan interrupted her.

"She goes through phases," Susan babbled on and Fiona had no option but to replace the book and move across to stare at the framed drawings on the wall.

"They are beautiful." The admiration in her voice was not lost on Susan.

"She is very talented." She then went on to tell Fiona about Cindy's work at the cat sanctuary. "It used to be voluntary but now they have taken her on part-time for the summer. It is a very busy time, people going on holiday and leaving cats to fend for themselves. I am surprised at the cruelty."

"Is the sanctuary local?" Fiona asked with interest and mentally noted the location as she wandered across to the desk. A sketching block lay in the centre with an array of pencils beside it. Fiona bent down, about to turn over one of the pages when she stopped. Her trained eyes had noted the precision with which the sketching pad and pencils were laid out on the desk. She laid her briefcase on the chair. Opening it up, she took out a small nail file.

"What on earth are you doing?" Susan stared at Fiona, watching as she slowly bent down and, without moving the pad, gently inserted the file between the cover and the first page. "What are you looking for?" Susan asked as she stood in the background watching the operation.

"Well, I am assuming Cindy is absolutely paranoid about her privacy," Fiona replied.

"I wouldn't say paranoid. But yes, she does get irritated if anyone has been into her room," Susan admitted. "What made you ask?"

"See!" Fiona pointed down to the page she was holding open with the nail file. "The hair ...!"

"Hair? Where?"

"Along the spine of the book, there!"

"So?"

"Look at the precise way the pad is placed on the desk in relation to the pencil. Geometrically, see ..." Fiona indicated to the edge of the desk. "Measured, I think and then the hair."

"You mean she's setting a trap to see if someone looks through her things?" Susan stared at Fiona.

"Probably another on her wardrobe door – yes. I can tell you, Cindy will know for sure if anything gets moved."

"That's ..." Susan paused. She couldn't admit Cindy's oddness, even to herself. But why go to so much trouble to set traps? For that is what they were.

"I wouldn't worry too much. Privacy can become an obsession amongst teenagers. They need to forge their independence, loosen ties with the family." As she talked, Fiona withdrew the nail file, gently inserting it further along the page. A sketch of a cat met her eyes. She smiled, "Pandora I take it?" She turned over another page to see another cat. The sketching block contained nothing less innocuous and she felt sure it had been planted there for her benefit. Fiona closed the book; it had been interesting.

Fiona noted the television and the expensive hi-fi equipment and formed the opinion that Cindy was probably an over-indulged child who was used to getting her own way and would no doubt sulk when she did not get what she wanted. When Cindy was initially refused the car, she would not have been pleased.

"Where did Cindy get the money for the all this equipment?" Fiona asked as she looked down at the small television and video tape recorder. "Did she work for them?"

Susan shrugged her shoulders. "Grant bought them for her."

"Did Cindy know I was coming?" Fiona asked casually as her eyes scanned the room.

"She may have done. I can't remember," Susan replied, and then followed on quickly, "Yes, of course she knew." Susan wasn't going to let this woman feel that she didn't know her own daughter.

"Tell me about Pandora."

Susan smiled, "Oh, Cindy loves her. We all do. I think with her being blind they have a special bond." Briefly Susan went on to explain how Cindy had rescued the cat.

"What a nice gesture," Fiona said thoughtfully, adding, "So Pandora was not here when Cindy says the offences took place?"

"No," Susan replied, shaking her head. "Is that important?"

Fiona frowned, "I think everything about Cindy is important at this stage." She walked to the closed door on the opposite wall to the bed. "Is this her bathroom?" Susan nodded as Fiona looked at the door closely, seeing the hair between the lock. She had come prepared. Returning to her briefcase she took out a roll of tape and cut off a small piece, which she stuck to the hair.

"This is ridiculous!" Susan said as she watched the performance.

It was ridiculous, Fiona knew that, but her object was twofold. If Cindy was very astute then she would know Fiona had identified her little traps and counteracted them. She would leave the mark of the tape on the bathroom door. She opened it. The room was clean and tidy, the towels neatly folded to hang on the rail. "Does Cindy clean and tidy her own room?" Fiona asked as she inspected the glass shelves over the basin.

Susan nodded.

Fiona closed the door and removed the tape. The mark where it had been was faint but visible if one really looked.

Feeling rather like an estate agent, Susan showed Fiona her bedroom, then the small box room. She noticed that Fiona had registered the fact that one wall of Cindy's room adjoined the main bedroom.

"No," Susan said to the unanswered question, "We cannot hear Cindy in her room. That was the attraction of the house, privacy in the bedroom."

Fiona did not comment. It seemed an unusual reason for buying a house. Perhaps Susan was nervous. And she had a point; thin walls and creaking beds were not conducive to a relaxing sex-life. But Fiona wondered if Susan had a particular anxiety about bedroom noise. She would have to ask Grant; he had not yet spoken about the physical side of his marriage.

"I am not a prude." Susan sensed now that Fiona was making a judgement. "Our married life is very good." Her voice was frosty.

Back down in the snug, Fiona looked at the various trophies and school pictures. As so often in these cases, all seemed absolutely normal. Susan insisted Fiona sit down while she went out to the kitchen to make a pot of tea.

It was a comfortable well-furnished room, Fiona thought. She got up and idly picked up a framed photograph. It showed a laughing Grant with his arm round Cindy in a playful mood. Cindy was laughing up into his face, looking perfectly carefree. She looked at another picture but suddenly returned to the first, peering more closely.

"Tea!" Susan pushed the door open and Fiona went to help her put the tray down on the small table.

"I was admiring the picture of Grant and Cindy," Fiona said after she had complemented Susan on the scones, the jam and the cream.

"Oh that was taken, let me see, when she was thirteen." Susan picked the picture up and looked at it. "She was such a sweet child." She sighed as she placed the picture in Fiona's outstretched hand.

"Does Cindy still wear the ring?"

"Ring?"

"I couldn't help but notice the ring on her wedding ring finger."

"Oh, that ring. It used to be mine. It was the first thing Grant bought me. Unfortunately ..." and she glanced in embarrassment at her hand, "... it became too small. Cindy took to wearing it, saying it was her wedding ring. Silly really!"

Fiona sipped her tea before replacing the cup down and asking lightly. "And who did Cindy say she was married to?"

Susan stared at her. "Grant, of course! She shared so many things with him, scarf, gloves, even used his toothbrush once."

"Did you think of having other children?" Fiona shot the question at Susan as she made notes.

"After this, one is enough," Susan attempted a smile but it didn't work. Nor did the answer satisfy Fiona.

"Doctor Stevens," Susan said in a formal tone, "all this is truly a nightmare. Sometimes I wish I could wake up and everything would all be as it was. But then I ask myself do I really want that?" There was a break in her voice and Fiona saw the hand that was holding the cup and saucer was shaking. "I don't believe he did any of the dreadful things Cindy said, and yet..." She stopped again.

Skilfully Fiona steered the conversation into the realms of Grant and Susan's marriage. It was a difficult area to explore, but one Fiona felt it was essential they talk about. She learned that Susan was not an overly sexual woman in the sense of abandonment and experimenting. Then she asked how Grant's sexual behaviour correlated with Cindy's account of his demands with her.

There had been a touch of embarrassment as Susan had shaken her head. "It just doesn't fit Grant. He is not sexually perverted."

Fiona had gently explored what Susan thought sexual perversion was and knew Grant had not attempted such acts with Susan. On the surface their sex life seemed ordinary and she wondered if Grant had found it dull. Was that reason to violate your daughter?

It was not conclusive, but then such cases seldom were. They talked about Cindy and Fiona learned there had been a period when she had been difficult. "A typical teenager, I suppose." Susan dismissed it. Then she mentioned the song that Cindy continued to play. Supertramp's, *Take The Long Way Home*. Fiona made a mental note of the song. "Nothing else?" she asked.

Susan paused. "Well," she started to say something more and then stopped.

Fiona encouraged Susan to expand, knowing by her hesitation that there was something more.

Susan bit her lip. "She can become very irascible during her periods."

"That is not uncommon," Fiona replied and thought about the implication. "How about her temper?"

"No, Cindy has always been a very even tempered person, rarely given to shouting."

"And lying?"

"That is the worst part. Cindy doesn't lie. She can be manipulative, especially with Grant. Oh yes, he spoiled her." Susan conceded and then in a firm tone added, "I am sure, as a mother, I would have know if Grant had been … you know, with Cindy." Fiona heard the faint note of doubt, but despite her continued and gentle probing she left the house knowing Susan was still unsure who to believe.

Monday, 11th July

With Grant still residing at the hotel Cindy had decided to move back home. She had finished school and the rest of her life stretched endlessly ahead of her. It wouldn't be long before she started at university. She was tempted to let David teach her to drive in her red Escort but thought it perhaps better to wait until the situation at home was resolved.

Would it ever be resolved? Tired and hot, she was laying on her bed thinking about Fiona Stevens's questions and asking herself why she had said all those things about her father. Now there was no hope of the family being put back together again. But people got broken. Like dolls, thrown down and smashed into little pieces. He had done that to her. She had been his angel and he had ripped her wings off.

That Fiona woman. Cindy now sat at her desk and drew her face, and then she ripped it down the centre. Two halves of Fiona Stevens; two halves of everyone. All the good and bad bits joined together.

It was a mixture of impulsiveness and curiosity that took her down to the garage. It was still there, her car.

"Keep the bloody thing," Grant had snapped when Susan had asked if they should sell it. But it was of no use now. Would she ever learn to drive? Emily had told her that the family had been destroyed and it had been a statement, not an accusation. But Fiona, that nosy woman who hovered like some malevolent stranger, was trying to desperately balance the scales. Cindy knew all about judging and retribution didn't she? Fiona was their judge and jury. Why had her father felt it necessary to bring in some outsider? Why had he protested? He was as guilty as hell.

But hell was where she was living – wasn't it?

She entered the garage and ran a finger lightly over the shining bonnet before walking to the driver's door and opening it. She slid into the driver's seat and held the steering wheel lightly in her hands, then slowly bent forward and rested her head on the wheel.

I miss him, she thought. The house seems so empty. She thought of Susan, how she had aged, and felt a twinge of remorse. "I wish ..." she whispered to herself, but it was too late.

CHAPTER TWENTY-ONE

Susan had sometimes wondered what sort of people phoned *The Samaritans*. Now she knew the answer. Desperately she dialled the number for the umpteenth time. She listened to the standard reply before balking and hanging up. Even to an anonymous voice and with the security of confidentiality she couldn't tell anyone – not about this.

There was no one she could talk to. One didn't bring up incest at the golf club. She was painfully aware of the speculation her distracted manner and disintegrating game were causing among her golfing colleagues who, she well knew, liked nothing better than a good subject for their endless gossip.

She met Grant twice weekly. These were strained, difficult meetings and somehow there seemed to be nothing left to talk about. She tried to imagine him with Cindy. The thought made her feel sick. She watched Cindy closely. It wasn't spying, she convinced herself. She was just trying to find out the truth. Would they ever know for sure? Could they prove Grant was not lying?

At night, alone in her double bed, Susan fought with the realisation that she could remain alone for the rest of her life. Tears of self-pity regularly dampened her pillows. She was becoming nervy, jumpy and snappy, Emma had observed. Poor Emma, it was too much for an old lady to comprehend; too much for any of them.

Now the house felt like a hostel, Susan mused. No, she thought again. It was more like a prison. They were all Cindy's prisoners.

Thursday, 14th July

Cindy had woken that morning feeling lethargic and nauseous. Susan had twice stuck her head round the bedroom door, asking when she would be getting up. Finally she managed to drag herself out of bed at half past ten and enjoyed a relaxing shower. As she walked down stairs she noticed two envelopes lying on the hall table. One was junk mail, the other looked more serious in a brown manila envelope. To her surprise it was the vehicle registration document for her car; her father had even bought it in her name. She had half anticipated that the car would have been registered in his name, but this was a genuine gift and she felt the tears prickle behind her eyes.

It was not a good start to her day.

"I don't feel like any breakfast," Cindy muttered as Susan came into the kitchen. She hastily placed the document and envelope into her pocket and refused her mother's offer of a mug of tea. "I think I'll just walk to the shops for a paper."

Susan gave her a swift glance, noticing Cindy's drawn face.

It was only a ten-minute walk to the local shops and it wasn't until Cindy was returning home that she felt the familiar, acute pains in the base of her stomach. It was her time of the month again. She walked as quickly as she could, just wanting to get home and perhaps have a doze on her bed. Once inside the house she went immediately to the kitchen and took two pain killing tablets, washing them down with water. Pandora sidled round her ankles, but she had no inclination to pick the cat up.

Slowly she went up the stairs and into her bathroom – she'd lie in a hot tub, which always eased the pain. Cindy folded her clothes neatly on the bath stool before immersing herself in the warm water. She felt a moment's relaxation but then the pain returned and her head felt like a band of steel was tightening around it. She finally got out of the bath and wrapped herself in the white bath towel.

The pain subsided and Cindy dressed with her usual care. She blow-dried her hair and brushed it slowly. The rhythm of the brush strokes helped her to think and seemed to ease the pressure in her head. She sighed, feeling her body relax. Slowly, she got up and went to her desk. Now there was no need to hide the sketching pads. The family didn't understand her drawings and it amused her to let Susan peer at them, knowing she could not comprehend what she saw. Susan would probably tell Grant, as well as that Fiona woman. Did Doctor Stevens really think she could counsel her?

Picking up the gold pencil, she ran her fingers up and down its slim shape and then placed it between her lips, allowing her tongue to touch it in a sensual manner. Pandora strolled across the carpet to silently jump onto the desk and sit beside the sketchpad where she could hear the pencil on the paper. She purred contentedly, oblivious to the turmoil in Cindy's mind. Under Cindy's hand a building took shape, a large building and then, so quickly, a human face. Cindy's hand moved rapidly over the page until another face appeared. Two faces, one imposed on the other, inter-linked. They looked stark, blank eyed against the blank windows of the building. Cindy ran her tongue over her dry lips. The picture frightened her and she quickly drew hearts, flowers and birds. Then, in the corner, she added a quick sketch of a cat in its hunting profile, face drawn back, eyes vicious and the clawed paw ready to inflict hurt. "There you are Pandora, I've drawn you like they are."

Cindy's head had ceased to ache. She got up, yawned and stretched before picking up the cat and hugging it.

"I think I'll go into town." Cindy placed Pandora back on the bed and walked down the stairs.

Susan was surprised when Cindy told her she was going out. She watched as Cindy walked down the front driveway, holding her shoulders back. You'd think she was without a care in the world, Susan thought, shaking her head. Then on impulse she went up the stairs and into Cindy's room and was surprised to see the open sketchpad on the desk. She couldn't resist going over to look at it. She shivered when she saw the building and the faces staring up at her, and wished she could analyse what was in Cindy's mind, what had prompted her to draw such a sinister scene. Somehow she had imagined that as a parent she would automatically know the inner dynamics of her child, that there would be some empathetic bond; but there wasn't. She is from my womb, and that is all I know for certain, Susan thought sadly, feeling depression surge over her as she unconsciously ran the forefinger of her right hand over the drawings.

Was this sketch a silent message? A clue to what Cindy wanted to say? She would tell Grant about it, see what he thought. No! She could only trust herself now, not Grant and not Cindy.

It had taken Susan some time to look at the map and work out a route; it was no great distance, especially by car. She had never wanted to make this visit, but now it seemed strangely imperative. She dressed casually in a trouser suit and bought flowers and chocolates to take with her. She felt a surge of anticipation as she pulled out of the driveway.

A faint summer drizzle splattered on the windscreen and the

wipers smeared her vision. After two wrong turnings she arrived in a shadowy, tree-lined avenue that had once been a highly sought-after residential area. The huge mansions with their carriage drives and walled gardens belonged to an era of servants and privilege. Now their glory days were over and they had been converted into flats, bed-sits or residential homes. She had forgotten the exact location and she was forced to drive slowly, peering at each moss-covered gatepost in an attempt to decipher a name or number. Then she saw the sign, almost covered by the overgrown laurel hedge. She felt the nervous flutter in her throat as she gripped the wheel so hard that the knuckles of her hand shone translucently. Well, it was too late now; she was turning the car through the open iron gates and down the gravel driveway, which was in need of weeding and raking.

It was a solid sandstone house, its walls covered in ivy. But as Susan approached the door she saw the peeling paintwork and rotten woodwork, signs of slow decay; rotting remnants of a past era – like the people housed within. Shuddering at the morbidity of her thoughts, she walked up the stone steps and found herself in a large porch. In front of her was a solid oak door with black studs. She pulled the bell chain and listened as a great chime reverberated through the interior.

After a short wait the door creaked open. "Yes?" A pleasant-faced girl dressed in a blue overall stood smiling at her.

"I've come to see Olive Howard."

"And you are?"

Susan hesitated again, for the words did not come easily to her lips. "Her daughter-in-law."

The girl's eyebrows shot up in surprise. "Oh!" she replied. Then the door was held open and Susan followed the girl into the large, once imposing hallway. A chair lift destroyed the symmetry of the beautiful wide wooden staircase, and zimmer frames and wheelchairs cluttered the walls. A small band of tottering ladies, dressed alike in sloppy cardigans, wrinkled stockings and old slippers, shuffled their way into one of the lounges. Age was rarely as dignified as it should be, Susan thought to herself.

The smell of stewed greens curdled with the ever-present odour of urine made Susan shudder but she managed a bleak smile as she followed the girl into a large lounge. "How is she?"

"Oh, she has her good days. She is very frail now. Her stroke didn't help. Sister will tell you more."

"Stroke? I didn't know Olive had had a stroke."

"It was just a very minor stroke," the girl went on. "It has left her with a slight facial disfigurement, and of course she does have dementia. Mind you," and the girl faced Susan, "I've only been here a month, but I tell you, she's well named."

"Well named?"

"Well, you know, Olive by name and bitter by nature." She paused, realising she had said too much. "Sorry, but Olive has a sharp tongue."

"Don't apologise. I know all about her sharp tongue," Susan assured the girl. From the entrance to the lounge Susan saw the circle of chairs and the bent figures, sitting like ghosts of a bygone age. She sighed sadly. They had been people, but now they just seemed to blend silently in with the shadows with only the occasional voice raised for attention. There was an air of despondency, a waiting for death.

"There she is," the girl pointed. "Over in the corner. She likes the darkness."

Susan was shocked as she stared at the shrivelled form sitting in a high backed chair, a knitted cape round her shoulders. Her hair was straggly grey and cut without style, and her hands moved constantly, tweaking and folding the magazine that lay unopened on her lap. Was this the same vindictive woman that Susan remembered? She really did seem a shadow of her former self.

"Her son, my husband, visits her sometimes," Susan said as brightly as she could.

"Mmm, well, I haven't seen him." There was a note of condemnation in the girl's voice. "They're quickly forgotten once they are out of sight. Relatives don't like to be reminded."

"Well, my mother-in-law and I have not had an easy relationship," Susan said, irritated and embarrassed by the accusing eyes.

Susan followed the girl into the lounge, smiling into the vacant faces.

"You have a visitor!" the girl said as they stood in front of Olive's huddled form. Red-rimmed, runny blue eyes dragged themselves up to look at her. There was no recognition in them, just empty windows in a thin grey face. A trickle of saliva came from the corner of the still bitter mouth. But it was the hands, with the thin bony fingers constantly washing and pleating the magazine, that Susan remembered.

"Hello Olive," Susan managed to say, knowing before she sat down that it had been a wasted journey. There was nothing to be gained here.

"Is that you?" The voice was thin, almost a crackle. "Have you come back?"

"She has problems with her sight," the girl said as she patted the thin shoulder.

"Who is she talking about?" Susan asked.

"Someone from the past; time sort of slips back and forth with them. Yesterday, tomorrow and today are often all the same."

"Who are you?" the voice asked as a long finger pointed at Susan.

"I'm Susan, Grant's wife."

"You're not her. She comes to me and I tell her what to do. She does it all for me." The mouth moved but it was not a smile. The eyes clouded over and as a shaft of light caught them they looked almost diabolical. For a brief moment Susan was reminded of Pandora's eyes, opaque windows leading to a mysterious world. Susan shivered, pulling a chair up to sit down. She could not touch this old woman, not even her hand.

"What does she mean?"

"Oh, I dunno." The girl gave a shrug. "Must go." She glanced at her watch. "Almost tea time for them."

Susan lowered her eyes as she suddenly remembered *The Seven Ages of Man* at the drama group. How true! How horribly inevitable human decline was.

"Olive, dear," Susan whispered, knowing it sounded false but unable to put any true warmth into her voice. They stared at one another, the observer and the observed. No flicker of recognition came into Olive's eyes. No, this is pointless, Susan thought. It was stupidity. There was nothing here but an old woman who seemed to have lost her grip on reality. She knew she should feel pity, perhaps she did. Her eyes saw the worn black handbag resting against the chair. What possessions did Olive have Susan wondered? Then, seeing a box of confectionery, she smiled. So Olive still liked her plain chocolates. Grant must have been here, she thought. Nobody else would buy or bring them.

"She is mine now. I've told her, told her what to do, what to say. He left me, but she won't leave me!" Suddenly the voice rose, the eyes became coals of fire, the mouth twisted venomously and the claw-like hands gripped Susan's fiercely.

"They won't take her from me! She's mine. Mine!"

"Hi Olive!"

Susan turned, taken aback by the overly familiar attitude of the young nurse who stood smiling down at them both. It seemed inappropriate for a young girl to address an elderly lady in such informal terms. She bent over Olive, "And how are we today?"

"Tell her to go!" Olive's voice was croaky. Her face closed, the shutters coming down like an engine switching off. Only the hands started to slowly tear at the pages, ripping the paper into long, thin strips.

"I think she's upset," the nurse said, giving Susan a sympathetic smile.

"Perhaps I should go." Susan got up, giving a last look at the crumpled figure. All the venom and hatred were still there behind the old face. Nothing had changed. It had been a useless visit.

"Good afternoon!" the voice was educated.

Susan looked up to see a smart figure, dressed in a navy blue uniform. It was the Matron and Susan asked about Olive as she walked through the long and dimly lit hallway.

"Oh, she has moments of lucidity," the Matron said. "She needs more visitors."

"My husband ..." They had reached the front door. Matron's hand was on the lock.

"I haven't met your husband, but I do know how much she loves having her young visitor."

"Young visitor?" Susan raised her eyebrows.

"Yes, Cindy. Such a beautiful girl with her long hair. Sits with her for hours, drawing and making her laugh."

CHAPTER TWENTY-TWO

Susan stormed into the house and slammed the front door behind her.

"Cindy?" she called as she went into the kitchen. Struggling out of her blazer and throwing her car keys down on the table, she unplugged the kettle and filled it with water. She turned to see Cindy leaning nonchalantly against the door, her eyes downcast.

"Do you know where I have been this afternoon?" Susan snapped as she waited for the kettle to boil.

Cindy shook her head.

"I have been to visit your grandmother, Olive." Susan sat down, shaking with anger. Her eyes did not leave Cindy's face. Apart from a faint flicker in the watching eyes Susan could detect no change in her daughter's attitude. "You never mentioned you visited her!"

"Didn't I?"

"What is going on Cindy?"

There was a faint pause. Cindy walked across the kitchen floor and stood with her back to Susan, making herself a mug of coffee. "Going on? There is nothing going on." Cindy screwed her face up and her eyes narrowed, then she turned round and faced her mother. "I'd just forgotten, that's all. We were talking about the ageing process at school. I don't know, it was some project that required visiting an old people's home." She sat down in front of Susan. "I've always been afraid of her so I wanted to kill a ghost."

"No, my girl that just doesn't wash with me!" And with that Susan got up and left the kitchen en route to phone Grant.

Grant had agreed to meet Fiona in the lounge at the local hotel. It had taken him time to persuade her to meet him outside the formal confines of the centre but he had been determined.

"I can't come here again. I don't find it easy in these surroundings: it makes me feel I'm being interrogated, that I'm to blame. And I'm not," Grant had said on his last visit.

Fiona had given him a sharp glance and he'd smiled ruefully.

"I know," he'd acknowledged. "I should feel at ease. But you've got to understand, it's taking me time to open up and talk to you about these problems." He sighed and got up to gaze out of the window. There was no view, just a back yard. "Look, why don't you have a drink with me?" he'd suggested.

Fiona hesitated. It was her discretion as to where she met clients and if Grant felt happier meeting outside the centre then perhaps it was time for a change of location.

"This isn't friendship, Grant," Fiona advised quietly. "I am still your counsellor. The problem hasn't gone away."

Grant agreed, but knew somewhere in his mind that in changing the location he was trying to escape from the reason they were meeting.

Grant appeared a little tense. He played with the stem of his glass and fiddled with the beer mat. When he finally met Fiona's eyes, she smiled so he knew she understood his discomfort.

"Does talking about Cindy make you feel disloyal?" Fiona asked.

Grant shrugged his shoulders but he realised that it did.

They were a family unit; it was their problem and they should have been able to resolve it themselves. "There is so much about Cindy that I don't understand." He went on to explain about Cindy's extraordinary visits to Olive.

"I need to get Cindy's confidence," Fiona declared. "It isn't being disloyal if we are helping her."

"You believe me?" Grant felt compelled to ask.

Fiona gave an enigmatic smile. "It's early days yet."

"But you've formed an opinion?" Grant persisted.

"Opinions are merely that; what is required is evidence."

Grant nodded.

"Evidence is hard to find, but I do need to be able to assess whether Cindy is truthful or not."

"God knows how you'll do that!" Grant said, holding his hands out in despair. "If you think about it, I suppose you could say nobody really knows anything about her, except that she loves cats." Grant sighed. "Oh, and James. She seemed really fond of him."

"James?" Fiona frowned. "Tell me about him."

"Oh, he was just a friend," Grant told her. "There was nothing in it. He's gone away; he and his family moved up north."

"Did they stay in touch?"

"I don't think so," Grant revealed. "I don't know if it's important, but you see, well, James went to a special school, the one near the cricket club. He was badly dyslexic, that's why he has never written to her."

"Could he and Cindy have been more than friends?" Fiona asked quietly.

"I never met James properly and I never spent time with them together," Grant admitted. "So I don't know."

"James has never telephoned her?"

Grant shook his head. "Not to my knowledge."

"Has Cindy ever telephoned James?"

Grant gave a sigh of exasperation. "I really don't know. She has received two over the top romantic gestures recently though," Grant admitted.

"From James?"

Grant shook his head, "I don't think so."

"Who sent them?"

"David who lives on the close."

Fiona referred to her notes. "The young man Cindy has a flirtatious relationship with?"

Grant nodded, surprised that Doctor Stevens had recalled his exact description of Cindy and David's friendship.

"Didn't you like her receiving the cards?"

"I am protective about my daughter, nothing wrong in that, and in my opinion there was nothing wrong in the cards she received." Grant replied with a self-satisfied smile.

Fiona made a mental note to mention David to Cindy when they next met.

Tuesday, 19th July

Fiona's visit was not to spy on Cindy, for that would have been totally unprofessional. She was motivated by curiosity, and a wish to see the girl in different surroundings. Fiona had a vague interest in cats and watching Cindy relate to them would give an insight into the other side of this mysterious person; a chance to delve a little deeper, perhaps. Fiona admitted that Cindy intrigued her. Was she the sort of person who felt superior to everyone because of her looks? Or was she a girl who couldn't live up to her appearance? Visiting Cindy would add a further aspect to the case study for her forthcoming book; the book that could be the start of a new career for her.

It was lunchtime when Fiona parked her car in what was laughingly termed the car park. She was already wishing that she had had the sense to wear slacks and sensible shoes as she stumbled over the potholed pathway that lead to the door marked office. Pushing it open she found herself in the large reception area with its small claw-marked desk. She rang the bell and waited until the back office door swung open and a rather harassed elderly woman appeared.

"Can I help you?"

Fiona smiled. "I am a friend of Cindy's. She is always talking about working here and I thought I could visit and perhaps make a donation." She saw the scepticism in the eyes as they swept over her outfit.

"Come with me," the woman said abruptly. "Cindy is doing the kennel cleaning." She stopped and pointed to a corridor lined with mesh-covered cages.

Slowly Fiona walked down the concrete pathway hearing the plaintive meows, noticing the variety of cats prowling round, sleeping or merely watching and waiting for someone to like them.

"Doctor Stevens!" Fiona turned round, startled and vaguely annoyed that it was Cindy who had seen her first.

"Hello Cindy. I could say I was passing but you wouldn't believe that, would you?"

"No, Doctor Stevens I wouldn't." Her attitude was tense but under control. "Is it a cat or curiosity that has brought you here?"

Fiona gave a rueful smile. "Perhaps a little of both."

Cindy was dressed for the job in green Wellington boots, jeans and a sweatshirt with her hair tied back beneath a baseball cap and her hands encased in rubber gloves. The padlock on one of the cages was proving troublesome and Cindy had no option but to remove the rubber gloves, allowing Fiona to see her long red-painted fingernails. Once inside the cage Cindy bent down and picked up a black and white cat. It seemed contented in her arms and purred loudly.

"I wish I could keep my nails like that," Fiona commented.

Cindy raised her eyebrows. "All cats have claws!" she said jokingly.

"Working here doesn't seem to fit in with your image," Fiona commented, knowing the remark would irritate Cindy.

"And what image would that be?"

"Beautiful hair, painted fingernails. You look more like a model than a kennel worker."

The remark infuriated Cindy and she placed the cat down. "I object very strongly to your observation, Doctor Stevens. It implies that all attractive women only want the attention of men." Her tone was cutting.

"Oh, I didn't mean that, but you are a contradiction," Fiona kept on.

Cindy turned her attention to a tortoiseshell cat before saying, "Perhaps if I hadn't have looked like this, my father would have left me alone."

Fiona bit her lip. This was not going to be as easy as she thought. Cindy was not submissive, nor had she been threatened by her approach. "Will you have lunch with me?" she heard herself ask and was surprised at her own invitation. "There's a good pub near here. Very countrified." There was now a challenge in Fiona's eyes that was not lost on Cindy, who accepted the invitation with a smile.

Susan was alone in the house. She decided to put the time to good use and have a thorough look through Cindy's room. Pandora meowed her protest as Susan stood looking round Cindy's possessions. The room was almost clinically tidy. Susan, remembering Fiona's comments, could see that Cindy was putting her belongings at odd angles. She would need to be very careful; she couldn't afford to arouse her daughter's suspicions any further.

Slowly, methodically and with great care, Susan started her search. She didn't know what, if anything, she was looking for. Quite by accident she found it. It was a page from a magazine that had been Sellotaped to the back of the bedside cabinet. Somehow the tape had come loose and the page was dangling down.

Carefully opening the page out, Susan saw a paragraph was outlined in blue biro and read:

Have you anything in your past you'd like to write about? Any problems or experiences you think may help other people. If you have, jot your story down in no more than a thousand words and we'll pay you one hundred pounds if it's published.

Surely Cindy wasn't thinking of writing about Grant?

Susan closed her eyes in horror. She looked quickly to the closing date but it was three months ago. Now she turned the page over to find a sheet of paper with Cindy's writing on it.

She started to read:

"When I was eight my father came into my bedroom ..."

Susan just wanted to replace the piece of paper and walk out of the room but there was something about the opening sentence that jogged her memory. She re-read the first paragraph before realisation dawned.

Slowly she made her way downstairs hearing the grandfather clock chiming in the hall. The second post had been delivered and there was a small bundle of letters on the hall mat. Bending down she picked them up and threw them onto the kitchen table. Cindy's seemingly fictitious story was all Susan could think about. She turned, waiting for the kettle to boil and idly flicked through the mail. From the corner of the last envelope, something caught her attention.

A postcard. She pulled it out and there was a picture of Edinburgh Castle. On the reverse side she read the badly written message.

She stared at it, slowly absorbing its significance. Without a moment's hesitation she retrieved the magazine and with the postcard firmly grasped in her hand she left the house and drove to Grant's office.

Their car journey was short and the pub was, as Fiona had implied, mellow and reasonably comfortable.

"Is this all right?" Fiona pointed to the corner table in the bar. "I think they have a sandwich menu."

Cindy smiled, determined not to be thrown by Fiona. She ordered competently, choosing a sandwich but refusing a drink, saying she would prefer a coffee later.

There was a pause as they assessed each other. Cindy was sitting quietly, relaxed and waiting. The use of silence was a method Fiona employed regularly. Some people were unable to hold onto silence. They felt a need to chatter or fidget uncomfortably, but Cindy was well at ease within the containment, very much her own person.

"I suppose you want to ask me questions?"

"Not if you don't wish me to."

"I've nothing to add to what has already been said," Cindy gave a faint shrug. "I would rather talk about your work. Tell me about it?"

The question took Fiona by surprise. She wanted to laugh and say, we are here to talk about you, but suddenly she found herself talking about her own life in a way that she had not talked for a long time. Cindy, she learned, was a good listener and a skilful questioner.

"I am surprised you can give advice." Cindy paused.

"Excuse me?" Fiona replied, not fully understanding the statement.

"After your divorce, which is surely the failure of a relationship, you still see fit to advise others. It seems a little arrogant."

"My experience has helped me to perceive and empathise with other people's problems," Fiona replied haughtily. Then, realising she was being goaded, managed a quick smile.

"Mmm," Cindy was not convinced. "You said your husband was interested in art?" she asked. Her voice was light and friendly, her eyes smiling warmly across at Fiona. "Do you miss him?"

Fiona found herself nodding and admitting that she did miss him.

"You know, I am considering art as a career," Cindy volunteered after a short pause. "It would have to be on a commercial basis, but I would prefer to paint and draw beautiful pictures of animals all day long." Cindy paused and a touch of humour came into her eyes as she asked, "You found the traps in my bedroom, didn't you?"

Fiona threw her head back, laughing. "Touché!"

Cindy laughed too and for a brief moment there was empathy between them.

"Tell me a little about the Cindy the family doesn't know?" Fiona asked, as the dishes were cleared away and a jug of coffee was placed before them.

"Is there one?"

"Your life outside the family; your friends. David Carter for instance?" A closed look crept into Cindy's eyes, but her composure did not alter as she replied,

"Are you implying that David is my boyfriend?"

"Is he?"

Cindy shook her head.

"But you're such an attractive girl," Fiona added and saw the swift change in Cindy's attitude.

"That is all people see in me, isn't it? The way I am packed, as if I am just hollow inside, no intelligence, and no feelings; just an attractive wrapper. It's like someone looking at a book jacket and passing an opinion without reading the contents."

"Have you been out with David?" Fiona pressed the question.

"David is very nice and he gives me lifts in his car, but that's all it is," Cindy replied thoughtfully.

Fiona wondered if Cindy felt disadvantaged by her appearance. It was an interesting subject to analyse; something that she would add to her book. How does a beautiful girl regard herself? Changing the subject she asked, "You do a great deal of reading, I couldn't help noticing …"

"Oh, my *odd books*, as mother calls them," Cindy cut in. "I don't like novels, silly imaginary stories about make believe people. I like to know why people do things." She stopped and glanced round before saying quietly, "Why did my father have sex with me?" She laughed humourlessly. "No book can give me that answer!"

"The Occult?"

"Doctor Stevens, people get frightened at that very word, as if it is all devil worship and Satanism. It only means that which is secret, and let's face it, we all have secrets."

"But you're a Catholic," Fiona said briefly.

"A liberal minded one!" Cindy went on to talk about the ancient beliefs of Paganism and Wicca. Fiona found her knowledgeable and fascinating to listen to but wanted to get the meeting back onto a firmer footing.

"Why did you and your friend coax your father into a lingerie shop and persuade him to buy you a revealing night dress?" Fiona shot the question and saw Cindy once more go on the defensive.

"I'm sorry, Doctor Stevens." Cindy stared directly into Fiona's questioning eyes. "My father bought me the night dress as a present."

"Your father says you coerced him into the shop."

Cindy shrugged her shoulders dismissively. "I can't really remember." Fiona realised it would be useless to continue that line of questioning. "Do you like puzzles?" Fiona asked and noticed the wariness creep into Cindy's eyes. "I have something for you. I am sure you can solve it with ease."

"A puzzle?" Cindy raised her eyebrows.

Fiona smiled. "Oh, it's just one of my peculiarities, I suppose." She could see Cindy was disinterested until she mentioned that her father had not been able to solve it in the time limit of a minute she had given him.

"But he's not very bright!" Cindy said seriously.

"You simply have to choose the odd word out and give the reason."

"Okay."

"Asphalt; delight; uncle; leave." Fiona stopped and glanced at her watch. "You've a minute," she said, watching as Cindy sat silently clicking her nails. At forty-seven seconds Cindy looked up.

"Asphalt is the odd word," she said.

"Why?" Fiona asked.

"Because the others can be country orientated."

"Explain."

"You can have Turkish Delight, Dutch Uncle and French Leave."

Fiona offered a small smile. "Very good," she said quietly, not divulging that her little game had allowed her to assess the agility of Cindy's mind, and had confirmed that she seemed able to adapt to difficult situations and could process information correctly whilst under pressure. Now Fiona believed Cindy would not divulge anything unless absolutely sure of her facts. It would have been so much easier if Cindy had got the puzzle wrong. Without preamble she attacked from a different direction.

"Your father mentioned that he made you a doll's house and was surprised when you seemingly lost your temper and smashed it one day. Do you remember the incident?" Fiona's eyes never left Cindy's face. She saw the flash of suspicion that swept like a tidal wave across the demure expression. "You remember the doll's house? From your father for his little angel?"

Cindy's hand suddenly clenched and her face went pale.

"Are you all right?" Fiona leaned forward and placed a hand on Cindy's arm.

"It's the heat and smoke! I need some fresh air. Do you mind?" Cindy got up and Fiona watched her walk to the door.

Bingo! Fiona thought, finally I have found Cindy's weak spot. The waiter brought the bill and she gave him her credit card and then hurriedly followed Cindy into the deserted beer garden.

"Please go away! Leave me alone. You're just prying. What

do you know about the doll's house? What do you know about my life?" Cindy's face was now contorted into such bitterness and hatred that Fiona felt herself recoil.

"I didn't mean to upset you." Fiona held her hand out in a gesture of contrition and watched as Cindy closed her eyes and then shuddered visibly.

"No, I'm sorry." Cindy's face was now that of a seventeen year old. "It got broken up, my doll's house. And all the family inside too." She gave a faint grimace. "It was just a part of growing up."

The barman touched Fiona's arm, indicating the credit card slip for her to sign.

"Can I borrow your pen?" she asked Cindy.

"Sorry, I've only got a pencil."

"Pencil will do, as long as my signatures are on all the copies." Fiona held her hand out. Cindy had no option but to reach up into the top pocket of her shirt and reluctantly hand over her gold pencil.

Fiona moved away in the pretence of resting the credit slip on a nearby table. In so doing she gave a swift glance at the pencil and saw that it was expensive and bore the inscription *Geoffrey*.

"Thank you." Fiona handed the pencil back to Cindy. "Very nice! Was it a present?"

Cindy did not reply but turned away, just as a young woman struggling with a baby in her arms and a toddler lagging behind, came up from the garden area.

The baby started to cry. As the mother tried to calm it down, the toddler broke free and ran across the patio, catching his foot on an uneven surface and falling down with a thump.

"Oh, you stupid boy!" the mother admonished him.

"Can I help?" Fiona asked. "Perhaps I can hold the baby while you comfort him."

The woman nodded in gratitude. Willingly she placed the

crying baby in Fiona's arms and attended to her son. Fiona rocked the distraught baby gently and then laughed as she turned to Cindy, who was standing impassively watching the scene, making no attempt to help her or the woman.

"Do you want to hold her?" Fiona asked nodding to the baby in her arms.

"No!" Cindy almost spat the words out and Fiona stared at her in surprise. Cindy's eyes seemed to blaze from their sockets with distaste. It was a look Fiona had seen before.

"Thanks, all's well again!" the woman said, reclaiming her baby and cuddling her close to her body.

"You don't like babies?" Fiona asked Cindy quietly.

"Of course I do. Why?"

"You seemed a little frightened of it, that's all."

" I just didn't want to hold the baby."

"Are you sure that's all it was?"

"What else could there be?"

But Fiona was not convinced. She had sensed there was something in Cindy's attitude towards the baby that merited further investigation. There had been a very powerful emotion of dislike, something more than natural wariness of a crying infant. Many girls would have been only too happy to hold and cuddle a baby; but of course Cindy wasn't like most young girls.

"I'll walk back," Cindy said as she held her hand out. "Thank you for the lunch." And with a wide smile she left.

When Cindy returned to the sanctuary the office was deserted. She immediately picked up the phone and dialled *Directory Enquires*, noting the number given on a pad. Then, with a look of determination on her face, she picked up the receiver again and dialled the number.

CHAPTER TWENTY-THREE

Grant was not in his office when Susan arrived and she felt a moment's irritation that she was not able to share this new information with him. She decided to return home. It was only as she drove along the familiar road and into the cul-de-sac that she wondered whether she should tell him of her findings. She was still wondering about the right thing to do when she arrived home. Then, on impulse, she picked up her handbag and searched for Fiona Stevens's business card.

Fiona had just arrived back at the voluntary centre after her meeting with Cindy and was surprised to receive a call from Susan. She was conscious of the urgency in Susan's voice and agreed to meet her in the coffee shop of the local hotel in an hour.

Susan wasted no time in telling Fiona that she believed that Cindy had actually written the article *Daddy's Girl* under the pseudonym of Shona Widdry.

Fiona had held group counselling sessions where she had encouraged people to write down their fears, phobias and innermost thoughts. It was easier for many people to put words onto paper than to actually speak them; words that told about an incident, perhaps for the first time. She immediately realised the significance of Cindy writing the article.

"I can't believe that Cindy wrote the article herself." Susan shook her head in disbelief.

"It really proves how little we know about people," Fiona said. Cindy must have written the article at least four months ago, long before her friend Elizabeth had been given the car. So were they wrong about the car being the trigger point for the accusation?

"What else have you got?" Fiona asked.

Susan handed over the postcard from Edinburgh.

"It's from James. He used to be a sort of boyfriend. He's dyslexic."

"Does he ever phone her?"

"Not to my knowledge."

"Odd how he's now chosen to write. The message doesn't tell us much. It's hardly romantic. But it must mean something. Watch Cindy's reaction and keep all this information to yourself."

When Fiona returned to the counselling centre late in the afternoon she was immediately summoned to the office of her superior.

It was late when Cindy arrived home. She entered the house with a disgruntled expression and dumped her bag down on the hall chair. Sighing she walked into the kitchen.

"There's a postcard for you. Something to brighten your day up!" Susan announced, cursing herself for sounding so eager.

Cindy's eyes narrowed as she moved across to look down at the card that was prominently displayed on the breadboard. Reluctantly she turned it over, reading the message without comment.

"He must be thinking about you," Susan could not resist saying, her eyes never leaving Cindy's face. "I mean, why would he send you a postcard otherwise?"

Cindy shrugged her shoulders.

Susan sensed annoyance in Cindy's attitude. "Are you going to reply?" she asked.

"No. Why should I bother replying?"

"I just thought ..."

"That's your trouble, mother. You're always assuming a right to other people's thoughts," Cindy retorted sharply.

"Okay! Don't bite my head off," Susan said.

"Sorry!" Cindy replied. "I've had a rotten day." She placed the card carefully in her bag and walked upstairs.

In her bedroom, Cindy took off her coat and placed it on a hanger in her wardrobe. She needed a shower and to be by herself.

After her shower, she wrapped herself in her robe and sat down in front of the dressing table mirror and began to calmly brush her hair. What had James written for? And why did Mum have to see it? I'll have to be more careful. Stupid, stupid girl. She glared at her reflection in the mirror and put her tongue out at herself.

Thursday, 21st July

Fiona telephoned Cindy at the sanctuary and asked if she would come into the centre for a short session. She was surprised by Cindy's initial reluctance.

"Will my father be there?" Cindy asked.

"No."

There was a pause.

"It's my half day tomorrow. I'll be there at two," Cindy said in a businesslike manner.

They sat opposite each other in the interviewing room. Neither of them was relaxed. Cindy sipped the coffee Fiona had put before her, her manner wary after their lunch.

Fiona watched as Cindy placed the cup down on the saucer then started to rub her hands together before clicking her nails.

There was an uncomfortable pause before Fiona asked quietly, "Tell me, Cindy, why did you feel it necessary to phone the centre after we had lunch? Apparently you questioned my methods." Fiona leaned forward to pick up her cup of coffee, her eyes on Cindy's face. She saw the eyelids close, the mouth tighten into a line of displeasure. Then the eyelids opened and Cindy's eyes stared at her with an intensity Fiona found disconcerting. "I was reprimanded," Fiona said lightly, as she leaned back in her chair. "Did my visit worry you, Cindy?"

"Why would it?"

"Why indeed?"

There was a short silence before Cindy bent down and opened her bag and extracted a roll of art paper held together with a rubber band. She pushed this across the table to Fiona. "I've done this as a small apology. I realise I shouldn't have made that call."

The apology was unexpected, but there was no doubting the remorse on Cindy's face. Had she come prepared? Fiona couldn't tell as she glanced down at the roll of art paper on the table. She picked it up, slipped the rubber band off and unfurled the paper. She wasn't sure what to expect but the sketch on the paper took her by surprise. It showed a hand outstretched and in its palm were three human figures. Fiona looked at the title in the bottom right hand corner – *In the Palm of Your Hand*. Cindy heard Fiona's intake of breath before Fiona said. "You are very talented."

"You sound surprised, Doctor Stevens." There was a faint note of mockery in Cindy's voice.

"Is this the way you see things, the family in the palm of my hand?" There was a pause as Fiona looked at the sketch again. "Or is this your hand, Cindy?"

The question threw Cindy. She lowered her eyes and shrugged her shoulders, declining to reply to the question but asking one of her own. "Doctor Stevens, you never answered my question. What would I have to gain by lying about my father?"

"No I never did," Fiona agreed, sitting back and clasping her hands together. "Revenge perhaps?"

Cindy's face screwed up. "Revenge for what?"

"I understand that you expected your father to buy you a car and," she paused, "he didn't buy it when asked."

A sudden frown came over Cindy's face and she closed her eyes, clenching her fists. Slowly, trance like, she recounted more events of the alleged incidents she had suffered at the hands of her father, detail by nauseating detail. Fiona listened to the voice; it was almost as though Cindy was reading from an unseen script. "That's what he did to me. The Ford Escort has nothing to do with it."

Fiona allowed silence to envelop them, broken only by the irritating clicking of Cindy's nails. Cindy was not comfortable with this silence, Fiona realised.

"Tell me about your grandmother?" Fiona shot the question at her, seeing Cindy bridle in surprise. She listened as Cindy recovered her composure and described Emma. "And your other grandmother?" she queried lightly.

"There's not much to tell," Cindy muttered.

"You visit her?"

"I am sure you know I have visited her recently," Cindy replied.

"But in the past, you were frightened of her?" Fiona asked.

"In the past I was a child. Yes, I was frightened of her. Mum used to say that she'd tried to break up their marriage, how wicked she was, all sorts of things. Then Dad took me to see her. It sounds silly," Cindy paused, "but I'd seen *The Wizard of Oz* and when I saw her she reminded me of the Good Witch of the North and the red shoes." She bit her lip. "I was eight years old at the time. Where she lived seemed such a bleak and shivery place, no warmth, people put away, out of sight, their relatives ashamed of them. The staff creeping round and all those batty women watching you."

"They're not necessarily batty," Fiona felt obliged to say, "Just sad and lonely old people."

"I know that now, but Dad told me they were batty, that his mother had gone mad and he'd had to put her away. He said she was evil and wicked; that she had tried to possess him. I didn't understand, but it sounded horrible. She screwed her eyes up. "He said it ran in the female line of the family, madness." Cindy started to shiver. "I don't like remembering it.

He told me all sorts of nasty things about his mother, how she always wanted him for herself. But that is how he wanted me. I was his little angel. I used to like it, but then it got scary. Cindy's face was white and drawn. "I only remember Grandma sitting staring at me and him whispering that I could end up like that."

Fiona listened quietly. She could see the distress the memory was causing. Fiona thought about what that visit had meant to each of them. Cindy, seeing it as oppressive, with Grant not as a dutiful son, but as a father who wished to instil fear into his daughter; fear of what she might become. It had all grown out of proportion. These descriptions were more fitting to a Greek Tragedy than the atmosphere in a modern nursing home. She watched as Cindy clicked her nails, uncertain now whether this betrayed lying or nervousness. There was fear there, that was obvious, but was Cindy afraid of her own imagination?

On Fiona's note pad was a list of reminders. On it were the gold pencil and the title of a book that she had seen in Cindy's bedroom. Susan's name was underlined at the top of the list and Fiona decided to ask some intensive questions. She started with, "Tell me more about your mother?"

Pushing her hair back, Cindy relayed a brief, non-committal opinion that told Fiona very little. A similar question about Grant produced an abrupt reply. Fiona couldn't decide whether Cindy's remarks were because of genuine hatred for Grant's alleged interference with her or because he was Susan's husband. Fiona proceeded to write her notes and Cindy watched.

I don't like this woman, Cindy thought. She thinks she is so clever, trying to tie up the loose ends, but she will never be able to unravel my thoughts.

Fiona allowed another silence to develop. The interview was not going as well as she had hoped. Cindy was certainly answering her questions but her replies were infuriatingly opaque. She hesitated and then asked, "The examination by the doctor, tell me how that affected you."

"How should it affect me? It was a medical examination."

"You are not a virgin?"

"No, I've been sexually interfered with, remember?"

"By your father?"

"Yes, by my father."

Fiona glanced down at her pad and toyed with the idea that was in her mind. This was brutal questioning, she knew that, but she had to try and derail Cindy. "Who is Geoffrey?"

"Geoffrey?" Cindy shook her head and frowned.

"The name Geoffrey. It's inscribed on your pencil?"

"Someone I don't have to tell you about," Cindy said sarcastically.

Fiona sighed and opened her desk drawer to extract a hard-backed book. She placed it face down on the desk, seeing Cindy's eyes following her movements. This is like a cat and mouse game, she thought. But who is the cat and who is the mouse?

"So, what is your next question, Doctor Stevens?" Cindy said, her eyes on the book.

"This," Fiona said, quickly turning the book over and holding it up for Cindy to read the title.

"Yes, I've read it," Cindy acknowledged. "It's a book about a father and daughter's incestuous relationship; a horrible story. You found the same book in my bedroom, didn't you?"

"It's also a book about a daughter's jealousy of her mother's relationship with her father," Fiona went on. "An odd coincidence, you having read it?"

Cindy smiled briefly. "Purely that, Doctor Stevens."

Fiona felt a little deflated. She continued to cross-examine Cindy relentlessly but, try as she might, she could not find a break in her story.

"I understand you have accused your father of coming into your room recently, is that true?"

"Yes. I had to put a chair to the door."

"Doesn't the door have a lock?"

"No."

"You never thought to put a lock on?"

Cindy didn't reply.

"Mmm, tell me again, do you love your father, Cindy?"

"No."

"Did you ever love him?"

"No."

"You do a great deal of sketching?"

"Yes."

"Do you sketch your father?"

Cindy stared at her, shrugging her shoulders. "Maybe," she muttered.

"You must know if you've sketched him or not."

"Yes."

"So why? If he has done so many bad things, why this?" Fiona placed the sketchpad in front of Cindy. She was pleased to see the confused expression in Cindy's eyes as they both stared at the sketch of an exaggeratedly handsome Grant, surrounded by love-hearts.

"Just a doodle, Doctor Stevens," Cindy tried to dismiss it.

"A doodle of a father who has supposedly abused you!" There was incredulity in Fiona's voice.

There was a pause and Fiona could see Cindy mentally weighing up her reply. "You think you're clever Doctor Stevens, but I can assure you that you are merely reading more into these inconsequential happenings ..."

Fiona raised her eyebrows. "Why do you think that?"

There was a moment's silence before Cindy met Fiona's eyes. "You know I don't have to sit here and listen to this. I am trying to be co-operative but you are constantly undermining my answers and are obviously biased."

Cindy was pleased to see Fiona flush then lean forward and rub her eyes before saying, "You may leave if you wish."

"I will, but before I go, let me give *you* a puzzle, Doctor Stevens." Cindy smiled now and there was a faint amusement in her eyes for she knew she had won the conversation.

Fiona allowed a small smile to creep over her lips. Cindy had again skilfully steered the conversation away from the difficult questions that had been asked and had placed herself once again in control of the interview. This in itself told Fiona quite a lot. She allowed herself to listen as Cindy outlined the puzzle.

"In a room there are three sacks of gold coins. One sack is full of artificial gold coins and they weigh differently."

Fiona nodded and Cindy went on.

"The solid gold coins weigh a pound each. The artificial gold coins weigh one pound and one ounce each." Fiona made some notes. "You have a penny scale and one penny, giving you only one chance to weigh the sacks. How do you know which sack contains the artificial coins?"

Fiona finished making her notes and glanced up to see the watchful expression on Cindy's face.

"I'll accept the answer the next time I see you, Doctor Stevens." And with that Cindy got up, ignored Fiona's out stretched hand and walked to the door.

CHAPTER TWENTY-FOUR

Fiona returned to her desk, slowly going through the notes she had made on Cindy's case. *An Angel with Two Shadows*, she had labelled it. They had reached stalemate, she knew that. There was nothing to persuade her of Grant's innocence except a gut feeling that he was telling the truth. And there was nothing to prove Cindy was lying. Fiona was troubled by her reluctance to even entertain the image of Grant as a sex fiend that had raped his daughter. She closed her eyes and sat in silence, the evidence sifting through her mind.

A girl jealous of her parents' relationship? A girl obsessed with sexual fantasy? A girl mesmerised with her appearance? Well, the mind was a strange, complex twister. It could turn you blind through hysteria, it could produce an alter ego. But was Cindy a hysteric?

Crucial evidence lay in the fact that Cindy, while never apparently having had a serious boyfriend, was not a virgin. Her denial that her relationship with James had been anything other than platonic was important, as was both parents' certainty that there had been no other boyfriends. She did not believe Cindy and David were secret lovers. She knew she had to find out more about the girl. It was going to be difficult and she would have to compromise her impartiality by probing more deeply.

Cindy was pleased that she finally had the house to herself, her mother having decided to visit Emma. She made herself a mug of tea and took two chocolate biscuits from the tin and then relaxed in her favourite chair in the conservatory, her bare feet resting on a magazine on the small coffee table. Pandora too was relaxing, methodically rubbing first one paw over her ear and then the other. Cindy gave a gentle smile; there was something very relaxing in watching a cat washing itself.

Outside the garden was at its summer best and Cindy felt almost at peace. But no matter how much she tried to relax, the house did not feel right. The atmosphere had changed. It had been such a traumatic period for the family that sometimes she wished she had never uttered those fateful words. But life was made up of sentences starting "If only…"

If only she had waited for the car. If only she had kept her mouth shut, they would all still be together. Had it really been worth it? The question hung unanswered in her mind. Was it really her moment of retribution? That was a powerful word. Retribution. Had she been churlish? Or worse, had her actions been unnecessary? Sometimes she wished … But it was no use wishing. The car in the garage was proof of how unnecessary it had been. She couldn't drive it and every time she entered the garage it sat there, silently accusing her.

Her father had kept his promise and the thought upset her. As if sensing Cindy's disquiet, Pandora jumped up onto her lap and Cindy bent her head and kissed the soft fur. Her thoughts were interrupted by the sound of the doorbell. Sighing audibly she placed Pandora on the floor, struggled into her slip-on canvas shoes, and went to answer the front door. She swung the door open and saw Elizabeth smiling at her.

"It's been ages, Cindy, since I saw you. What's been happening to you?"

Cindy pulled her face into a smile and shrugged her shoulders as she invited Elizabeth in.

"So, tell me what you've been doing. I've got a summer job

at a hotel," Elizabeth said as she perched herself on one of the kitchen stools.

"Not much," Cindy murmured.

Elizabeth started to relate what had been happening to her over the summer but soon realised that Cindy wasn't interested. Instead she suddenly asked, "So, where's your car?"

Elizabeth was looking at her through narrowed eyes and Cindy knew she had suspicions about her actually having the car.

"It's in the garage," she said, trying to put some enthusiasm into her voice as she went to the small cupboard under the stairs where Grant kept the garage keys. "Come on," she said opening the back door. "I'll show you it."

"I'm surprised you aren't out in it!" Elizabeth said, following behind Cindy. "I've called mine Madonna."

"You can't call a car a name," Cindy said dismissively.

"Well I have," Elizabeth snapped as Cindy inserted the key into the garage door and swung it open. "So you still can't drive?" Elizabeth was determined to get the last word.

"Dad's been busy," Cindy muttered.

"Oh, you don't want your Dad to teach you," Elizabeth replied haughtily. "Get a proper driving instructor, but in your case a woman!"

Cindy frowned. "Why a woman?"

Elizabeth sighed; sometimes she was astounded at Cindy's naiveté. "If you get a guy he'll be too busy looking at you and not at the road."

Cindy managed a faint smile as they stood back to admire the red Ford Escort.

"It's two years old!" Elizabeth remarked as she ran a hand over the rear hatch. "Of course you really can't beat a new car!"

Cindy shrugged as she made way to the driver's door. "Have you got a sunroof?" she asked knowing very well that

Elizabeth did not. Cindy unlocked the doors and slid into the driver's seat. But the car represented a negative part of her life and she experienced no sense of enjoyment as she sat behind the wheel.

"Stop day-dreaming!" Elizabeth cut through her thoughts as she opened the passenger door and plonked herself beside Cindy. "Come on! Reverse it out," she urged.

I can't, Cindy thought, remembering her father, who was now living in a hotel, and Susan, almost demented with worry. It was all because of this car and she wished to God that she'd never seen it on the garage forecourt.

"Come on, take it out." Elizabeth was getting impatient.

"I can't," Cindy said.

"Don't be such a wet. Of course you can. It's your car isn't it?"

"Of course it is," Cindy replied, slowly inserting the key into the ignition.

"Press the clutch before you start the engine!" Elizabeth advised in a superior voice that made Cindy cringe.

Feeling the sweat on her hands and conscious of the beating of her heart, Cindy checked the gear lever was in neutral and with the clutch pedal depressed she turned the key.

She bit her lip as she heard the engine fire, then selected reverse and without gauging the take up on the pedal, released the clutch quickly so that the car shot backwards, narrowly missing the garage pillars. She slammed on the brakes and the car came to a rest half in and out of the garage.

Cindy was shocked. She had never driven a car before and thought it was far easier than it looked. Elizabeth, giggling in the passenger seat, did not help.

"Damon Hill, you're not!" Elizabeth said and Cindy was about to answer back when she saw David's Mazda come slowly down the cul-de-sac. It turned into the adjacent drive, but David had seen them and after parking his car he walked across.

"You could ask him to teach you," Elizabeth gave another irritating giggle, "to drive as well!"

"Oh, do shut up," Cindy muttered as he approached.

"What's all this then?" he asked as Cindy got out of the car.

"Cindy's *trying* to learn to drive!" Elizabeth replied with a laugh as she slammed the passenger door.

"You don't have to shut the door so hard," Cindy cut it.

"Sorry, I forgot it's an older car." Elizabeth raised her eyebrows provocatively at David who was grinning.

"So, when are you going to get the L plates on?" David asked Cindy.

"Dad's been busy," Cindy said dismissively.

"I haven't seen him around lately," David said and there was curiosity in his tone. "His car's not been here either."

Elizabeth turned and gave Cindy an inquisitive glance. "Left home has he?" she joked.

"No, he has not," Cindy, replied testily. "He's away on business."

She wished she had had more time to think up a suitable excuse. It was obvious that people were wondering where her father was. She started to click her nails. What had Susan told people? They should be getting their story together instead of ignoring the situation.

"Stop doing that!" Elizabeth said, irritated at the sound of Cindy's nails clicking.

"I'll teach you," David offered, giving the Escort the once-over. "Seems in good condition and it's no use to you stuck in the garage."

"I'm parched," Elizabeth said after Cindy had persuaded David to drive the car back into the garage. She didn't want Susan to be aware that the car had been moved; somehow it didn't seem right. But what was right? She no longer knew.

"Come into the conservatory and you can have a juice," Cindy said, conscious it was not the most pressing invitation she'd made, but Elizabeth was impervious and turned to David.

"You may as well come in with us," she said.

They sat in the conservatory talking and Cindy found herself relaxing. David always made her laugh and she tentatively accepted his offer to teach her to drive.

When Susan returned she noticed Elizabeth's car outside. As she soon as she entered the house she heard the sound of laughter from the conservatory where she found Cindy openly flirting with David. The scene inexplicably disturbed her.

Monday, 25th July

When she realised that they had not yet broken up for the summer holidays, Fiona had decided to visit the school. Mr Arthur, the principal, was a short middle-aged man with thinning ginger hair. His pale brown eyes beneath ragged ginger brows were encased in rimless spectacles. As Doctor Stevens was shown into his office, he stood up, extended his hand and gave a weak smile of welcome. His voice was pleasant as he said, "We are all ready for the holidays. We have all of August off. I am not sure precisely what it is you wish to know?"

"I hope you'll tell me a little about your school," Fiona said, accepting his invitation to sit down.

He nodded in a precise manner and prepared to deliver the speech he gave to all new visitors. "This school caters for pupils who have learning difficulties. They are not, as some would wish to class them, stupid." His voice was firm and he sat with his fingers together as though in constant prayer.

"I'll come straight to the point. I am interested in one of your past pupils. It goes without saying that any information you give me will be treated in confidence."

Fiona dug into her bag and handed him her card. He studied it for a second or two and then said, "You are very well qualified. Which pupil are you interested in?"

"James Simmons."

"Mmm, I see."

"Mr Arthur," She made her voice sound reassuring, "I'm sorry not to be able to tell you the reason for my questions. I can only hope you'll accept that there is a very real need to know. All I want is for someone to talk to me about James. There are no unethical questions I want to ask."

Mr Arthur fingered the card and then said quietly, "James Simmons, yes, I remember him." He straightened his spectacles. "There was nothing academically remarkable about James Simmons."

Fiona crossed one leg over the other and sat back. "I suppose you must have a picture of him – a school photograph?"

Mr Arthur frowned before getting up and walking across to the opposite wall of his study. He peered at a series of annual photographs. "Yes, here he is!" He took the framed photograph down and handed it to Fiona, who peered at the figure indicated by Mr Arthur's index finger.

A tall, good-looking boy, dressed neatly in the school uniform, smiled back at her.

"What age would he be?"

"That was taken just five years ago – fifteen going on sixteen."

"Fifteen!" Fiona handed the photograph back. "He looks older."

"Don't they all these days? James was a nice boy, helpful and yes, now I remember, he was extremely talented at woodwork. His craft master thought him an exemplary pupil. They had a good working relationship and that helped James.

"I wonder, could I talk with the woodwork teacher?"

"Yes, I am sure he is in today."

Mr Arthur picked up the phone, "Mrs Marshall, would you take Doctor Stevens across to the woodwork class."

Fiona followed the dumpy figure of Mrs Marshall, Mr

Arthur's secretary, through the dark corridors. Apart from a murmur about the weather she was disinclined to talk to Fiona.

"In here." Mrs Marshall opened a door and pointed to a small man who was hovering over a class of boys quietly engaged in various aspects of carpentry.

"Mr Stewart, someone to see you," Mrs Marshall announced and then left.

Fiona extended her hand, asking if they could talk privately for a few minutes. Mr Stewart gestured in the direction of a small office. He brushed a coating of sawdust from the stool before indicating that she should sit on it. He perched on the table.

She showed him her card.

"James Simmons? Oh yes, I remember him." The teacher's accent was broad Scottish. "Good with his hands, a natural carpenter. Not many about now. All the boys these days want to be yuppies in fast cars. I told James he could do a lot worse than being a successful carpenter." Mr Stewart grinned at her and gave a lengthy account of how he himself got interested in carpentry.

"And James?" Fiona said gently, bringing him back to the subject.

"Doing well until he upped and went to Glasgow with his Dad." He gave a rueful laugh. "Probably won't bother up there. Very few real craftsmen left."

Fiona smiled in sympathy. "He lives in Glasgow you say, with his father? What happened to the mother?"

He shook his head. "James was a victim of a broken home. His Mum went off with a young guy. That didn't help James. He was a soft one; needed a lot of love. He took it badly when his Mum left. Dads are never quite the same." He shook his head. "James had another wee problem, his girlfriend."

"A girlfriend?" Fiona raised her eyebrows.

"He met her on his way home from school, so I gathered.

And it went from there, as they say. He was upset at having to leave her, losing his mother and then his girl. Love comes harder when you're in your teens, and James, well, like I said, he needed love."

"You talk of love, not friendship?"

"Oh, there's no age limit on love, is there?"

"No, it was just ..."

"He was young and so was the girl, but as far as they were concerned it was love all right. So, he was devastated at having to leave her. I told him, he'd meet other girls, that he'd forget her, and probably just as well, I thought. Though it was nothing to do with me, that girl was not right for him. I didn't know her, only ever saw her from a way off, but she changed him. He became secretive. James had always been open and honest with me, told me everything. Then, when he met her, I suppose he transferred his trust to her. He closed up."

"Who was this girl?" Fiona asked casually.

"As I've said, I never really met her and he didn't mention her name. She was nice looking, I'll give you that. Went to the private school with the posh uniform. James was impressed and anxious to please, I said he'd learn ..." He paused and frowned and Fiona waited, hoping that some memory was being triggered. "Mmm, it's of no consequence," he said and his face broke into a smile, "But I do remember James making her something in woodwork. An odd present, I thought. A miniature family for a doll's house."

"A miniature family?" Fiona tried to keep her voice steady. "How unusual. Do you think ...?"

"I think it was probably as well he went away. I think there could have been complications, if you follow my meaning."

"You're implying his relationship with his girlfriend was a physical one?"

"I'm not implying, I'm telling you. No doubt about that at all!"

"What makes you so sure?" Fiona queried.

"Well," Mr Stewart smiled and tapped his nose, "You just know!"

Back at home Fiona opened and took out the CD she had bought that afternoon. She inserted the silver disc into the machine and selected the appropriate track. As she adjusted the volume in preparation her evening paper was delivered through the letterbox.

The words of *Take The Long Way Home* started to play as Fiona bent down and picked up the newspaper. The headlines hit her eyes and she stared in disbelief. Then, newspaper still in her hand she walked back into the lounge and sat listening to the words of the song, whilst reading the story below the headlines.

Cindy was also reading the evening paper. The headlines jumped at her from the front page. *Sex allegation dropped against local priest.* A thirty-two-year-old woman had apparently retracted her allegation that Father Patrick had acted in an improper way with her.

Cindy felt sorry for the woman, knowing how difficult it must have been to retract such an allegation. After all, what would people think of you if you had lied? Cindy felt more disgust at the thought that she had condemned Father Patrick without knowing all the facts. She had been prejudgemental and didn't like to think of herself in those terms. The report concluded that Father Patrick was taking a sabbatical.

Sunday, 31st July

Grant and Fiona met for lunch to review the situation. Briefly, she told him of her visit to the school, but did not divulge any of Mr Stewart's information. She parried his questions, asking him to consider what he knew of Cindy's relationship with boys outside school and to think again about James. She saw the flash of annoyance in Grant's eyes and that surprised her, until she realised that he was angry at her suggestion that Cindy and James could have had a sexual relationship.

When it became clear that he could not believe the full nature of Cindy's relationship with James, she felt justified in breaking her promise of confidentiality and told him all she knew. She also went back over the discovery of the article *Daddy's Girl* and how Cindy herself had written it. There was a stricken look on Grant's face. Fiona felt a moment's sorrow that she had put him through so much in such a short time.

"Go and find out all you can," he insisted quietly.

Before he left, she casually asked if Grant knew of anyone called Geoffrey. He shook his head.

The gold pencil was now worrying Fiona. Who was Geoffrey? Had he given Cindy the pencil? Had she stolen it? It was a very expensive pencil that no one in the family knew about and, because Cindy had been so defensive when asked about it, Fiona felt it had some peculiar significance.

Cindy wished her mother had not decided to celebrate Emma's birthday. It seemed inappropriate. It also meant, to her great annoyance, that she had to cancel her day with the cats.

At 11am Cindy wearily struggled out of bed and by the time she had showered and dressed and come down stairs, Susan had done most of the preparation for the lunch and was fussing about, checking that everything was in order before leaving to collect Emma.

They sat round the dining table, the family conscious that this was the first time they'd had lunch together since Grant had left. Susan worked hard to help the meal along, including each of them in the conversation, trying to instil a false sense of jollity. Now it was nearly over and they sat drinking their coffee in the lounge. Emma had not enjoyed her birthday any more than anyone else had. Sipping her coffee, Emma listened to Cindy talking about Elizabeth's experience of working in a hotel.

"Apparently all sorts of people book hotel rooms these days," Cindy said, and as she glanced round the table she knew she had their attention. "Elizabeth said that one time a perfectly nice chap came in and said he had booked the room for the night and that he was on a business trip." She paused for effect. "Well, the next morning the chambermaid said two people had slept in the single bed."

"Perhaps he smuggled his girlfriend in?" Susan replied with a laugh.

"No," Cindy shook her head. "Apparently he smuggled in his gay lover." The smile left Susan's face and was replaced by a look of repugnance.

"It happens," Cindy commented, "whether you like it or not." Then she added with a defiant look in her eyes, "Like molesting your own child, it's something no one can understand."

Susan's face was taut as she glanced across the table at her mother.

"Not the subject for lunch!" Emma said cuttingly.

After lunch Cindy walked to the shops.

"Thank you," Emma said to Susan when they were finally alone. "It must have been a strain for you having this party. I do miss Grant!"

"You miss him?" Susan said in despair as she sat down on the settee beside her mother. "I feel like the cement holding the bricks together on a building with a sandy foundation." Susan's eyes, Emma could see, were tired and the stress of the unresolved situation was pulling her down more with each passing day.

"I don't know why Grant couldn't have come today. You did ask him?" Emma turned to stare at Susan who was shaking her head.

"No. I wanted to, but Doctor Stevens felt it would be wiser to keep Grant and Cindy apart. It was either him or her."

Emma frowned. Over the past weeks she had been hearing a great deal about Doctor Fiona Stevens. Now she made no secret of her mistrust. "This Doctor has a lot to say for herself. Everybody seems to need counselling today. I don't understand it."

"I've told you, mother, it brings problems into the open."

"Well, in my day you sorted out your own problems. Now it's all big words that mean nothing. All new-fangled ideas of paying for people to meddle in your business." She sniffed audibly.

"Oh, mother." Susan took the vein-lined hand in hers. "If only we were as down-to-earth as you are." She wiped a tear from her cheek.

"I worry about you, Susan. What is going to happen to you all?"

"I worry too. I am so frightened. I don't know what lies

ahead. I don't even know if Grant and I have a future." There was a silence and then she went on in a broken voice, "I feel torn between two people I love. Which one will I lose? Dear God, *when sorrows come, they come not single spies, but in battalions.* I never fully understood that quotation from *Hamlet* until now."

CHAPTER TWENTY-FIVE

Wednesday, 3rd August

Grant was feeling tired and defeated. He was the outcast, pushed out of the family home because of an unjust accusation. He missed them, his two women. He missed turning in bed to wrap his arms round Susan, missed the laughter and love of the house. He should not have left; he should have insisted on staying. Cindy wouldn't have left, it was bluff, words said that could not be retracted through pride.

But during the long, lonely nights, Grant's future looked bleak. Even if his innocence could be proved, what about his life with Susan? Susan was proving to be the linchpin of the family, her strength and purpose had sustained them all and Grant knew that without her, they could have disintegrated. But, in the future, would she flinch at his touch as she did now? Would they ever be able to eradicate the accusation? And Cindy? What would happen to her?

He also took hope from Fiona. Her belief in his innocence, and her confidence that they could break Cindy's accusation sustained him. He had started to write down incidents as he remembered them – accounts of Cindy's possessive behaviour in his journals. Cindy wanting to be cuddled, kissed and hugged by him. Cindy demanding his attention, watching him, waiting for him to come home. His little angel, wanting to possess him – blurring now into a vision of his mother.

Fiona caught the early morning flight from Glasgow. By mid morning she was back home, tired after her hectic visit. The interview with James had been complicated, but so worthwhile, and she was pleased with the result.

James had asked if he could return and help Cindy in any way he could. Fiona had agreed. James had turned out to be a nice, open boy, anxious to tell her all he knew. His father had sat in on the interview and had confirmed the truth of all that had happened. Now as she sat at her small desk in her living room, Fiona congratulated herself. It was all there, on the tape and she had a notebook full of asides and descriptions. The visit had given her a wealth of insight, providing information that would be invaluable to her as a therapist.

She had brought James back to England with her and dropped him off in a nearby village to stay with his aunt. How would Cindy react to meeting him, she wondered? She glanced again at her notes; it was time for a confrontation with a family who had to learn the truth about each other.

Yes, she could afford to congratulate herself, this was family counselling at its best, proving that it could and did work.

The sound of the phone interrupted her thoughts. It was Grant, asking her to meet him for lunch. Fiona hesitated. She did not wish to divulge the details of her meeting with James and she could have done with a little relaxation, but because Grant sounded agitated and anxious she eventually agreed.

In a local pub and unable to contain his worry and anger Grant banged one fist down onto the table. "I'm bloody sick of this! I can't concentrate any more. I feel like some criminal on the run!" He stopped, turning his face away.

Fiona was unable to find the words to console or comfort him. She waited until he had control of himself and then asked, "Grant, are you all right?"

"No, I'm not all right," he snapped. "None of us are, as you put it, 'all right'."

"There is hope, Grant," Fiona said. "You have to believe me."

"Hope?" His voice was bitter. "My innocence you mean? I have had to lose my wife, my family, my home, my whole bloody life to quash an allegation made by a jealous daughter."

"You haven't lost it all yet, Grant."

Grant took a long drink of his beer, wiped the froth from his moustache and sat back. "So you saw James then?" He was taut and the lines round his eyes and mouth seemed to have deepened. He was clearly impatient to hear what Fiona had unearthed.

Briefly Fiona told him of the journey she'd made and the difficulty she'd had in locating where James lived. "But what happened?" Grant cut in. "Did he say anything useful?"

"He was very interesting. What I have learned was given in confidence but I've explained to James that what he tells us could help Cindy and he is willing to tell you everything that he told me."

Grant frowned. "I don't understand."

Fiona gave a smug smile. "You will. I'd like to arrange a meeting with all of you and, of course, James." She knew she had the reason for the accusation in a nutshell.

"So what do we do?" Grant asked.

"We have to be very careful," Fiona advised. "Cindy can be, as we all know, very intuitive; any slight difference in our behaviour and she will pick up on it. However, as a counsellor I have to give her the opportunity to talk to me in confidence once more."

Friday, 19th August

Cindy sat in front of Fiona Stevens's desk, clicking her nails in irritation. She had refused a cup of coffee or tea. She had only agreed to come because she hoped some process was under way to prove her father was guilty. The expression on Fiona Stevens's face made it clear that this would not be the case.

Fiona waited before speaking. The idea was to give Cindy time to retract, to allow her some dignity. But Cindy sat in stubborn silence until Fiona was embarrassed into asking further questions.

"Have you read this?" she asked, picking up a newspaper from the desk and showing Cindy the headlines about Father Patrick.

Cindy had no option but to nod her head and say, "Yes, I've read it."

"What are your comments?" Fiona persisted.

"I'm glad Father Patrick has been vindicated." It was all Cindy wanted to say on the matter.

"But you thought he was guilty?" Fiona was like a dog with a bone.

Cindy paused to think of her reply. "I only knew what I read in the papers. They painted a very negative picture of him."

"But you thought him guilty?"

Cindy reluctantly nodded.

"It is hard to retract something you've said," Fiona continued but Cindy interrupted her.

"There is no connection between this and my predicament. Either change the subject or I will leave." Cindy's voice was emphatic and Fiona had no option but to agree.

"Tell me about *Take The Long Way Home*." Fiona asked.

"There is nothing to say; I just like the song." Cindy replied.

"Do the words mean anything to you?" Fiona picked up a sheet of paper on which she had written the song's lyrics. She read, *"forever playing to the gallery,"* and paused before meeting Cindy's eyes. She continued, *"when you're up on the stage it's so unbelievable."* Cindy didn't comment and Fiona had to continue. "It sounds like fantasy," she observed. "Maybe like your life?" She knew it was a brutal statement but one which had to be made.

Cindy threw her head back and laughed. It was the first time there had been genuine amusement in her eyes and it took Fiona by surprise. "You're making something out of nothing, Doctor." Cindy laughed again. "The song also has the lyrics, *"cos you're the joke of the neighbourhood,"* and *"does it feel that your life's become a catastrophe?"* You can read anything into my reasons for liking the song, Doctor Stevens."

Fiona knew she wasn't getting anywhere with that line of attack so asked Cindy again about her feelings for Grant.

Cindy responded by becoming unusually angry. "Doctor Stevens," she said, rapping her watch. "I have been here for almost an hour. I have answered your questions again and again. You want me to withdraw my accusation but I'm not going to. You want me to lie, to say it never happened."

"Of course I don't wish you to lie."

"But you think I'm already lying."

Fiona leaned forward. "I want to give you a chance, Cindy. A chance to tell me about incidents, important incidents you have chosen not to relate. I want to help you." Fiona paused, she saw a faint shadow pass over Cindy's face and watched as Cindy sank her teeth into her lower lip. There was a moment's hesitation; a moment when Fiona could see that Cindy was balancing her scales, considering her options. Waiting in the stillness of the office, Fiona knew Cindy was fighting indecision.

"Doctor Stevens..." For the first time the voice was uncertain.

"Cindy, I can help you. I know you love your father." It was the wrong approach. Instantly Cindy's expression changed and a derisive smile crept over her face. She stood up.

"You can't help. Not if you won't believe me."

"I will be seeing you and your parents shortly to disclose my findings. I hope they don't upset you," Fiona said, as she too stood up.

But then Cindy retook her seat. A change of expression swept over her face and Fiona could almost sense the transformation in her attitude. "Well Doctor Stevens, do you have an answer for me?"

Fiona knew Cindy was referring to the puzzle she had set. Fiona had thought long and hard about it and had been tempted to cheat by asking a colleague but had refrained. Slowly Fiona said, "the three sacks each contain gold coins, one sack contains false coins and they weigh differently."

Cindy nodded as Fiona continued.

"If you put all the sacks on the scale and remove them one by one."

But Fiona saw Cindy shaking her head, a self-satisfied smile on her lips.

"No, Doctor Stevens. You only have one reading on the scale and one chance to weigh the sacks. I'm afraid Doctor Stevens you have lost your penny."

Fiona felt a wave of irritation. It had been important to her to give the correct answer and now she had to grit her teeth as Cindy told her the solution.

Cindy went to Fiona's desk and retrieved a number of paper clips. Sitting down she methodically placed them into three little piles.

Fiona watched as Cindy demonstrated the answer.

"You take one coin from bag one, two coins from bag two and three coins from bag three. You place them all on the scale." Cindy looked up. "Do you follow me?"

Fiona gave a reluctant nod.

"If the artificial coins came from bag one then the scale would weigh, six pounds and one ounce, from bag two six pounds and two ounces, from bag three, six pounds and three ounces."

"Very good, Cindy, but…" Fiona said and before she could continue Cindy cut in.

"You see, Doctor Stevens, I think this proves that things are not as easy as you think they are." Cindy stood up and walked to the door. "When you talk to my parents, I too will have something to add to my accusation that will put the matter beyond doubt." She walked out, leaving the door to close behind her.

There was something in Cindy's tone that caused Fiona enormous disquiet as she listened to the girl's retreating footsteps.

CHAPTER TWENTY-SIX

Saturday, 6th August

*I*t was half past seven in the morning when the ringing of the telephone shattered the silence of the house. Startled, Susan immediately thought of Grant. Had he had an accident? She picked up the receiver and muttered, "Hello? Yes, who is it?"

She was surprised to hear Grant's voice asking her to be ready to see him at eleven o' clock. Before she had time to ask why, the line went dead but there had been urgency in his voice so it had to be important. She showered and dressed before padding across the landing to Cindy's darkened bedroom. Pandora stirred as Susan placed a hand on her daughter's shoulder and gently shook her awake.

Cindy watched the bedroom door close and then got out of bed. After her shower, she sat in front of her dressing table mirror brushing her hair, the steady strokes calming her mind. Whatever her father wanted, she sensed it was going to be an ordeal.

At precisely eleven o'clock the front doorbell rang. Susan, who had been sitting in the conservatory watching the minutes go by, hurried to answer the door. When she saw that Grant was accompanied by Doctor Stevens she stood back and gave them both a curt nod to enter.

Cindy stood at the top of the stairs. Not for the first time she felt entirely alone. They were going to accuse her now; bring out some evidence to prove her father was innocent. They would try to show her up as a liar so that she, her father's victim, became the perpetrator of the crime. But I don't care, she thought, I still have right on my side.

By the time Cindy walked into the room Fiona had sat down. She watched carefully as Grant looked at his daughter.

Cindy threw her father a withering look. She had quickly assessed the atmosphere. She saw Fiona Stevens and a feeling of dislike swept over her, but she controlled it, realising that Fiona's presence was designed to throw her off balance. Ignoring Grant who had stood up to greet her, she forced her lips into an easy smile, and went across to Fiona.

"Hello," Cindy said ingenuously. They were all taken aback for this was not how the reception had been planned. "So, why are you here?" Cindy asked. There was no irritation in her voice. Her eyes were bright, open and clear, almost friendly. "You wanted to see us?" Cindy turned her head so her eyes met Grant's. There was a pause. Susan bit her lip and waited for the outburst she felt would come, but there was no aggression in Cindy's manner as she asked again, "Dad, what is it?" Cindy stood in front of him, her eyes not leaving his face.

Fiona could feel the surge of emotion that passed between them, but whether it was hatred or love she could not tell. What was evident was the change in Grant's attitude. From wanting revenge on Cindy he seemed now to almost want to comfort her. Fiona had not anticipated this response and was struck again by the complexity and strength of the relationship between them. Giving him a swift glance of warning, she gently shook her head, hoping he would stick to their plan. But to Fiona's dismay he spoke.

"Cindy!" he held his hands out in a gesture that begged for reconciliation. "I need to understand you."

Cindy looked at her father and thought, to think I loved

you and now you are grovelling before me. She pulled her mouth into a smile and replied, "Would you really?" With a faint sigh, she walked across to the chair opposite Fiona and sat down. "If you wanted us to be a family why did you want sex with me?"

Grant ran a hand over his hair in a gesture of despair. He had made one last stand and that had been thrown in his face. His manner changed, his tone became brusque as he said, "Right, if that's the way you want it, young lady, that's the way I'll deal it."

"Grant, can we get to the point? You've got us all wound up." Susan was tortured by Cindy's pain and Grant's sorrow. She was certain too that Cindy's outward show of indifference was a cover-up. Grant looked across at Fiona who nodded reassuringly before starting to talk directly to Cindy.

"You know Cindy, sometimes people find it difficult, balancing the truth against lies. Someone, like you, who is very creative, with extraordinary ability, may live in their own world, a dream world. This takes on a shadowy reality so that they are unable to separate the truth from the fantasy. Now," and she smiled, "I want to ask you a question."

Cindy sat back on the settee and listened as Fiona asked, "Describe how you think people see you."

Fiona saw Cindy give a start and knew she had been taken aback by the question. Cindy's brow furrowed in concentration. "I don't see the relevance of this question," she said and her voice indicated that she did not wish to pursue the subject.

"I am sorry," Fiona persisted, "but you must have some views."

"Well," Cindy sighed after a pause, "if you really want to know, men want to shag me and women want to kill me. Does that satisfy you?"

Fiona noticed the distress on Susan's face but went on. "And how do you see yourself?"

"As a victim and I shouldn't be that. I have a right to look this way."

"But you do nothing to play down your attraction."

"And why should I?"

There was a pause as Fiona gathered her thoughts. It was clear that Cindy was not going to alter her contradictory views regarding the attention she brought to herself. "You see, Cindy, your allegation regarding your father is, I believe, tied up in your physiological outlook."

"Load of rubbish," Cindy said and made to get up, but stopped when Susan asked her to stay. Fiona went on, "We are here to try and find out what you see as truth, because sometimes it appears that you exaggerate quite seriously. The truth has become confused with fantasy."

Cindy sat back. It was as she had suspected. They were making a case against her. What did she know about it – this so-called expert? She screwed her eyes up in an exaggerated play of attention and asked, "Why would I lie about him?"

"Cindy," Fiona continued quietly. "You lied about your father because you are possessive about him. In fact, Cindy, the basis of your accusation is jealousy of your mother and father's sexual relationship."

"Rubbish!" Cindy snapped angrily. "Why would I want to be with someone, who ..." she broke off and turned her face away.

Fiona's voice was firm. "All the attention during the last few months in this family has been on you and your relationship with your father. You have frozen everyone else out. Don't you see it is about you and him?"

Cindy sat impassively.

"Let me ask you a question. How do you feel about your mother's relationship with your father?" It was a question that Fiona knew merited a thoughtful answer, and Cindy did not respond immediately.

Finally she gave a half smile and said, "What am I expected to feel? They are my parents."

Susan shifted in her chair, obviously uncomfortable with Fiona's line of questioning.

"I would say," Fiona replied, "that there's one word to describe your feelings regarding that relationship, and that is envy." Fiona was sure that the girl was beginning to crack. For a moment she allowed her attention to stray as she considered how she would record this confrontation in her book. "You confuse fantasy with reality," she went on. "So, what is fantasy and what is reality; what are lies and what is truth? To you, the boundaries have become blurred." She met the mocking stare in Cindy's eyes but Fiona also saw that the girl's hands were clenched and the body language indicated that Cindy was on the defensive. "You accused your father of sexually interfering with you when you were younger, but this just isn't true."

Cindy did not reply. Instead she lowered her head so a curtain of hair covered her face as she started clicking her nails. Her head had started to ache. It had been real; it had happened. They were trying to confuse her, trying to make her believe she was mad. Mad like her grandmother. But her grandmother wasn't mad, she was just a sad old woman, driven mad by him. She bit her lip and tried to concentrate on what was going on, it was important.

Susan had leaned forward. "I'm confused. You will recall that the lady doctor examined Cindy."

"You were present at the time?"

"No I waited outside. Cindy was embarrassed. The doctor called me in, she told me ..."

"Exactly what did she tell you, Mrs Howard?"

Susan frowned. "Well, she said something to the effect that Cindy was not a virgin."

"Didn't you think that was an odd statement to make?"

"No. It was an answer to the question I asked."

"How did you imagine Cindy came to lose her virginity, Mrs Howard? You either have to believe her accusation or she had consented to have sex with someone, or that the results of the examination gave a false assumption …"

Susan sat staring ahead unable to answer.

"Don't you agree that the answer to that question is fundamental to the entire allegation?" Fiona persisted.

Reluctantly Susan nodded.

Fiona picked up her notes and leafed through them. "You made this statement, Mrs Howard. I quote: *Cindy isn't the sort of girl to go around having sex*. I am right? You did say that earlier on?"

Susan closed her eyes. Fiona Stevens was playing games with them, she knew that, but they were powerless to do anything but listen.

Fiona met Grant's eyes; she was finding it difficult to get the break she wanted. "So Cindy, how did you really lose your virginity?"

Cindy's eyes stared at Fiona as her mind flipped over unrelated incidents. It should have been him who was going through this barrage of questions, she was innocent. Susan watched, feeling the silence that Fiona was allowing to envelop them, a sticky, cloying silence that was generating a tension, an under-current. Susan shivered despite the heat, feeling that she was being drawn into a swirling vortex, whirling round with no end and no beginning. Her body felt heavy, her mind confused. She forced herself to look at Cindy, seeing the face white and drawn. What are we doing? Why have I allowed my daughter to suffer? Susan took a deep breath as she saw Grant staring at the carpet, small beads of sweat on his brow. Only Fiona remained calm, her eyes shadowy as they went from one to the other. She is in control and she is thriving on our misery, Susan thought. Fiona turned and Susan saw her nod to Grant, who quietly got up from his chair and left the room.

There was an uncomfortable silence until they heard the sound of voices in the hall. Instinctively all eyes slowly turned as the door pushed open and Grant returned. She paused, glancing across at Cindy and Susan knew instinctively this was evidence against her daughter.

I should stop this woman, Susan thought. She enjoys playing God. This isn't therapy; this is an inquisition.

"You remember John, don't you Cindy?" There was a glint of satisfaction in Fiona's eyes and she heard Cindy take a gulp of breath as through the open door came a thin, good-looking youth dressed in jeans and an American baseball top. Fiona watched the colour drain from Cindy's face and her expression went blank. She looked almost petrified. Susan could only watch, a feeling of nausea coming over her as she realised the enormous lengths Grant must have gone to, just to locate him.

John glanced across at Grant and then his eyes were on Cindy. He muttered that his father had told him to come. He sat down next to Cindy.

Cindy stared at him. Everyone saw the blankness leave her face to be replaced by angry patches of colour. She turned a look of pure hatred first on Fiona and then on her father. She almost spat the words out to John. "Why have you come?"

As John told them about Fiona's visit, Fiona was suddenly aware of the striking resemblance between Grant and John. They were both tall with thin features, the same facial contours and a similar attitude. As Fiona watched, she saw the shy smile that spread across John's face as he looked at Cindy. For a brief moment they seemed oblivious to the onlookers, and Fiona felt the emotion between them. She remembered suddenly how it had been for her when words had no importance and a look could say it all.

"Remember, Cindy," Fiona said, "when we had lunch at the pub, there was a moment that changed my whole concept of this situation. Can you remember what happened?"

"You bought me lunch, Doctor Stevens. We talked."

"We talked, Cindy, about the things you wanted to talk about. You manipulated the conversation so I could not ask the questions I wanted to ask, and then you went outside and I followed. The incident outside cast a different light on the whole scenario. You must remember what it was?"

Cindy looked at Fiona's face, seeing the sympathy there. She is a two-faced bitch, who thinks she knows it all. She is trying to corner me, trying to break me down. "I remember the incident with the baby," Cindy replied and regretted it immediately. She cursed herself for not concentrating, realising she had played into Fiona's hands.

"Exactly!" There was a naked note of triumph as Fiona went on. "More significant, from my point of view, was not that you wouldn't hold the baby but the look of revulsion that you gave the baby. It was mixed with what I felt was self-hatred. It was an expression I have seen before when I have spoken to mothers who have rejected their children."

"There is a point to this, I take it?" Susan cut in, seeing the distress on Cindy's face.

"Oh yes," Fiona replied, abruptly returning to look at Cindy. "So are you going to tell them Cindy, about the relationship you had with John?"

Cindy glanced at John and there was a faint undercurrent between them that was not lost on Fiona. Neither replied.

"At such a young age, John was an important and significant part of your life, wasn't he, Cindy? He is the key to what I think is a confusion that exists in your mind; a part of your life you have shared with no one. I am right, aren't I?" Fiona asked.

"I didn't rape Cindy if that's what you think." John was close to panic and he tried to get up from the settee but Cindy held him back.

Susan sat with a horrified expression on her face.

Fiona turned to John, "John, we are not here to judge you, or worry about what age she was when it happened." She softened her tone as she saw the look of confusion spread across his face. "I think Cindy must have enjoyed play-acting. Tell us about that. What did you play at?"

Susan saw Cindy's shoulder droop as she slowly shook her head from side to side. Was it an admittance of defeat? She couldn't tell, the scene had become unreal to her as she listened to John in disbelief.

"I guess it was all sorts of childish stuff!" John gave a laugh as he now felt on safer ground.

"What was the game Cindy liked to play?" Fiona prodded him along.

There was a pause and John sighed and gave a sideways glance towards Cindy.

"The game, John. What was Cindy's game?" There was an urgent quality in Fiona's voice and they turned towards her. She repeated. "John it is important, believe me – you must tell us so that everyone can understand." She saw him hovering between wanting to tell and reluctance to divulge a secret he and Cindy had shared.

He turned to Cindy but she was staring straight ahead. "It was stupid really – it was a game called ..." He stopped. "I can't – it's too stupid. It was just a game to do with you, Mr Howard. Cindy liked to think that I was you and I would come in to Cindy's bedroom and ..." John gave an embarrassed snigger.

"Go on, please John. It is very important for Cindy that you tell us all you know." Fiona gave him a reassuring smile. "The game, John, it became real and you had sex with Cindy, didn't you?" she pressed for firm answers.

John reluctantly nodded and started gnawing the side of his thumb. "She then asked me to make her a family for the doll's house her Dad had bought her years ago. I made a wooden man and a wooden woman, I did it all in carpentry – it was good. Then Cindy wanted something else ..."

"What else did she want?" Fiona asked.

"Something in the house to make it seem real."

"Explain what you mean," Fiona urged.

"She wanted a cradle so I made a small wooden cradle for the doll's house. It rocked back and forth. Cindy thought it was great." He paused. "I guess with me at a special school they'd have sent me away and Mum, when she was still around, didn't want that. She was great and saw to all the problems, no hassle – we broke the cradle then ..." He was crying now, the tears coursing down his cheeks.

"I don't understand." Susan glanced from one to the other. "This doesn't make sense. Cindy and John used to play mothers and fathers. That's it, I'm right aren't I?" She glared across at Fiona who nodded.

"Yes, you're right, of course, but it went a stage further, real mothers and fathers produce ..."

Susan stared at her. "You seem to be implying that there was a baby!"

"Yes."

Susan's face suddenly drained of colour. "Is it true?" she asked Cindy, who had lowered her eyes. Her body twitched and her hands started to fiddle with the edge of her shirt. "Cindy?" Susan got up out of her chair and walked across to her daughter. Kneeling down, she put her hand under her daughter's lowered chin and raised her head so their eyes were level. I don't know this girl, she thought, as she gazed into the beautiful eyes. So many emotions I cannot read, so much I do not know or even understand. I have failed as a wife and a mother. She brushed Cindy's hair back from the face, seeing in that brief moment the vulnerability, the fear. Susan walked back to her chair, her mind in turmoil as she said, "This has got out of hand. I can't believe we are sitting here, calmly discussing the fact that Cindy and John had a child. Did you know?" She looked wildly across at Grant.

He didn't reply.

"I'm afraid it is true," Fiona continued. "It was a game that had disastrous consequences." Fiona's voice was soft. "Yes, there was a baby, wasn't there, Cindy?"

Susan could only sit and stare at her daughter; her mind was numb as unanswered questions besieged her.

Cindy suddenly laughed, a thin childish laugh. "Mothers and fathers have babies, so I had one, but who was its father?" There was something in her manner that filled Fiona with a sense of foreboding, and involuntarily she shivered. I don't understand her, she is not mad, just disturbed, horribly disturbed.

"In 1990 you were pregnant – weren't you?" Fiona asked very softly, watching as Cindy dug into the top pocket of her shirt and produced the gold pencil. She held it between her fingers and as Susan started to speak, she placed it between her lips in a sensual gesture.

Fiona smiled encouragingly at Cindy. "You had a baby aborted?" she closed her eyes briefly. "Why in the name of God didn't you tell someone? Cindy, you were so young!" John put his arm comfortingly round her shoulders and muttered how his mother took over the details of the termination.

"My Mum arranged it all, paid for it too. She took Cindy one morning. My Dad didn't agree. They split up, my Mum and Dad. He took me away."

"Cindy how old were you?" Fiona asked.

Cindy stared at her, her eyes blank as she muttered, "Thirteen. I was thirteen."

"Thirteen and you'd had a full sexual relationship, the trauma of pregnancy, a termination and being left alone." Fiona turned to Susan. "I am sure as her mother you can realise the effect this has had. It can't be overestimated, the effect of facing this on her own. Immediately afterwards John, her lover, her only friend leaves. She loves her father, she is emulating the relationship between her father and mother – the sexual relationship – that is the crux of this accusation. Confusion exacerbates the trauma and she becomes seriously disturbed."

Fiona paused, wanting her words to have their full impact, feeling a sense of exhilaration as it all came so neatly together. Her original assessment of possessiveness and jealousy had been proved. She had seen the look of relief on Grant's face and the bewilderment on Susan's as they heard Cindy's accusation being torn apart piece by piece. Had she been too ruthless, lacking in compassion? Someone once said to her, "Your ambition over-rides your compassion." She dismissed the thought. "Cindy," she continued, "is hovering between promiscuity, fantasy and revulsion. It has culminated in this accusation. I believe Cindy wanted to wash herself clean of the abortion. Break up the family and finally have, in her own mind, Grant to herself," she paused.

"That is your conclusion?" Susan asked. "But why accuse Grant? You say she wants him for herself…"

"The mind, Mrs Howard, does not always reason. I think we have proved Grant's innocence, and the reason for Cindy lying. Of course, if she and John had used precautions then their precocious experiments would have been largely harmless."

This is like a third rate play, Susan thought, with the playwright, unable to think of a satisfactory ending, rushing blindly for closure, for resolution. Loose ends knotted hurriedly and delivered to the audience. Only I am the audience, Cindy is the package. Why do I feel this is so contrived? But there is no other answer, only the totally unacceptable one that Grant is guilty. She looked across at Cindy who seemed to be in an alarming, almost catatonic state;

her eyes closed, her face white. She wanted to go to her, but she felt too emotionally drained to do anything but sit and try to reason.

Then quite suddenly the silence was broken as Cindy gave a humourless laugh that made Fiona feel an inexplicable apprehension.

"Doctor Stevens, you know nothing! Why do you assume the baby was John's?" Cindy's voice was merely a whisper.

Susan felt the room suddenly start to spin round as she sat unable to comprehend the awfulness of what her daughter was saying. There was a silence, then she felt the coldness of the glass in her hand and heard Grant's voice as if from the end of a tunnel saying. "Here, drink this brandy, it'll help." Gratefully she took the glass and moistened her lips with the liquid. Slowly the room came into focus once more.

"Are you all right, Mrs Howard?"

"No, of course I am not all right!" She managed to snap the words out.

"I had to pretend I was pregnant by John to make it all right, didn't I?" Cindy was smiling now. "I couldn't have Dad's baby, or tell Mum, could I?" she stopped. There was a hush before she said. "It wasn't all dirty, nasty, touching with John. Not like it was with him."

"Cindy, there is no point in continuing with this. We have discussed it. We understand!" Grant croaked hoarsely. "How could you even think of saying I was the father? Oh my God!"

Cindy bit her lip and her fingers grabbed the pencil. She pointed to Grant, "Jealousy, that's what she's saying, that I was jealous. That I've done it all to be her." She pointed to Susan. "I murdered a defenceless creature." Her voice had risen and they watched as she controlled her outburst before turning her eyes on Fiona. "But it was my father's baby!"

There was a horrific silence as the implication of what Cindy said sunk in. Fiona blinked. She had not planned this change of direction. She was irritated that what had seemed a reasonable explanation was now opening up into another maze of unknown dimensions.

"It's all damned lies. Lies!" Grant shouted and pointed a finger at Cindy. "You're ill. You need help."

"It was my baby, Cindy, it had to be." There was despair in John's voice.

"Cindy," Fiona's voice was the calm in the storm, "you are confused." Fiona was determined now to retrieve control of the situation. "Cindy, your father did nothing to you. It was imagination, possessive imagination."

Fiona waited for the denial and had anticipated it would now end with Cindy in tears; Cindy saying she was sorry but there was an awkward pause with nothing being said.

"Daddy, tell them why you stopped?" Cindy now shot the question at Grant who bridled in surprise. "Tell them, Dad. Tell them why you could no longer do it?" Her voice sounded like a hypnotic whisper and Fiona suddenly found herself gripping the arm of her chair as they waited fearfully, the scene seemed frozen in time. They were set like characters in a charade, but Cindy saw only her father.

"Tell them Dad!" she repeated but Grant could only stare at her. Then, as the silence deepened and the tension mounted, there was a change, an imperceptible change in the atmosphere, a subtle change that Fiona picked up on.

"Tell them." Cindy's voice had a sing-song quality as her eyes bore into Grant's.

Realising Grant was not going to say anything, Cindy turned and met the querying look in Fiona's eyes. "You've never asked me one, very obvious, question." There was a hint of victory now in Cindy's tone.

"And that is?" Fiona said.

"Why did my father stop having sex with me?" Cindy glanced at Grant and then back to Fiona. "You see, I know something that I couldn't possibly know unless my story is true." The words hung in the air for a moment as they all stared at her.

Cindy turned towards Grant. "You tell them, Daddy."

"Why don't you tell us Cindy?" Fiona said.

"Shall I tell them Daddy, about our little secret?"

"I don't know what new lies you have, Cindy; whatever you say is a lie." Grant looked for support from Fiona, but her eyes were on Cindy now.

"For God's sake, Cindy what is it?" Susan said in desperation, seeing the fraught look in Cindy's eyes.

"Oh, you must know, Mum." Her voice broke as she looked from Grant to Susan. "He could no longer do it. Someone heard my prayers. He became impotent."

After an initial gasp of horror there was a deathly silence and then Fiona looked directly at Susan. She knew from the expression on her face that Cindy's revelation was true. Grant had lowered his head into his hands, his shoulders shaking with sobs.

Fiona sat with disbelief written all over her face. She had thought she had correctly analysed the situation, listened to both sides fairly, but still she had come to the wrong conclusion. Grant was guilty.

CHAPTER TWENTY-SEVEN

Seven years later: January, 2001

*C*indy came out of the downstairs room that acted as her art studio and yawned before rubbing her hands on her old paint-stained jeans. Flicking a loose strand of blonde hair from her eyes she crossed the passageway into the small sitting room and switched on the light. Glancing round the sparsely furnished room she smiled, acknowledging that it was slowly taking on the feeling of home. The cottage had stood empty for some time before she had bought it, late the previous year. But its remoteness from the nearby village and the spectacular views of Coniston Water had outweighed the disadvantage of its near dereliction. Obtaining a mortgage had not proved easy and she had eventually succeeded by stretching her meagre finances to the absolute limit.

But if getting the cottage hospitable was an uphill struggle, Cindy had been surprised at the warmth and generosity of the villagers, who had welcomed her into their community. Despite her wish for isolation she had been glad of their help and support. They had not intruded into her life as she had originally feared they might, but had been there when required, the women soon realising that she posed no threat, that she was quiet, unassuming, private and always polite. As time passed she had felt more at ease within the community and started to integrate and form tentative acquaintances. She did not make friends, for friends had to know you, and no one here knew the real Cindy.

Cindy's sitting room was an odd blend of mis-matched furniture, bought from garage or jumble sales. She had spent many an evening cleaning and painting the cottage, even turning her hand to restoring a few items of furniture. Now it all now blended in with the white walls, oak beams and the stone built fireplace with its crackling log fire. There was also the familiar and reassuring figure of Pandora who, in the autumn of her life, always waited patiently on the living room window ledge for Cindy to come home every evening from work.

The living room always gave her a sense of belonging, the uterus warmth cocooning her from a still harsh outside world. She glanced at the small clock that rested on the thick railway sleeper of wood that had been put over the fireplace to serve as a large mantelpiece. It was early evening, time she made herself a meal, nothing like the Sunday dinners of the past, but a simple vegetarian dish prepared in the galley kitchen that had recently been gutted and modernised.

This Saturday and Sunday was her monthly weekend off, a time she always set aside for herself; a time when she would divide the hours between her artwork and the more mundane task of completing the decorating of the two cottage bedrooms. And walking. Cindy now took long, soul-searching walks on her own through the hills and farmland adjacent to her property. She always returned to the cottage feeling rejuvenated.

The cottage had become an important and integral part of her existence. Years of studying and living in halls of residence or in cheap and cheerful accommodation had made her value privacy and peace. The small front room had been set aside as her studio. It was a tidy clutter of sketches and paintings as she compiled material for her first autumn exhibition. Her artwork was both relaxing and rewarding. Today, she had worked solidly on the commissioned portrait of a cat, taking only a short break for lunch, which consisted of a cup of black coffee and a cigarette. She glanced down and smiled, hearing the plaintiff meow and then scooped to pick up the small black and white kitten that had made its home with her and Pandora, along with a tortoise-shell cat called Tiffany.

"Come on, Oscar, you're all right." She gave the cat a small kiss on the face and heard the comforting purring as she cradled it against her chest.

The villagers knew Cindy's soft spot was cats, but the observation was an affectionate one. Not only was she known to take in any stray cat, she sketched it to advertise it's whereabouts or find it a new home. She was also extremely well thought of as one of the female veterinary surgeons working at the prestigious practice on the outskirts of Keswick.

Now as she stared again at the clock her eyes rested for a moment on the long white envelope with the distinctive handwriting of her mother. She had read the letter eight days ago and had propped the envelope up next to the clock until she decided what to do. It needed to be answered, she knew that, and the dilemma it posed lay heavily on her mind and deeper in her conscience. She gave a grimace as she placed Oscar down on one of the chairs. Then she dug into the top pocket of her denim shirt and produced a packet of cigarettes and, after lighting one, blew a thin curtain of smoke into the air, her eyes still on the envelope.

What had happened to that young girl with the long fair hair who frequently played hide and seek with her fear? That vulnerable Cindy now resided in a lead coffin, in a deep grave of memory. The images and voices still lurked in the recesses of her mind but would now only come occasionally to haunt her. She walked across to the sitting room window and looked out, seeing the mountains shrouded in mist, denoting the start of the year. It was, she always thought, the most beautiful time in the Lake District. The tourists had gone and the peace and tranquillity had returned.

Cindy had become used to living in solitude with just cats for company, her paintings for solace of the spirit and her veterinary work for her continued love of animals. But it had been far from easy. Her carefully crafted re-creation was in the early years difficult to master, and she could still remember her resentment as Doctor Fiona Stevens had crashed back into her life, deliberately goading her out of the constraints of the prison she had made of self-doubt and misery.

Cindy gave a grim smile, remembering the beautiful, impeccably dressed young woman who had allowed her father to use her so she became a person of utter worthlessness in her own eyes. It had been a hard and desperate struggle; a balancing act between the depths of depression that could have engulfed her and a need to survive. But she had survived, so the end had turned into a new beginning. Cindy could still recall the disbelief and anguish on her mother's face. The accusation had hurt their relationship although she had been thankful that Susan had initially listened to her and that had been the first important step to rebuilding her life.

Grant had seen Susan's repugnance as she had moved away from his touch. Seen the incredulity turn to horror in Fiona's eyes.

Cindy had felt alone and vulnerable as he had stood in front of her, his eyes behind his spectacles emotionless, resembling skull-like holes in his head. His hands had moved slowly in a dry washing motion, reminding Cindy of Olive. In that instant she had grown older, her childish dreams had evaporated as she realised that she didn't really know this man who called himself her father. Even now she would ask herself numerous questions that remained unanswered. Cindy wished she knew more of his early life with his mother. Perhaps he too had demons in the night. We should have all talked to each other by being honest. He should and could have helped me understand. But more importantly he should have just said sorry.

On that terrible day she had stood before him, her whole body trembling; her hands clenched as she met his eyes and waited for an apology that never came. Instead he seemed almost arrogant as he stared into her eyes. Grant left the house and the family, with no sorrowful goodbye, no words of remorse just a slamming of the front door. It was, Cindy thought, as if he felt he had done nothing wrong, as if he was incapable of understanding the gravity of his act.

Susan had been devastated. There seemed to be no basis on which she and Grant could build any type of future. Susan had not wished to talk about it, saying only. "We must put it all behind us."

But Cindy found it desperately hard and often saw Susan looking at her in an accusing manner. They had suffered the curious glances from the neighbours and veiled, inquisitive questions from friends.

After three months Grant had asked for a separation. "How will we live?" Susan had whispered and there had been fear of the unknown in her eyes.

So the house, they had lived in since 1979 and so heavily mortgaged had been sold. The car, that red Escort that had arrived an hour too late, had gone. Their life had crumbled away. The parties, Grant's laughter and fun all now forgotten. On the day of the move, Cindy had stood in her bedroom with tears running down her cheeks at what she had lost. She wished, not for the first time, that the clock could be put back.

She and Susan had packed what they could and stored the rest. What affected Cindy the most was her mother's resignation from the golf club and the weekend she put her treasured golf clubs up for sale. Susan simply didn't deserve that humiliation.

Grant had returned when the house was empty to take his clothes, his books and belongings. But he had moved into a top floor apartment in a prestigious development. He had retained the white Jaguar, and seemed to be totally unaffected by the change in his circumstances.

Susan often said there was not much justice in the world and Cindy could only agree, for they had both become the victims.

"What happened?" Elizabeth had asked curiously.

"Life happened," Cindy had retorted as she walked out of their friendship and moved with her mother into Emma's cramped house with Pandora, who did not take kindly to the change.

Cindy could not fault her mother's behaviour. She had sacrificed her marriage, but in an odd sort of way Cindy felt that Susan resented her, almost blamed her. Perhaps she felt degraded that her husband had gone to their daughter for sex. "As if I couldn't give him what he needed," Cindy had once heard Susan whisper to Emma.

Cindy had taken full time work in the cat sanctuary. Her hair was pulled back and her fingernails gradually lost their luscious length and style. She no longer wished to go to university. That was a dream that would remain unfulfilled. Her life was bleak. She had stopped going to Mass. With no direction in her barren life she became withdrawn and, apart from her work, almost reclusive.

Cindy had thought about her sin, even about ending her life as she had her baby's. It was a treadmill of existence and there was no light at the end of this mythical tunnel, and if there was it turned out to be coming from the wrong direction.

Cindy had been working full time at the cat sanctuary for four months and still found a sense of comfort with the animals. If Pam knew there was something wrong she did not enquire until one afternoon she saw Cindy looking at the cats' cages with a plaintive expression etched on her face.

"You don't sketch them any more?" she said and Cindy shrugged her shoulders. It was then Pam realised how drawn and thin Cindy had become and her nails, once her pride and joy, were cut and filed short.

"Come on, tell me what's happened?" Pam asked and guided her to the deserted office, where Cindy blurted out a half-truth about the termination, but nothing about her father. If Pam thought there was more she didn't enquire, merely nodding in a reassuring manner.

For Cindy the irony, or perhaps her saving grace, came on an innocuous Monday afternoon. Looking back on it now she realised it may have been a guiding hand that had made her decide to go into town for no specific purpose except she did not want to return to the cramped living conditions they all shared with Emma. She had changed into her jeans and trainers, and taken the bus to the terminus. Once she had enjoyed walking round, spending the money that fell into her hand from her father's wallet.

She walked aimlessly along the under cover shopping area, dodging the prams and colliding with the occasional person. Cindy noticed a smartly dressed woman walking towards her and then looked a second time. Suddenly realisation dawned, but before she had a chance to make herself inconspicuous she had been recognised.

"You!" Cindy said involuntarily.

"Yes, me!" Fiona swiftly took in Cindy's drooping shoulders, the bleak face, sad eyes and the mocking curve on the lips.

Cindy's eyes held a flicker of envy and for the first time in her life she felt disadvantaged by her own appearance, for Fiona was smartly dressed and well groomed. They hovered, each remembering their last encounter, each unsure whether to walk on and dismiss the meeting as merely a blast from the past. It was impulse that made Fiona say. "Come and have a coffee with me."

"You must be joking!" Cindy said abruptly and turned to walk away. She felt a swift and sudden wish to cry. A wish to have someone hold her; someone who knew her; someone who, more importantly, would listen to her rambling thoughts. For questions still raged inside her mind. Why did he feel the desire to have sex with me? What fantasy turned him on? Was it the thrill of my young body? She slowed her pace and half turned.

Fiona watched her, wondering where the beautiful eye-catching young girl had gone. She blamed herself. I should have listened and not been so judgmental. I should have seen beneath the attraction of her face to the hurt she had undoubtedly suffered. It could have been so different. She had rewritten the part of her book that Cindy had seemed to fit so neatly into. Yes, she too had learned a lesson, albeit not as hard as Cindy's.

They had gone out of her life, Susan, Grant and Cindy. Except the memory of Cindy nudged constantly at her conscience. Their case was closed and resolved, placed now at the back of a filing cabinet in a yellow envelope and marked simply C & G.

The after effects of the case had lingered and came back to haunt her one afternoon when she was looking through her bookcase. As she pulled a book out for reference a rolled up piece of paper fell to the ground. Picking it up she slid the rubber band off and a memory unfurled before her eyes. It was Cindy's sketch and she looked at the words *In the Palm of Your Hand*. It was then she had wished she had eased her guilt by seeing Cindy, but too much time had passed.

Now Fiona bit her lip and then started to walk after Cindy,

conscious that she was increasing her pace as Cindy was dropping hers. Then Cindy stopped and half turned and Fiona saw the veiled misery in her eyes.

"Cindy, please, let's have a coffee!" She placed her hand lightly on Cindy's arm. There was an appeal in Fiona's voice and Cindy shrugged and managed a slight nod. She felt she had nothing left to lose by seeing her.

They sat across the table of the *Olde Tea Shoppe* each with a cappuccino before them, talking in stilted tones, uneasily bogged down with memories. The house, Fiona learned, had been sold and Cindy had moved in with Susan to live with Emma. Instinctively Fiona knew Cindy was finding it claustrophobic.

"You didn't go to university?"

"No, Doctor Stevens, I didn't."

Fiona watched as Cindy dug into the pocket of her anorak and produced a packet of cigarettes and as she held the match Fiona saw her hand was shaking.

"You smoke?" It seemed a stupid, unnecessary comment that produced a glimmer of long forgotten amusement in Cindy's eyes as she said.

"Obviously!"

"Cindy," she paused before saying, "I was mistaken. I owe you an apology. I really am so very sorry." She saw the flicker in Cindy's eyes and a faint relaxing in her body language. "Cindy, please let me help you."

"I think you have helped me enough already." There was unexpected mockery in the tone.

"I do understand your bitterness."

"Do you really?" Cindy tried to make her voice sound hard and disinterested but there was a faint catch in the words and Fiona saw the tears come into her eyes as she turned away.

"Cindy, I too need …" Fiona stopped and there was a pause before she heard Cindy whisper.

"To make reparation?"

"Yes," Fiona said seizing on the word. "I feel guilty ... but most of all I want to help ..."

"Me or yourself?" Cindy asked, her voice low.

"You are right, of course. I want to help both of us," Fiona replied and saw Cindy purse her lips.

"Did you write your book Doctor?"

"No, I re-wrote my book," Fiona said quietly.

"I'm sure we all did," Cindy said and then paused before adding, "You shouldn't give up as a counsellor," she lowered her eyes. "You're good at it."

"I got it wrong."

"Maybe next time you'll get it right." They talked in a desultory manner, each wary of saying too much, neither fully at ease with the situation.

"I must go," Fiona said as she glanced at her watch. "I have a meeting this evening. Look, if you ever want to talk ..." She opened her bag and retrieved her business card. "Call me!"

CHAPTER TWENTY-EIGHT

On the journey home, after her unexpected meeting with Fiona, Cindy saw the full-page notice in a magazine she had bought for herself, advertising an exhibition of cat paintings in a small London gallery. Suddenly she felt the need to have a break and decided the exhibition would be a good reason to spend her forthcoming day off in London. Although she had passed her driving test, Cindy elected to travel by train. The exhibition had proved interesting but tiring and now, after an exhausting day, she finally boarded the home-bound train at Euston station.

The train was full and Cindy made her way from one carriage to another, her long raincoat flapping as she passed chattering and screaming children, young men who winked and old men who leered until she finally reached a suitable seat. She sat back remembering the time the family had all travelled first class and lunched at Harrods. Accepting the reality of her life she knew the journey would be crowded and uncomfortable and Cindy shuddered as she looked out of the dirty window for she still hated public transport. As the train bustled forward, Cindy opened her bag and took out a packet of cigarettes and a box of matches. She held the cigarette in her hand and then, giving an involuntary shudder, she placed the cigarette between her lips. Inhaling deeply, Cindy looked out of the window as the train entered a tunnel and saw the gaunt features, unsmiling mouth and lack-lustre hair of her own reflection in the darkened window. But try as she might, Cindy could not disguise the fact that even without make-up the remnants of her natural beauty were still visible.

It had been a long time since Cindy had smiled, even longer since she had really laughed. Life moved out of one day and into the next without joy and without hope. She closed her eyes as the smoke curled like an ethereal mist from her nostrils.

A young man came to sit across the aisle from her. Cindy briefly met his eyes and feared that he would try to engage her in chit chat. She braced herself for banal conversation but, much to her relief, he said nothing. Instead he opened his briefcase and took out a copy of The *Daily Telegraph*. Watching him flicking through the pages reminded her of watching her father reading the paper at breakfast.

There was a sudden jolt as the train pulled into a station. Cindy peered through the window at the crowded platform and, when the doors slid open, the carriage seemed to be invaded by seat grabbing passengers. A worried looking man who was trying to guide a pretty, fair-haired girl down the narrow aisle caught her attention. Cindy saw the flash of impatience and the furrow of his brow as the little girl started to chatter with excitement.

"Come on, sweetie," the man urged the girl. Seeing the two empty seats in front of Cindy he smiled, and she knew they would sit down opposite her.

"Here, you can get in by the window," The man guided the girl to sit opposite Cindy. Then he too sat down and smiled across at Cindy. He placed a large plastic carrier bag down on the table in front of the girl and reached across to kiss her head. Surreptitiously Cindy observed him. He was ordinary looking, with a brown tweed sports jacket, a green shirt and a green tie. She saw his eyes turn and watch the young girl as she sat, nose pressed against the windowpane. He had a faint smile on his lips. The child turned and smiled at Cindy. She had deep blue eyes and a pert prettiness. Cindy reckoned she was about seven years old. Cindy managed a faint acknowledgement of the child's smile, which disappeared when the man leaned forward and placed his arm round her shoulders, giving her a quick hug.

"Don't Daddy," the voice was plaintive as she pushed him away. She rummaged inside the carrier bag, finally bringing out a packet of crisps.

The man took the crisp packet and opened it. "Can Daddy have one?" he asked, as he held the packet in his hand.

The child hesitated then murmured, "Oh go on!"

He dipped his fingers into the packet and produced a crisp, which he bit into. Then he held the other half out to the girl. She snatched it from his fingers with her mouth.

"You'll take my fingers off," he laughed as his eyes caught Cindy looking at him.

"We've been to visit Grandma!" he said, looking at Cindy as if waiting for a reply.

She nodded and murmured, "How nice." But her eyes were on the child, who was now busy devouring the packet of crisps.

The man glanced at his watch. "It's getting late. Almost past your bedtime." He turned and hugged the child and then kissed her hair again. "You're Daddy's girl, aren't you sweetheart?" He stroked the top of her head in a gesture that reminded Cindy of someone stroking a cat. Watching them made her feel uneasy and instinctively her hand went to the cigarette packet as the man continued. "It's been a long day for her."

The girl produced a *Milky Bar* from the carrier bag and handed it to him. "Peel it, Daddy." The child smiled up into his face as he took the chocolate bar and pulled the wrapping off it.

"Don't make crumbs!" He dug into the top pocket of his

jacket and produced a pale blue handkerchief. "Wipe your hands on this." He handed it to her and watched as the small mouth closed over the chocolate bar and sharp white teeth sank into it. Cindy noticed the girl's red tongue lick her lips and then her fingers.

"Well, that's all gone!" he whispered.

The girl giggled and looked up into his face as he took the handkerchief, spat on it and slowly wiped round her chocolate-covered lips and then her fingers. "There, that'll do until we get you in the bath!" He replaced the handkerchief in his top pocket and then put his arm round the child's shoulders. The girl laughed and snuggled into his chest and he kissed her hair once more.

Why do I feel a sense of disquiet, Cindy wondered as she continued to watch them from beneath lowered eyelids. Is this how it was with Grant? Did he always want to touch and paw me? Was this the way a father's illicit love for his daughter started, by innocent affection? She drew heavily on her cigarette. The man was whispering in the child's ear and Cindy closed her eyes as memories started to play through her mind. I don't really need this, she thought and felt the tears behind her eyes.

Her ordeal wasn't over; she knew that. The memories she had tried to ignore could still return and she would again be filled with self-doubt, hatred, and a longing to understand the situation. I need someone there for me. Not my mother, but somebody who would listen and advise. She gave a slight sniff and opened her eyes. Conscious that they were tear-filled she made a pretence of wafting away the smoke from her cigarette. But the man had closed his eyes.

"I've been away with my Daddy," the little girl told Cindy. "Have you got a Daddy?" she went on.

Cindy stared at the child. Seeing the innocence she gave a faint nod and reached into her bag for another packet of cigarettes. Rummaging inside she felt her fingers touch a small white card. She withdrew it and frowned as she read the embossed name of Doctor Fiona Stevens. She was about to tear it in half and place it in the ashtray but then she looked again at the young girl and her father who were whispering and giggling. With a decisive gesture she replaced the card in her bag.

Cindy knew it had been the encounter with the child on the train that had made her decide she needed someone to talk to. She could not go on pretending that the situation regarding her father and family had not happened, and reluctantly accepted that Doctor Fiona Stevens's offer to meet her had merit. Cindy had little time for Doctor Stevens, who she blamed completely for the break up of her family, but she had come to understand that she would not rest until she had had the opportunity of airing her grievances with the Doctor.

The following evening Cindy slipped out of the house after supper and walked to the local telephone box. She felt the sweat on her hands and the sudden beating of her heart as she punched in the number and waited. Finally Fiona answered the call. Her voice was warm and welcoming and they agreed to meet in two days time, with Cindy going over to Fiona's for coffee.

As Cindy walked back to Emma's house she had second thoughts and decided that meeting Fiona would achieve nothing. She was tempted to go back to the phone box and cancel the appointment, but she didn't because she had so many questions in her mind and Doctor Stevens was one of the few people capable of answering them.

The following two days passed slowly and, on two separate occasions when the house was empty, Cindy attempted to call Fiona and put off the meeting. But each time she hung up before the call was answered. Why, she wondered, was she so reluctant to meet Fiona? Was it that she was afraid to be told that she had been responsible for the break up of her comfortable home? That, she Cindy, had wrecked the family single handily. What would Fiona's reaction be? Sympathetic or accusing?

For the first time since the accusation, Cindy wanted to revert to the beautiful young woman she had been. She wanted to appear in control of the situation even though inside she was in a thousand pieces. She chose her outfit with particular care, discarding the usual jeans and T-shirt for a more stylish pair of well-fitting black slacks, high heels, a silk shirt and patterned waistcoat. She washed, dried and brushed her hair and applied her make-up thoughtfully. As she glanced into the mirror in Emma's dimly lit bathroom she felt a sense of security behind her armour of glamour.

"You're meeting someone?" Susan asked and Cindy saw the weariness and depression in her mother's eyes and knew that her menial job at the local supermarket was taking its toll.

"A friend. I won't be late." Cindy said. She had no desire to tell Susan where she was really going, suspecting that her mother would not take kindly to her daughter spending an evening with the woman who had helped to destroy her life.

Fiona lived in the more fashionable part of the next town. The bus took twenty minutes to get there. Now, clutching the piece of paper with Fiona's address on it, Cindy walked along the tree-lined avenue of residential houses. It was a good, middle class area and Cindy felt a stirring of resentment as she stopped at the five-bar wooden gate of the house she sought. Cindy felt strangely nervous as she pressed the doorbell. Fiona quickly opened the door and welcomed Cindy with a warm smile. Fiona was dressed casually in denim jeans and a matching denim shirt, her hair was loosely tied back and she wore little make-up. Cindy followed her down the small hallway and into a spacious sitting room. She noted the comfortable chairs, log fire, expensive paintings, a large bookcase and the general ambience of well-being. It reminded her of the life she had once had at *Henderland*.

After removing her jacket, Cindy sat down and nervously rubbed her hands together while Fiona went to the kitchen and reappeared with a laden tray, which she placed on the long table in front of the fire.

"Please, help yourself," Fiona invited as she turned the handle of a coffee jug towards Cindy. Then she handed Cindy a glass ashtray.

"You don't mind if I smoke?" Cindy asked, knowing how much Emma disliked the smell of smoke in her house.

Fiona gently shook her head.

There was a pause as Cindy poured herself a cup of black coffee and lit a cigarette. She felt uneasy and then Fiona asked, "Why did you decide to telephone me?"

Swiftly Cindy told her, in a voice braced with concealed irritation, about the incident on the train. She told Fiona how the father had fussed and pawed his daughter and Fiona saw disgust on Cindy's face. The tenseness of her hands and the quick nervous puffs she took as she lit her second cigarette indicated that Cindy was far from relaxed.

"I don't think you can say every father would be like yours," Fiona admonished as Cindy went on with a diatribe of how perverted men are towards young women.

"I know what all men want." Cindy shivered and Fiona knew the scars inflicted by Grant lay very deep. She realised the wounds would never heal but could Cindy learn to live with them? Not on the evidence so far. But the more Fiona listened, the more she realised that here was someone in desperate need of proper and sympathetic counselling; someone Fiona had walked away from without giving any consideration to how Cindy would deal with the situation. It was another reminder that her handling of the family's trauma had been nothing short of negligent. As Cindy talked, Fiona got the impression that she had lost interest in herself, and almost in living. Fiona wondered whether Cindy had the characteristics that would make her likely to commit suicide. She certainly hated herself enough, and yes, Fiona sensed, it could certainly be a possibility. There was no animation in Cindy's face and although she had obviously taken trouble with her appearance, the zest of youth had been firmly extinguished. Fiona dared not think of the consequences if Cindy opted out of her life and their casual meeting took on greater importance. Fiona was determined to help the sad and lonely girl who sat before her.

But Cindy wanted to blame everyone for her predicament and took verbal swipes at her mother and grandmother for not listening to her initially. "And you, Doctor Stevens, did you enjoy playing Miss Marple?" The challenge in Cindy's voice was not lost on Fiona but before she could answer Cindy had added, "*Doctor* Stevens, why didn't you believe me?" Cindy's eyes were hostile as she inhaled deeply on her cigarette.

Fiona heard the biting words and knew Cindy was hoping she would rise to a confrontation. Instead she met the mounting hostility with an understanding smile. The question, after all, was not unexpected. Indeed, Fiona had asked herself why she had doubted Cindy's recollection of events and had to admit she had no logical answer. Now she sighed and held her hands up, saying with a note of contrition. "I have to confess that I found it incomprehensible that any man would come for help knowing he was guilty. It seemed an enormous gamble."

"He called your bluff and you fell for it," Cindy said with contempt.

Fiona nodded. "But I also think you opened your memory box not fully realising the impact it would have on you and your family. Am I right?"

Cindy bent her head low, refusing to meet Fiona's eyes. With a voice cracking with emotion she told Fiona that all she wanted from her father was a sincere apology, not the stupid game of cat and mouse that ensued. "I felt he was playing with my emotions, that he had no regard for me whatsoever." She looked up and there were tears in her eyes. "I would have attended therapy, we could have talked. We all needed help but all we got was an inquisition about who was telling the truth."

Fiona felt an overwhelming sense of pity for Cindy and could only nod her head in silent agreement. She had thought about the dilemma many times, but Grant had been her client and the problem he presented to her was the one she had had to work with. She ended up by saying, "If you had come to me Cindy I would have believed you. I would have helped you."

"At a price!" Cindy retorted and the statement left Fiona speechless. "I don't have much time for these privately run organisations," Cindy went on with a dismissive sniff as she glanced round the comfortable surroundings. "But I can see it obviously pays well."

Fiona allowed the remark to pass. There was a pause and Cindy felt the visit had been pointless. Fiona saw the frustration on her face and, desperate to keep the girl talking, asked what she intended doing with her life.

"I don't know." The answer was abrupt.

"What about your art?" Fiona pressed and Cindy said that she had lost interest in putting pen to paper. She then went on to condemn Fiona for going behind her back to locate James.

Fiona, resentful of the constant criticism of her counselling skills, snapped, "What did you want to happen Cindy?" Cindy was clearly stumped for an answer so she went on, "You said your father abused you as a child. That has now been proved. What more do you want?" The question clearly shook Cindy and slowly her composure deserted her as realisation dawned that there was nothing further that could be done or said. She lowered her head into her hands, sobbing. Between body-racking gulps for air she muttered that she wished the clock could be turned back.

"Oh Cindy," Fiona whispered as she put her coffee cup on the table and walked across to sit on the arm of Cindy's chair. She placed her hand on the girls shoulder and instinctively hugged her, feeling the thinness of the body and an intense sympathy for her. Cindy repeated that it was all her fault and she wished she had just left well alone. Her mother had been reduced to ridicule in front of her friends, they had very little money, and the only person who had come out of this unscathed was her father.

"I don't think he has come away completely unscathed," Fiona said.

Cindy viciously wrenched herself free of Fiona's arm and shouted, "Stop arguing his corner!"

Fiona's body shook with the depth of bitterness in Cindy's tone and she sank slowly back into her own chair, not knowing what to say to help Cindy.

Cindy stood by the window and cursed herself for losing control. It had achieved nothing and her vocal cords were sore from the force of the outburst.

Fiona waited until she felt Cindy had calmed down and then said, "If you want justice, then you can press charges. I will back you up, if that's what you decide to do."

Cindy turned from the window shaking her head. "No. I can't go through all that again."

"Then Cindy, you really have to get on with your life or you will be a victim forever."

Cindy had returned from that meeting realising just how much the whole episode had affected her, both mentally and physically. She had never fully admitted that to herself until now. The horror of the termination, a sin the church described as murder, had had a terrible effect on her, denying her even the comfort of the church. She had been unable to even make a confession and felt abandoned by God.

She settled back on the hard single bed in the small bedroom in Emma's house, looking out through the open windows. She could feel Pandora nestling at her feet but her mind would not be stilled. She knew she would find no peace until she had unburdened herself. Fiona's offer of help seemed tempting.

"It would not be counselling," Fiona had assured her before she had left that evening. "Just talking and perhaps, who knows, we might even become friends. It's up to you now, Cindy. Your future is in your own hands." She had murmured her thanks and heard Fiona reply. "I think perhaps you could drop the Doctor and call me Fiona."

Fiona was rewarded by the faint glimmer of a smile in Cindy's eyes.

So the weekly visits to Fiona's house began. They shared confidences, ate suppers together and laughed over their dreams as Fiona slowly, and with a great deal of patience and skill, peeled the layers of hurt and doubt away from Cindy's personality. Finally they arrived at the stage where they were able to discuss rationally the impact Cindy's accusation had had on the family and herself. From these meetings Fiona learned of the significance of the gold pencil and the song Cindy kept on playing.

"They were from the day I had the termination." Cindy refused to use the word abortion and her eyes became distant with unwanted memories. "The song was playing on the radio when I got dressed in my bedroom that morning, supposedly for school. The pencil belonged to the doctor who came to initially examine me. He accidentally left it on the bedside cabinet."

It had taken a great deal of persuasion on Fiona's part to get

Cindy to place the pencil and the CD out of sight. It was essential that, during the early stages of her rehabilitation, she was free from those constant reminders. It worked, for Cindy no longer used the pencil and never played the song. The pencil and CD now resided in an old shoe box, along with the gold ring that had once been Susan's and the infamous bed sheet. Curiously, she also stopped eating *Toblerone* chocolate.

Gradually Fiona saw Cindy learning to relax. Slowly the long lost animation was starting to return. Not as before, but the dullness of her face and eyes was being replaced by amusement and tolerance. Fiona had always found Cindy very intuitive, but now she could add *intelligent, with a strong point of view, and an amusing companion* to her description of the younger woman. They found they were enjoying each other's company and the bonds of an easy and trusting friendship started to form between them. Occasionally Fiona would call unexpectedly into the cat sanctuary to take Cindy out for a lunchtime snack. It was during one of the lunches that Fiona, seeing Cindy still looking tired, pale and drawn, steered her into making a huge change in her life.

"You can't shovel cat shit forever."

Cindy stared in astonishment at Fiona who waited, unsure how Cindy would react. She was surprised when she threw her head back and laughed. "Very descriptive, doctor!" she replied mockingly and then shrugged her shoulders dismissively.

"I mean it," Fiona replied, resisting the urge to get up and shake some motivation into her, knowing Cindy was allowing things to drift purposelessly.

Cindy finished her lunch of a baked potato with a cheese filling and sat back to light a cigarette. Fiona saw the frown on her forehead and knew Cindy had taken her words to heart. Cautiously, and without making it seem she had given the idea any degree of thought, she casually inferred that she had friends who were veterinary surgeons. She extolled some of the attributes of working in veterinary medicine, adding that it would give Cindy stability, a means of earning a reasonable living, and something to keep her in contact with animals. Finally she suggested that perhaps Cindy would like to meet her friends and look over their practice.

Cindy laughed, then nodded and said she'd think it over. But Fiona had sown the seed, and later that afternoon as Cindy cleared out one of the cats' cages in the sanctuary she found herself thinking seriously about Fiona's suggestion. She even asked Pam about training to be a vet and took up her suggestion that she talk to the vet who visited the sanctuary.

But it was Fiona who, not wanting to let the matter rest, pressed ahead with the proposed visit to her friends' veterinary practice. Initially Cindy was quiet and withdrawn as Fiona introduced her to Mark and his wife, Jane, who ran a thriving practice on the outskirts of town. Dressed in Wellington boots and green overalls, Cindy went out to the farms with Mark in the morning and in the afternoon stayed with Jane, seeing small animals in the surgery. It had been the appearance of a badly hurt black and white cat that had set Cindy's mind into overdrive. Knocked down by a car, it had dragged itself back to its owner, who now stood tearfully by the table. The cat was in pain and not friendly and Jane was wary of the claws. But Cindy bent down and whispered to the cat and then skilfully drew it from its wicker basket. She gently placed it down on the table and watched as Jane skilfully felt the fragile bones, assuring the owner that none of the injuries were life threatening.

"She's a natural. The animals will love her," Jane said to Fiona that evening as they sat in the large farmhouse kitchen having a late supper.

Fiona congratulated herself on her masterly stroke and was pleased when Cindy enrolled at Bristol University. Cindy had talked it over with Susan who showed little interest in the decision, realising that her daughter was about to move away and get on with her life. Emma, on the other hand, was enthusiastic and offered to help with the tuition fees. It was only when Susan asked where Pandora fitted into the plan that Cindy told her she had met up with Fiona who had agreed to look after the cat for her.

The biggest hurdle Cindy faced was to be living away from home. Despite the cramped conditions in Emma's house she was reluctant to venture forth into an unknown world. She was wary of men and worried about sharing a flat with other students.

She talked it over with Fiona, voicing her fears of having a relationship with anyone. She was, Fiona learned, still unsure of herself and frightened of getting involved in any type of sexual commitment. Grant, Fiona learned with disgust had been brutal with her at times and the violence had made sex something to fear. It had been Fiona who had accompanied her to Bristol and helped to get her a single room in halls of residence so that she did not have to share a flat with other students.

Susan and Emma had also visited. Now an element of pride was beginning to return to Susan's face. Having watched Cindy move on, she also had progressed and had obtained a reasonably well-paid job with an estate agent.

Cindy found herself enjoying the academic challenge. She made no real friends. She was pleasant to everyone but refused to join in the drinking sprees or the partying, still preferring her own company. She eased the financial burden by managing to find part-time weekend work, mucking-out at some local stables. By the end of the first year, Cindy knew she had found her vocation.

Cindy was in her third year of study when a phone call came from Susan to say that Emma had died peacefully in her sleep. Cindy travelled home for the funeral and found Susan thinner and with short blonde hair. In an overly bright manner she told Cindy that she was planning to sell Emma's house and move in with a man who cared for her. "He's fifteen years older than me!"

Cindy recalled the tall, nondescript man who had shaken her hand with intensity.

Cindy also learned that Susan still kept in touch with Grant, albeit it on a very casual basis. His business appeared to be prospering and he had bought himself a new Mercedes. Occasionally he sent Susan a cheque, which she used as holiday money. He had not embarked on another serious relationship. His mother Olive had died, but Susan did not elaborate.

CHAPTER TWENTY-NINE

So the years of studying passed and Cindy was offered, and accepted, a temporary position in a prosperous practice in the Lake District. It covered a large area and apart from farm animals dealt with everything else that was under a vet's remit. Because it was part of her contract to be on call when required, Cindy was given a small bedsit on the premises. So, after renewing her friendship with Pandora, Cindy moved north. She quickly proved competent and willing and the senior partner suggested she join them on a permanent basis. That was when she learned of the derelict cottage in the hills.

Cindy finished her evening meal and cleared away the dishes, washing them in the small sink in her back kitchen. Occasionally she remembered the large American style kitchen they had enjoyed at *Henderland* and wondered if her mother ever thought back to those days. It had seemed that money had come out of the taps when you turned them on. As she picked up the tea towel to dry the dishes her thoughts reluctantly went back to the letter on the mantelpiece. From its position there it continually attempted to nudge her into making some sort of decision and she felt resentful that her family were intruding into her life.

Walking back into the living room she lit a cigarette before picking the envelope off the mantelpiece. Sitting down in the armchair beside the fire, she curled her legs beneath her and held the envelope in her left hand, watching, as if mesmerised, the spiral of smoke wending its way from her cigarette to the ceiling. Resting the cigarette in the ashtray she extracted the single sheet of paper from the envelope. Although Cindy had read the letter many times her heart started to thump as she scanned her mother's neat handwriting. As she did so, the lid of her personal coffin of memories, which had been so successfully buried in the deep recesses of her mind, began to creak open.

After deliberating over the contents, she felt the stirrings of panic followed by a deep-seated anger. How dare they infringe on her life! Was her reaction callous and cruel? Perhaps she should let reason enter her mind. This was a big decision and it merited a thoughtful response. Suddenly she felt the tears nudge the back of her eyes and she shook her head irritably at the situation. Never, in her wildest dreams – or would they be nightmares? – had she imagined this dilemma. I will not cry, she whispered and only Pandora heard and remembered how it had been all those years ago when tears had often made their familiar journey down her face.

Cindy still had no idea as to what to do and, picking up her cigarette, she took quick, nervous puffs allowing the smoke to invade her lungs. Then swiftly she stubbed her cigarette out and changed her sitting position so she was upright with her hands loosely clasped in front of her. She closed her eyes and started to breathe deeply as Fiona had suggested if a panic attack presented itself. Slowly she felt the tension release from her body as she whispered the words of the mantra over and over again in her mind. It was, she had learned, an effective method of divorcing herself from times of stress. She could cut herself off and only her breathing and the words mattered as she felt the much-welcomed calmness invade her mind. The past disappeared and the words baptised her with strength. But was she strong enough for this?

Fifteen minutes later she stood up and stretched her arms

above her head. An answer to this letter had to be given but first she needed to contact Fiona for she valued her opinion. She leaned across and picked up the phone from the bookshelf and pressed the key for the preset memory number. She heard the familiar voice and felt herself relaxing as she said, "Fiona, it's Cindy."

Reassuringly she heard the calm reply and taking a deep breath said, "I need to read you a letter from my mother." As she began to read the tears ran down her face. They were not tears of sympathy, but tears of irritation for being put in such an invidious position.

"I feel so gutted. You know, one step forward and now I'm being dragged back into their vortex. How could Mum even suggest I consider it?" Cindy's voice broke as she gripped the telephone receiver. She tried to concentrate on Fiona's calm response, to her soothing and understanding words of comfort. Eventually she felt the tension leave her body.

But there was too much to discuss on the phone. Fiona was utterly shocked at the seemingly uncaring request from Susan. Had this woman no feelings for her daughter? To write without even having the sensitivity to go and discuss it in person. It made her wonder if Susan really wanted Cindy to help Grant. By writing such an informal letter was she merely fulfilling what she saw as her moral obligation? Fiona knew the trauma such a letter would have on Cindy. The guilt and fear would be re-awakened and could easily undo progress gained through hard work and therapy. The confident person Cindy had now become was under threat.

Fiona thought it essential that she and Cindy meet so that the letter and its implications could be fully discussed. She offered to put Cindy up the next weekend, arranging to meet her at lunch time at a country hotel not far from her house.

"Don't drive down; relax and take the train. I'll meet you for lunch at The Langden Chase Hotel."

Her partners at the veterinary practice agreed that Cindy could take some extra time off, but instead of taking the train, Cindy left early on the Saturday morning, driving down the M6 with only her tumultuous thoughts, her old Land Rover and *Radio 2* for company.

Thursday, January 18th 2001

The Langden Chase was a prestigious country house that had been converted into a four star hotel. In had been an establishment that Grant and Susan had often used, giving Cindy a feeling of apprehensive about going there.

Fiona had arrived early and was sitting in the corner of the lounge in a deep chintzy armchair. She glanced at her watch expectantly. It had been almost a year since she had seen Cindy, although the many letters and phone calls had kept her continually in touch. She got up and went into the powder room where she touched up her lips and hair. Her thoughts went momentarily to Michael, the kind man who had recently moved in with her. Michael was in IT and treated her with far more respect than her first husband had done. Their relationship was still in the preliminary stages but Fiona felt confident of the future. Unlike Cindy, whose family seemed intent on emotionally blackmailing her.

Fiona returned to the lounge nodding to two guests who murmured their good mornings as she sat down to wait. It was a crucial meeting for Cindy. She had to keep her perspective throughout and not for the first time Fiona felt saddened that yet again Cindy had to make an agonising decision.

Fiona was suddenly conscious of being observed. As she raised her eyes she saw the still figure standing in the archway.

She smiled and stood up, and held her hands out in a welcoming gesture as Cindy approached. Her eyes were hidden behind dark glasses, her hair was cut short and her face seemed older, thinner and taut.

"Oh it's so good to see you again!" Fiona was conscious that her voice was ragged with emotion as she hugged Cindy.

Cindy murmured, "I'm so very glad to see you Fiona."

Eventually they disentangled themselves and sat down, opposite one another. Slowly Cindy pulled the folds of her long raincoat around her but Fiona noticed the thinness of her body as she crossed one jeaned leg over the other, displaying scuffed leather boots.

They did not speak initially, and then Cindy removed her glasses and Fiona saw the misery in her eyes before she lowered her head and delved into her capacious leather handbag to bring out the inevitable cigarettes and lighter. Fiona watched the thin trickle of smoke escape from the mouth and nostrils. "Smoking is a disgusting habit!" Fiona remembered Cindy saying years ago.

Fiona knew Cindy was still unable to have any meaningful relationship with a man and it saddened her that she was so sexually crippled. They had talked about it openly when Cindy had gone to Bristol and Fiona had heard the fear and disgust when Cindy had talked about the possibilities of having sex. Fiona understood that to someone who had been raped so forcefully with such devastating consequences, sex might not be a pleasurable, loving and rewarding experience. Time and an understanding man would be Cindy's only hope. "For the meantime, I'll remain with my paintings and animals," Cindy had replied. "I can trust both."

"So tell me about your life in the Lake District," Fiona asked.

"I like it," Cindy hid behind a smile, not wishing to relate the intricacies of her fragile life. It had improved but there were still remnants of self-doubt. She admitted she was lonely and suffering from a poor appetite.

They talked vaguely about Cindy's journey and her work, and Fiona saw the flicker of enthusiasm sweep over the still face and the quiet smile as Cindy talked contentedly about the animals, her work colleagues and the cottage. She also spoke briefly of her forthcoming exhibition to be held in Keswick, "I'm just an amateur painting animals," she remarked in a self-inflicted put down.

Fiona sighed loudly and rebuked her gently, "Cindy, be proud of yourself! You built a bridge and you moved on."

Fiona poured out two cups of coffee and suggested Cindy take her raincoat off and make herself more comfortable. She was surprised to see that Cindy wore a loose denim shirt over a tee shirt and realised that the days of Cindy worrying about her immaculate appearance had gone. The hair was no longer long and luscious, the fingernails were short and there was an air of pragmatism about her. As if reading Fiona's thoughts Cindy raised her eyebrows and gave a quick smile that lit her face up so that Fiona felt drawn by her warmth. Yes, Cindy was still beautiful.

Silently Cindy produced the infamous letter and handed it across to Fiona. She sipped her coffee, her eyes never leaving Fiona's face, as she watched her scan every word on the page. At last she slowly folded it up and handed it back.

Fiona had given the matter considerable thought since the phone call but even now, having read the letter, she felt unable to give an opinion. It was so personal and only Cindy could decide.

"This is a difficult for you," Fiona temporised, drawing her brows together. "You've been, in my opinion, placed in an invidious position."

The tension reappeared on Cindy's face. "Tell me what to do?" There was a plea in the voice.

Fiona shrugged. "I can't do that."

Cindy lowered her eyes. "I resent mother writing to me like this. I've moved on, built my own life and now this ..." She felt the anger welling up in a red tide of fury that she had not felt in years. She wanted to put a lid on it but couldn't. It was all such a waste; the bloody waste of her life, her youth, the relationships that had fallen apart because she couldn't bear to be touched. Men had called her frigid, and more hard and hurtful names when she had suddenly pushed them away, crying and unable to respond.

Fiona saw Cindy's hand tremble as she went on. "I should have made him pay for it all, had him rot in jail. Made him know that I'd be waiting for him when he got out. I wanted to follow him for the rest of his life, so he would know no peace, as I've known no peace." She brought the cigarette to her lips. Her eyes were hard and unyielding and Fiona was reminded once again of the vulnerable, mixed-up girl she had met all those years ago.

"Please," Fiona reached across and placed her hand over Cindy's, feeling the thinness and murmuring, "Don't let this letter bitch up your life." Her voice was gentle and her words comforting as she reaffirmed the years that had lapsed, how Cindy had grown in confidence. As she talked the words calmed Cindy, who lowered her head.

"Thanks, but this letter makes me feel used all over again. But you're right. Anger and hatred are pointless." She sighed. "I need to make a decision."

"Have you spoken to Susan?" Fiona asked.

Cindy shook her head vehemently, adding she didn't care if Grant lived or died. But Fiona saw the faint hesitation creep into her demeanour and, as if noticing the observation, Cindy whispered, "I played God when I had my termination. I am cautious about doing it again."

Fiona realised that Cindy still deliberately avoided the

word abortion. The guilt was there, perhaps buried far deeper than she had imagined. Years ago it had taken Cindy a long time to talk to her about the horror of walking into the clinic, knowing she was carrying a life within her. The detached approach of the staff and the veiled sympathy of the doctor were as distressful as the termination of her child. Fiona had been shocked when Cindy had used the word murder to describe what she had done. To her, an abortion, although an agonising decision, was in many instances necessary. But she knew she could never comprehend the physiological trauma of aborting a child whose father was your father.

"I wonder if mother still sees him?" Cindy asked, her eyes half closed, her body still and tense.

"Sometimes it is not easy to have a complete break," Fiona temporised.

Cindy gave a harsh laugh. "Obviously not." She pressed the tips of her fingers against her temples.

"What will you do?" Fiona asked. There was a long pause while Cindy lit another cigarette. The question hung in the air as they stared at each other. Despair, hope, regret and guilt; the lost years of childhood and youth; revenge, retaliation – it was all there without a word being spoken.

"You have to face this head on," Fiona said as she glanced up at the hovering waiter. "Will you have a sandwich and a glass of wine?"

Cindy nodded disinterestedly and Fiona ordered two tuna fish with mayonnaise on brown and two glasses of white wine.

It was ironic, Cindy thought, that this woman plays such an integral part of my life now. We haven't seen each other for a year, she is in a relationship and yet she spends time with me and understands me. She is right, I have to face this, and it is a challenge to really put the past where it belongs. She met Fiona's eyes and saw in them a friendship and compassion.

Cindy felt the anger burn itself out, only the ashes remained; ashes to be scattered into the wind of time.

"It is guilt," Cindy said quietly. "My decision hinges on that one word." She had occasionally prayed that one day she could balance her scales once again, that sometime in her life there would be a chance to expunge the sin, to possibly return to a guiltless state of mind. She had murdered his child. Could she now save the life of a man who had dominated her existence?

"Go and see your mother," Fiona advised after they had talked and Cindy had nibbled at the sandwiches, sipped at the wine and smoked numerous cigarettes. She had seen the moment of conflict and the shudder before Cindy had nodded her head in agreement.

CHAPTER THIRTY

Cindy sat in her Land Rover outside the hotel. Fiona had told her she would meet up with her in the evening but the afternoon was hers. She had the faint inclination to seek out her mother. Her fingers lightly tapped the steering wheel, then she started the engine. She knew where she was going.

She stopped the car outside the gates of her old school and saw the fleeting glances of teacher and pupils within the dark red brick building. Even now she could still hear his voice. "Have a nice day, Cinders!" And his smile, intimate, knowing and watchful as he kissed her on the cheek. Now she slipped the Land Rover into gear and drove to the cul-de-sac, knowing the route so well that she didn't have to think about it. Cindy pulled in to the kerb at the top of the road and looked across at *Henderland*. There was a swing in the side garden where her mother's rockery had been, and a dog was running up and down. It was in beautiful condition and it looked a happy house. She gazed upwards and her bedroom window stared blankly back at her. Did the house remember as she remembered? Did it have a stored memory of creaking boards and the door handle slowly moving. Cindy shuddered and reversed out of the cul-de-sac.

There was another visit to make on her journey of remembrance. She drove into the industrial estate and parked outside his office. It was still there, with lights on in the second floor. It looked prosperous with a new van parked outside with the company's name emblazoned on the side.

Fifteen minutes later, Cindy parked the Land Rover in Maple Avenue. Susan's new house was in a small housing estate, nothing like *Henderland* but still comfortable. She was pleased her mother had found happiness in another relationship. She realised she should have used her mobile telephone to warn Susan that she was coming but it was too late now. She glanced at her reflection in the door mirror, the outward shell, seemingly sophisticated and accomplished. The inward – afraid!

There was a small car in the driveway and she hoped this indicated that Susan was at home.

The doorbell seemed to echo through the house.

Cindy heard the noise behind the door and then heard the voice asking faintly, "Who is it?"

There was a pause and Cindy felt suspended in a time warp, her lips would barely make the sound. "Cindy."

She heard the gasp as the door opened slightly on the chain and Susan stared suspiciously at her through the crack.

"Cindy – is it really you?"

"Yes, it is really me, mother," she whispered, conscious that her own eyes had filled with tears as the chain was withdrawn and the door slowly opened.

They stared at each other. Incredulity followed closely by disbelief passed through Susan's eyes as they flickered over her daughter's figure. "Cindy!" It was a cry from the heart.

Cindy bowed her head. "It's been a long time." She did not disguise the shame she felt. The years had not been kind to Susan. She has shrunk, Cindy thought. She looks an old woman. "I should have stayed in touch." She moved forward to enfold Susan in her arms. She felt a sudden rush of affection as she kissed her mother's cheek.

She followed Susan into the front room. We are strangers, she thought, as she stared round the unfamiliar surroundings whilst Susan fussed in a nervous way that Cindy had not remembered.

"I guess I've moved on!" Cindy said diffidently dropping her eyes under the close scrutiny. She didn't quite know what to say, seeing so many emotions on her mother's face. "I am so glad to see you, mother," she held her hands out and took Susan's hands in hers. "I have missed you!"

"You suit the short hair," Susan started and then stopped as if suddenly remembering. "I'll make some tea!" she finished in a rush. "You sit down, I won't be long."

Cindy sat down on one of the armchairs and sighed. Fiona had been right. She felt it had been a good decision to come here. A flood of memories invaded her mind as she listened to the once so familiar sound of china teacups rattling on their saucers.

"Here." Susan broke through her thoughts as she set the tray down on the small table beside Cindy and proceeded to pour.

"You are still the only person I know who uses a tea-strainer!" Cindy remarked.

"I like to keep my standards," Susan replied as she sat down opposite Cindy and smiled across at her. "How's the Lake District?" she asked without preamble.

Cindy took a sip of tea and then went on to relate her life, experiences, and work, finishing with, "I still can't forgive him."

"I understand," Susan murmured. "But his life has changed."

"I would have expected it to!" Cindy snapped and then shook her head in annoyance at the sharpness of her remark. "I'm sorry. I don't want to sound bitter. I've tried to forget."

The eyes in her mother's face were full of sadness. "We'd all like to forget." The words rushed out of Susan's mouth, then there was a silence before she went on, "Tell me more about your life, you look..." she floundered.

"Normal?" Cindy raised her eyebrows and the word hung between them. Normal. Had she ever been that? She saw the consternation on her mother's face and waited for her reaction. But did it matter what she thought? Slowly she smiled and relaxed realising that she was at peace with herself. "Normal." She repeated the word. "I try to be."

Susan looked more closely at her daughter. She had anticipated anger, frustration, and a need for revenge. Her face broke into an answering smile. "I was going to say contented."

"I am. I have a good job. I have caring friends. I still have Pandora!"

"Oh Pandora!" Susan sighed with affection. "How is she?"

"Getting old!" Cindy replied with a hesitant laugh.

"Is there somebody in your life?" Susan asked with growing confidence and watched as the lids dropped over the eyes before her and there was a gentle shake of the head.

Susan instinctively glanced at Cindy's hands, seeing no obvious wedding ring.

Cindy read her thoughts and continued. "I can't face that type of relationship yet." Her tone indicated that she did not wish to pursue the subject. Instead Susan related how she had met Peter.

"Cindy, I have to know, do you still hate your father enough not to try and help him?" There was a faint quaver in Susan's voice as her eyes searched Cindy's face for a reaction.

Cindy watched her mother, seeing the entreaty in the eyes, "Hate is such a strong emotion. It warps and destroys you. It could so easily have destroyed me. It would have meant so much if Dad had said sorry and we could have remained a family. But he chose not to do that." Cindy lowered her eyes and for the first time in years attempted to click her finger nails together but was unable to do so.

Susan sat staring down at the carpet. A small tic played in the corner of her left eyelid. She removed her spectacles and wiped them with a clean paper tissue, then she replaced them and her eyes met Cindy's again. Her voice was faint and she sat wringing her hands in an unfamiliar gesture. "Grant's business prospered, but in the last two years he has not been well, thus the reason for the letter."

"Did he ask you to write to me?"

Susan shook her head and there was a deathly silence.

When Cindy did not offer any comment, Susan had no option but to go on. "If I tell you that he spends one day a week on a dialysis machine, you can imagine what that is like for a man who hated illness." There was a pause as Susan looked into Cindy's face for some type of reaction, but there was none. "If I tell you that the veins on his arms are bruised and knotted from the needles, that he sees no future and gets tired and has not the energy to do the things he used to do."

Cindy remained impassive as Susan continued, "If I say he has lost hope of ever finding a suitable donor, I wonder what your answer will be if I ask again if you will take a test to see if you are compatible."

"It's a lot to ask, mother," Cindy whispered.

"Yes, but it would be the ultimate act of forgiveness," Susan replied thoughtfully.

"I am meant to forgive him, am I?" Cindy asked bitterly.

Susan shook her head. "It may heal many wounds."

Cindy tried to murmur something appropriate for it was obvious that Susan wanted an answer, but she found her lips were dry and could only nod at the mention of his name. She could feel her heart beating and the pulse in her throat seemed to constrict her breath. She watched as Susan slowly started to rub her hands together in an agitated manner. "Don't think he hasn't suffered because he has. Yes, I love Peter, but there is still a part of me that will always feel something for Grant."

"Does Peter know?"

Susan shook her head, shocked at the thought of telling him.

Cindy felt her hands shaking uncontrollably as she contemplated her decision before looking up, her eyes bloodshot with tears that now ran down her cheeks. Faintly she nodded her head whispering, "In answer to your letter, yes I will take the test."

The Foot and Mouth crisis that had affected many of parts of the UK was making its presence felt in the Lake District. Tourists were staying away and the towns, normally bustling with holidaymakers, were almost deserted. The local economy was in sharp decline and there was a feeling of panic amongst some of the villagers. Would the crisis ever end?

If anything the crisis in the countryside had made Cindy *almost* forget the situation she found herself in. It had been a traumatic time for her but in a strange sort of way she had been glad that an opportunity had presented itself for a reconciliation with her mother and a chance had come along to truly test her mental resolve. In retrospect Cindy had known it had been stupid and perhaps stubborn on her part to allow the silence between herself and her mother to increase until it had been almost impossible for either to make contact. Her visit to Susan had taught Cindy a great deal and she wondered if there would ever be an end to the sharp learning curve she constantly found herself on.

The visit south had turned out to be almost therapeutic. Not only had she had the strength to visit her old teenage haunts but the initial visit with her mother had showed her that Fiona was right, she had moved on, moved away from the incestuous relationship that had developed between the three of them, and that she was no longer the girl with the fragile personality. She was a person in her own right. She didn't need her parents any more. Ironically they needed her.

Cindy had visited Susan again on the Sunday before driving back north. There she met Peter for only the second time and her opinion that he was a thoroughly decent man who had Susan's best interests at heart had not changed. Yes, she liked Peter and as Susan fussed around in the kitchen he had asked about veterinary work, even enquiring about Pandora, a cat he had never seen but had obviously heard a great deal about from Susan.

Cindy had asked that Grant was not informed about her participation during the living donor transplant assessment period. Susan frowned at the request, and worried that there might be an underlying reason for Cindy's secrecy. Surely, her daughter would not back out at the last minute in a spiteful revenge attack? No, Susan was sure that would not be the case, so the promise had been kept. Neither the hospital nor Susan would mention Cindy's involvement. As she prepared to leave, Susan handed her a small card with the words: *Walk With Me*, a Diocesan Prayer, and Cindy read it with a thoughtful expression on her face. There was emotion in her voice when she said her goodbyes.

Cindy had not realised the lengthy period involved during what was called the assessment process. When she received notification from her Transplant Coordinator regarding the tests she would need to undertake, she learned that they involved four lengthy and separate appointments, and a fleeting doubt entered her mind. The tests were thorough, time consuming and tiring and, coupled with the journey south, it all became an exhausting process.

Her partners at the veterinary surgery had been more than understanding after Cindy had explained about her predicament. Her hectic schedule was eased by the knowledge that she had the full support of her colleagues, who implied she could have as much time off as required. But Cindy did not abuse the privilege and except for one extra day when she felt emotionally drained, she was always was back at work on the day she promised.

The Transplant Centre at Addenbrooke's Hospital in Cambridge had superb facilities and the staff, including the renal nurses and kidney doctors spent a great deal of time explaining the procedure. At no time did Cindy feel pressurised into taking further tests. On her third appointment the schedule had to be altered to fit in with her request that Grant was not told of her involvement. On this appointment Cindy was taken round the transplant ward by her coordinator, a middle-aged woman by the name of Elaine, whom Cindy had warmed to during their first meeting. Elaine was adept at putting Cindy at ease and reminded her of Fiona in one of her most persuasive moods. Fiona herself was a strong support and as Cindy divided her time between Fiona and her mother she wondered, not for the first time, if Grant would thank her for the trouble she had gone to. But she was not doing this for a thank you from her father, but for her own solace of mind.

CHAPTER THIRTY-ONE

Tuesday, 10th April

*T*he letter arrived with the morning post and it lay on the mat until Cindy arrived home from work. She picked it up along with two bills and the usual junk mail. The franked postmark of Addenbrooke's Hospital stood out.

She walked into the living room and placed the mail on the window ledge, then bent down and stroked the cats before taking off her green waxed jacket and placing it over the back of one of the chairs. She ran a hand through her short hair and then dug into the top pocket of her denim shirt and took out a packet of cigarettes and her lighter. Then she picked up the envelope and held it for a moment in her hands before finally opening it and extracting the single sheet of paper.

Fiona received Cindy's telephone call moments before she sat down with Michael for their evening meal. As Cindy told her the results Fiona got the impression that Cindy was no longer sure if she wanted to go ahead with the transplant. Fiona signalled for Michael to put her dinner back in the oven. It was obvious that Cindy needed to talk.

"The transplant coordinator is suggesting I make an appointment for the operation," Cindy said, but instead of relief Fiona had heard doubt in her voice. A doubt that Fiona picked up on, though Cindy had tried very hard to conceal it.

The results of the tests had not come as a shock to Fiona. There had always been a high possibility that Cindy would be an ideal candidate for a living donor transplant and she had tried to help Cindy think through all the implications. As so often in these cases, when the time came to actually act in a positive manner, reasons for not going ahead became more important that the reasons for going ahead.

Fiona had questioned Cindy's motivation for even considering the transplant surgery. The whole scenario seemed strange and didn't fit in with Cindy's careful reconstruction of herself. Why should she help the father who had made her pregnant? It seemed more fitting to a badly written television drama than real life. But then life was peculiar with its twists and turns. Fiona remembered Cindy saying, years ago, that she never wanted to see her parents again. Had time helped to heal the scars to the extent that Cindy felt able to risk her own life for a man who had denied her all hope of a normal, loving relationship?

"He's still family," was all Cindy would say on the matter when asked about her reasons for going ahead.

A week passed. Cindy was unable to concentrate on anything other than the dilemma she was now in. It had been different before. Until now she was merely complying with her mother's wish to take the compatibility test, but now a new challenge was opening up before her.

Did she really, after years of wiping away the hurtful and wicked memories, want to be remotely associated with her father again? The answer was a resounding no! But could she face the responsibility of knowing that his health was in decline because of her? Could she ignore the fact that her father could die if she didn't go ahead? She had killed his child but would ending his life make hers any easier?

Cindy had the Wednesday afternoon off and although the cottage was now more like a home than a junk shop, she had no inclination to continue with her home improvements. Returning after her morning work, she ate a light salad sandwich for lunch and sat in her studio, looking out across the mountains. Although Fiona and Susan were a telephone call away, she felt entirely alone and cursed God for giving her such a difficult decision to make. Hadn't she had enough of living through life changing incidents? Wasn't her cup overflowing with trauma?

Sitting on the stool in front of her easel she smiled at the images of the walrus and carpenter on the paper in front of her. She had recently diversified from painting and drawing animals; now it was fantasy creatures, monsters and angels that occupied her talents. Well, she could use her own experience for drawing the monsters! She had even sold a few examples to a craft shop in Kendal. Now the shop wanted more and she should be finishing them off, but suddenly she felt a stab of pain at the back of her eyes and knew she was going to have a migraine attack.

Her inhaler! She cursed herself for leaving it in the bedroom, and now it was too late for medication. She would go upstairs, lie down and wait for it all to pass. The room slowly swayed back and forth and she felt nausea rising in her throat.

She stumbled to the bedroom like a drunk, swaying from side to side, and threw herself down on the bed. The room was spinning and she felt like Alice in Wonderland, dropping, dropping down her personal rabbit hole. Down and down and she felt the sweat breaking out on her forehead now and her heart beating like a drum in her ears. I hate it, she thought as she tried to focus her eyes on an object, tried to still the flicker of vision.

The afternoon was wasted but by early evening the attack had worn itself out. Cindy got up and walked into the bathroom to splash cold water over her face. The migraine attacks were all due to stress. She thought they had subsided but this recent attack was quite severe. Was she surprised! In the kitchen she boiled the kettle and made herself a drink of warm water; food made her feel nauseous.

She wandered slowly back into her studio and opened the large chest of drawers that had been placed against the back wall. It was a long time since she had retrieved this particular item but she felt it necessary to reacquaint herself with these possessions. Fiona had said bury them, or even throw them away, but she had attached too much importance to them for that. Placing them out of sight had been a better alternative. Had she also placed them out of her mind? Well, they would never be that. Even when she had moved around the halls of residence in Bristol and then to this cottage she had refrained from opening the box that now sat innocently at the back of the drawer.

Reaching in she retrieved it and placed it on the window ledge. Carefully, and with a deep breath she removed the lid. The bed sheet had long since been cut up but the section with her blood on it had been kept. It now stared back at her from within the box. She removed it, seeing underneath the gold *Cartier* pencil, a few humorous cards, Susan's wedding ring, the Supertramp CD and a few other items. These were memories of a different Cindy. But the possessions meant nothing to her, indeed the gold pencil looked old through lack of use and she knew there would be no reason to hold it in her hand again.

Just as she was about to replace the items back in the box, she saw it, lying face down in the corner. Suddenly her knees felt like jelly, and a slight feeling of nausea rose in her stomach. She picked up the piece of white plastic and turned it over and in doing so began to gently sob. They were not long body racking sobs of the past but just a gentle cry of remembrance. Sitting down on the stool she covered her face with her hands before wiping away the tears from her eyes. Turning the white plastic strap over she saw her name and a number. It was the medical identification strap that had been issued to her at the clinic, the name and number that identified her as the person who had killed the unborn child that lay within her.

For years she had asked for forgiveness, so much so that it had become a focal point in her life. Prayer after prayer of an asking for understanding until one day she could simply pray no more. Reparation came in many disguises. Was this decision regarding the transplant the final test on her journey of faith? If it was she dared not think of the consequences if she ignored it.

And so with her leave of absence agreed and her cats placed with a work colleague, Cindy packed her suitcase on the Friday afternoon and took a taxi to the train station.

"You can stay with us, Cindy." Fiona's voice had been warm in her mind as she sat listening to the song of the train as it sped over the lines. This weekend she knew she would rely a great deal on Fiona's understanding and support. Cindy had hesitated to accept Fiona's invitation, knowing Michael had moved in as Fiona's partner. But Fiona had understood her concern and reassured her that Michael fully understood the situation and would welcome her as a friend.

Tomorrow she would meet her father for the first time in years, although he was yet to know of this. She closed her eyes, conscious that the woman opposite was hovering on the brink of a conversation. She wanted only a quiet journey into memory. Her father was all she could think about.

Cindy had tried to visualise him ill, and it had allowed her a brief moment of grim satisfaction. Now he was the one suffering pain and fear. Had he changed or did he still posses his charismatic personality, good looks and that bon-ami attitude? Had he, and she shuddered at the thought, found someone else? Another young girl perhaps? Susan had not said anything and she had not asked. She remembered his fear of death, or even illness. How he had disliked visiting Olive.

Would he too become bitter like his mother? As the train sped along she turned her face to the window; she looked gaunt and weary. Would he still think she was beautiful? Did it matter? She sighed and bit her lip. How would she cope with his eyes on her? Would he still desire her? Dear God, what a thought, and with that Cindy nodded off.

Fiona parked her car in the station car park and then walked in glancing at the arrivals board to ascertain the platform number. She wondered how Cindy was coping; knowing this would be a traumatic weekend for her. Fiona wished she could talk with Susan, to find out more about Grant's current lifestyle, but realised that was an impossibility. Cindy had had no option but to tell Susan about their friendship. Susan had not been bitter and recognised her daughter's need to have a confidant, but she had no wish to meet Fiona again.

The train was slowly coming into the platform. Fiona watched as the doors opened and people tumbled out. She saw Cindy, her suitcase in hand, her face thin and taut, her long, loose coat flapping as she walked briskly towards her.

They hugged each other and exchanged the usual greetings before Fiona led Cindy to the car park. Fiona drove with competence through the traffic and familiar surroundings to stop outside her house.

"We'll have a cup of tea. Michael's at the football. Then I've booked a table in the local restaurant where we can relax and talk."

They chatted over their mugs of tea, not broaching the subject of the meeting, and then Cindy went into the small bedroom and unpacked. She looked at her make-up bag and wondered why she had felt the need to pack it.

The restaurant was full and noisy. Fiona ordered a half bottle of red and felt guilty as Cindy had to make do with mineral water. Smoking and drinking had been prohibited since the tests. Gently Fiona probed Cindy about the meeting. How would she feel seeing her father? Would memories overshadow the reason for the visit? Cindy shrugged and Fiona could only listen to the varying doubts and concerns that Cindy expressed.

"Why did you really feel you had to take the tests?" Fiona asked after they had finished their main course and had declined temptation from the array of ice-cream desserts and just settled for coffee.

"Retribution!" Cindy said and her eyes were sad. "I want to exonerate the guilt. I want to feel comfortable enough to go to Mass."

"A life for a life," Fiona added quietly and Cindy gently nodded her head.

Michael was waiting for them when they returned, he had gone out of his way to ensure Cindy felt comfortable and relaxed and now they sat in front of the fire. Cindy was sipping a cup of coffee.

"I think it is appalling the slaughtering of fine healthy animals," Fiona said with a shudder as the news report highlighted the increase of foot and mouth cases in the United Kingdom.

"Killing the few to protect the many," Michael said philosophically.

Cindy did not reply, her mind was too occupied with the forthcoming meeting. Suddenly she wished she could opt out, wished she had never taken the damned tests, wished she had no decision to make. She slept fitfully, unable to get used to the room with its bright streetlight shining through the windows. Even the curtains could not dim its insistent glow and she remembered the streak of light in *Henderland* and the shadows on the ceiling as the door slowly opened. She heard again the creaking of floorboards and felt her heart start to race in panic before she realised it was Michael in the adjoining bedroom.

She missed the gentle snoring of Pandora at her feet; she missed the quietness and overpowering darkness. Car doors seemed to slam throughout the night shattering her thoughts.

The red Ford Escort. What would they all be doing now if that car had arrived an hour earlier? Would Grant still be ill? Would her parents still be living in the land of parties and laughter? Would she have become the famous artist? One thing is for sure; she would not be here in Fiona's house!

Saturday, 14th April

Cindy woke early and crept into the bathroom wanting to take her shower before Fiona got up. She heard the sound of voices and a tap on the door and Fiona popping her head round to ask if she was all right. Cindy reluctantly nodded.

The relaxing breakfast helped and after she had sipped half a mug full of black coffee and made a token gesture of nibbling a corner of toast she excused herself saying she would go and get ready.

Cindy stood for a few seconds in front of the bedroom mirror. It had been a source of anxiety to her as to how she intended presenting herself to her father. Her clothes were an important factor. To play it all down, to appear nondescript, would surely indicate he had won; she had become submissive. He had diminished her, taking away all her self-esteem and confidence. She had mulled this thought over with Fiona the previous evening. Fiona had initially disagreed with her, emphasising that she had to get the balance right. Finally she had ended up saying it was Cindy's decision, that she had to feel comfortable and dress in accordance with her frame of mind. But what was her self-image, what was her frame of mind?

Slowly she slipped into the coolness of the expensive black silk shirt, the fashionable black trousers and high heels. The black jacket hung on its hanger. Black, the non-colour, mourning and death, ravens' wings and nuns' habits. It cocooned and protected her in the colour of bereavement. She stood staring at her reflection, cool, slim and impersonal. She picked up her towel and placed it over her shoulders and then sat down in front of the small mirror and brushed her hair. She smiled, knowing that Grant would dislike her new, closely cut style. Then picking up her make-up bag she started to apply her makeup. This was the visor in her helmet, like knights in the battles of old; it was drawn down to protect her, not from spears but from curious glances and the invasion of her soul. She applied the pencil to her eyebrows accentuating the natural arches. She highlighted her eyes and outlined her lips. This was her mask, the person she wished to present to Grant, not the fear, not the guilt, not the angel. That was the past; this was her step forward.

She heard the tap on the door and Fiona came in as Cindy stood up. Fiona frowned as she scanned the sombrely dressed figure. Then she glanced at the face. It was devoid of expression; a mask full of make-up. She hesitated and Cindy sensed, not her disapproval for Fiona had not disapproved, but a degree of disquiet.

"Well?" Cindy asked.

"If you feel the need." Fiona indicated the clothes and the face with her hand. She smiled but somehow Cindy felt her disappointment. She sat down on the edge of the unmade bed and stared round the room.

Fiona went downstairs and entered the lounge. "I don't think I will ever fully understand this extraordinary case," she said to Michael.

"What do you mean?" he asked, glancing up from the paper.

It had been on Fiona's mind ever since she had met up again with Cindy. Here was someone who had irrefutable proof that their allegation was true and yet stubbornly refused to use it. And now her appearance this morning. "She is going like a plastic princess, but it won't protect her. Only she can do that." She glanced at the clock. It was getting late and Cindy had still not appeared.

After a few minutes Fiona heard the noise of footsteps on the stairs. She glanced round as Cindy stood in the doorway. Gone were the black widow's weeds, gone was the overly made-up face. Instead Cindy stood in clean jeans and a white tee shirt, over which she wore a casual denim jacket. Slightly scuffed trainers had taken the place of the high-heels.

They looked at each other and Cindy gave a faint shrug and then a self-conscious grin. "You're right, I don't need the armour." She walked across and held her hands out and then instinctively hugged Fiona close.

Their journey to Maple Avenue was subdued and Fiona knew that Cindy was as well equipped for the meeting as she could be. She dropped her at the end of the avenue, placing her hand on Cindy's in a reassuring gesture.

"Don't lose the plot through emotion!" was her parting shot.

Cindy heard Fiona's advice ringing in her ears as she watched the car disappear round the corner. Then she started to walk slowly down Maple Avenue, asking yet again why she was putting herself through this. She gave a grimace for she could not help thinking that if the situation had been put to her six months ago she would have smiled at the absurdity of it all.

She walked up the pathway, seeing the small neat garden, and then mentally primed herself as she rang the doorbell, conscious now of the butterflies in her stomach. The door opened and mother and daughter stared at each other and nodded in acceptance that this was going to be a difficult meeting. Cindy saw that Susan was dressed with her usual meticulous care, although the quality of the clothes were no longer in the league of past designer labels. She had tried, and Cindy felt another sudden rush of sympathy for this woman who had once achieved the pinnacle of her dreams only to have them shattered and to lose everything.

Susan held the door open and Cindy saw her mother's eyes flicker over her casual attire with a degree of disapproval, but Cindy knew their relationship had moved past comments and criticism.

Cindy stood in the small living room and watched Susan fussing round getting her belongings together.

Susan turned suddenly and saw the tension on Cindy's face and the tautness in her body. She moved across and placed her hand on Cindy's arm. "I do understand and if you don't want to go through with it..." She sighed. "You are free to make your own decisions."

The gesture took Cindy by surprise. Here was an escape route. She was momentarily tempted, but a feeling of a commitment stopped her.

"Thanks," she said softly, "but I'll be all right. He doesn't know I am the proposed donor does he?"

"No," Susan confirmed. "He doesn't even know I've contacted you. Be prepared for a change. He has suffered this last year." She saw the cynicism in Cindy's eyes and for the first time Susan was beset with doubt, suppose the meeting all went wrong?

Susan's car was old and the journey uncomfortable. They did not talk. Susan had become an erratic driver who clenched the steering wheel with intensity. Cindy closed her eyes to try and quell the panic she felt taking control of her.

Cindy had deliberately refrained from asking Susan about Grant's lifestyle. She knew he had no current serious relationship but was sure there had been female skirmishes of one sort or another.

As if reading her daughter's mind Susan said, "Like I've

said before, Grant has changed. Don't expect to see the father you remember."

"I bloody well hope he has changed." Cindy's voice was rough, and she saw Susan's quick sharp glance and was annoyed with herself for voicing her inner thoughts.

CHAPTER THIRTY-TWO

The apartment building took Cindy by surprise for this was no middle class development but ostentatious luxury. The three storey apartments sprawled behind iron railings and mature trees. Susan pulled up outside the iron gates and lowered the driver's window and then keyed in a security number on the pad. The gates swung silently back on their well-oiled hinges and Susan drove down the red tarmac driveway to the discreet car parking area.

Cindy saw the small inlays giving each apartment owner two parking spaces and watched as Susan parked alongside a red BMW convertible. She gave a sigh of disapproval when she recognised Grant's personal registration number.

They got out of the car and Cindy took in the general ambience of well-being noting the quality of cars parked in their designated areas. The lawns were beautifully attended and two gardeners were busy preparing the flowerbeds.

"Not exactly living in hardship is he?" Cindy commented, but Susan chose to ignore the remark as she walked to the main entrance and spoke into the intercom system.

"It's me," Susan said in a more friendly voice than Cindy had expected. The double glazed outer doors automatically clicked open and Susan walked forward and gestured for Cindy to follow. They entered the opulent lobby area with its thick piled carpet, flower arrangements and brass mailbox slots. It was obvious to Cindy that Susan was very familiar with the surroundings as she walked purposefully towards the elevators.

He hadn't suffered, Cindy thought with a touch of resentment. He's living better than any of us. This place was as far as you could get from her northern retreat. She was living in a ramshackle cottage with no disposable income and here was a guilty man living thus and begging for someone to help him.

The elevator whisked them up to the top floor and Cindy knew they had to be making their way to the penthouse suite.

She followed Susan out of the elevator and walked along the plush corridor to stop outside the heavy oak door, noting the discreet brass plaque. She saw the small peephole in the door and moved to one side as Susan pressed the bell and then gave Cindy another worried glance.

"Remember," Cindy said quickly, "I will decide when I tell him if I am going to be the donor."

Susan gave a nod and a smile of understanding, realising that Cindy, having seen the surroundings, was beset with doubt.

"Be brave," she whispered. "You are saving a life."

The door swung open and Cindy gave an involuntary gasp. She wanted to turn her head away, to avoid seeing his face. She felt her heart start to thump as she took in his slim figure, the well-cut jeans, the Tattersall shirt, open at the neck with the cuffs turned back. She saw the glint of his gold watch, the gold chain on his wrist before her eyes travelled up and she looked at the face that had once been imprinted on her mind. She had forgotten that years and illness would have taken their toll and was shocked at what she saw. The hair, once so thick and black, was receding and grey, cut in a fashionable, short crop. The moustache had been shaved off, making the mouth seem thin and small. The eyes minus their spectacles no longer seemed to be full of life but peered at Susan with a tired expression. There seemed to be little of the charismatic charmer left. He looks ill, this old man who is my father, she thought.

"Susan," he smiled and the fleeting ghost of a his charm peeped through and then, as if conscious that Susan was not alone, he turned his head so that his eyes met Cindy's. She saw him swallow and then blink his eyes rapidly, as he stared at her. It was as if he was mesmerised and she wondered what thoughts were passing through his head.

"My God, it's Cindy!" He finally uttered the words with a note of disbelief in his voice as he continued to stare. The silence between them became memories as Cindy found herself biting her lip to stop the tears she felt coming into her eyes. Seeing this man standing before her was far more emotional than she had envisaged. This man needed her, but then he always had.

"Come in." His voice was low and he seemed ill at ease, as though he had sensed that this was no father and daughter visit. He stood aside to let them pass and Cindy's nostrils quivered to the still familiar aroma of his after-shave. She wanted to turn and run; to run far away from this man. Even the emotions he evoked frightened her. She felt Susan's hand on her arm and the gentle pressure of reassurance.

Cindy could not speak for there seemed to be no appropriate words. She followed Susan down the hallway and into the living room as if in a dream. She thought she could handle the situation but knew now she was totally unprepared for this reunion. They stood in the middle of the room, the fragmented family that had once seemed so united and so safe.

"I didn't expect this," Grant said, his eyes on Susan. "You should have told me."

"I told Cindy you were ill," Susan filled in for him and they saw him shake his head.

Cindy dragged her eyes away from Grant's face and

allowed them to flicker round the room, taking in the expensive furnishings. They remained standing awkwardly in the centre of the room until Grant pointed to the chairs and they sat, Susan and Cindy on the sofa, soft and yielding, and Grant opposite in an easy chair.

Susan and Grant spoke in short jerky sentences, trying to include Cindy who remained tight lipped, only half listening to the interplay. Conscious of the tension and emotion, Susan suddenly started to chatter inconsequentially about the journey and Peter, but neither Grant nor Cindy paid much attention as each took stock of the other.

It was still there lurking between them. Cindy could feel that tenuous bond of unspoken words, thoughts and feelings conveyed only by a gesture or a look. She sensed his disquiet at the situation.

Grant met her eyes with a faint, almost imperceptible raising of his eyebrow and Cindy remembered the silent language that Susan had so resented.

"It's been a long time," Grant eventually said and Cindy could see he was vaguely embarrassed.

"Yes," her reply was monosyllabic. *I don't know what to say to this man. I have no words. My father, he is a stranger and yet …*

Grant rubbed his hand across his top lip where once the moustache had been, the familiar gesture caught Cindy by surprise and she remembered with vivid accuracy the cream tea with Elizabeth and how she had scooped cream off his moustache. She closed her eyes. *I want to go. I want to get back to the life I understand, my cats and my solitude.*

She heard Grant's voice and knew he too was caught up in a time warp.

"I'll go and make tea," Susan murmured with more diplomacy than Cindy had given her credit for.

"This is difficult isn't it?" his voice was oddly gentle. "I have often wondered how you were." She could still not speak with ease; she just stared mutely across at him. He continued to look at her. Was it appraisal, or just curiosity? Either way she felt uncomfortable beneath his scrutiny.

"I liked your hair longer." The words made her close in on herself. The remark seemed inappropriate, a reminder of forgotten intimacy.

Now they were alone together. He leaned forward and held his hands out in a gesture of supplication. She wanted to turn away but could not for she saw the horrendous markings on the veins where the dialysis needles had been inserted. She also noted that the gold bracelet was not vanity but a medical bracelet informing strangers of his condition and medication.

"Mother wrote and told me you were ill." How cold the strangulated voice sounded and she saw him nod his head. She wanted to whisper retribution, but it no longer seemed appropriate, for it was already there before her in his face. Slowly they talked, not quite as strangers but certainly not as father and daughter. She saw the pride flicker in his dull eyes when she told him briefly, so very briefly, about her life. He asked no intimate questions and she knew he was struggling, unsure as to why she had come, unsure as to what she expected of him.

Then the remnant of the anger she had buried for so long re-emerged and she heard herself say, "Don't you want to say anything to me?" Her voice broke with emotion and gave vent to all the bitterness and hatred she had felt.

Grant lowered his eyes and mumbled, "I am so sorry."

"Say it again!" she rasped.

He raised his eyes as if her thoughts had been transposed to his mind and she saw his discomfort as he whispered the words she had waited so long to hear.

"Dear God, I never meant to hurt you. I can't explain why

I did it." He sounded oddly humble and contrite before adding, "I can only live with my guilt."

She got up, her head started to ache. He had finally apologised and there was no denying the contrition in his voice. Perhaps he hadn't the energy to fight with her any more and she quickly reassessed the situation. He certainly had all the trappings of money, but he was alone and ill. He needed her more than she needed him. She felt a wave of sickness and flinched from the pain. As if reading her needs he pointed to the hallway.

"First right."

She washed and dried her hands and was returning to the living room when she saw his bedroom door was slightly open. Curiosity got the better of her and she went in. The room was masculine and she could smell his presence. She saw the double bed and then her eyes travelled round the room and she frowned seeing the silver framed photograph holder. She walked purposefully across to the bedside table. She might have known there was someone else in his life.

Picking up the silver framed photograph she stared into the young face with the long blonde hair.

It was herself and her feelings were confused, surprised that he kept her photograph on his bedside table. She continued to stare at the photograph for a few moments, for she could not recall when it was taken. An unwanted tear came into her eye and she quickly replaced the frame and was about to leave the bedroom when she saw two other photographs. Her frown deepened as she peered at them, seeing the family as it had been. Her mother laughing up at Grant, his hand on her shoulder and she was between them – the divider – she remembered this incident. It was when he had bought his new camera, he had activated the timing device and run across to join them; they had laughed as the camera clicked.

The other photograph was formal, Susan and Grant at a

function. Susan groomed and gowned and Grant in his dinner jacket, so handsome. She sat down on the bed and rested her head into her hands and started to cry for the years that had gone.

"Cindy." It was Susan's voice coming from the doorway. "Are you all right?"

They walked back into the living room and Susan poured out three cups of tea and they tried to talk in strained staccato sentences.

"So why have you come Cindy?" Grant asked suddenly. "Was it to see me like this? Or to hear me say I am sorry? Because I am really sorry." He swallowed and screwed his eyes up and clenched his fists and she knew he was making a desperate effort, as in a whisper he said. "What I did was wrong. I panicked when you told your mother, I should have …" He stopped. "I've told your mother, I was totally to blame." He opened his eyes and held his arms out and rolled his sleeves back to the elbow and she now saw the full extent of the damaged arms. "This is retribution. Don't feel sorry for me."

Cindy felt a rush of pity. It took her by surprise for Grant, as always, had been his over-dramatic self, but beneath it she saw his fear and loneliness.

She stared at him. "You could have written, contacted me. Why this contrition now?"

"Would you have answered if I had?" he asked quietly and saw Cindy gently shake her head. "You had to make the first move and I'm glad you have."

Cindy felt her body go taut, it was like that infamous door of her bedroom opening, except this time it was a door closing on a memory. She saw him run his tongue over his dry lips and realised he wanted to say more. She waited.

"I can't say sorry any more than I will be able to thank the person whose kidney will be used to save my life." He shrugged. "You know, Cindy, sometimes there are just no words to express the emotion you feel."

Cindy chose to ignore the comparison for it seemed all too dramatic.

"How do you feel about the operation?" she asked.

Grant realised the question deserved a considered response and paused before glancing across at Susan. "I am very frightened. I don't like hospitals and the dialysis treatment has been horrendous. It's an odd sensation watching your blood circulating out of your body."

"It's not pleasant being frightened, is it?" Cindy replied and Grant could only lower his eyes in silent acknowledgement of her comparison. Her voice was emotionless as she continued. "Blood outside the body is something I had to get used to." She bit her lip for she was now verging on retribution and that was not the purpose of the visit. She felt Susan's eyes on her.

But before she could say anything Grant asked, "Will you ever forgive me?"

Cindy ignored the question and said, "You asked me a few minutes ago what was the purpose of my visit. The reason I am here is to tell you that I am your saviour."

Grant's face became expressionless as his eyes darted from Susan and then back to Cindy. At first he did not realise the significance of what Cindy was telling him. She reiterated it softly. "I am your donor." She saw his eyes widen before frowning and him shaking his head in disbelief.

"It's true, Grant," Susan said.

"You would do this for me?" There was incredulity in his voice and a deep frown on his forehead.

She nodded, not wishing to speak, not wishing to hear the quaver she knew could be in her voice.

Slowly he shook his head. "I can't, I just can't take from you again," he muttered.

It was not the response Cindy had anticipated and she

heard herself saying. "Last time you took without asking. This time I am offering."

He stood up and ran a hand through his thin hair. He stared down at her. "But why would you do this for me?" He lowered his head and gave a self-deprecatory shrug. "I'm not worth it."

Cindy again chose not to answer and watched as Susan went over to place an arm round Grant's shoulder. But she still felt the outsider. A mirage of unspoken words seemed to pass between Cindy and Grant.

"Does this mean you have forgiven me?" he eventually asked and there was a pleading note in his voice.

"Does that matter?" Cindy replied not wishing to be drawn.

"Yes, it does." And she knew from the tone of his voice that it did matter to him, almost as much as receiving an apology had mattered to her.

There was a brief silence as Cindy weighed up the question Grant had put to her. Did she really want to continue on her course of self-pity and attempt to exact revenge on this sick man? Could she afford all the time and emotional turmoil that such an undertaking would entail? She was only young, her life still ahead of her; yet here was an opportunity to finally balance her scales of injustice. She asked curiously, "And if I agreed to forgive you?"

"Then I will accept your donation and go ahead with the operation," Grant replied.

It was almost a replay of a past situation, Grant out-manoeuvring her with clever words. But this time Cindy could exonerate her life-long sin by saving a life, and that thought appealed to her more than dealing out retributive justice. At last she could be at peace with herself. She felt Susan's eyes on her and knew her mother was thinking Cindy was considering giving Grant the ultimate repayment by saying no; that this was what it had all been about.

Cindy felt the moment of power she now had over her

father. She had climbed the mountain and was now looking at the scenery below. She savoured the feeling, her learning curve had come to an end. In a voice she barely recognised as her own she heard herself saying, "I forgive you father."

Bank Holiday Monday, 27th August

It was late summer and Cindy stood at the lounge window of her cottage. She had spoken to Fiona on the telephone the night before informing her that according to her mother, Grant had recovered well.

Her own rehabilitation had been far quicker than anticipated. Her stay at Addenbrooke's Hospital had lasted for eight days, in which time she had visited Grant on two separate occasions. On each visit there was a mutual respect and understanding between them. What struck Cindy more than anything was that their relationship had changed so dramatically that she was now the one in charge. No longer was she Daddy's girl, Cindy had become a person of considerable worth and ironically, in Grant's eyes, someone he could respect. After all, she had saved his life and there was no greater debt than that.

Looking back on those traumatic and unpleasant months during which she'd had numerous tests and faced the dilemma of what to do, Cindy now felt it *had* been worth it. Although she was not cured of the mental anguish she felt regarding her childhood, a lid had been put on it, a door had been closed. Her life had moved on and although the hurtful scars remained in her consciousness, Cindy, for the first time in years, felt at genuine ease within herself. The memories would always linger, perhaps getting smoothed out by the passage of time.

She had even returned to the church and took Mass regularly. The congregation had welcomed her and she quickly integrated into their fellowship.

She lit a cigarette and remembered her promise to Fiona to cut down. Perhaps she didn't need to smoke now; after all she had managed to stop for three months before the transplant. It was a habit she could do without.

Cindy talked to her cats as they followed her into the hallway – it was time to feed them.

CHAPTER THIRTY-THREE

Eight years later: Tuesday, September 8th 2009

*F*iona returned to her office after escorting her three new clients out. With a sigh, she sat down, her elbows resting on the desk, the tips of her fingers gently touching. Deep in thought, she frowned; it had been a difficult session. In an act of near frustration she ran her fingers through her hair before glancing once more over her notes. *Perhaps I am getting tired of other people's problems swirling around in my head, trying to decipher the truth from fantasy. Maybe I should pack it all in and live my life at a steadier pace.* How often had she thought about that in the last two years?

Her office was now a purpose-built extension on the side of her detached house. The concept of Fiona gaining more counselling qualifications and establishing her own specific clientele had come when her partner, Michael, had decided to take a job abroad. Fiona had deliberated long and hard whether she should go with him, but had decided to stay in England. They remained friends, but it was nothing more than a long distance relationship and they are never easy to sustain.

Cindy had got on well with Michael, and Fiona smiled affectionately remembering how Cindy had been there, quietly and compassionately helping her to get her life back on track after the separation. The irony of the role reversal had not been lost on her.

It was Cindy who had suggested that Fiona move to a new area to start afresh and extend her private practice. However, Fiona had been ill prepared for the trauma of moving house. After collecting numerous house brochures and visiting what seemed like a never-ending list of unsuitable properties, she had settled on this house in a small village outside Oxford.

Fiona leaned back in her leather chair and glanced round the room. It was a balance between office, consulting room and personal study. Framed diplomas graced the walls while on the bookcase stood a silver framed photograph of her daughter, Joely. The titles in the bookcase covered all types of complicated subjects; two of them had been written by Fiona. It was a relaxing, compact house with a spare bedroom that Cindy used when she came to stay.

That did not happen as often as Fiona would have wished, but when Cindy did stay, she always brought her two beautiful German Shepherds in the back of her Land Rover.

Her visits were special times for both of them: a meal, perhaps a walk to the local pub, or just an evening in together. Over the years a strong empathetic bond had grown between the two women, but Fiona accepted the friendship would always be on Cindy's terms.

Joely was now a talented twenty-nine year old, a high earner living in London. The real surprise was how close Joely and Cindy had become over the years. There had been a tentative dawning of friendship after the tumultuous time of Grant's transplant and this had grown as Joely and Cindy had discovered that they enjoyed each other's company. They were similar in age, but were direct opposites in personality. Fiona smiled, thinking of Joely the extrovert, the avid collector of designer handbags with her iPhone, her high-heeled friends and her swish London lifestyle. She had carved out a successful career with a leading asset management group in the City, where all the current talk was about the increasing budget deficit, the effect of quantitative easing and the possibility of a double dip recession. Joely's career had survived the credit crunch, but it was during the unpredictable and stressful autumn of 2008 that she had started to think more seriously about a change of career. Despite her trappings of success, Joely had often remarked to Fiona that she envied Cindy's rural lifestyle.

Cindy had not encompassed the technological revolution to the same extent, though she did manage to send emails and had, somewhat reluctantly, learned to text. Her disparaging remarks about social networking sites always made Fiona laugh. Cindy described them as, "similar to sitting in a restaurant, getting up and going over to an adjacent table and saying to someone you have never met, I have just eaten my lunch!"

Joely often took a long weekend away from her cosmopolitan life to travel up to the Lake District and visit Cindy, where she thoroughly enjoyed the invigorating change of lifestyle.

Cindy remained an incredibly private person, very good with her veterinary clients and a pure natural with animals, but she could be infuriatingly distant at times. She had left the veterinary practice in Keswick and gone into partnership with a highly qualified female American vet who dealt solely with domestic cats. Their practice was well respected and had a clientele that spanned the whole country. But there were still no boyfriends, no relationships, and Fiona accepted this was the way Cindy chose to live.

Fiona got up from her chair and watched her clients reverse out of her drive. It was a disturbing case and she was in two minds as to whether she wanted to take it. The allegation of a female teacher forming an inappropriate relationship with a female pupil was nothing she hadn't heard before. The girl claimed she had fallen in love with her teacher, while the teacher said the relationship was nothing more than friendly teacher/pupil behaviour. The girl did not want to press charges and the teacher felt she had done nothing wrong. Nevertheless, the teacher had been suspended from the school. The parents wanted answers and compensation.

For some inexplicable reason, the case brought back flashes of memories about Cindy and Grant. Both had had believable explanations and even today, after all the years that had passed, their case remained something of an enigma.

The ringing of the telephone interrupted Fiona's thoughts. She picked up and immediately recognised the voice of a colleague. She listened to his request for advice, but was reluctant to give any without the backup of an official handbook. She sighed, knowing the handbook she wanted was in one of the filing cabinets in the loft.

After clambering up the loft ladder and searching for the light switch, Fiona stood in the boarded attic area and grimaced as she saw the three grey metal filing cabinets. She peered at the indices she had so painstakingly put on each drawer and then knelt down to read the contents of the bottom drawer. They were all past cases, their details forgotten. She slid the drawer open and started to scan through the metal folders and then paused, staring down at the file with the title C & G. Fiona knew immediately what it was, but that didn't stop her extracting the folder and flicking through it. Then, remembering her mission, she resumed her search for the information her colleague had requested. She did not replace the yellow folder in its allocated slot.

Back in her office, she telephoned her colleague saying she would drop the handbook at his house the following morning. Her eyes now rested on the yellow folder. Somehow, the file demanded to be read.

The folder contained details of one of the few cases that

Fiona had got dramatically wrong. Curiosity now made her open the file and take out the pages of notes and typescripts annotated with comments in red ink, explanation marks and question marks. She remembered the title she had given the case: *An Angel with Two Shadows*. A used airline ticket to Glasgow, dated August 1994, had been stapled to a bundle of papers. As she picked it up three photographs fell out. She placed these to one side and then, leaning back in her chair, she began reading.

Half an hour later she came across a closely typed report with five comments in the margin. They read:

Would Cindy have made this accusation if she had got the car?

Toothbrush and ring.

Descriptions.

Baby!

Article.

Now, 15 years later, Fiona reassessed her thoughts on those five subjects.

1. Grant had always claimed that if he had brought the car home earlier, Cindy would never have made the allegation. It was an odd remark that had somehow been overlooked, lost in the quagmire of information that had followed.

2. Fiona had forgotten the odd fact of Cindy using Grant's toothbrush and Susan's wedding ring for, as she called it, *fun*. Why did Fiona now feel that she had missed something very important? Or was she just being over-imaginative, too suspicious? Sharing a toothbrush was such an intimate thing to do; young lovers often did it, newlyweds also, but a father and his daughter? The thought of it suddenly made Fiona shiver; it was something she really did not wish to think about. And why had Cindy worn Susan's wedding ring? Had there been more to that than was immediately apparent?

3. Fiona glanced back at her notes and saw a sentence had been underlined. *Never says the word abuse.* Try as she might,

Fiona could not remember Cindy ever using that terminology when describing what happened.

4. Cindy's pregnancy had been terminated. Although Cindy claimed the unborn child's father was Grant, there was never any conclusive evidence to back this up.

5. Fiona had kept a copy of the article that Cindy had written. Reading it again after all those years brought back how effective Cindy had been in communicating her despair at what had happened. No wonder she had won the writing competition. She had used a pseudonym and Fiona's eyes now rested on the name Cindy had chosen.

Fiona frowned; Cindy seldom did anything without purpose. Instinctively her hand picked up the pen that lay on her desk. She found herself writing the letters down – with spaces in between. She studied what she had written.

SHONA WIDDRY.

Fiona re-arranged them and eventually came up with:

SINDY HOWARD.

Cindy had disguised the anagram by spelling her Christian name with an S. "Clever girl!" Fiona said shaking her head.

Then she saw an added entry, in newer ink and on different paper, referring to Cindy's act of donating a kidney for Grant. Did such a compassionate gesture indicate remorse or forgiveness?

Fiona realised that were she investigating the case now, it might not appear so black and white. Yes, Cindy had been the victim of horrific, perverted abuse, but there were also events that Fiona knew she had pushed conveniently to the back of her mind, or that Cindy hadn't fully explained.

Grant's death, seven years ago, had been a shock, even if it hadn't been totally unexpected; Cindy had told her that he was still not well.

Cindy, her voice devoid of emotion, had related the news of his death over the phone. "I am going to attend the cremation," she had said matter-of-factly. Fiona remembered how the ensuing silence had indicated her surprise. It was several seconds before Cindy had added, "I have to."

It was a statement that Fiona had felt did not really need an answer, but had found herself asking, "Do you?"

"Yes," had come the reply. It had been sharp and abrupt and Fiona had realised it would not be wise to say any more.

Cindy had got time off work, placed her animals with work colleagues, and travelled down the familiar route to stay with Fiona. Once unpacked, Cindy had become surprisingly quiet and withdrawn.

Fiona had accompanied her to the bleak crematorium and had watched as Susan, with her new husband, and Cindy, who was dressed in black with her eyes hidden behind dark lenses, walked at a slow pace behind the coffin to the faint rendering of *Canon in D*.

Fiona still remembered the look of hostility on Susan's face when her eyes met Fiona's. Fiona knew she still found her friendship with her daughter difficult to comprehend or accept.

Cindy, her face strained, had offered no emotional support to Susan and chose to sit alongside Fiona on the front row, on the opposite side of the aisle to her mother. She had shed no tears as the service progressed, but Fiona was suddenly conscious of a faint sound, not immediately recognisable until she glanced down and saw Cindy attempting to click her nails. The nails had not been long enough to give a decisive click, yet it had still brought Fiona up with a start. This mannerism of Cindy's was something she remembered so well and thought had long been buried.

The coffin had borne a single spray of flowers. Fiona had placed a hand on Cindy's arm as the curtains parted and the coffin slid silently from view. Fiona had heard Cindy give a deep sigh. She felt that Cindy had come to the end of a long lane with no turnings, and had won what seemed like an insurmountable emotional battle with herself. Maybe she could now start being the other Cindy that had momentarily surfaced from beneath her personality. Fiona, however, had been ill-prepared for Grant's parting shot and the effect it would have, not only on Cindy, but on their friendship.

Cindy had chosen not to join Susan in the porch of the crematorium to shake the hands of the congregation, but had waited to one side until the final cars had left. Then she had walked across to Susan and kissed her on the cheek.

At Susan's request, Cindy had gone with her the next day to see Grant's solicitor.

After the visit, Cindy had returned to Fiona's home in a contemplative mood. Fiona did not ask any questions and it wasn't until they both sat down for a coffee that Cindy, a deep frown on her brow, had lit a cigarette and said, "Of course, the solicitor had to be young and blonde." Her voice was tinged with sarcasm. "I inherit the lot apart from a bequest to mother. I guess you could now call me a woman of substance!" Cindy had ground the cigarette stub into the ashtray on the coffee table.

Fiona had nodded, recognising a subtle change in Cindy's attitude.

"They asked if I required the assistance of a financial adviser. I said no."

There had been a pause and Fiona recognised the hesitancy and knew Cindy was balancing whether to tell her something. She had sipped her coffee and waited.

Then in a matter-of-fact tone, Cindy had said, "There is something else he left me." She had lowered her eyes and took out another cigarette. "It was a sealed package."

Fiona had known that her face had betrayed her curiosity and had been annoyed to hear herself ask, "Have you opened it?"

"They are his personal written journals," Cindy had replied, a small, almost secretive smile touching the corners of her lips. Fiona had again been reminded of a Cindy from the past.

"His journals?" Fiona had repeated and waited for Cindy to disclose more information.

"His journals," Cindy repeated, but her tone had still made it hard for Fiona to ask further.

Then, deliberately Fiona thought, Cindy had changed the subject.

Fiona could still see the closed expression on Cindy's face and as they continued to talk, Fiona had realised from past encounters that it was best not to ask any more questions.

The journals had become a significant point in their relationship and Fiona pondered if that had been Grant's intention in leaving them to her. Cindy had left to go back to the Lake District that evening and Fiona had realised that her sudden unscheduled departure had been because of the journals and Cindy's unconcealed desire to read them.

That was the last Fiona had heard from Cindy for almost six weeks, an unusually long time for them not to talk. The only other time there had been silence for longer than a week was when Cindy's beloved cat, Pandora, had died from cancer in 2005. This time, even Joely was finding it hard to get in touch with Cindy. In the end she had resorted to phoning her at her practice one evening. The soothing message that Fiona was worried about her had got an uncharacteristically short response before Cindy said she had to go.

Then, one Sunday afternoon, Fiona got a phone call from Cindy, who had apologised for not being in touch, but said that reading the journals had really upset her. Fiona had wanted to ask what was in them, but again Cindy had become cagey and said that she would tell her one day.

Fiona sighed and sat back in her chair. Cindy had never referred to the journals again and they were as much of a taboo subject as her termination. Taking everything into consideration, since Grant's death, Cindy had imperceptibly changed. Yet, there were odd idiosyncrasies in her life that still took Fiona by surprise. Cindy had purchased an expensive and powerful German sports car that one would normally assume would be driven by men, claiming she got a thrill from driving it. Fiona wondered if it gave her a sense of superiority over the family men driving their hatchbacks and people carriers. Strangely, Cindy had decided to use Grant's personal registration number on her Land Rover. Then there was Grant's business: she had sold 51% of the company to a rival firm, but still kept a foot in the door with her share. It was when Cindy decided to let Grant's penthouse, rather than selling it, that Fiona had finally got the answer to the question she had asked herself many years ago.

Over the years, her instinct had often tapped her on the shoulder, claiming that Cindy would have never made her accusation had the red Ford Escort arrived on time. She brought herself up with a start for it was quite an admission to make and she didn't really want to dwell on it, but it was the truth. The pivotal point in all this had been the car. If it had come an hour earlier, then Fiona was convinced that she would never have heard about the Howard family.

Her conclusion was far too dramatic, judgmental and traumatic to contemplate. It was almost a story within itself. Yes, Cindy had played the role of the molested child very convincingly, but Fiona now believed it was a part that Cindy had never thought of auditioning for until she mentally rolled her small snowball down what became a *very* steep hillside.

Fiona returned her attention to the photographs that had fallen out of the file. One was of Cindy's family, the other something unconnected with the case that had been filed incorrectly, the third was of Cindy at the time the allegation was made. Fiona compared the photograph to the Cindy of today. Gone were the flowing locks of blonde hair, replaced with short stylish black hair. Fiona had once said to her, 'a woman who cuts her hair is a woman who is about to change her life.'

Cindy had definitely made the best of her life. She was now a published author. Her book about the intricacies of drawing life-like animals had enjoyed reasonable sales. Her hands were still thin and artistic, but devoid of jewellery and nail varnish, the clothes, expensive and well chosen. And the shoes? They hadn't changed; Cindy still loved her high heels.

Fiona glanced at the clock and was about to get up from her desk when the telephone rang. She picked it up, frowning at the interruption. Coincidentally, it was Cindy.

"Hello Cindy," Fiona said in a bright voice. "I've just been thinking about you!"

Twenty minutes later the call ended. Cindy had said she was coming to visit Fiona at the weekend and they would go out for an evening meal together. Fiona leant back in her chair with a thoughtful expression on her face. It had taken Cindy seven years to decide whether to let her read Grant's journals, but this weekend Fiona was going to do just that.